WANDERING WARRIOR: BOOK 2

JURY

MICHAEL HEAD

Editing by James Kelly
Cover by Paganus
Typography by Paganus
Formatting by Christine Cajiao

CONTENTS

PROLOGUE 1

The city of Greendown was old, but it had been built upon ancient ruins from a civilization that was even older, and far more advanced. The integration of the aging sewer system left by those who had come before had cut down on outbreaks of disease and helped Greendown flourish, even after its borders stretched beyond the bounds of the ancient ruins. Only the people living in the slums closest to the outer walls had to deal with the smell of raw sewage in the streets, making the more central regions of the city more sought-after.

Naturally, the center of the city is where the vast majority of the guild halls were located, along with a few governmental buildings dedicated toward running the city. In the exact center, in the place of prominence, there wasn't a palace or keep for a king. Instead, what rested in the spot of distinction was the guild hall for the Hunter's Guild, which served as the headquarters for the Western Wardens. This late at night, it was almost abandoned, except the few people still working to prepare for what was coming from the mountains and forests to the north.

"Commandant, there's still been no word about the missing people from the guilds, or your nephew and Captain Cross." The aging figure hunched over his desk looked up to see his scarred secretary standing in his doorway. Commandant Beck held in the sigh that tried to escape, not wanting his loyal servant to see him feeling the strain he was under.

Years ago, the secretary had been badly injured when he refused to stop running back into a burning building, determined to save every person inside that hadn't been consumed by the flames. He had saved nearly a dozen, most of them children. It had been a heroic feat worthy of songs and stories told by bards up and down the banks of the Mighty Reka for generations. As was the way of things, he had quietly retired from his position in the Black Wardens and been offered his current position, where he worked to help Commandant

Beck keep the region from descending into chaos. Such a man was a reminder to Beck that his own struggles were only a pittance of what the men and women under his command went through every day they wore the uniform.

Taking Beck's silence as a reply, the secretary cleared his throat and moved on to the next issue. "Lieutenant Lucente is here to speak with you, as you requested."

"Send her in." Commandant Beck stood, leaning backward to stretch his lower back. "We don't have much time left to finalize our plans." The light drizzle outside made his bones ache, and in such dreary weather he could always feel every injury he'd sustained over his long career. He thoughtfully fingered a thick scar where a goblin spear had caught him in the back when he was a much different man, still filled with the fire and zeal of youth. He knuckled the spot with a fist and stretched, seeking a modicum of relief from the uncomfortable hours in the chair before he had to meet with the Lieutenant. Then he checked himself over quickly, making sure he was presentable.

Appearances still had to be kept. Although he wished he could cast them all by the wayside, appearances were valued by those who only had such things to rely upon. Commandant Beck knew, however, that it was a man's actions that truly mattered. He'd tried to ensure his actions had always been to a standard he would have pride in, and remembered to measure those around him in the same manner.

While old age was catching up to him, Beck knew he could still hold his own on the battlefield. His old friend and guard captain would attest to it loudly after their spars, especially while nursing his shield arm. Beck's frame still held enough muscle to carry the burden of heavy armor, and carrying a shield and lance was something he practiced with the men when time allowed. Morning practice with his longsword kept him in good enough shape that he didn't fear any of the younger men in a duel. Especially since they hadn't learned the tricks that experience had brought with time. Not to mention the few magic spells he knew that could tip the scales in a real fight. Being replaced by a younger man was still a few years away, which boded well for the city. Beck had yet to find a replacement for himself that he felt could handle both the responsibility of securing the region, and the balancing act in the political arena required to hold the peace. His nephew, Commander Gleason of the White and Captain Alexander Cross had been the two most likely to succeed him, but Cross was from the Blue branch instead of the White–making him politically unprepared for the role–and Gleason had proven himself to be… problematic.

He shook off his internal concerns about his personal situation and walked over to the place on his wall where he had carefully removed some paintings of his forebearers. There, he had hung a map of the surrounding area, with Greendown in the center. It didn't show all the details he would have liked, but it was enough for the purposes of planning the defense of the city against what was coming.

Beck wished the map's colorful lines and hand-drawn details held the answers to the questions plaguing his mind, like where all the craftsmen kept disappearing. It was never the best who went missing, like the guild leaders and their vice heads, but the fourth or fifth in line. The ones not quite good enough to warrant top security details, or rather–a major diversion in manpower to investigate. Enchanters, blacksmiths, armorers, bladesmiths, leatherworkers, alchemists, all had disappeared into the night without a trace, sometimes with their entire families in tow. The uproar it had caused somehow landed on his shoulders instead of the various guild leaders, and the people wanted answers. So did he. Many of those men and women were his friends, people he had known for years. His investigators could only determine that it wasn't the witches' type of magic that had taken them. Something else was loose in the city, and he didn't have the manpower to hunt it down at the moment.

"You wanted to see me, sir?"

Beck turned around to see the highest-ranking Blue Warden left in his command, at least until Captain Cross could be found.

Lieutenant Lucente hadn't bothered saluting. The two were familiar enough that she knew he didn't care about such frivolities in private. Beck knew she was the illegitimate child of some noble from somewhere far to the east, which gave her the raven-haired and tan-skinned features that stood out this far north. Many men would have found her beautiful, before the battle with a wendigo had caused her to lose an eye and given her two long scars across the left side of her face. Now, most men found her black eyepatch intimidating, and kept their distance. Her uniform was stained with blood, and a dirty bandage was wrapped around her left calf, giving her a slight limp. She was dripping mud onto the floor and smelled like she hadn't seen what a bar of soap looked like in at least a week. Commandant Beck was quietly impressed. Such dedication was only one of the things that Beck admired about the woman.

"Yes, Lieutenant." He motioned to the map on the wall. "I know you just came back from the field. Show me where the largest concentrations of undead were located, and where *you* think the witches are going to make the next push with their monsters."

Located at the juncture of two major roads, and along the banks of a mountain-fed stream deep enough that most boats could make the voyage from the Mighty Reka, Greendown was a strategic location for ore, lumber, furs, and food production. It was also home to a major branch of the Alchemist Guild, and the thick forests and mountainous regions were rife with ingredients important to their craft. Unfortunately, those same forests and mountains were home to many of the worst kinds of monsters, beasts, and unsavory characters that could find a home nowhere else in the world. Which is why they were now dealing with an undead uprising while simultaneously fending off a monster horde lead by a witch coven, hellbent on taking the city for their own unknown, but certainly nefarious, purposes.

The Lieutenant pulled a dagger from her belt and used the tip to be as precise as possible. "Sir, the largest concentrations of undead are here, here, and here. We managed to push them back, for now, and my men hold the intersections that run roughly along this line."

Unsurprisingly, the points coincided with major routes to the north. Undead tended to travel along the path of least resistance, congregating in hordes on trails and roadways until they ran into something that interested them. They all expected orcs, ogres, and goblins to make an appearance at some point, but they hadn't materialized in any great numbers yet.

"But, sir, that isn't the only thing." She paused, digging into a pocket to pull out a small scroll. As she unrolled it, a small black stone fell out. Drawn on the parchment, Beck saw the rough drawing of a ghoul, but one unlike any he had seen before. "There's something new. It's not just vampires occasionally leading the undead when the sun goes down. During daylight, there's these new kinds of smart ghouls, who are tougher, faster, and stronger than they should be." She passed over the black stone. "Inside of them, we found this."

"Interesting." Beck held up the stone to the light of his lanterns, noticing the glittering swirls that seemed to come alive as he touched it. The feeling of foreboding coming from the pebble was disconcerting, and he sat it on his desk before wiping his hand on his shirt. "How much has this affected the battlefield?"

"Honestly, sir?" Lucente sighed, seeming to age a few years before Beck's eyes. "Even with twice the number of Wardens, we wouldn't be able to hold for more than a week. Their numbers are growing too fast. I don't know where all of these undead are coming from, but whoever is doing it must be gathering every undead there is in the entire mountain range. On top of that, with the ghouls handling the daytime, and the vampires at night, it makes the zombie numbers even more effective than normal. We don't have a chance to rest our best fighters, and it's only a matter of time until they start to fall to exhaustion. Once the witches muster their additional forces, particularly the orcs we've seen in the past, it's going to turn on us quickly."

"Is it really that bad? We have a pair of Green Wardens on their way up from the south. Once they get here, things should get much easier." Beck was pleased to see the Lieutenant perk up at the news.

The Green Wardens were the strongest of their forces. A single Green was practically a platoon by themselves, with incredible magic, equipment, and physical damage capabilities. There were usually only ten of them in the entire Guild, and getting more than one in a single location was almost unheard of. "Can you hold out until they make it upstream? Three days. Four at the most, as long as the weather doesn't turn."

She pointed to a second line on the map, where another road intersected with the northern trails. It was the last row of intersections before the actual city, where their supply stations were currently set up for their field operations. "We are probably going to *need* to pull back in the next day or two, if we want to keep our defenses intact. Then it's just going to be a fight to hold those positions long enough to pull as many supplies as we can into the city before the siege starts. If they can get here soon, we can hold this line. If they take their time, or the witches start casting curses and using their big spells, we'll have no choice but to hide behind the walls."

Beck took a long look at the map, thinking over his options. He knew the Green Wardens were on their way because of a mission from The Oracle, and not because of the undead, but once they arrived, there was no doubt those battle maniacs would jump at the chance to fight. Whoever James Holden was, he would die quickly and allow the Green Wardens the opportunity to save the city. He would also get answers as to the whereabouts of his nephew, and Captain Cross, whatever their fates might be. "I'll give the order to start pulling in supplies. You do what you need to do, Lieutenant. Hold the line for as long as you can, and I'm sure our city will come out the other side of this fiasco unscathed."

She gave him a sharp nod of agreement before saluting and turning to leave. Both of them knew they were in for a long slog of a fight, but with the Green Wardens on their way, the weight didn't seem to burden their shoulders quite as heavily.

Hope was on its way.

PROLOGUE 2

Chilly mountain air from the north blew through the trees, causing the trio of witches to shiver. The presence of the supernaturally beautiful vampire in their midst didn't help curb their discomfort, and the dense power coming from her magical staff cowed all but their most rebellious thoughts.

"You *still* don't have the goblins in position? What's taking so long?" The vampire princess stalked across the clearing, causing the shadows cast by the bonfire to jump across the forest clearing in a macabre dance. "Do you need me to do it for you?"

"No, great lady." The oldest of the witches, a hunched crone, shuffled forward into the light. "The orcs had to be convinced to stop eating them. Now that they are willing to allow the greenskins to muster on the surface, we should be ready for the next phase of the attack by sunset."

"*Sunset*!" The vampire stabbed her staff into the dirt, causing a flare of power to erupt from the gem set in its top. "What's the point of having forces that can fight during both the day and night, if you only attack when the sun goes down?" She paused, cocking her head to the side, as if she were trying to hear something whispered from far away. Thc undcad princcss took an unnecessary deep breath and let it out slowly, calming her sharp temper. "Fine. One more day won't matter in the long run. The important part is keeping the pressure on the city's defenders, both day and night. Stage the forest and cave dwellers for daytime raids, and my ghouls and vampires will continue to push them during the night."

"We'll make it so, great one." The old crone pulled a clay tablet from within her heavy robes, her gnarled fingers showing a surprising level of dexterity as she gave it a twirl. "Once we have them behind the city walls, we'll crack their fragile shell like a rotten goose egg!" Her deranged cackle ended in a phlegm-filled cough, forcing the crone to spit into the fire. The orange flames sputtered and danced green for a moment before returning to their normal hue. "Drats. Now I'm hungry for scrambled eggs."

The vampire winced at the disgusting display, turning toward the edge of the clearing that led to the largest concentration of her own forces. "I'll leave you to it. Make sure your monsters are ready the following sunrise. No mistakes or delays this time, or I'll be forced to punish you. Again."

Now it was the witches turn to wince, their eyes flashing to the fourth member of their coven. She was still staked to the ground where the vampire had left her, the whimpers of pain long ago ending.

"If she survives the change, send her to me. I'm interested to see what kind of abilities a vampire witch might have." With that, the undead princess left, her heavy presence lifting off the coven like a wet blanket shrugged from their hunched shoulders.

The youngest of the witches, a woman who had yet to see gray in her long black hair, was the first to speak once they were sure the vampire was gone. "Now what should we do? There's only three of us left! Without a full coven, the moment the vampire returns to the mountains, we won't even have the power to keep the orcs in line. They'll turn on us, and eat us, or worse, we'll–"

"Enough, Danika." The old crone slashed her hand through the air, tucking away the clay tablet in the same motion. "We were forced into this by circumstance, not by choice. We'll make the best of it, as we always do."

"But–"

"Trust us, Danika." The third witch, who was closer in age to the leader of the coven, with pure white hair and a slightly hunched back, patted the younger woman on the small of her back. "This isn't the first time we've been in a tight spot. There's plenty of time to make plans for what comes after, whether we win or lose against the Wardens."

"Orcs are the least of our concern. Either they get wiped out trying to take the city, or they are distracted enough when we win that sneaking away will be child's play." The oldest of the three was struck by another coughing fit, hacking her phlegm into the fire once again before continuing. “Our true enemy is the undead. The princess already let slip that she wants the power a vampire witch under her thrall might provide. We can’t let that happen.”

To accentuate her point, she pulled a small pouch off of her belt and sprinkled some of its contents onto the body of their fourth member. The powder hissed and bubbled when it made contact with the open wounds covering the corpse. After a few moments, the body trembled and thrashed against the ropes holding it. As suddenly as the movements started, they stopped, and the body stayed still.

“What did you do?” Danika approached the body of her coven sister cautiously, afraid of what might happen next. “Is she…a vampire now?”

“No. She’s passed on to her next life. I released her from the bonds of the undead.” The old crone hunched down a little lower, sadness haunting her features. “I had hoped to never see another sister pass before me, but the fates deem my wishes to be nothing but wasted words on the winds.”

“So, if the undead are our true enemy here, what should we do next? Try to help the Wardens? Try to make a deal with the guilds?” Danika wrung her hands in worry, her thoughts on the idea plain for her coven mates to see.

“The Wardens and guilds are just as much our enemies as the undead.” The old crone shuffled her way over to a chest near the edge of the clearing, where the majority of her personal supplies were kept. “We’ll continue with the plan, and try to sack the city. It’s what we do afterward that matters. Now, come help me. We need to prepare.”

The two coven sisters nodded in agreement before hurrying to her side. They didn’t know how much time there was before the vampire princess returned, and every second could make all the difference.

****

"You called for me, milord?" The princess made her way through the trees, using the light from her staff to illuminate her way. "Is there something wrong with the Demon Gate?"

"No." The voice of the Destitute came through the pendant on her necklace, as strong and powerful as if he were standing next to her. "I wanted an update. Have you found out anything about the interloper who killed the lich?"

"The witches are barely competent, but I have hopes that they will be enough to take the city. Once the population has been converted, I'll march them to the mountains immediately, and the new numbers should be enough to provide the push we need to close the gate." The princess took another deep breath and let it out slowly, a habit she maintained from a time when breathing was necessary for her to live. "As for the interloper, there's been no sign. I've had my forces looking everywhere south of the city working outward from their last known location, but all they found were some old campsites and faint traces of someone using magic."

"Hmmm…" The Destitute's displeasure was palpable, even through the speaking device. "Make your attack on the city. We need those extra units if we're going to have a chance. Don't forget to arm and armor them as best you can while you're in the city, even if it takes a little longer."

"Of course. I know the value of properly prepared troops, milord." The princess finally made her way through the trees to the road where the majority of her forces were staged for the evening's attack. "If there's nothing else, I have a city to take."

"Yes, there is something else." An invisible force pushed down on the princess, forcing her knees to buckle under the pressure. "You will find out who the interloper is, and inform me immediately once you do. There can be no mistakes this time, Princess Starnight. I have a feeling once you make your assault on the city, the interloper will make themselves known. I *will* hear about it immediately afterward. Don't forget our ultimate mission. We're the only ones who can save the world, after all."

“Yes, milord. I understand.” The pressure disappeared, and she made it back to her feet. “I *hate* that name. Princess *Starnight*.” The vampire dusted off her clothes as she made her way over to the ghouls that would be leading the push against the Wardens. “If I could find the bard that stuck me with that name, I’d feed him his own entrails for an eternity.” Pushing aside her anger, the princess focused on the forces arrayed in front of her. “Enough delays! Forward, and kill them all! We have a planet to save, and no time to spare!”

The horde of undead roared in response, rushing out of sight in the darkness like a wave. The restless dead howled ravenously on their mission to protect the world of life as they charged away, off to kill every living thing in their wake. The princess’s full lips curled into a grin at the irony.

CHAPTER 1

Pain was the best teacher I had ever known. Not because it taught me what I *should* do, but because it showed me exactly what *not* to do. Like, say, trying to teach a barmaid lycanthrope shifter some magic spells with the potential to wipe out entire buildings. Not that such a situation would ever in a million years come arou–

Boooom

"Okay, nice try, but this time you should be sure to aim the cone of destruction *away* from us. Sound good?" I coughed, waving away the cloying dust in the air. "And maybe also away from…" I gestured vaguely at the destruction all around us. "All the things." The ever-present headache and pain in my chest that had stuck with me for the last month reminded me that I still wasn't back to my peak, and my body certainly didn't appreciate the heavy impact of rocks and dirt clods that had hit me after the explosion. "It would go a long way toward keeping us in one piece."

"Sorry about that, James. It got away from me right at the end." Jess, the cat-eyed apprentice that I never asked for, but possibly the one I deserved, did her best to shake out the dirt from her hair. She avoided looking at me as she surveyed the destruction of the forest clearing around us. "I'll try it again with a focusing rod."

I cleared my throat and looked at her meaningfully, raising one eyebrow.

"…like you said I should."

I nodded in approval, keeping my face stoic. You could never let them see you sweat. I gave her a once over, thinking back over my own attempts to grasp the elemental forces of the universe. Had I ever been this bad? The unasked-for memories of accidental explosions came to mind as an elven instructor shielded himself behind multiple layers of energy.

Was I that bad? Worse. Much worse.

Her training over the last few weeks had been steadily working toward these bigger spells, and I had been dreading it for exactly this reason. Jess had a natural affinity with earth magic.

Earth was big.

Not simply the planet, though that was true as well. Earth, magically, was *big*. It had weight, not simply in the tangible sense, but in a gravitational draw that exceeded the pull of the other elements. In broad terms, fire was fierce, water was nourishing, wind was sharp, but earth was present and solid in a way that was intimidating to grasp.

Especially for someone that had never seen a globe, or had a hard time understanding that stars in the sky weren't dead heroes looking down on their descendants. Attempting to control such a force with the level of affinity Jess possessed? It was like throwing gasoline on a bonfire. Or, maybe giving a toddler the big red button to launch some nukes. That kind of Taco-Bell-with-a-hangover-level of explosiveness.

"First, we need to move again. Destruction like this is bound to draw attention, and we don't know who's still looking for us." I picked up my gear and tied it to the back of my new horse. It had once belonged to the White Wardens and was trained not to run when things started to go boom, making it a great choice for a mount. "Once we reposition to the west, you can try *Earthen Eruption* a few more times before we have to return to camp."

Jess gave me a thumbs up as she packed up her own gear. Her horse was another of the White Warden's horses we had gathered up after they had been wiped out by the undead forces of the lich I had barely managed to kill a month ago. I'd been surprised that the horses had survived at all. The undead didn't discriminate much when it came to flesh. In fact, the horses hadn't been the only ones to barely survive the battle. I rubbed my aching joints and muscles. Even with my advanced healing and spells, the recovery on this world was far too slow.

The damage I had suffered during the fight hadn't been simply physical. Well, it had *definitely* been physical, but it wasn't *just* physical. I didn't have a quantifiable way to describe how I had been injured.

When I battled the undead monster, events had gone in a direction where all twenty years of my experience fighting across twenty worlds hadn't prepared me for. The lich had *wrested control* of my body away from me after I absorbed a fountain of energy from a place of power it had already claimed for itself, something I probably should have expected. I failed to account for it because I had never seen anything like it in my past.

Memories of my eleventh world hit me. The last time I had faced a serious threat from the undead I was… not ready. Especially a damned lich and their twisted kink of hijacking bodies. My mistake allowed it to take over and use my body like a puppet, even without actually possessing my mind. I'd fought back using techniques learned fighting mindflayers to regain control of myself, and eventually found a way to break free. The hippies on world fourteen had used singing and dancing like a bunch of fruitcakes, but thankfully I was never that desperate. Still, the wounds from that confrontation hadn't yet closed properly. My body was perfectly fine, of course.

Somehow, the lich had damaged my soul. And I regretted nothing. Especially not having to sing. World fourteen had done *far* worse things to my soul.

"How much longer until you think we can risk going into the city?"

Jess broke me from my inner thoughts, forcing me back into the present. I answered with a shrug of my shoulders, not willing to voice a reply. We'd hashed over the same arguments dozens of times, and always came back to the same answer.

Not yet.

Avoiding Greendown and all its hazards was the best choice for now, even if it meant I might fail my gods-given quests by running out of time before I was yanked off of this planet and sent to a different one. Completely against my will, of course. Like the gods always chose for me, year after year.

Being stuck in my twenty-seven-year-old body over the past two decades had made it hard to keep the sense of urgency necessary to accomplish the tasks I knew were expected of me. It felt like I was an old man trapped in a young body. I guess that's kind of what I was, but I also knew if I ever wanted to make it back to my own world, I couldn't hold back for too long. We would have to go to Greendown sometime soon. Just not today.

"All I'm saying is, I think I'm ready. Even the Button Guild would have to think twice before coming after me now." Jess held up a hand as we led our horses side by side down the dirt track, making a fist with only her pinky extended. "*Stone Spears*!"

Faint light glowed under the edges of her bracers and pauldrons for a brief moment before a good twenty perfectly pointed rods of black rock erupted from the ground in two neat rows along either side of the trail. The runes I had carved into the underside of her armor plates were meant to focus and enhance the spells cast through them, which made Jess even more deadly to our enemies. When she remembered to use them, of course.

"See? That didn't tire me out at all, and I placed them all perfectly, with no mistakes." Jess looked over at me with a smug grin on her face, obviously proud at how far she had come.

"That isn't the point, Jess. In my experience, assassins in general, and if I had to guess, the Button Guild in particular, are not the kind of people who would confront you face-to-face anyway." I snapped my fingers, and her stone spears sank beneath the surface of the trail like they'd never been there.

None of my armor pieces lit up like hers had, but I did have my own copies of the runes just in case I needed a little extra juice. I'd practiced with them a few times, and the results had been as dramatic as I had hoped. The only downside was the materials the runes were carved in. My armor was mostly formed from hardened leather with wooden reinforcement, so using the runes too often would burn them out quickly. Which was why I didn't use them all willy-nilly.

"I know how the Button Guild works. They make a chimney fall on you, some bad wine gets served only at *your* table, or a runaway freight wagon runs you over in a freak accident. Supposedly, you never even see them before you die. You end up in the cemetery, and weeks later the rumors start to spread that it wasn't really an accident at all." Jess guided her horse around a stump in the trail, looking at her feet to avoid tripping over old tree roots. "Between the five of us, I think we can keep anything like that from happening."

"Look, I'm tired of sleeping on the ground, same as everybody else. That doesn't mean we should rush the process here. Your training is going well, but that hasn't been the case for everyone else." I held back the sigh that tried to escape at the thought of what I had been going through with Cross over the past few weeks. "There are still plenty of…issues we need to work out before I trust everyone can handle themselves in a crowd if we get separated."

Jess didn't have an easy answer for that one. She knew as well as I did that the three former Wardens in our group would definitely have a harder time in Greendown than the two of us would, despite the probability of hired assassins trying to kill us.

During the battle with both a member of the White Wardens–from what I had seen, they were basically this world's version of the Spanish Inquisition–and the evil undead lich who had nearly killed me, I had redeemed Captain Cross from a disgraced member of the Blue Wardens to a fellow member of my own order.

I had made him a Judge.

Now, there were two of us on the entire planet. I scrubbed a hand over my face. Sometimes I felt like it was one too many. Most of the problems I was having came from the differences in culture between Cross and myself. Passing on the skills of a Judge wasn't all that hard. The knowledge and wisdom of *how* and *when* to use them was a completely different issue.

"Does this work?" Jess had led us to another clearing, this one much smaller. From the small pile of weathered lumber left on the far side, one made for a purpose long-forgotten by the people who had clear-cut it years ago. "We've been walking for quite a while.

I'm sure we've made enough distance between the other clearing and this one."

I took a moment to look around and gave her a thumbs up. "Looks good to me. Try using the large focusing rod this time, and then you can move down to the more specific ones after you get the hang of keeping the spell under control."

She moved off, taking the premade tools I had prepared to help with her training weeks ago. I should have started with them in the beginning, but the mad rush of my first arrival on this planet hadn't been very conducive to proper preparation. Especially when I hadn't even wanted an apprentice mage in the first place. Now, I had both an apprentice mage, and an apprentice Judge to deal with.

At least I didn't have to worry about what Jess would do when I left. She was going to be a powerful earth mage, sure, but I had no doubt there were plenty of even more powerful mages running around somewhere that could reel her in if she got too far out of hand. Cross, on the other hand…that was leaving behind a very real legacy, and I couldn't afford to mess it up.

Cross was raised to believe the guilds on this planet were doing good things for the people, and they only needed slight adjustments to be put right back on the top of the proverbial food chain. From what I had seen, they needed to be burned to the ground and then the earth salted. Twice.

That wasn't even mentioning his views on some stupid book called *The Oracle*, which was supposed to be a direct line to the gods. I was about ninety percent sure it had been hijacked by somebody decidedly *not* this planet's gods, if it ever had actually been a holy relic of some kind in the first place. The person, group, or god behind the persona of the Oracle was not simply misguided, as many of the Wardens were. They were the ones actively misleading others. To me, that was a different level of unacceptable, and wasn't something I would stand by and allow to continue.

Whoever was communicating from the other side of the book had known I'd arrived on this world and that I was a threat to their agenda, and since *my* agenda was preventing injustice and the wanton killing of innocents, well, let's just say that I don't think we'd get along.

Cross, however, lacked my experience and worldview. If I wasn't around in the future to argue the finer points of right and wrong with him, he might end up taking orders from some dusty tome like some medieval form of text messaging straight from the desk of the bad guys. Hence the importance of instilling a strict moral code that at least pointed in the same general direction.

A powerful explosion rocked the forest clearing, nearly knocking off my straw hat. I looked up to see a rather sheepish grin on Jess's face.

"Sorry!" She lifted up the baseball-bat sized focusing rod of carved wood and banded iron I had fashioned from a broken axle we had salvaged off of an old freight wagon at the cheese factory south of Greendown. The runes running up and down its length were meant to help control and focus the mana of a large spell. They were essentially training wheels for a new mage. "I already know what I did wrong. Too much push into the end of the spell, and not enough emphasis on the targeting portion."

"Look, you've already made enough noise to alert half the forest. Take your time and it will come quicker as you go. Slow is smooth, smooth is fast. Think of it as a form of motivation. When the bad guys show up, you can use your fancy new spell on them." I shook the hilt of my sword in its sheath, making sure it was loose enough to draw in case I needed to pull it out quickly. "It's only a matter of time before we have some kind of uninvited guests. I'd rather face them now, than lead them back to camp."

"R-right." Jess gave me a shaky nod as her hands tightened around the focusing rod. Talk of real enemies had her jittery, but I knew from experience that she'd get it together quickly if things popped off. By now, she was a veteran of several battles, and even I couldn't call her a rookie anymore. Well, I could, and still *would*, but that was my prerogative as her teacher, after all. I had to take advantage of every perk I could from this gig if I wanted to stay sane through the experience. "I'll get it this time. No more mistakes."

I positioned myself to better see both directions up and down the trail while she got back to work. The rapid series of booms behind me seemed much more controlled, and I only had to brush off the occasional clump of dirt that came raining down from the sky. It's amazing how the threat of real danger could improve performance.

She kept at it for another hour, only taking a single five-minute break to get a drink of water and allow her mana to recover a bit. The drastic improvement in her ability to recover from spell casting was the biggest change I had seen in Jess over the last month. It wasn't nearly as pronounced if she was using non-earthen spells, but since that was our sole focus, I had no doubt she could keep it up for at least another hour or two.

After the fight with the lich, our little band of misfits had scrounged what we could from the remains of the battle, and traveled farther east, circling the edge of the forest surrounding Greendown. It was the least inhabited section of forest even before the undead uprising due to the lack of natural resources, and now it was absolutely empty.

We had stayed on the move, avoiding the few major hordes of undead moving through the area, and taking down any smaller groups we thought wouldn't be missed by the undead leadership we knew were still out there somewhere.

There had even been a few Warden patrols, but they made more noise than the undead. The patrols had stopped completely over the past week, however the presence of orcs during the day and undead at night had increased with measured efficiency. It made for a miserable month of camping in the ever-present damp and almost daily rainstorms. Keeping out of sight while we recovered had been essential, though. Necessity always had a way of making hard times more bearable. One semi-ambiguous positive of our situation was that we still ran into enough groups of enemies that keeping our skills sharp wasn't a problem.

"Movement to the north." I didn't exactly shout, but I wasn't trying to keep my voice down, either. There was no question whoever was coming had already heard all the noise we had been making. "Grab the horses and swing to the west. You can hit their left flank while I hold them at the front. Make sure none of them escape, whoever they are."

"You got it, James. No one gets away." She gave me a sharp nod as she led the horses off, and even though I was sure the anxiety of possible combat was coursing through her, she hid any signs of her earlier jitters.

I noticed a bit of heaviness to her steps that hadn't been there before. Maybe I should have stopped training sooner, especially with the expected confrontation coming.

No. Jess would have to fight when she was tired far more often than when she was well-rested and fully recharged. This was far better training for her in the long run.

Pushing aside my thoughts, I stepped out of the bushes and into plain view of the group approaching on the path. I still didn't know if it was wild animals, monsters, undead, or people, but it didn't really change how this would ultimately go down. Whoever it was, we would fight, and I would win. There was no room for any other thought process.

Until Jess came running right past me, ducking low to stay out of sight. I had no idea where our horses had gone, but her frantic waving caused me to let out a long sigh of frustration. Having an apprentice was hard.

"What is it, Jess? Why are you hiding?" I motioned behind her, clearly peeved at the lack of horses. "And where are our things?"

"Forget all of that! We have to run, right now, or we're going to die." The whites of her eyes were visible all the way around her irises, and I began to realize just how freaked out she really was.

"Calm down. Tell me what's going on." I leaned back to look up the path, my view still partially blocked by all the foliage and shadows cast by the trees. If I couldn't clearly see them, then they couldn't clearly see me, either. "You should know by now there isn't much in this forest that I can't handle. What is it? More dinosaurs? Wendigo? Some of those one-legged fae creatures that like to sneak up behind people and kick them in the butt, and every one of them calls themselves Paul?"

"No. It's much worse. Green Wardens. There's *two* of them, and they have lots of friends. A full platoon of Blue and White Wardens."

"Well… shit."

CHAPTER 2

I didn't have a solid gauge for how powerful a Green Warden might be, and I wanted to meet one in person. According to how Jess was acting, they were no pushovers. But, I wasn't exactly a pushover myself, either. I had long ago maxed out the system granted to me when I was sucked through a portal and forced to become a world-hopping patsy for a bunch of mystery gods who never deigned it necessary to speak to me directly.

Since then, I had found a way to increase my personal power past the limits of the system. By absorbing the mana found at places of power, I boosted my stats over what should have been possible for a human, even a system-enhanced one. It had also created some kind of mana generator inside my body, an orb of energy that rested behind my belly button like a ball of barely contained liquid lightning that empowered my body and magic. While I still wasn't sure what it was, exactly, I wasn't afraid to use every tool at my disposal to give me an advantage. Before jumping into a possible fight with an unknown enemy, I checked my status to see how far my healing had come along.

Name: James Holden (Earth v7.2)
Title: Chief Justice/Arbiter/Justicar/Executioner/etc…
Level: 100/MAX
Rank: 2/10
Age: 27 (Physical) 47 (Actual)
Class: Warrior/Soldier/Knight/Paladin/Mage (5/5)
Profession: Healer/Alchemist/Blacksmith/Runesmith/Judge (5/5)

Status: [Currently suffering from the effects of Soul Strain]
Strength- 65 [59]
Flexibility- 65 [64]

Vigor- 65 [61]
Mind- 65 [57]
Mission:
Mythical Quest: Deliver Justice - World Count 20/???
Legendary Quest: Return Home - Requirements not met
Epic Quest: Find out why - Requirements not met
Rare Quest: Track down Silver Star - Ongoing
Unique Upgrade Quest: Find ten places of power - 2/10

Soul Strain- Grade 1/5 - An injury to the connection between the body and soul. Can cause a myriad of issues, including but not limited to the temporary reduction of status points, nausea, headaches, hallucinations, reduced magical control, impulsive behavior, and bouts of rage. Recommended cures include extended periods of rest, items or potions intended to cure or assist strengthening of the soul, or absorbing places of power attuned to life or soul energy.

My quests hadn't changed, but my stats had gotten closer to their max level, meaning I was getting better all the time. Right after I had woken up from the fight with the lich, everything had been in the mid-forties. The incremental daily increases back to where I should be was a good sign.

The total sum of knowledge I had about items and potions meant to strengthen the soul couldn't fill a thimble, and I had even less information about 'attuned' places of power. That meant rest had been my only option over the past few weeks of recovery. I had already improved from grade three all the way to grade one on my soul strain, so I was feeling pretty good about dealing with these guys.

"James, we're wasting time just standing here! We've got to go!" Jess grabbed my arm and tried to pull me away. "They're going to notice you any second!"

"I'm just going to talk to them. There's no reason for them to fight a random stranger they find in the woods." I gently peeled her hand off my arm and waved her back. "Go get the horses and find the others. Let them know what's happening, and pack up everything. No matter what happens, we're going to have to move sites before we bed down for the night. These people are already too close to our camp for comfort."

"You don't understand, they won't–"

"Go, Jess. This isn't the time to argue."

She opened her mouth one last time, but finally gave up when she saw the look of determination on my face. Jess quickly disappeared into the underbrush, her steps as silent as a hunting cat. Which made sense, considering she was part cat-shifter.

I took a moment to prepare my shield bracelet, making sure it was ready to go at a moment's notice. It would block a few projectiles, or one big spell. In a fight, that often made all the difference. Fights were dirty, brutal, messy, and above all shockingly fast. At least, for the majority of fights it was like that. It wasn't my habit to give my enemies the chance to get off multiple shots at me if things came to blows.

I also pulled out two of the items I had been working on over the past few weeks from my pack and hooked them on my weapons belt, next to my mace and sword. Each of them were things I had been able to create from the leftovers of the battle with the lich and his undead army. They were the culmination of both my alchemist and blacksmith professions while exploring the rules of chemistry and physics specific to this world. The results had been… mixed. Especially given the lack of proper tools, work stations, and limited ingredients. I cast my *Identify* spell on the first item to make sure it still registered as a functioning device, and hadn't been damaged in my ruck.

Item: Grenade
Type: Choking Smoke/Bone Shrapnel
Grade: 3/5
Description: An alchemical mixture of ash, herbs, and gunpowder in a skeletal bone and metal frame that explodes upon significant impact. Purity level is moderate. Smoke causes temporary blindness and irritates lung tissue. Effects are variable based on environment and resistances of target. Area of effect is two paces for shrapnel, five paces for smoke under ideal conditions.

There were only four of those, considering my limited supply of gunpowder. I still needed to save enough for my three-barreled wrist cannon, and the grenades weren't as important to me as my 'trump card' that had saved my life time and time again. I looked at the other creation and cast *Identify* once again.

Item: Potion (Blend)
Type: Healing/Stone Skin
Grade: 7/10
Description: An alchemical mixture of herbs and minerals that greatly speeds healing over a short period of time. Purity level is high. If the entire potion is taken at once, the effect 'Stone Skin' will activate. Vigor will increase by 35%. Strength will increase by 15%. Flexibility will reduce by 20%. Status changes will revert to normal levels based on activity levels. More than one potion used in a thirty-minute period will result in adverse side effects.

While the time limit on 'Stone Skin' was a bit vague, I figured it was metabolism-based. It would wear off faster if I was running around a whole lot. I was also going to make sure I didn't ignore the warning about taking more than one potion every thirty minutes. After all, none of my healing abilities could cure an erection lasting longer than four hours, and who knows what kind of things might happen. It definitely wasn't worth the risk.

"And what do we have here?" A woman dressed in the uniform of a Blue Warden stepped out from behind a large tree to my right, near where Jess had been training. "A lost villager in need of help, or perhaps a bandit in need of a lesson?"

I didn't react to her popping out of nowhere beyond turning to face her. Since I didn't sense her before she appeared, it meant she either used magic to hop there, or she was an incredible scout. My bet was on some kind of magic tied into her armor, similar to the speed enhancements Leedy had on his Blue Warden armor. It did mean that her perception and spatial targeting was on point though.

"Hello." I raised a hand in greeting, making sure to keep my other hand relaxed but resting on the hilt of my sword. Always the carrot or the stick with these types. My spear-staff was currently on loan to Cross until he could find a quality weapon for himself, leaving me with only my magic-eating ninjatō sword, starmetal mace, wrist gun, and the grenade. Oh, and my folding pocket knife, shield bracelet, and the potion. I guess I was still okay if they wanted to throw down.

"That's all you have to say for yourself? Hello? After all that magic you were tossing around–*without* displaying a guild sign–you didn't even try to hide or run away. My, you are an interesting one." The woman took a step back into the shadow of the tree and disappeared, using whatever magic had allowed her to sneak up on me.

I paid closer attention this time, and there was a definite glow around the armor covering her calves before she disappeared, along with a faint spatial tremor that I picked up on now that I was looking for it. This was looking like a more diverse and well-prepared group compared to what I had seen from the Wardens in the past, marking their group as the sort of elites that I'd heard rumors about. It seems there was more substance than exaggeration to the rumors and fear when people talked about the Green Wardens and their followers.

Just to be safe, I activated my shield bracelet. The low hum and faint bubble of clear energy quickly faded away as it settled into place, conforming to my shape like a second skin. If that skin floated about an inch from my body, anyway.

There was a commotion back at the larger group as the scout reappeared near them, and I heard some shouting. A few barked orders had them spread out, some going off the trail in an obvious flanking maneuver to either side. I thought I could see two members of their party stay toward the back, both wearing distinctive green cloaks that would hide their features even if they were close enough for me to get a good look at them.

"Well, you've stepped in it now, stranger." The woman scout came out from the shadow of a much smaller tree to my left this time, two long daggers drawn and ready in her hands. "You match the description of a certain someone we've been ordered to find. It would go much easier if you would drop your weapons and surrender yourself for questioning. No need for you to feel any extra pain, beyond what the White Wardens are going to do to you."

"You have *got* to be kidding me." I took a moment to rub at my temples, feeling a headache coming on. "All I said was one word to you, and now I'm to be tortured and possibly executed because I *might* be someone you're looking for?" I waved my arms around. "Look at where we are right now. In the middle of nowhere, and you just *assume* I'm your target based on a general description and the fact that magic was cast nearby? Well, lady, I wasn't even the one who was casting the magic. Your assumptions are wrong, which could lead to the death of innocent people."

The fact that they might be after me in the first place didn't matter. It was the principle of how she came to her conclusion that I was upset with. They were more heavy-handed than a sumo wrestler filling his plate at an all-you-can-eat buffet line. I mean, seriously. These Wardens were absolutely out of control.

"That doesn't matter. You don't get to decide–"

"No, *you* don't get to decide who to torture and who to kill based on half-assed information. You are no better than a group of bandits. A bunch of murderers wearing fancy armor." I felt the mantle of Judge settle over me, straining to be released. My voice deepened, changed by forces older and more powerful than those controlled by mankind. It was an ancient authority that had shaped and molded civilization itself since before recorded history. "You are *guilty*, and I *Judge* you as unworthy of your position and station."

"Uhm, what's happening?" The scout took a step back, stumbling over an exposed tree root as a wave of energy pushed against her. "What in all the hells below are you?"

While we had been talking, most of their group had managed to encircle me. I counted at least twenty that I could see, which was far too many for me to take on all at once safely. What was supposed to be a simple conversation to gauge the power of a Green Warden had quickly turned into a mess.

So be it. If these people wanted to throw down, then that's what I'd do. A quick shot from my wrist gun would surprise them, taking the scout out of the fight and giving me a chance to throw my grenade at the largest concentration of Wardens standing on the road. Then, I'd break free of their circle and use my mace to crush the legs or skulls of anyone in my way. If they tried to follow me, I could–

"Wait." The voice cut through the mounting tension like a knife, causing the Wardens to take a step back and the knotted tightness in my shoulders to relax a fraction. "There's no need to jump straight to violence. Not when the forest is filled with enough undead to make me suspect the end times are near."

The speaker stepped out from behind the scout, using her shadow to travel from where they had stood behind the encircling group. I checked the rear of their group, and now only one green cloaked figure was standing back there. Which, of course, confirmed their identity if the emerald cloaks weren't enough of a give-away. It was a Green Warden.

As they dropped their hood, I saw it was a woman. She was younger than I expected, with a slight build, and blonde hair that fell in crumpled waves, framing her face. She reminded me of someone important I had left behind, and for a single aching heartbeat, I was somewhere else.

"You're always so ready to do violence." Sinthia shook her head, the breeze coming in off the ocean providing fresh air from the coppery stink of blood and burnt smell of ash as it blew strands of her hair across her stormy green eyes. "Will you ever take a moment to just try *and talk your way out of things? This was supposed to be a peaceful negotiation."*

"These people were never going to stand with us. And in a fight like this one, you're either with us, or you're against us." I wiped the tip of my spear clean on a nearby curtain, ripping it down in frustration. The heavy material felt expensive, which only made me even more angry. The open window showed hints of an oncoming storm, one that would help cover our tracks as we made our escape from the city center. "It isn't like this so-called council *cared about the people anyway. Just look around us! There's enough wealth in this one room to feed everyone in the slums for a week! Maybe two weeks! Instead, they were happy to sit up here, getting rich and fat, while their own people suffer, and the lich runs free to do as it wants unopposed. Stealing children off the streets while they watch! No, Sinthia. This time, violence* was *the answer."*

"One day, James, I hope you grow to see there are more than just two options. More than right and wrong, black and white. And I hope even more to be by your side when it happens." Sinthia bent to grab the key to the treasury from the neck of the dead councilman seated to the right of the council leader, the man I had roasted to death with a lance of flame hot enough that it melted the golden armrests of his chair. "Come, we have to hurry. The enchanted equipment should be in the vault, and we need to get it out before the guards find what you have done."

I blinked, coming back to myself. Sinthia and I had been trying to gather support for an assault against a disgustingly powerful lich on my last world, making deals with every local and regional power in existence. Most of them had gone poorly.

At least the armor we had found had helped lead us to the true hiding place of the phylactery that made the lich immortal, ultimately allowing me to kill it and free the children held captive by the insane undead.

The pain of remembering Sinthia again–even under those bloody circumstances–was as strong as a physical stab to the chest. I could still feel the part of me that I had left behind when I was forced to abandon her, throbbing as if it was an open wound. The mantle of Judge seemed to stutter, shifting uncomfortably on my shoulders before dropping away. I looked back up at the woman that had reminded me of her, noticing her eyes were blue, not green. I let out a small sigh of relief. No need to get lost in the past. She was not Sinthia, and this was not the same world.

"Are you okay?" The Green Warden took a tentative step forward, holding up her hand questioningly. "You looked to have suffered an extreme injury just now."

"I'm fine, thank you. You reminded me of…someone I knew once." I straightened my back, rolled my shoulders, and shoved down my emotions into the pit of my stomach where they belonged. "Now, where were we?"

"My subordinates were sent to apprehend you, before you revealed the fact that it was not you who was casting the large works of magic here earlier." The Green Warden held out her hand, motioning to the torn earth where Jess had practiced. "Do you know who was doing magic? Before you say anything, I encourage you to answer truthfully. We will know if you are lying."

"Wardens. Right." I looked around, noticing that they were an almost even split of White and Blue Wardens, both of which might have the ability to see if I was telling the truth. "Yes, I know who was casting here. She's long gone by now, and I won't give you any more information about her beyond the fact she's out of your reach.

And once again, in case you wanted to make sure I wasn't lying, it wasn't me casting spells in that clearing."

Her eyes flickered to someone standing behind me, getting confirmation from someone else that I was being honest. It meant she either didn't have the ability, or wasn't using it herself right now.

"Hmm. You're telling the truth. Tell me this, stranger. Why didn't you run when you saw us coming?" The Green Warden took a step closer, putting her just out of range of my sword if I were to draw and swing it. She obviously didn't understand what the cannon on my wrist could do to her if I lifted my arm about four inches. "Most people unaffiliated with the guilds would run at the sight of a group of Wardens approaching them."

I shrugged. "I was doing nothing wrong. If Miss Blue Warden over here is any indication, if I'd gone running off into the forest at the first sight of your group, you'd now be asking me why I'd run away if I hadn't done anything wrong. But now you're asking me why I *didn't* run? Guilty if I do, and guilty if I don't. I'm sure you can understand my frustration here, Warden. Currently, my only intentions for being in the woods are to kill monsters and undead, as well as resupply, rest, and recuperate before going to Greendown. Why should I run from you?" I hooked my thumbs in my belt, relaxing my posture. I was also aiming my wrist gun at the Green Warden's stomach. "You can ask your people, that's nothing but the truth."

"Resupply? Is there a merchant caravan we missed?" The Blue Warden scoffed. "Your story makes no sense."

I glared at the contentious woman. "How many deer and game animals do you think are running around in the city, *Warden*? From what I can see the city is being besieged day and night. That kind of situation doesn't tend to be very beneficial to food stocks, in my experience. Coming into the city loaded up with meat could keep my belly full whether I eat that meat or sell it." I gestured around me. "There's not exactly a lot of hunters out here gathering fresh meat, what with the *horde of monsters* running around. I bet meat is selling for a premium right now. So yes, *resupply*. It's not that difficult of a concept if you stop assuming that anyone talking to you is a liar or a criminal."

Glaring, the woman opened her mouth to retort. "Who do you think—"

"Enough of this." The Green Warden raised a hand to forestall any more arguments. Her eyes looked over my shoulder again, and she flicked her hands to either side. "We're taking too much time accosting this man for no reason. Gather up the gear and carts. This task force is back on the move in five minutes."

The Wardens started to disperse, moving quickly back the way they had come. The other Green Warden hadn't moved from their place, holding position with the few carts they had apparently been pulling by hand.

"Since you seem to be a local, do you have any news of the area? Is there some reason why so many undead infest this region, stranger?" The Green Warden pulled her hood back up to hide her features once again, as if the few stray beams of sunlight that made their way through the thick canopy hurt her fair skin.

"You haven't heard? Greendown is nearly surrounded." I was genuinely surprised by her question. "They'll be under siege by the undead and the armies of the witches within a few weeks if things keep going like they have been. Orcs, goblins, trolls, all kinds of monsters have banded together to crush the city. As it stands, they'll be lucky to last more than a month without reinforcements from the south. Isn't that why you're here? To help save the city?" I was hoping that was why they were here, and not because of little-ol'-me, like that scout had hinted at.

"No, we had no idea. We were sent after a single man, one who might even be behind this uprising. In fact, given who our orders are from, I now have no doubt. It's imperative we reach the city before the siege falls in place."

The Green Warden's hand flashed out, grabbing me by the forearm hard enough I felt my bones shift under my muscles. At least that answered one question. Green Wardens were *strong*.

"I hate to impose on you after the way we met, but time is of the essence. You *must* take our task force through this forest to the city as quickly as possible. We *must* speak with Commandant Beck at the Hunter's Guild, and then use whatever information he can give us to track down our target. Finding and killing James Holden is *all* that matters now."

"Am I… being deputized right now?" I asked cautiously.

She smiled brightly, her grip firm on my arm. "Something like that."

"I'd sure hate to be this James Holden guy right about now." Suddenly, I had a thought that perked me up a bit. "Hey, I don't suppose I could I at least get a fancy badge, or maybe–"

Her grip tightened in warning. She gestured vaguely in the direction of the city, her eyes providing a fierce heat that I could almost feel against my skin. I sighed.

Sometimes, I think the gods thought my life was all one big joke.

CHAPTER 3

"I'm not alone out here. I have a group of friends I can't abandon just because you want a shortcut through the forest." I pulled myself free, surprising her with my strength. "What I can do is *tell* you how to get through the forest quickly. Does that work?"

"That's… that's fine, yes. Thank you." Having someone tell her no, especially as one who wore the cloak of a Green Warden, must've shaken her a bit. Her face and voice couldn't hide her age, the indecision of the moment making her waiver from her earlier firm stance. "Can you draw us a map?"

"Sure, but you won't need it." I crouched down, tugging on her sleeve to pull her with me. I drew some lines in the dirt, and placed a few rocks as place markers. "This is the trail we're on now. In a few miles, you'll run into a branching trail with an old shack at the intersection. Take that trail past the shack until you see a burnt-out stone building that used to be a dairy farm. The city is just north of it. All you have to do is follow the cobblestone road from there. I've done most of my hunting in that region so it should be mostly clear, unless something's moved through there recently."

"We're that close?" She looked the map over, trying to gauge distances. "Why can't we just cut straight north through the forest at the intersection?"

"Because you have carts, and the trees are too dense. Not to mention all the Pauls running around in that section. They're a kind of one-legged creature that sneaks up on you and kicks you when you're not looking. You don't want to stir up fae who are that devious if you don't need to."

"Pauls." She said the word with surprising disgust. "I've heard of them."

"Yeah. They're real assholes." I tapped the rock that symbolized the city. "Besides, you want to approach on a road. That's where the gates are. If you come in through some other way, you'll just have to circle around until you find an entrance. Also, due to the terrain the other entrances to the city tend to be the ones attacked more frequently. Only one gate has it easier than the rest. Which, if I'm not mistaken, is this exact gate I'm telling you to take."

"Oh, right." She looked back at the rest of her group. "Only Tew and I could jump the walls. I have to think of the others." She stood, brushing off the imaginary dirt from her knees. "Thank you again, stranger. I hope to see you again, preferably under better circumstances."

"Sure. Maybe I could buy you dinner sometime." I flashed her a grin that had made actual queens blush. She didn't even notice, already walking back to her group. "Or not, I guess."

Her shouts made them pick up their pace, and they were quickly marching past. I stood to the side, watching the platoon of Wardens march along. Every one of them wore enchanted armor and carried rune-covered weapons. They would be a welcome addition once Greendown was under siege. The two Green Wardens brought up the rear, and I gave a little wave to them as they went by.

"*You.*"

I swear, the ground actually rumbled when the second Green Warden, the one I hadn't met yet, stopped to speak to me. It was impossible to see what he looked like under the hood, but he was taller, broader, and I got the impression this one was much older. I would also bet he had the experience to go along with the strength he wielded.

"*Name.*" The rumbling growl coming from under the cowl was strong enough to shake my chest. There was more than a little mana used in whatever he was doing.

"What?" I almost took a step back, but I didn't let the clear attempt at intimidation push me. "It's hard to understand you over the fluttering in my chest, big guy."

"*Give. Me. Your. Name.*" The Green Warden shifted under his cloak, exposing his hand gripping the hilt of a thick-bladed dagger hanging from his belt. It had a green gem cap that flickered with an angry light.

I kinda wanted to steal it.

"Tew, leave the man alone. He helped us." The Green Warden who reminded me of Sinthia tugged on his elbow, but she might as well have been trying to move an oak tree. "We wouldn't even know about the upcoming siege if it wasn't for him."

Apparently, being helpful didn't count for much in the big guy's book. He gently stiff-armed his fellow Green Warden, pushing her away without moving from where he stood in front of me.

"*Name.*"

"Well, since you asked so nicely…" I thought furiously, knowing what would happen if I told him my real name. Violence and blood would just be the start.

Now that I had stood next to both of the Green Wardens, I had a better gauge of where their power levels were at. If I wasn't suffering from Soul Strain, I wouldn't even hesitate to take both of them on at once. Stat-wise, I put the woman somewhere in the high thirties of my system for strength, flexibility, and vigor, while Tew's presence felt like the middle forties. They were certainly the strongest humans I had met on this world, but I bet I could beat them like a drum in a purely physical contest. Humans were usually much easier than monsters in a straight-up fight, especially on unprepared ground.

The first thing holding me back was that it wouldn't be a straight-up fight. From where they sat magically, I *should* be able to crush them. *Should*, didn't mean *could*. Both *felt* like they were in the low thirties for their mind stat, but it was impossible to gauge what their gear and weapons could do to boost them.

I also didn't know what kind of spells they might know, or what their expertise was in. It would really suck to have something crazy and exotic like an illusion spell or something trip me up. And, just because they seemed to be weaker in their magic, didn't mean they weren't suppressing their own abilities. Kinda like I was doing right now, to keep them from knowing how strong *I* was.

The second thing was that they were just too damn *useful*. I already knew that there was some kind of vampiric cabal out there that had at least one now-dead lich working for them, and to say we didn't get along would be an understatement. Sure, the Wardens wanted me dead as well, but if the vampires weren't involved in the attacks against Greendown, I'd eat a whole bowl of wendigo mushroom stew. After twenty worlds with various factions in conflict with one another, I'd become somewhat proficient at finding the gaps between the chaos, and sometimes even stoking certain flames when necessary. Why fight one enemy, when you can get another one to do it for you? Then, it was too easy to swoop in and put down the weakened winner if necessary. No, I definitely didn't want to kill the Green Wardens. Unless I *had* to.

Since I took too long to answer, Tew got fed up with me and growled in anger, drawing his oversized dagger. Holding up my hands, I activated my Paladin class and cast one of only four spells it gave me when I gained it. "Be at ease. *Blessing*."

The flare of pure white light that pulsed over Tew made him pause, and he slowly sheathed his blade. My magic slowly faded from the world, making it seem washed-out and gray. It's why I hated using that spell. I'd feel…off, for at least the next day or two, and the only tangible benefits were going to be felt by Tew. He'd be a little faster, stronger, and tougher for a few days, and sleep like a baby tonight. Lucky jerk.

"You are a Paladin." Tew's hidden features seemed pleased, and his voice didn't try to shake the trees free from the ground anymore.

"For some time now." I nodded in agreement, thinking back to when I had gained the class.

That'd been fourteen years ago, to be exact. It was my sixth world, and it was the first world that I felt with any kind of certainty it would have a successful future as a direct result of my actions when I left. It was a turning point for me. The first real indication that what I did, *mattered*.

I didn't know how I knew Tew was suddenly in a better mood, but I just knew it was true. Maybe the voice was a clue. The gem in his dagger dimmed as the tension between us ratcheted down, and I could literally feel my palms itch at the urge to snatch that thing. It was a very nice dagger.

Tew nodded and held out his hand for me to shake it. Now that he wasn't enhancing his voice with mana, he sounded more like someone from my original world who had smoked two packs a day for the last twenty years or so, and less like a natural disaster with a voice. "Should have said so. Or wear your accouterments, like a normal Paladin."

"Vampires and other greater undead underestimate me a lot more when I don't show off my abilities. Also, well, you guys aren't exactly the best at communicating. Some of you seem to like to jump straight to the fighting before I can even get a word out." I motioned at Tew's dagger with my free hand as we clasped wrists, making my point. His crushing grip was unsurprisingly stronger than the other Warden's, and I squeezed back just hard enough to keep him from injuring me, and to send a little message of my own.

"Hmm…" He turned away from me once he let go, looking back at his compatriot. I still hadn't seen his face under the hood, but I had the feeling he didn't want to admit how close to the mark I had hit. "Oriana, come. This siege will be good training for you. To become our new Tenth, you must have many leadership challenges." Tew looked over his shoulder at me, letting me catch sight of a close-trimmed beard that had gone completely gray. "I'll see you in the city. A Paladin is meant to fight against the undead."

It wasn't a question.

I casually reached into my pocket and pulled out the broken remnants of a shattered perfume bottle with the old-fashioned squeeze ball still connected to it, although partially melted now, and gently tossed it at the man. I knew I'd kept this thing for a reason.

"I know."

He caught it, surprised, and more than a little confused. "What is this broken–" His voice cut off abruptly as he ran his magical senses across the item. Once he realized what he was holding–the storage container of the lich I had killed–his eyes flew wide. "This is… a phylactery? How?"

I simply gave him a smile. The two Green Wardens gave each other a look I couldn't see under their hoods before the man gave me a grim salute, fist to chest. I returned the salute with a nod of acknowledgement and they turned to leave. I let out a slow breath as they walked away without saying anything more, and did my best not to slump in relief. Next time, I should listen to the native of the planet and just run away.

I watched the pair hurry to catch up to their departing platoon of Wardens, and caught the woman, Oriana, glancing back at me. She gave me a little wave before they disappeared around the gradual curve of the trail, and I raised a hand in return. That's right, still got it, baby.

After they were out of sight, I started walking in a completely different direction than where our camp was located. I didn't know if they would leave someone behind to watch me or not, but I wasn't going to take any chances by leading them right to us.

While I was walking, I replayed the encounter with the Wardens in my head, trying to suss out any nuggets of information I might have missed. The detached feeling created by my Paladin spell actually helped for once, dampening any emotion that might have colored events.

The obvious exchange between Tew and Oriana about her being in training felt like the most important bit I had heard. Well, that, and the small matter of their plan to hunt me down and kill me. I had no doubt the orders came from their *Oracle* book, same as they had the last two times. Somebody had a real murder hard-on for me, and I was more than ready to return the favor. The murder part. As for the hard-on, well. I'd play it by ear.

As soon as I found out who they were, of course.

If Oriana was only a Green Warden in training, that meant Tew better represented their normal baseline for power. Considering there were only supposed to be ten Green Wardens, and Tew's age was getting up there–a guess based entirely on the brief glimpse I caught of his beard–it was likely that Tew wanted to retire. Oriana was going to be his replacement, and he had to get her up to snuff before he could hang up the hood. I didn't know what to do with the information, but it was never a bad thing to know more about your opponents.

There was no question they were my enemies, especially since they were the enforcers that propped up the guilds that kept average people as little more than serfs. Until I could convince them to change their ways–or crush them under my heel and force those who remained to see things my way–I'd remain at odds with everyone in a Warden's uniform. Didn't mean I hated them, though. I thought about Gleason, the asshole White Warden I had crushed.

Well, maybe some of them, but it definitely wasn't a blanket hate. No, my hate was targeted. Discerning. Nuanced. It was based on Judgement.

"You were meant to be a protector, fuckstick. Instead, you became a nightmare to the people you were supposed to protect. Try and do better in your next life." I raised my mace over my head, but before I could swing it down, the floor under Gleason gave way. Meaty tentacles from some undead abomination reached up from the sub-basement, forcing me to scramble back so I didn't join him.

His screams disappeared as he was dragged away into the darkness below.

Meant to punish the guilty.

After a few miles of wandering around in the middle of the forest for a bit, I was sure I didn't have someone following me. There were insect noises and little forest creatures running around all over the place, so I felt okay letting my guard down a bit as I swung back around toward camp. Generally, fauna were the best indicator for predators and unnatural things like the undead. When they went quiet and still, it meant something nasty was around. Frankly, in this place, I trusted their senses over my own. This was their home turf and they had a long history inside of it. They knew what belonged better than I ever would.

While I walked through the underbrush, I thought over the plans I had been putting together over the past few weeks. There had been a lot of gold and treasure we collected after killing the lich, and my very first step when we got to the city needed to be upgrading my wardrobe and armor. If I was going to be rubbing elbows with the rich and influential, I needed to look like I belonged in the room.

It was an annoying lesson I hadn't wanted to learn, but a particularly spiteful mentor who taught me my Soldier class from world three was very good at completely ignoring what I did and didn't want to do. Eyide had been the craziest woman I had ever been in a romantic relationship with, and I had learned *a lot* of lessons from her.

She once tied me up–naked–in bed, thinking something exciting was going to happen. Well, something exciting *did* happen. Once I was secure, she opened the bedroom door and let in four men with clubs to try and beat me to death. Eyide had considered it a training exercise. From my point of view, it felt more like attempted murder. She didn't see any difference. Our relationship didn't last much longer after that.

Okay, two or three weeks longer. Six at the *most*.

Her crazy was only matched by her hotness and flexibility, but my stats had only been level fifteen or so at the time. I wasn't strong enough to handle that kind of combination, so I snuck out in the middle of the night while she slept. The rest of my time on world three I had to watch my back, looking for the knife between my shoulder blades that I was sure she was planning to put there. That was one world-hopping portal I was happy to see when it showed up.

Finally, I could smell the makeshift smokehouse Leedy and Murphy had set up to make some jerky. It had the distinct aroma of burnt pine sap and too many herbs, which seemed to be the norm for this world. They liked a thick crust of whatever-the-hell on their meat, while I preferred mine a little more plain. No sense disrespecting the animal like that, but to each their own I suppose. I couldn't complain too much, especially since I wasn't the one making it.

We had set up against the edge of a tiny spring in a particularly thick section of forest, making it much harder to find our camp. Unless you had a nose, of course. Then all you had to do was follow the smell. Which was why I had tried to say we didn't *need* a smokehouse. It was an argument I had lost almost immediately, especially since we *did* need some way to preserve meat when one of us killed something bigger than a rabbit, and I had unfortunately left my salt mine in my other pants.

Another point the others had made was that we moved often enough that the odds of someone finding us were really no different than random chance. I brought up the fact that random chance had a bad habit of stabbing me in the face, but they just laughed at me. For some reason, I don't think they understood how serious I was when I said it. Showing them the scars had only made them laugh *harder* if anything, the bastards.

The wind had picked up as I got closer to camp, and the few distant clouds in a mostly blue sky had quickly turned into heavy thunderheads that looked ready to let loose as they grew closer and the shadows got darker. One of the worst things about this planet was the weather. It was always changing, and somehow that change tended toward bad. It had even snowed in the middle of the night with no warning a few weeks ago. *Snow*, when it had been hot enough earlier during the day to make me miss air conditioning.

It didn't match any weather patterns I knew about, but I wasn't a freaking weatherman, and each world certainly had their quirks. At least it wasn't world eleven, where they had only one hour of daylight every twenty-four-hour period, and it was covered by living nightmares constantly on the hunt for human flesh. Or even worse, world fourteen, where they had perfect weather all the time, except everyone was absolutely bug-nuts crazy and went around dancing and singing everywhere they went. They hadn't even been *good* at singing, either. Their church snapped up anyone with talent when they were young, and spirited them away to various monasteries and convents to 'protect' them from all the mindflayers running loose. It was like being stuck on a planet filled with 'Got Talent' tone-deaf rejects. I *still* woke up in cold sweats from that one.

Really, I had bad dreams from both of them, but the first one was expected. The second one was something completely new. PTSDD, or Post-Traumatic Singing-and-Dancing Disorder. If I ever got back home and found a shrink that didn't immediately lock me in an insane asylum and melt down the key for scrap, they would be able to discover a whole new field of study. A real breakthrough for clinical psychology. I'm sure they would appreciate it, even though I didn't.

I shook my head, imagining what that conversation would sound like. There wasn't a situation where I stayed outside of a padded room, no matter how free-thinking the doctor. Talking about my experiences to other people from my world would never work.

A branch snapped to my right, and I shifted up against a tree, clearing my mind and focusing on the here and now. That stupid Paladin spell had made my mind a bit foggy, causing it to wander all over the place, otherwise I would have noticed the complete lack of sounds coming from small animals and insects much sooner.

I strained my ears, enhancing my senses and focusing on my surroundings. There was no *way* I had been followed–at least a ninety-nine percent chance I hadn't been–meaning the odds were heavily in favor of me stumbling across somebody already here. From what I was hearing, I had walked up on a group that was slowly creeping up on the camp. I had no way of knowing if it was Wardens, bandits, dinosaurs, wendigo, chupacabra, or undead, but the most likely enemy had to be undead. Intelligent undead, because they knew to be quiet. The worst kind.

Another twig snapped to my left, and I slowly turned my head to try and see through the thick underbrush. A spur of bone scraped against a tree as a monstrously overgrown ghoul took a graceful step into the open before disappearing again out of sight. It wasn't fair that something so ugly could move so smoothly, or so quietly. Three more cut through the same gap while I watched, each of them looking more deadly than the last. The one in the back even turned around and checked their tail, like a proper rear guard.

Yep. Intelligent undead, and they were headed straight for camp. This was bad.

Thunder rumbled overhead, and the skies opened up, dumping buckets of rain in the blink of an eye. I was soaked before I could pull up the hood of my waterproofed cloak.

It could be worse. At least nobody was singing.

But it looked like it was time to dance.

CHAPTER 4

Warning the camp was my first priority, but I needed to do it without getting mauled or isolated from the others. Linking up with them and fighting a running retreat toward our fallback location was the best choice, especially since I had no idea how many ghouls were running around. Charging straight into camp would only spring the trap on myself, and ruin any chances of making it to my friends. Especially if I ran into a group of the ghouls with cores.

This planet's ghouls weren't like regular ghouls, and somehow they had been getting worse over the past few weeks. Their skin grew a kind of natural bone armor covered in deadly protrusions–sometimes with nasty barbed spikes over the knuckles, knees, and elbows–protecting joints and vital areas. Instead of being wiry and uncoordinated cowards, they were beefy, over-muscled undead knights in plate armor of bone that doubled as deadly weapons.

When I fought the lich, there were only a few of them to deal with, and they seemed…dumber. The ones we had been seeing recently had been in larger numbers, with a certain kind of animal cunning that made them more dangerous than a pack of wolves.

They also frequently carried inside them something called an 'artificial monster core' that my system told me was used as a way to control them. What made the ones with a core a genuine threat was the boost in intelligence to near-human levels. I'd even heard them speak, and their capabilities went far beyond mere animal cunning when it came to tactics. The cores were made from a solid hunk of death mana that made my skin crawl when I touched one, and I still hadn't figured out how it could be used to control an undead monster, or more importantly, where they were being made.

No matter where these ghouls were coming from, it made warning my friends they were coming that much harder. They would zero in on me in seconds, and make it almost impossible for me to join my group.

A flash of lightning overhead lit up the forest in harsh lines of bright light and deep shadows. The deafening boom of thunder that followed shook rainwater from the trees, adding to the deluge drenching the forest floor. Already, footing was getting precarious. The leaves and needles covering the dirt had created a skim of mud and detritus that was almost as bad as an icy sidewalk outside a gas station too cheap to use enough salt to get the job done.

In the distance, I heard horses neighing, upset by either the storm or smell of nearby undead. Given the heavy rain, it was probably the storm, which is exactly what the others would think as well. Time to change that.

My grenades and wrist gun would work as a warning, but that knife cut both ways. The ghouls would know exactly what direction to go to come after me. Same thing with a flashy spell, or just straight-up shouting. That meant I needed something that would cause everyone to be more alert, but not give a specific direction from where it came from. I took some inspiration from Tew, the Green Warden, and decided on trying to cause a localized earthquake.

It might have seemed like an extreme choice given the circumstances, but besides the benefit of not revealing my location, Jess would definitely be able to recognize my magical signature. Her abilities with earth magic meant she wouldn't take the quake as a natural phenomenon, so she would be looking for something that stood out. Although, considering the level of the disturbance I was about to create, I doubted it would matter much. No one was going to ignore the ground shaking like a wet dog. It would be just the thing to warn them that something was wrong and that they'd need to be ready.

Dropping to one knee, I placed both hands flat on the muddy ground. I dug my fingers in as deep as they would go, creating furrows that quickly filled with water. The mana inside me thrummed along with my heartbeat, circulating throughout my body. There was no way I could power an earthquake large enough to affect the area I needed by myself, so I had to tap into the energy of the world to help me.

Not something I was used to doing often, but I could do it. As with everything, there were risks. World sixteen had been extremely low on mana, so I had learned to tap into the local environment for a boost. Not often, since magic had been illegal there, but I'd helped change those laws before I left. Hopefully, they had stopped burning 'witches' at the stake every time somebody sneezed wrong.

Focusing on my hands, I pushed the need to connect with the earth beneath me into the wet soil. I felt the world slow down around me as a connection snapped into place between my own energy and the energy around me. There was no longer any worry about Soul Strain, no concern for ghouls, or quests, nor anything beyond the epic calm that settled over me. The earth and stone beneath me had been here for eons, and it would continue to be here for eons more, no matter the struggles of the beings that walked above it.

It was as if the land itself were trying to prove that quantity had a quality of its own. Though there was no explicit thought or will to be found, the simple *boundlessness* that the earth possessed gave rise to a strange, heavy resolve that very nearly approached conscious intent. The earth pulled at me in an effort to merge my will with its own, to set aside the burdens of the flesh and the sentient and be wholly given over to a vast unconscious collective.

No. I refused to lose myself in the perspective of the inorganic. That was always the risk in something like this. Reaching out to something greater than yourself meant you opened up your mind to other viewpoints, other ways of seeing the universe. It would be too easy to fall into that sense of peacefulness, and lose yourself forever.

Instead, I held on to my own mind, and started shifting the tiny flows of mana through the forest beneath me. Earth, and by extension, earth magic, can only be accurately described with terms like 'massive', 'enormous', and 'heavy'. The physical mass of the earth lends similar properties over to its branch of magic.

Earth–the planet–is constantly under tremendous forces, the most notable of which is gravity. Combine gravity with the rigidity and brittleness of stone and earth–the dirt–and when something gives way the forces involved make sure that everyone hears about it. Knowing that, a competent mage can use such information to locate, or even create and manipulate the various natural faults that can be found underground. To my senses, these fault lines and forces were highlighted and defined by flows of mana. They were virgin streams, never twisted to another purpose beyond what nature formed on its own. All that was needed from me was a slight magical nudge, a perfectly placed snowflake that would begin an avalanche. I was thankful, because the strain was already making me shake like I was lifting a refrigerator over my head, only made worse by the ache of the Soul Strain that throbbed around the mana generator pulsing behind my belly button.

Luckily, it didn't take long for my spell to take shape, and the power started to build. I made the spellform fragile enough that it would break on its own when the shaking of the earth grew strong enough, and pulled away before the tremors were barely noticeable. It would build into something *everyone* would notice soon enough.

As I stood, there was another flash of lightning, turning the forest around me into a world of light and shadow. I used the rumble of thunder to sprint along where I thought the line of ambushers were closing in, trying to find the edge of their encirclement. When I ran full-out, I could move faster than a horse could gallop. Considering the trees and storm, I wasn't quite going that speed, but I was pushing it, zipping around like a roadrunner on speed, raindrops stinging my eyes. The slick footing and heavy rain actually helped make it easier for me to stay unnoticed.

Until I ran head-first into a ghoul.

The undead was crouched behind the root ball of a half-fallen tree. It was hard to tell which of us was more surprised, but it was most definitely me who ended up on the worse end of the collision. I'd been clipped by the ghoul's heavy elbow spike somehow, and its barbed end tore free a chunk of my tricep as we separated. Which hurt.

A *lot*.

The impact was about as violent as a car crash, and both of us went flipping into the trees and underbrush with heavy and hard impacts that hurt even with my high vigor stats. The ghoul's shocked face and wide eyes were my only comfort, and even downright hilarious as I saw it tumble away in a spray of black blood and shattered bone armor. A thick tree was helpful enough to stop my uncontrolled flight when I hit it with my legs, and I fell to the ground in a heap. I laid still for a moment, trying to gauge how injured I was, and thanking my lucky stars that the grenade on my belt and the ones in my pack hadn't gone off. I'd been too cocky, and I was paying for it with a messed up left arm and a left shin bone that was bruised badly enough that it might have been better if it had just broken instead of taking the massive soft tissue damage.

Before I could sit up or even be given the satisfaction of a pained groan, the earth had already started to shake. There wasn't time to feel sorry for myself, and there most especially wasn't time to sit around meditating to heal up. I unclipped the blended healing and stone skin potion on my belt, noticing the vial was cracked along the neck.

I simply snapped the top section off completely and poured the whole thing down my throat, slamming what would have been the equivalent of about five shots of burning alcohol all at once. It hit my gut like a bomb, shaking my stomach harder than my spell was now quaking the earth.

Pushing aside my discomfort, I used the tree that had stopped my impromptu aerial excursion to help me get back on my feet. The burning sensation was spreading out from my stomach, moving quickly up my chest and down my hips. I could feel my strength already beginning to increase. My aches and pains started to fade into nothing more than memories as the effects finished working down my limbs. I flexed my injured arm, amazed at the results. The missing piece of muscle and skin was knitting itself whole as I watched. There wasn't even a scar left when it finished repairing the damage, and the bruised shin I had worried about felt better than ever.

Making more of these potions just moved up on my to-do list, because I felt amazing. There was bound to be a downside when it wore off, but I couldn't imagine it being anything that would make me want to pass on these upsides.

The ghoul I had run into wasn't up and shouting about our little incident, so I took off again, still trying to circle around the edge of their group. By now, the earthquake spell was picking up momentum, and I had to be more careful about my footing. There was an obvious slow-down in my reactions caused by the stone skin potion, but there was an increased strength that balanced it out enough I didn't have a problem adjusting.

A loud crack announced the end of a tree's life, the increasing earthquake making the whole forest sway. It fell with a crash somewhere closer to the campsite, accompanied by more thunder and lightning. I could hear shouting from what had to be Cross, and the horses losing their shit at the earthquake. All of them would know the shaking wasn't natural, and they were under attack. I could most definitely check the box about warning them that something bad was coming.

Ghouls started hooting and howling, giving away their presence to the camp, along with a rough estimation of their numbers. There were a *lot* of them. Like, a concerningly large amount, even more so if they were all the intelligent versions of the ghouls I had seen approaching the camp. I might have been cocky about my speed, but I had made the right decision not to try and rush straight through their lines. It would have been very bad.

Their hunting noises also told me I was on the edge of their line, with only a few more yards to go before I could finally circle around and make it cleanly back to camp. I used a thick tree limb to help me turn a hard corner just past the final cluster of ghouls holding the end of their line.

Not wanting to waste the opportunity, I unclipped the grenade on my belt and pulled the pin before side-arming it at the group of six or seven enemies I could see trying to stay on their feet while the earthquake kept them unsteady. I poured on the speed, not wanting to get caught in the blast radius. The rain would cut down on the smoke–not that it would affect the undead much anyway–but shrapnel didn't discriminate. It was an equal opportunity ass-kicker.

The explosion pushed me in the back, shoving me forward between two trees. I managed to stay on my feet, despite spalling slapping against the back of my calves and thighs. I hissed a complaint as some pieces embedded themselves into any bits of exposed skin and past any thin fabric. There was no way to tell if it was actual hot metal and bone fragments, or pieces of rock and dirt kicked up by the explosion. It didn't matter, because the stone skin potion pushed out whatever it was before I cleared the forest edge and made it into the campsite.

It was as if I walked into a wall of water, the rain slapping me in the face with a vengeance. Mother nature on this planet was a real bitch. Blinking my eyes clear, I saw I was almost too late. Not too late to save them, of course. The team I was building was turning into an efficient little force, and I needed to remember that. I was almost too late to be able to link up with them before they left the area for our fallback point. They were already leading our train of overloaded horses on the narrow trail out, with two people trailing behind as a rear guard. I was genuinely impressed that they had managed to pack up so much of our stuff on such short notice, but then I remembered that I had sent Jess earlier to tell them to load up because we were moving. This time, we had blind luck on our side.

"James! Where have you been?" Leedy, one of the former Blue Wardens I had somehow ended up with, was the first to notice me. "It doesn't matter, you better hurry up! A bunch of ghouls are about to attack!"

I scrubbed at my face with my hands, fighting back the groan of pain and frustration that wanted to escape. A sharp quake made us all stagger, only made worse by the muddy conditions of the clearing.

"Let's go. We can catch up when we're clear. There's too many of them to fight under these conditions." Cross, the other guard in the rear–and my apprentice Judge–was in full captain mode. He liked giving orders, and sometimes, he was even good at it. "I can hold them here while you gain some distance."

And then sometimes, he said some stupid shit like that.

"How about you shut up and we all run? That earthquake spell I put in place is going to get a lot worse before it gets better. The only reason those ghouls haven't charged us right now is because they are trying to figure out what's happening before they commit to the attack. These ghouls are the smart ones, remember *them*?" Cross paled as I jogged forward at the pair of them, making shooing motions with my hands. "Come on, we don't have much time. Once they realize it's not an actively controlled spell, they're going to rush us."

"This was you?" Cross turned to follow me as another hard rumble caused him to nearly trip and fall. "How? I thought you were still on the mend."

"Not important. Run now, talk later." Leedy was in the rear, considering he was usually the slowest of the three of us. His armor was glowing, meaning he had already activated the runes used to enhance his speed and strength. It would tire him out quickly, but the man had enough grit to push past the inevitable exhaustion he would soon get hit with. "They're going to be right behind us."

"He's right." I slowed down a bit to let Leedy catch up. "I'll have to show you how to do what I did some other time, but we've got bigger concerns at the moment. If we can make it to the stronghold in time, I think we can hold them off. If they get the chance to surround us, though…"

I didn't need to finish the sentence. They had heard how many ghouls were behind us, and it wasn't good. Even with my stats, Jess being a fledgling mage, Cross developing well as a Judge, and Leedy and Murphy in their Warden armor, we would be hard-pressed to make it through in one piece. It was important to remember the enemy always got a vote, and none of us were invincible.

A bolt of lightning struck a tree nearby, adding to the chaos. Leedy sprinted even harder, eager to catch up with the horses. Behind us, the earthquake spell was reaching its crescendo, and the ground started to split apart in great rents that cut through the forest. We had made it past the epicenter, so we only caught the edges of the attack, but the ghouls bore the brunt of the assault. Their hoots and howls that normally meant they were on the hunt took on a more desperate tone.

There was a final mighty rumble as the spell formation shook itself apart. Miniature canyons yawned open, creating small mudslides as trees and huge amounts of earth fell into the gaps. We had all fallen to the ground, unable to stay on our feet during the heavy shaking. Each of us looked back to watch the end of the spell, and it was downright apocalyptic for the section of forest caught in the strongest area of the earthquake. Anything within the morass was crushed into a pulp while the ground settled back to stillness.

A screen popped into my vision, telling me how effective my spell had been.

New Title Earned: Crack Kills -Your unique use of earth spells has managed to crush more than 50% of the enemies arrayed against you. Destroying a pristine section of the forest in the process has gained the attention of one of the gods. Lucky you!

Skill Imparted: Large-scale earth magic uses 3% less mana per minute. An additional 2% will be applied if the earth magic being used is outside of combat, including construction, training, and enchanting.

Well, a useful title for once. A major downside from my experience, however, was that the attention of a god was, in fact, the exact *opposite* of lucky, but I was beyond caring at this point. Either way, it was time to get out of here.

"Come on guys, we need to go. There's still a lot of ghouls who are going to want revenge, and we need to get ready for them." Leedy panted, forcing himself on despite the obvious affects his Warden armor's enchantments were having on him.

"Normally, I'd tell you that undead are definitely *not* going to 'want revenge', but you might actually be right in this case. One way or another, whether it's the orders they're getting from their controllers, or they have enough intelligence to want vengeance, they'll definitely keep coming after us." I brushed myself off after I stood, only managing to smear the mud into a more even layer over my clothing and armor. It was a small thing, but I hoped the rain would clean it off a bit before the storm blew away.

Both Cross and Leedy were looking back at the destruction, so we all saw as the mud-covered forms of ghouls rose from the earth like angry murder mushrooms. Now that huge swaths of trees were gone, we could get a better idea of how many there were coming for us.

Even after killing more than half of my estimated number of undead, we were still going to be pushed hard. I stopped counting at twenty, and grabbed my two compatriots, shoving them to get them started.

"Go. We've got to get to the castle. These things aren't going to kill themselves and we need to put a wall to our backs."

CHAPTER 5

The screams of the tortured captives made it impossible for Gleason to concentrate on the designs and diagrams in front of him. He knew it was necessary for their cooperation, but his underlings weren't nearly as effective as he was at getting what he wanted from people. They just didn't have the same *passion* for the art that he did.

Being a White Warden had opened the door, but recent events had changed him from someone who liked his work–forcing the truth from people, no matter how recalcitrant they might be–to a man who *loved* what he did. Hurting others had been a necessity for Gleason to perform his mission as leader of the White. Now, it was still a necessity, but he no longer bothered with the song and dance of pretending to find an excuse.

Gleason used pain as a method to force other people to do as he wished, and–as he'd learned from his time on duty–as a way to make himself feel good. The screams were far too distracting for him to finish with the plans for the recently captured blacksmith. Gleason would rather torture the man through his family for a few more days, just to make sure the final product came out as perfect as the man could make it. If he was properly motivated, it might even be possible to get a masterwork out of the man.

He swept the drawings for the new armor into a neat pile and put them into one of the waterproof pouches stacked on the shelves that currently served as his filing system. It was necessary to use the expensive pouches, since the dampness of the sewers would ruin parchment and paper in only a few days. The plans he'd already put in motion were outlined in the numerous documents he had in other locations, but here were the ones still to be finalized.

There were plenty of ways Gleason could move forward, and he knew most of them would hinge upon the actions of those who weren't even in the city yet. He double-checked the seals on the pouches, making sure nothing would be ruined while he left for the surface.

For Gleason, finding the old abandoned sewer maintenance station under the Merchant Guild District was another sign of the Trinity's favor. It had everything he needed, all in one place. A small barracks, kitchen facilities, enchanting tables, forges, blacksmithing workshops, alchemy stations, offices, and even a small temple dedicated to the Trinity. The pervasive smell and toxic fumes had probably been what forced the maintenance crews to the surface ages ago, but such trivial matters didn't bother him anymore.

Ever since the lich had cursed him, and then the vampire had bitten him, he wasn't affected by the same things as a normal person. He held up his hand in the dim candlelight, studying the black veins that throbbed under his skin. Once, a few candles wouldn't have been enough light for him to see such fine details. Now his eyes could see no matter how dark it was. He only needed light to see colors.

At first, he had thought himself abandoned by his gods. Cursed by the undead, defeated by some human monster calling himself a judge, and doomed to die a horrible death. After his trials–no, his *awakening*–he understood the truth. Gleason had undergone a transformation. A series of trials that would damn and destroy any other man had remade him, shaped him into a tool the Trinity could use to cleanse the filth from the world. The Trinity had made sure he didn't turn into an undead, as that would mean he was no longer fit to serve them. Instead, they had made him something more. Something *new*.

"Sir!"

Gleason turned, surprised to see one of his men had been brave enough to disturb him. The eleven followers he still had were once thirteen. Two had been turned into lessons for the others, so they would know not to make the same mistakes. He cleared his throat and motioned for his underling to get on with it. "Given the price of disturbing me without reason, I take it this is important?"

The man flinched, reminded of the two previous object lessons. "Sir, I know you don't like it when we come in here, but you told us to tell you immediately if any of the prisoners escaped."

Instead of reacting, Gleason studied the man. The formerly white robes and pristine armor of the White Warden were now gray and dingy, the steel accents and protective layers were scuffed in several places and going to rust in others. A few blood splatters stained the uniform, layered in both old brown and a newer red that created a mosaic of his deeds that Gleason could appreciate. He decided then and there he would rename them. They were no longer White Wardens. These were his Blood Wardens, and they would do his work as the Trinity intended. He would have an announcement and ceremony to inform them of their new designation and ranks tomorrow, after all of this excitement was dealt with.

"What would you like us to do, sir?"

"Who escaped? And who was on guard when it happened?" Gleason grabbed the thick metal bar he had been using as a weapon off the table before limping swiftly out of the room, ignoring the stiffness in his limbs that persisted even after all the healing he had been through. The broken limbs given to him by that damned judge seemed cursed, forever causing him problems. The guard stepped back so quickly as Gleason swept by that he almost fell over. Righting himself, he both rapidly and meekly trailed behind his Commander. "It wasn't you, was it?"

"N-no! I mean, no, Commander. No one was on guard. It was in the section of tunnels we had secured last week. There wasn't supposed to be any way for them to get out." The Warden waved a gauntleted hand toward the east, closest to the region where both the slums and the river encroached on their section of the sewers. "From what we could tell, it looks like they found a secret passage, or maybe a hidden door. It leads to an area we've never explored, close to the docks."

"Who originally inspected the tunnels and cleared it for work?" Gleason continued his barrage of questions doggedly. A long silence followed his question.

"I… I did, sir." The soldier stuttered.

Gleason came to a stop so quickly that the man had to scramble to not slam into the back of his leader. Whipping around, Commander Gleason was suddenly inches from the man's shocked face, studying him with a cold, calculating scrutiny. From boots to helm, Gleason took in the man's value with a frozen efficiency.

"Three lashes." Gleason stated firmly.

The soldier paled, but nodded, daring not to argue. Gleason leaned into the already miniscule space between them, whispering menacingly.

"And who is this 'they' you mentioned? A crafter?" Gleason could afford a crafter or two escaping, as long as they weren't too highly placed in their guilds. If one of the politicians had escaped…

"Yes sir, it was a carpenter. One of the shipwrights in the Sailor's Guild. The man you…" The Warden trailed off, swallowing hard, not wanting to meet Gleason's eyes.

"The man I what? Spit it out." Gleason was getting tired of the man's timid nature. Perhaps the time under the lash would burn it out of him.

"Last week. The prisoner you maimed. When you got angry after he spit on you, so you cut out his eyes and tongue. It's him and his sons who are missing. We thought he was going to die, but…" The Warden slowed down, pulling free a ring of keys from his belt as they approached the section of sewer tunnels where they had thought there was no escape for those housed inside. "It's just above the water line, near the flooded sections."

"Show me." Gleason pushed through the heavy metal doors that served as their prison entrance for those broken enough that they no longer required such a watchful eye. All the people on the other side of the doors huddled in the dark around the few candles he allowed them to keep lit. They clustered as tightly as they could get on the narrow walkways on either side of the filth flowing through the middle. Threatening to take the light away was the easiest and most effective form of control he had at his disposal, especially when it came to mass punishment. His brows drew down as he glared toward the workers. “Move.”

His order meant everyone on his side of the sewers had to jump into the disgusting muck running through the arched tunnel, but none of them hesitated. Their skinny forms and shrunken cheeks cast jagged shadows on the ancient stones, somehow making their muted whimpers and quiet splashes more macabre than pitiful.

“I’ll get the lantern, sir. Give me a moment to find the matches, and–”

“Stop talking.” Gleason held out a clawed hand and furrowed his brows, concentrating for a brief moment before dark orange flames erupted from his palm. His magic had transformed even more than he had, and its power was far beyond what he could have managed in the past.

Gleason had been the most powerful White Warden in Greendown before the Trinity blessed him, but now he thought he might be able to rival even a Green Warden’s powers. He looked forward to the challenge, if he ever got the chance. After what they had done to his father, a chance at revenge against their order would be another gift from the gods. Gleason had his pride and he’d even admit, if only to himself, that on the very rare occasion his pride was in excess. That same pride twisted into a knot of ego and humility when he considered the many blessings from the gods he’d received in his life. Especially recently.

The former leader of the White Wardens looked over at the prisoners before motioning his yet unchristened Blood Warden to lead the way. Gesturing with his head toward the flame resting on his palm, he spoke casually to the air with a composed voice that carried far through the tunnels. “We’re going to check on this supposed ‘escaped’ prisoner. This door will be left both open and unguarded. However, if any of you try to leave while we’re gone, you will be caught and I’ll *personally* burn off the soles of all of you and your families’ feet, so you aren’t tempted to try and run a second time.”

It wasn't normal fire that he conjured, but something from a different place. It was laced with veins of black, that seemed to swallow most of the light the orange flames tried to emit. More concerning, it gave off an oily smoke that settled in the lowest places, such as the cracks between stones, and the slowly flowing sewage that cut through the tunnel. Anyone who looked too closely would swear sometimes there were faces that briefly formed in the smoke, screaming in agony before disappearing like they had been pulled back from wherever they'd momentarily escaped.

"We don't have to travel far, Commander. The flooded sections are closer to the river, so we need to go this way." The Warden, seemingly both grateful for and fearful of the dim light provided by the twisted flame, led Gleason through a series of tunnels that were in even worse disrepair than the rest of the sewers. This section was either older, or had seen heavier use due to its proximity to the river. Regardless, given the extra moisture, it hadn't weathered the passage of time nearly as well as the rest of the system.

They came to a stop just before the tunnels started to angle downward, and going even one more step would mean they would be up to their ankles in filth. Gleason could see a hole where a thick tube was placed, running along the edge of the channel, butting against the opposite walkway. His vision allowed him to see details that those who had inspected before him had most likely missed in the poor lighting. Gleason took in the environment, performing rapid mental calculations, his eyes leaping across the various contours and structures and quickly putting together their purpose before reaching a conclusion.

"It isn't some kind of hidden doorway, nor a secret tunnel." He gestured toward his left, a direction he was no longer even looking, having already grasped the particulars there at a glance. Dark eyes reflected the dim light, never stopping their rapid cadence of collecting and evaluating the information that was so straightforward and evident to himself. "That's part of an overflow relief system. From the clarity of water coming in, I would bet your life that it runs straight to the river. Two starving young boys and a blind man? They've certainly drowned themselves trying to escape." Gleason thought for a moment, trying to remember any large drain pipes that exited along the city wall near the docks. He couldn't think of any that were made from the old stone found in the ancient sewers. "Send some men to try and find their bodies. If they haven't been eaten, they're probably caught under the docks somewhere. Toss them where the undead or goblins will find them. There won't be any questions after that."

"Yes, Commander. What about the mission to pick up the new alchemist and his family? The guilds have all increased their security, and their new number four now has a guard detail at his house." The Warden hurried to keep up with Gleason, who had already turned to go back to the entrance. "Do you want us to take the risk?"

"Hmm…" Gleason paused, causing the Warden following behind to almost stumble into the disgusting causeway beside them. "No. Instead, send them an invitation to dinner at a nice restaurant. Make sure it's from someone they won't want to offend, and the location is far enough away they'll want to hire a carriage. That carriage will be ours." Gleason's hard gaze made that simple statement an order. The Warden frowned, indicating that he understood Gleason's meaning but that he had reservations. "Bring them here, and begin the integration process immediately."

"What if they have their own carriage?" The Warden winced when he saw the look on Gleason's face.

"Then you make *sure* they don't have a carriage *driver* available. You will then provide one, discreetly and through the proper channels. Do not leave a trail leading back to me. Do I need to explain *everything* to you?" The flames in his hand jumped higher, but somehow there was less light than before. "Or does the number four alchemist's carriage driver *also* have a guard detail to protect him?"

"I–I'm sure we can arrange something, Commander." The Warden swallowed heavily, stepping back from the thick black smoke that seemed to reach for his boots. "There shouldn't be any problems."

"Good." The fire returned to normal, and Gleason resumed his steady march toward the exit. "Now, I've got a few more designs to go over with the shield master, and a completely new idea I want the leatherworker to review for a different kind of whip. One I think the enchanters are going to really lose some sleep over." He looked over his shoulder at the underling trailing behind him. "So this time, I really *don't* want to be disturbed."

"Y-yes sir, of course sir. I'll make sure everything is taken care of." The trails of smoke grasping at his boots were more than enough warning for the Warden. Most of all, he decided right then that he would make sure the next time something happened, it was someone else that drew the short straw and had to visit their Commander.

The two quickly left the prison section, locking the doors behind them. There was no sign of anyone having attempted to leave through the open door. Quiet whispers burst forth as the light from Gleason's dangerous flames slowly disappeared. No one took a candle and ventured to inspect where they had come from. The carpenter and his boys had tried to get more people to leave with them, but none had been willing to take the risk. They understood what the carpenter hadn't. Sometimes, there were powers you didn't challenge. It was best to let those with the ability to stand against such things do so, while those who were mere mortals stood to the side.

Even though the heavy slabs of steel had remained open while Gleason had been deeper in the prison, not one person had tried to escape.

CHAPTER 6

Calling our fallback point a 'castle' was using some pretty strong words where they didn't belong. Our fortifications were nothing but stacked boulders with crumbled walls and broken, roughly hewn logs that had seen better days. All tucked behind a decrepit wooden fence and crude defense mechanisms built in a rush.

"Murphy, get the little barrels of oil we can set on fire placed in the trench. Leedy, help Jess get the horses in the corral. James will get the gate in position." Cross was shouting orders to the others, his blackened arm pointing where he wanted people to go. "I'll get the crossbows loaded and ready, and we'll all meet at the top when we're done."

"Sounds good!" Leedy dashed for the square fence of roughly cut logs behind our stack of boulders, knowing that it would be a pain for Jess to get the makeshift gate open by herself.

Considering it was basically just a few trees cut in half lengthwise that had been tied together with old ropes and brittle vines, it took some finesse to not have it fall apart when you lifted the stupid thing to swing it to the side.

That pretty much described our entire setup. What had initially been a clearing filled with boulders and a few encroaching trees, had been transformed by Jess and Cross into an improvised base during an extended training session. We had decided to make it the place where we stored our bigger items, and continued to add to it as the days went by. Now, we had a lumpy mess that was certainly defensible, but rough was putting it nicely.

I made it through the steep dry moat before I walked over to the palisade of stone spikes and pointed logs that lined the perimeter of the site. The dry moat wasn't completely dry, since it had about a foot of dirty water in the bottom thanks to the rain, but the slick mud would only make it harder for an attacker to climb out of it. I found the open section where we had left a gap, and lifted three pointed logs that had been lashed together to fashion a gate.

Dropping them into the narrow holes where they were supposed to fit was easy enough. They were a good two feet shorter than the rest of the wall of spikes though, and weren't nearly as steady, since the hole was loose around the logs. I kicked in some gravel and dirt to try and fill in the gap, and it made it sturdy enough that I didn't feel like wasting mana on a spell to fix it. I had a feeling I was going to need every bit of magic in just a few minutes.

A spike of earth mana spun me around, and I saw Jess had dropped the section of moat that functioned as a land bridge where the horses had come across. She raised a few more stone spikes to finish out the palisade so the corral was closed off. Now, the ghouls' best option was to come through the sections that had wood instead of stone. Which is exactly where we would be, and not the horses, or all our stuff.

"Uh, a little help?" Murphy waved at me from the other side of the wall. "I'd like to be on the *inside* when the monsters get here."

I guess I should have waited for him before dropping the gate in place.

"My bad, Murph. Hold on." I jumped to the top of the gate and leaned over, reaching down for him. His armor lit up, providing him with the physical boost necessary to make the six-foot leap so I could pull him over the eight-foot section of wall. We both hopped down, and started making our way up the stacked boulders to where Leedy and Cross were already waiting for us. "How many barrels were you able to set up?"

"We've got four along the edges, and two right in front of the gate." Murphy brushed back his sopping wet dark hair, the faint curls definitely longer than the regulations the Wardens had ever allowed him. His rugged good looks, dark stubble, sharp jawline, and muscular frame could land him on the cover of any romance novel in my home world. It was almost enough to make a guy jealous, if I had a little less self-confidence. At least I was taller. "They're going to get a nasty surprise when they try to go through the front door."

"Let's hope they do." I looked back at the possible approaches, noticing several places they might choose besides the gate. "We've got a lot of ground to cover if they don't."

Once we got to the top, Cross handed each of us a loaded crossbow. They were weapons we had recovered from the destroyed platoon of White Wardens that had tried to kill us while we were fighting the lich and his undead army.

"It won't be long now." Cross passed out a small quiver of the special bolts I had prepared to go with the crossbows as Jess finally joined us. "Everything's as well prepared as it can be. I'll handle setting off the barrels. You focus on hitting them with the crossbows. If the ghouls break through, we make our stand here. As much as we need them, horses aren't as important as our lives. They probably won't bother with them until they've killed us, anyway. Stay focused, and we'll stay alive."

"Actually…" Cross paused. "What I just said about the horses not being as important as our lives is true, but it also gave me an idea. Those are not common horses. They're Warden horses. Bred and trained for war. Leedy. Make sure they're untethered and able to move around in the corral. They'll be able to take care of themselves and act as a deterrent and distraction if one of the ghouls manages to make it past our defenses."

Everyone gave him a sharp nod, with Leedy even throwing in a salute. I guess old habits die hard. It made me happy to see Cross taking charge of the situation, because it meant I didn't have to do it. I knew it also made Leedy feel more comfortable, since the former corporal preferred getting orders from his captain.

As we settled in to wait, I noticed Cross was unconsciously flexing his darkened hand, the lich-cursed appendage drinking in the light around it. Wherever the blight spread, it caused him to feel a tingling numbness that I knew was hard for him to ignore. The curse was weird to see, almost like the eye didn't want to focus on it. Veins of throbbing black streaks went from the middle of his forearm to his elbow, much thicker than they had been when I had restored his hand and tried to isolate the curse to one spot. It seemed like the more he used magic, the further the curse spread.

I'd never seen anything quite like it, and that's saying something. Novelty was getting more and more rare for me as the years went by. No matter what I did to try and stop the curse, all I could manage was a series of magical roadblocks to slow it down. If we didn't find a cure or counter-curse before it made it to his heart or brain, things weren't looking good for the home team. I didn't know what would happen to him, but I was sure it wouldn't be very pleasant.

"They're here." Jess had the eyes of a cat shifter, so it made sense she was the first person to see the ghouls making their way to the edge of our perimeter. "They're spread out too far apart for any of my bigger spells yet."

She sounded glum, but I figured she'd be okay. Jess shouldered her own crossbow, the tip of the special bolt gleaming in the small amount of fading light that managed to make it through the clouds.

To make sure Cross had passed out the right set of bolts, I cast my *Identify* spell on it.

Item: Crossbow Bolt (Enhanced)
Type: Organic Corrosive Compound
Grade: 4/5
Description: A simple steel and wood crossbow bolt that has been treated with an alchemical mixture, making it brittle and prone to shattering. After striking a hard surface, the wooden portion will splinter, releasing the powdered acid hidden within. Any organic tissue will suffer immediate damage, dissolving most cellular membranes in seconds. Effects vary based on environment.

Yep, definitely the ones he was supposed to pass out. I had two other kinds made, but they wouldn't work nearly as well on the ghouls. Their heavy bone armor might be able to stand up to the corrosive powder contained in the brittle, bulbous heads, but all it needed to do was make it between a few gaps and they would start falling apart. Of course, we wouldn't be able to use them after the initial wave without risking getting some on ourselves. The acid would burn itself out quickly, so we would be okay as long as we played it smart.

"Aim for the big ones. They're usually slower, and won't be able to dodge." Cross was preaching to the choir, but I knew he was just talking to steady nerves. "Pick your targets early. Start from the edges and work your way inside. Focus on any that look like they might be trying to flank and come at us from a different angle. Don't forget to lead them a little. Center-mass is all we need, don't get fancy. Fire and reload as fast as you can. Once they get halfway to the moat, stop shooting. We'll wait for a few seconds to see how they handle James' little surprise."

There wasn't time for anyone to acknowledge his orders, because that's when they rushed us. It was outright unfair how something that big and nasty could move so fast over open ground. We all fired as quickly as we lined up our shots, the steady twang of the steel cords and crossbow arms finding a drumbeat-like rhythm that ran counter to the hunting howls of the bone-armored ghouls. Somehow, most of our shots managed to hit their moving targets, but they were shrugging off the hits as if the bolts caused little more impact than the rain.

While the storms had died down in intensity, there was still an occasional flash of lightning that lit up the skies. When one flashed overhead as I was reloading my third bolt, it made the charging line of ghouls look like twisted knights in demonic plate armor, their jagged faces warped beyond recognition of anything that could have ever been alive. It made both the Paladin and Judge inside me burn with anger, and I could feel the snarling electric thrum inside my mana generator thrash in sympathetic rage.

I tracked my third target, a ghoul with an unusually oversized head spike, and fired as it leapt over a tree stump. The bolt caught it in the hip, and it stumbled for only a moment before running for the moat. *All* of the ghouls were still running for the moat.

"Hold! They're getting too close. We'll melt our faces off if we keep shooting." Cross leaned closer to me, trying to keep his voice low. "Are you sure those bolts are going to do something to them?"

"Yeah, I'm sure." I finally had a solid count of the ghouls, now that they were in the open. We were facing exactly thirty-five of them. Even seven-to-one odds. There was no way in hell we could kill all of them without casualties. If the acid didn't work, some of my people were certainly going to die. "Just give it a minute to kick in."

The ghouls stayed spread along our front, either smart enough to know we would use an area spell on them if they did bunch up, or because they all wanted to be the first in line to eat our faces. Probably a combination of both. After all, based purely on the sheer number of attempts over my life, I'd bet a lot of gems that my face was delicious.

At some unspoken signal, they rushed the moat as one. Cross waved his cursed hand, activating the runes on the barrels. The newly appointed Judge grimaced and angled his body away from our group, but I caught the strained look on his face and the act of him shaking out and flexing his curse-riddled hand as well as the dark stain of magic creeping another slow measure up his arm.

I could have cast the spell. I wanted to, in fact. However, that cold and hated practicality inside of me reminded me of the consequences paid in the blood of previous worlds, the result of allowing my allies to grow too dependent on me and my presence. Though it gnawed at my conscience, I didn't argue when Cross said he would activate the runes with his magic. Cross's control and impact on the fight magically was limited, and so was my mana. It was the smart and necessary choice. It was the *right* choice. As I watched the magical glyphs flare into life, I shoved down the guilt and rage I felt over swallowing the bitter pill that was *necessity*. I stifled a sigh.

Sometimes, doing the right thing still sucked.

It would take a good five or six seconds for them to heat up enough to explode, which was enough time for the ghouls to find out that climbing out of the moat was much harder than jumping in. A few of the smaller and more nimble ghouls jumped straight over the moat, and immediately started climbing the palisade walls.

They managed to get about halfway up when the barrels went off.

I had to cover my eyes from the light of the sudden explosion, blinking away a few spots before I could see the damage. For the ghouls that had been close to the barrels, the results were… impressive. They were burning like candle wicks, unable to climb out of the moat as the flames cooked them inside their armor. The ones farther away were only knocked down, and unless any oil managed to splash on them, they went right back to climbing out of the trench. Of the thirty-five that had entered the moat, only twenty-six would be leaving. Better, but still not survivable for everyone. It was a good result, especially in comparison to my acid bolts, which seemingly still hadn't done anything.

The few ghouls that had been climbing the palisade had been knocked off the wall, but all of them were soon right back where they were moments before. Their claws had no problem finding handholds in the wooden sections of our wall. Things weren't looking good.

Jess knelt down, placing one hand on the ground and pointing the other toward the palisade. The runes in her armor lit up, and the mana around us thrummed in response. I was happy to see all the hours of practice we had put in starting to show dividends. She didn't even vocalize a spell as sharp stone thorns suddenly began to grow from the stone sections of our wall. The ghouls trying to climb were immediately tangled up, and left large chunks of themselves behind as they were knocked or forced to the ground.

"Nice job!" Murphy, who was bound and determined to one day marry Jess, scooped her up before she could fall over. "You're amazing!"

"Calm down, genius. She just exhausted herself before the battle's even halfway done. It was a great spell, but she should've stopped at the halfway mark." I shook my head, walking over to gauge how drained she was. I shook her awake, not being gentle about it. "Hey! Wake up, crazy!"

"Huh?" Jess opened her eyes, rubbing at her cheeks. "What's going on? Did we win?"

"No. You passed out for about two seconds. In the middle of a battle. Now you're a liability that Murphy is going to have to guard with his life, instead of helping us fight." I knew I wasn't being very nice, but I also wasn't wrong. This was the kind of rookie mistake that got mages killed all the time, and it wasn't always just the mage that ended up dead. What had upset me the most was that we had talked about this exact thing in the past. "Stay awake and concentrate on getting as much mana back as you can. And we're most definitely going to have *another* discussion about tactics for mages once all of this is over."

Jess gave me an unsteady thumbs up as Murphy helped her get into a comfortable position to meditate. Murphy didn't look happy with me either, but Leedy seemed to agree with me for once. He probably wasn't happy that he would be fighting without his normal backup, since Murphy usually watched his back.

As I moved back to the edge to see what the ghouls were doing to get over the wall, Cross leaned closer to speak privately with me.

"You know she only got excited. This is her first time defending a position like this." Cross glanced back to where Murphy was helping Jess sit up straight. "I've seen similar occurrences from young warriors time and time again."

"I know." I watched as a ghoul tried to leap over the wall and impale itself on the abundant spikes protruding from it. I admitted that the spell wasn't a total waste. However, it was still a mistake–and a deadly one–to take herself out of the fight without having won the damn thing.

Wrenching itself free, the ghoul fell back over the wall after leaving behind a chunk of the armor around its calf and lower leg.

"But after this–if we survive–she's not going to do it again. It was a fantastic spell, and bought us some extra time, but it would have been nearly as good at half its size."

"All I'm saying is, don't be too hard on her." Cross motioned to another ghoul that was defeated by her wall of stone thorns. "You don't want to stamp out ingenuity like that."

"You're right. All of that can wait. Right now, we need to worry about what happens when they make it over." I tried to think over what our next step needed to be. Whatever it was, it looked like my acid bolts had been a complete failure. Was there something different about these ghouls? Were the artificial monster cores giving them some kind of resistance that I hadn't taken into account? Finally, the undead decided to change tactics. "Get ready everyone, they're coming."

The ghouls had decided to stop trying to jump over, and were now moving toward the one spot on our wall where there weren't any thorns covering it. The front gate.

"Wait for them to get closer, and we can try to crush them with something nasty." Cross was leaning forward, anxious to attack. "Do you want to use fire?"

"I don't want you to do anything." I looked rather pointedly at his cursed hand and gestured below. "This is a great time to use some powerful area of effect magic, since they will be forced to bunch up. My acid bolts failed, so let me make up for it."

Cross looked like he wanted to argue, but he knew as well as I did that his life was on a timer. He nodded, conceding the argument. Every time he used mana, Cross was burning through what life he had left. He let out a long breath and motioned me forward. "Fine. I'll leave it to you."

I hopped down to the next row of boulders, wanting to get closer to the main gate. This time, I didn't want any mistakes. No more shrugging off my attacks.

When they clustered up to break through, I was going to drop the hammer on these bastards.

CHAPTER 7

It didn't take long for the ghouls to gather themselves. They were smart enough to wait and cluster together to rush the gate until the last possible moment, only giving me a few seconds to react. Unfortunately for them, a few seconds was all I needed.

The wood used to make the palisade was all fresh-cut timber from the forest. Not only was it still green, but it seemed to rain at least once a day on this planet, making it even harder for wood to become properly seasoned. There was a lot of moisture still in the logs that made up the gate. Not to mention the active ongoing storm that was just now seeming to lose momentum. So, I decided to use the newly hewn logs to show the ghouls how devastatingly a guy with a basic understanding of physics could ruin their day.

I had a spell I used that could gradually increase the temperature of an object until I cut off the flow of energy. In fact, it was how I melted the silver to make the bullets for my wrist gun. The flexibility of the spell allowed the temperature to go *both ways*. While standing above, I had placed one hand on a raised post, sending my magical senses down into the wood and gradually leaching heat from the wood around the gate, leaving behind partially frozen logs of fresh wood that steamed as the light rain splashed against them.

I held out my right hand, palm facing downwards, and brought my ring finger down to my thumb, making sure to keep the other fingers perfectly straight, and said the activation word. "*Heat*." Instead of a gradual influx of mana like when I had frozen the wood, I pushed enough of the crackling energy that flowed through me into the spell that the strain on my body made me drop to one knee.

As the frozen water inside the wood sublimated directly from ice to steam, the logs let out an ominous groan. None of the ghouls paid it any attention, rushing forward in a tight cluster. Air began to warp around the logs in a haze, the high temperatures causing even the rain that came close to the wooden barricade to boil off. I knew the rapid expansion would be too much for the logs to handle, and they would soon explode. I'd shaped my magic in such a way that I froze only the side of the gate and enclosure's wood on the side facing the ghouls, forming a crude version of a shaped claymore mine. 'This side toward enemy', assholes.

With my left hand, I held up my palm vertically in front of me with my fingers spread wide, visualizing an invisible wall of hardened air that would help direct the blast outward. I didn't vocalize anything for the spell, not wanting to divide my mana too evenly. The air shimmered, clashing with the waves of heat coming off the logs, adding to the intensity of my first spell.

As the first ghouls reached the gate, I activated one of my seldom-used titles. It had harsh restrictions, but I felt as though the moment called for it.

Title: Send Them into Orbit -Explosions are often overkill. That's exactly what this situation needs. More overkill! Blast those enemies straight to the moon.
Skill Imparted: Any explosion caused by the title holder is 50% more powerful. Secondary explosions will not carry this bonus. Can only be used during the waning phase of the moon or moons, depending on the world. Useable once per thirty-day period.

Warning

Be wary of friendly fire, as explosions do not know friend from foe.

I considered using my newly acquired Crack Kills title to flex my earth magic once again. It would serve as a great object lesson for my apprentice to see what could have been if she'd have left some mana in her metaphysical tank.

However, it wasn't often that the literal celestial bodies aligned to allow me to use this one. At least, that's how I justified it to myself. The truth is that my main motivation was that explosions are just super badass and a fifty percent increase of badassery was something that I just couldn't pass up.

I had gained the title back on world nine, shortly after gaining my Mage class. A spider, one big enough that you could put it in the 'nuke it from space' category, walked across my face while I was sleeping in the jungle. My companions and I at the time agreed to disagree as to whether I'd overreacted a bit or not, and the resulting title had been my reward.

The title was finicky enough that I honestly forgot about it most of the time. I had a ridiculous amount of titles, after all, and the majority of them were completely useless in my day-to-day life. Most seemed to be made solely to make fun of me, like the one called 'Donkey Kick' that I could use to kick a donkey incredibly hard, but only after it had kicked me first. I had gotten it after a donkey had kicked me into a ditch while on an escort mission on world four. All the title did was poke fun at me in the moment, which fit the mold for most of my titles. But, for once, this one could come in handy.

I felt the title's effects settle over me, and the first of the ghouls crested the pointed spikes of the gate. As it saw me, our eyes met, and it smiled a fang-filled grin meant to cause fear. I smiled back, and shoved one last burst of mana into my *Heat* spell, pushing the wood of the gate over the brink.

The sound of the explosion was underwhelming, considering the size of the fireball and flaming spears of splintered wood that blasted into the group of undead like the world's largest shotgun blast. That isn't saying it wasn't *loud*, just that it wasn't as loud as I thought it should have been. There was no doubt about the effectiveness of the last-second plan. It was even more destructive than I expected. Considering what I was looking at, I double-checked to see if there was a freaking mushroom cloud forming above the hole where the gate used to be.

"Wow." I took a moment to catch my breath before getting to my feet. Our palisade wall sagged inward along both sides for several yards, the ground holding the spikes wrenched upward in a rough-edged crater. A shockwave had torn the earth apart for well over two hundred yards. The destruction reached deep into the forest in a cone of wood shrapnel, flattened trees, and spots of burning brush where the superheated steam was hot enough to ignite the more flammable organic materials. "I need to use that title more often."

Apparently, my system agreed with me.

Title Upgraded: Send Them into Orbit II
-Your penchant for overkill astounds! If you keep this up, blowing your enemies into space might become an actual goal you can achieve!
Skill Imparted: Primary explosions are 50% → 55% more powerful. Secondary explosions now carry a 5% chance to also carry the same bonus as the primary explosion. This chance applies to each secondary explosion individually, not cumulatively. Can now be used during the waning phase of the moon, as well as days of the full moon and new moon. Useable twice per thirty-day period. Explosions are still dangerous to both friends and enemies.

Warning

Your continued destruction of the pristine sections of forest has changed your status from 'gained their attention' to 'angered' for one of the gods of this world! They have dispatched Icons of Wrath for your immediate execution. Leaving their area of influence as soon as possible is strongly advised.

Damn. Well, that's definitely not good. The title upgrade was definitely a nice bonus–especially having the extra activation and days to use it–but having a local god after me was a checkmark in the bad column. It wasn't the first time it had happened to me, of course. I'd done it a good six or seven times before, and each time it had meant fighting the avatar or champion of the local god or gods that didn't like me. I hoped the prompt was something like a pre-recorded message. After all, I understood how necromancy worked and whoever was behind these undead, their base of operations would be like an open wound to trees and nature around it. That *had* to be doing more damage to the "pristine sections of the forest", than I had, right? Those 'Icons of Wrath' were likely too busy being dispatched to take them out, surely.

When you go around flipping the power structure of entire continents, you tended to piss off everybody. Admittedly, this was probably a speed record for me, though. I usually didn't have a local god or two trying to kill me until I'd been on a planet for at least six months or so. Given the clues in the messages, I'd have to say it was some kind of forest or nature god that was mad at me. It was definitely time to spend some time behind the walls of a city, while the forest deity got distracted by squirrel politics or something and forgot about me in a couple of weeks.

"James! They're still coming!" Cross was making his way down to join me closer to the gate, so he was in the perfect position to see the ghouls that had survived the gate explosion sneaking their way toward the gap in our defenses.

The others were still at the top, prepping our crossbows and covering Jess, who was waving her hands around and working on some kind of spell. I was glad to see they were planning a proper division of forces and supporting fields of fire without me having to provide any input.

A loud crunch from a ghoul tossing aside some debris made me take a few shuffling steps over to where I could get a better view over the twisted remains of the walls. I was surprised to see so much movement through the steam and smoke the rain hadn't managed to tamp down.

"How are these things still kicking?" I pulled off my hat and wiped the sweat and rain off my forehead before settling it back on my head. My body and soul ached from the strain of the past few minutes, but I wasn't going to let it stop me. Letting someone else handle the magic for a while might be a good idea though. "Doesn't matter. I'll hold the gap, and you can provide support. There shouldn't be enough left to overwhelm me anymore. Once more unto the breach, dear friends…" I muttered, trying to shake off the exhaustion of mana expenditure. "And close up the wall with our… undead."

"Don't speak too soon." Cross joined me on my boulder as we watched ten surviving ghouls struggle through the steaming mud and rain. "You can't take on all of them by yourself. You're good, but not that good."

I gave him a grin for an answer. I honestly didn't know if I could take all ten ghouls by myself. Probably not, especially in this environment. It was too open, and they would be able to surround me before I could whittle down their numbers. Friendly fire would become a problem, and by then the closeness of battle would make it hard for the others to be able to help. If our walls hadn't been messed up so much, it might have been worth a shot. After I had a few minutes to recharge some mana for healing, of course.

We both watched as the group of undead got close enough for us to make out more details through the haze and fog. The ghoul leading their survivors through the disaster zone was the same one I had shot, with the distinctive bone ridge spike on his head. It walked with a noticeable limp, and I felt a little thrill of victory knowing that my corrosive crossbow bolts *had* hurt them. Even if it was only a little bit. They were just incredibly tough, and anything short of a kill shot wouldn't put them down. As they got close, it opened its maw of a mouth and hissed for a moment before speaking actual words.

"*Hssssss... Man-meat out of tricks. We fight. You die. We eat. Lady will give us more magic rocks.*" The ghoul's voice seemed almost up-beat and excited, if a gravel pit that had the ability to speak could sound excited.

"You feel like telling me more about this lady you mentioned?" I knew there were some witches further north that were causing problems, but the ghoul made it seem like there was a singular person he was talking about, not a coven. "Like, maybe a name? How about her number?"

It was never that easy. All I got in reply was a snarl before the leading ghoul charged. Cross and I leapt forward to meet them, both of us leaving one another some room to maneuver. I was a bit stronger, so my jump landed me closer to the undead. As I unclipped my mace from my belt and activated my shield bracelet with a flicker of mana, two crossbow bolts slammed into the ghouls on the edges of their line. It forced them to tighten up their group, lessening the amount of room they had to swing their meaty, bone-covered fists at me.

The lead ghoul fell back at the last moment, letting two of the biggest remaining bone knights take his place at the front. Lucky me, I guess. I used my forward momentum to help me swing my mace upward like it was a golf club, and the ghoul on the right became a golf ball sitting on a tee. The bladed head of my mace caught the undead creature full-force in the solar plexus, shattering its bone armor and sending the oversized bone knight flipping back into the monsters behind it. I didn't kill the robust creature, but it definitely wouldn't be getting up right away.

Cross caught up to me, wielding the spear I'd let him borrow for the time being. The paper-thin blade darted at the weak points in the ghouls' bone armor, piercing ankles and knees with the precision of an expert. He managed to tie up three of the smaller undead in the blink of an eye, their movements getting slower and slower as the damage built up against them. I was relieved to see that even these undead, whose capabilities seemed to exceed my expectation at every turn–needed things like tendons and ligaments to function, at least to their full capacity. I wasn't putting it past them to have some kind of magical equivalent that would allow them to move around even without the conventional reinforcement of biomechanics. At least for now the information was something I could work with.

I ducked as another volley of crossbow bolts flashed overhead. Leedy and Murphy were still targeting the ghouls trying to work their way around to our sides, cracking bone armor with the heavy impacts. Gratefully, they were using the heavily reinforced bolts intended for powerful or armored opponents and not the corrosive ones. It didn't stop them, but it certainly slowed them down.

The ghoul I hadn't smashed threw a haymaker of a punch at my face, and by reflex I tried to knock its fist up and away with my forearm, trusting my shield bracelet to handle the attack. That was a mistake. Even with both the bracelet active and my Vigor stat sitting somewhere in the sixties, the spikes on its knuckles tore through the shield like tissue paper, ripping into my arm. A shock of cold sunk all the way through my bone, stealing my breath in surprise. The pain tried to rob me of my concentration, and I silently berated myself for thinking I could fight ten of these things by myself. These ghouls were on magic steroids.

Some kind of power or ability made their armor much more dangerous to living flesh than any regular bone spikes should be capable of. My guess would be that the dark core it carried inside its chest was better than the ones I had seen before. The ache from the freezing magic it carried flashed into my arm when it connected, numbed the wound and made using my hand sluggish, but I continued to hold my mace in my right hand anyway. My natural healing fought against the creeping cold of the magic, keeping it from spreading further as I could feel the wound slowly–and painfully–trying to close.

While fighting against the shock of the ghoul's new ability, it managed to knee me in the ribs on the same side. The crunch of bone sent another wave of pain through me, thankfully this time there was no debilitating cold to go with it. I definitely wasn't doing as well as I should have been, but these were the survivors. The best of the ghoul forces. There were a bunch more left to kill, and this one had already torn up my arm and cracked my ribs.

Still, I guess numb arm and intel was better than getting eaten and being dead. As the ghoul wound up for a second haymaker, I torqued my shoulder muscles hard and brought the head of my mace across and downward onto its undefended hip and pelvis, crushing the primary hinge of the monster and bringing it onto its knees. The ghoul wasn't the only thing here that packed a wallop. I kicked away the disabled monster and looked up for the one with the spike on its head. Instead, I faced a fresh group of bone knights.

It was no surprise to me that the ghoul leader still held back. There was more animal cunning in its rotting brain than any of the others. It wanted us to be worn down and weakened as much as possible before it risked its own life. I wanted to include him in the festivities sooner–leaving people out of parties is impolite, after all–but the remaining ghouls wanted to turn this dance into a mosh pit.

There was no way for Cross to help me, since he wasn't done finishing off the three he was still picking apart. I danced back from the ones trying to surround me, my mace flicking out and making them pay for their eagerness when they got too close.

Jess finally emerged, turning the ground under our feet into a muddy soup. The heavy ghouls sank down in to the mud past their knees, while Cross and I only ended up a little past our ankles. Both Cross and I jumped high and backward, giving her the chance to turn the ground into solid stone, sealing the ghouls in place.

Since they'd certainly smash their way free quickly, the two of us capitalized on the moment. Both of us went all out, our movements a blur. My mace crushed the skulls of two ghouls before they put up any kind of defense to stop me, and Cross finished off the three he'd been wearing down. The rest of them managed to break free of the stone around their legs, and regrouped just inside the crater where our gate used to be, though I'd focused my efforts on previously undamaged knights to maximize the benefit of their entrapment, so old crushed-sternum and Mr. Bad Hip were among the gathered enemies.

The remaining ghouls consisted of the two big ones I had badly wounded, two speedy-looking ones that had a few crossbow bolts sticking out of their cracked armor, and the leader. We squared off against each other, gauging our odds of success.

Cross had taken a few wounds during his fight, and he was bleeding a red and black sludge from a cut on his ribs and another from his leg. It was concerning to see the lich's corruption had tainted his blood so thickly, but there was nothing I could do about it right now.

As for me, I had the torn-up forearm leaking blood, and I was breathing heavier than normal, my gasps were constrained painfully against the tightness from my cracked ribs. Most of my fatigue came from the strain of my earlier spell-casting, and now it was catching up with me. The strain on my body and soul after such a long day had me almost as close to my limits as I'd been since the fight with the lich. Despite that, I was silently pushing myself to heal my injuries, but the cold taint in my forearm fought against me. It was a steady drain that wasn't letting my mana levels recover, and our enemies weren't going to be kind enough to wait a few minutes.

As if agreeing with my thoughts, the ghoul leader motioned the four others toward Cross, while giving me a snaggle-toothed grin. "*You eat tainted one. I eat* this *one.*"

"I can assure you, I'm more than a mouthful, bub." I tried taking a deep breath, but my ribs stopped me. "You can ask your mom all about it if you want." Everyone stared at me in confusion. Even Cross. The traitor. I guess 'your mom' jokes didn't always translate well on this world. "Whatever. I'm funny. You can ask your mom about *that* too."

Understanding that I was at least poking fun at them, the ghouls snarled in anger before charging. Another pair of crossbow bolts cracked into the fast-moving ghouls going for Cross, and he steadily backed away from the four monsters trying to kill him. That was all the attention I had to spare for his fight, because my own fight went crazy with a quickness.

The leader of the ghouls held its position for a reason. The ground cracked beneath its feet as the bone knight surged forward, black and green energy crackling like lightning along its joints. I barely managed to knock away the sweeping kick it aimed at my midsection, my left arm buckling under the pressure as I took two quick steps backward. It was much heavier than it looked, the bone armor covering it was denser than steel.

As we parted, the ghoul only managed a few more steps before it tumbled to the ground in a thunder of splayed limbs and spraying mud. The earlier soft tissue damage from my acid crossbow bolt must have burned through something important in its hip, affecting its mobility.

Not one to pass up such a kind gift when one is offered to me, I darted forward with my mace held high over my head, ready to end the ghoul before it could get back on its feet. Trying to coup de grâce this bitch, I aimed at its head. That's how I found out the bone spike that made it stand out from the others was more than just a decoration.

Somehow, as my blessed starmetal mace was about to crush the vulnerable ghoul's skull, it twisted its head and neck so my weapon was deflected down and along the bone and shunted off to the side. I struck the wet ground next to the bone knight hard enough that it buried the mace halfway up the handle in the mud. It was immediately stuck, and I was forced to let it go as I rolled away from a spike-covered elbow aimed at my midsection. The ghoul was back on his feet in the blink of an eye, and he made sure to put himself between me and my mace.

"Damn!" I cursed both myself, and my bad luck. A rumble of thunder seemed to agree with my outburst. My ninjatō sword hissed against its sheath as I drew it out slowly, locking eyes with the lead ghoul. "I guess today just isn't my day. Want to call it for now and try this again tomorrow, preferably when I've had some time to recharge my mana a little more?"

"*Hungry now. No waiting.*" The ghoul's wicked smile showed how confident it was feeling, despite the earlier tumble. It held up both fists, and smashed them together. Despite them being coated in bone, it still sounded like two plates of steel ringing against one another. "*Lady send us to find you. Now, I eat you, and Lady make me most strong and fast bone ghoul ever.*"

"Wait. If she only sent you out to *find* us, are you sure she wanted you to *eat* us?" I was only mildly curious about the answer. What I really needed was the ghoul to keep talking. Every second we weren't fighting was a second I gained ground on the cold in my arm, not to mention my other wounds. I almost had it beat, and once

I did, my natural regeneration would let me roast this guy. "What if she wanted you to find us because she wants to *talk* to us?"

Confused at the new idea, the ghoul froze for a good three seconds. That's a long time to stay completely still, and both Leedy and Murphy were happy to have such a helpful target. Two crossbow bolts bounced off of the monster's chest, his armor too thick for them to penetrate. The kinetic force still transferred, and it knocked the ghoul back half a step.

Once again, I closed the distance between us, this time aiming for the tiny gaps in its armor. My sword ate every kind of magic it came in contact with, which made it a potent weapon against magical creatures, mages, and basically anything controlled or animated by mana. It was not, however, some fantastic longsword, greatsword, or claymore, that can hack off limbs with a single mighty blow. That meant I was forced to try and kill this thing by chipping away at it, or more accurately–its damned mana supply, bit by bit, without letting it hit me.

So, that's exactly what I did. It wouldn't have been possible if Leedy and Murphy hadn't helped me by plinking away at the ghoul leader, causing the occasional distraction. There was also the fact that it didn't have a fully functioning hip, so I kept forcing the ghoul to follow me in a big circle, dancing in and out of its reach as I gave it the death by a thousand cuts. Each time the ninjatō found a gap in its armor, it stole a bit of the black and green lightning mana that made the undead so powerful.

I lost track of time, slipping into the dance of blades taught to me by the elves on world eight. Dodging the attacks of the ghoul became a natural part of the dance, the two of us falling into a pattern I could follow with my instincts alone. It was as pure a representation of battle as I had ever experienced, the two of us precariously balanced. I slowly started gaining an edge, the margin of my dodges becoming narrower and narrower, enabling more varied and powerful return blows as my sword stole more and more power, and both the ghoul and I could sense the fight was coming to an end. I was going to win.

While I never matched the grace and speed of the elves when I had been at level fifty-five, now I couldn't help but wonder what the blademasters would say if they could see me after breaking past the limits of level one hundred. Probably some snide comments about my footwork, immediately followed by a lot of sniffing and sour looks as if there was something that smelled bad in their immediate vicinity. Elves could be jerks like that. At least they made delicious cookies.

The flow of our fight slowed, and I capitalized on a brief lull to recover my mace. After regaining the armor-crushing weapon, I swapped my sword to my left hand–which had healed enough to use again–and held the mace in my right. It allowed me to smash the armor protecting the ghoul's joints, slowing it down even faster. Eventually, the bone knight dropped to its knees, drained and defeated.

As I sheathed my sword and finished healing with a burst of recovered mana, my ribs and arm were finally made whole again. I walked up to the ghoul, pushing enough mana into the starmetal mace to be able to power a *Smite* spell. The bone knight watched me come closer, leaking undead fluids from nearly every inch of its body.

"Is there any chance you feel like talking about that 'Lady' person you mentioned earlier?" While I knew the odds weren't great, I couldn't help but try. "I'm willing to listen if you are."

"*Closer.*" It rasped at me, leaning forward in the mud. I carefully approached, fully aware it could still take a swipe at me. When I stopped a few feet away, it motioned with a curled finger. "*Come. Closseerrr...*"

"Yeah. I've seen this movie. It never ends well for the good guy. No thanks." I started backing away, and I felt the mana start to swell in the ghoul's chest. "Ah, shit. You're about to blow yourself up, aren't you?"

The ghoul started to chuckle, and I turned to run.

I only made it a few steps before an explosion of malignant death mana detonated behind me.

CHAPTER 8

As far as explosions go, it wasn't nearly as big as the one I had made at the gate. Because my magic-eating sword had drained the undead monster of a good portion of its powers, it just didn't have the 'juice' to make it any bigger. What it *did* have, was absolutely *wretched* chunks of shrapnel, and a mana type that tried to kill anything living on contact.

"*Ouch.*" I picked myself up off the ground slowly, and my whole back screamed in protest. There were dozens of small punctures through my armor and clothing, and I could feel blood starting to pool in my boots as it ran down my back and legs, though I'd only been standing for a couple of seconds. A large piece of bone armor–probably that stupid head spike–stuck out of the back of my thigh. I picked up my hat and brushed it off as I put it back on my head. "I really hate the undead."

The mana generator inside my body was working overtime to push the invasive mana the explosion and bone shrapnel carried with it out before it could get any deeper. Lightning thrashed from the fog as it billowed outward from inside of me, destroying the black and green miasma that tried to penetrate past my skin.

"Are you… okay?" Leedy was the first one to make it to me, since Murphy was helping Jess climb down the tower of stacked boulders. "From up there, that ghoul blowing up looked like it had to hurt." He saw the large shard of bone sticking out of the back of my leg, and went to grab it. "Here, let me help–"

"No!" I pulled away, the quick movement making me wince. "Don't touch it yet. Some of the ghouls were different. I think their cores are bigger, and even touching the bone armor can hurt you. You and Murphy don't know enough magic to protect yourselves from something like that, so you shouldn't touch them unless they've been dead long enough for the mana to fade to safe levels."

I could feel that I was essentially radioactive at the moment–magically speaking–and I wanted to avoid any potential issues with contamination. For all I knew, this kind of mana could turn normal people into one of those ghouls, or open them up to whatever influence the creator of the undead possessed. After all, I hadn't forgotten identifying one of the cores and seeing the very obvious description about it being an 'Artificial Crude Monster Core'. Like all undead, these things were *made*, though these seemed much more unconventional in their creation. Most Necromancers stuck with the black magic equivalent of peanut butter and jelly. Blast any old corpse with enough death mana and boom–instant slavering horde of undead. I'd never heard of an artificial monster core in any of the worlds I'd visited.

"Okay, sorry." Leedy's hand dropped, and he frowned. "I was just trying to help. I feel bad for not doing more during the fight."

I grabbed the chunk of bone and yanked it out myself, which felt exactly as fun as I thought it would. About the same amount of fun as a root canal without anesthetic. "You did help. In fact, you probably saved my life. Without you and Murphy shooting that thing, there were a couple of times it would have crushed me."

Leedy immediately perked up, and gave the crossbow on his back a pat. "From where we were, it was hard to tell if we were doing anything. That's why Jess focused on helping Cross with the other four he was fighting, and we kept shooting at the one you were dealing with. Less chance of us accidentally hitting a friendly as well, since Cross was all over the place. You were much more predictable."

"Predictable? What are you talking about?" I knew I had to have been moving fast enough at some points that I would have been almost a blur in their eyes. "I was going at ludicrous speeds."

"You were, sure, but you were basically circling the ghoul over and over again. We could time our shots based on that. Cross had *four* ghouls to fight, and he couldn't do the same thing over and over again like you did." Leedy play-acted jumping around a bit, swinging an invisible spear in his hands. "He was a true master, never where you would expect him to be. Those monsters never stood a chance. They looked like new recruits, stumbling all over each other while he picked them apart."

It felt like dealing with the elves all over again. I brought down a super monster with extreme skill, but I did it in a predictable manner, which of course made it less impressive somehow. At least the elves gave cookies after their critiques. Leedy probably didn't even know how to bake.

"Anyway, why don't you get the others and stack the bodies? Just be careful. I'm going to concentrate on healing myself." I motioned to the freshly killed ghouls near Cross, who was on one knee, still recovering from the battle. "Don't forget not to touch those yet."

"Sure." Leedy started toward Jess and Murphy, who had finally made it down the tower. He stopped and turned back to look at me. "James, what's next? This felt much bigger than anything we've faced since the lich. And Jess told us about the Green Wardens. If they went to the city, neither place is safe for you."

"It *was* bigger–much bigger–and this won't be the end. Things are changing in the forest." I paused, remembering the warning about the local god coming for me as well as the ghoul leader's words, '*Lady send us to find you*'. "While the Green Wardens are a threat, they're *one* we know about. We don't know what might come next if we stay here." I looked at the devastation around us. "Besides, I think it's time we head to the city anyway. There isn't anything left here for us." I looked into the distance in the direction that I knew stood the walls of Greendown, a gloomy certainty weighing down on me. "Also, I get the feeling that if we don't get in there now, we never will."

Leedy gave me a nod, and went to tell the others the plan. They would handle getting everything prepared, and hopefully get a meal ready once they were done moving the bodies. I would be hungry after healing.

I found a relatively clear spot further down the wall and gingerly leaned against a stone section after stripping off my clothes and armor. The pieces of leather and wood that had provided minor protection were covered in holes, making them all but useless. All the rune work I had done was destroyed as well, causing me to grimace in frustration. One of the first things I would need to do in Greendown was to look for something a little more sturdy, especially considering the increase in threat these new undead represented.

After confirming my armor was ruined, I focused on getting myself patched up. Healing would be easier sitting down, but considering where some of the bone shrapnel was located, that wasn't exactly an option yet. I needed to get to work, and fast. I didn't need to give any ammunition to the team to gleefully comment on whether taking some bone to the backside was the same as me getting lucky. Especially Jess. The kid was getting lippy. Someone was clearly influencing her, and when I found out who it was…

Closing my eyes, I focused on the mana generator inside me. The crystalline structure looked like a blue geode leaking a cerulean fog laced with yellow lightning. It still thrashed in irritation against the death mana trying to invade my body, slowly pushing back the evil-feeling energy as my Vigor stat helped push out the shards of bone.

The whole process felt imprecise–unfocused, and I knew I could speed it along with a little help. Even though my mana generator was still a mystery to me, I grabbed hold of it and put it back to its normal sense of flow. Once the fog inside it was spinning and pulsing with lightning like it normally did, I already felt an improvement. Then I started focusing on the pieces of invasive bone stuck in my back and legs, the bigger pieces first.

My initial target was a thumb-sized piece wedged against my backbone, right between my shoulder blades. It was extremely uncomfortable, and the death mana that leaked from it was uncomfortably close to my heart. As soon as I focused my attention on it, my mana generator sent out a concentrated burst of lighting that flowed up my spine until it met the invasive piece of bone. The bright yellow energy released by my body surrounded the shard, and it started to condense around it like a closed fist. Instead of pushing out the bone as I wanted, the piece of shrapnel melted, dissolving into dark, viscous mercury that the lightning pulled right back into my mana generator.

That freaked me right-the-fuck out. Dead ghoul pieces did *not* belong inside my body, thank you very much. I doubled down on my concentration, trying to force the dark liquid out of my mana generator. Instead, my focus seemed to give the lightning more power to assault the fluid it contained. Bursts of energy jolted through the material, each time making it a little brighter. Somehow, it seemed to be...purifying the death mana from the solution. In a matter of moments, it was a bright silver that gleamed with an iridescent shine, losing any traces of impurities entirely.

A strange sense of calm came over me as the cleansed mercury-like liquid was absorbed by my mana generator. The blue crystal walls might have darkened a bit, but it was impossible to be sure. What I *was* sure about was the screen that popped up in my vision.

Congratulations! Your Soul Strain has improved.

Status: [Currently suffering from the effects of Soul Strain]
Strength- 65 [59→60]
Flexibility- 65 [64]
Vigor- 65 [61→62]
Mind- 65 [57→58]

I guess I found one of the things that could help with my Soul Strain. Either that, or my mana generator used the ghoul's bone armor to *make* something that healed me. This... wasn't going to force me to start eating greater undead, was it? I had a brief thought of me staring down hungrily at the broken body of an ancient vampire, holding onto a steak knife like a crazy person. Whatever was going on, it created a lot of questions.

Understanding why the strange lightning inside of me would want to strip the bone shrapnel of the undead of its magical death affinity was one thing–it was dangerous, after all. However, why did that action suddenly change the bone into some kind of magical elixir for my mana battery? Were the undead wearing armor that wasn't biological, but instead made up of some kind of liquid mana, or converted into something similar through a different method? Is that what the artificial monster core did as a function and why these ghouls were so much smarter and stronger? How far could I take converting this strange energy to my own use? Could I achieve a similar result from *any* undead, or did they need a certain level of power… or conversion, or whatever level the ghoul leader had achieved? Was it just the bone armor, or all the bones?

The worst question of all came last. Let's say there was something about the bones that was unique and that my mana generator could use them to lessen my soul strain, and I had a nice big chunk of monster bone in my hand. Would I need to fucking *stab myself* with it in order to get the strange lightning mana inside of me to break the thing down into its magical components? I shuddered.

I looked up into the sky, searching for some sign of the sadistic god or gods that had sent me to this place. "You wouldn't do that, right? I'm just overthinking things. *Right?*"

Who was I kidding? This is just the kind of mechanic I'm sure those bastards would love to see. Want a power up? No problem. Just stab yourself with the decaying shards of pungent, grotesque undead. Easy-peasy. I shook off the thoughts, resigning myself for some rather unpleasant testing and analysis in the future.

After knowing that the lightning mana wasn't working against me, I stopped trying to fight it, and focused on clearing out the rest of the shrapnel. The process was certainly different from my normal way of healing, since my magical energy wasn't actually being drained, but the mental strain was certainly more than I was used to handling.

While the fist of lightning mana scooped up several pieces at once, my natural Vigor stat managed to heal the open wounds left behind. Then, the lightning would drag the bone shards to my mana generator, inundate them with a new and exciting form of electro-shock therapy until they were free of death mana and all other impurities. The walls of my mana generator would absorb the liquid, and the process would start all over again.

Losing track of time is easy when you're focused on something inside yourself, so it was no surprise that it was almost dark outside by the time I finished and opened my eyes. The clouds had been blown away, and an orange sunset colored the sky. As was the norm for this world, another bank of purple clouds growing in the distance meant more storms would come later, but for now it was a picture-perfect moment. I wasn't exactly dressed for the occasion, however, what with me wearing nothing but a coating of my own blood, of course. I was pretty used to stuff like that by now, considering my track record. At least, as used to it as a person could reasonably get.

After clearing out every tiny speck of foreign bone in my body, I confirmed that the crystal walls of my mana generator had definitely changed color. They were now darkened enough to almost be called purple, with heavy streaks of blue swirling throughout it in a mesmerizing design that mimicked the natural flow of my mana's normal path. It looked pretty cool, even if I didn't feel any more powerful than I did before. I also noticed there was a distinct silver tone to the lightning that flowed through my body, as if it had adopted some aspect of the mercury-like liquid I had absorbed. The final update was the best part.

Congratulations! Your Soul Strain has now been healed. Due to your resilience from such a special set of circumstances, your status has been permanently improved.

Status:
Strength- 65→70
Flexibility- 65→70
Vigor- 65→70
Mind- 65→70

> Extended rest cycles will reduce the risk of reinjury. Further steps can be taken to strengthen the ties between body and soul, increasing your resiliency and bond affinity.

It was the first time in weeks that I had felt whole, and I couldn't hold in the full-body stretch that came over me. Man, it felt good to be back. And apparently, with the new bonus, better than ever.

"Good, you're finally awake." Cross was sitting a little farther down the wall from me, his own wounds looking weeks old already.

"If the next words out of your mouth are something about trying to cross the border and running into an imperial ambush, it would explain so much of my life." I interrupted the apprentice Judge with an idle thought.

Cross looked understandably confused. I felt too refreshed to apologize or explain. "Look, I'm funny, okay? You're just not my target audience."

Condescendingly, Cross placed a consoling hand on my arm. "You just keep telling yourself that, Holden. You'll be funny to someone, some day." Cross was smiling now, though it was still only barely discernible. "Now, back to what I was saying. The others have been ready for a long time. Are you ready to go?"

"That depends. What did you guys do with the bodies of the ghouls?" I was seriously contemplating taking as many pieces of the bone armor as I could, no matter how long it took to harvest them. Considering the bonuses it gave me, I would be crazy not to.

"Oh, Jess practiced her fire magic on them after we threw all the bodies in the crater you made. There isn't much left." Cross shrugged as I felt my stomach drop. "It was good training in mana control and management for her, especially after she drained herself at the start of the fight. They were surprisingly flammable, once she got them hot enough."

"Damn." There was no one to blame but myself. If I had stopped for a moment and let them know to save the ghoul leader's bone armor for me, I would have a great resource to test increasing my strength right now. Instead, I got wrapped up in what I was doing and completely forgot the outside world. Rookie mistake. "Well, I guess it's time to head to the city, as long as everyone is okay. Do any of you need any healing before we head out?"

Cross flexed his light-absorbing arm, shaking his head. "No, we're good. The others weren't wounded, and I'll be fine by this time tomorrow."

"Hey," I got serious for a moment. "You took out four of those things with minimal support from an apprentice earth mage? How'd you manage it? That would've been a hard fight, even for me."

Cross's head tilted to one side for a second, before simply raising an arm and flexing a massive bicep, as if that should explain everything. "What is it you told me last week? 'I've got mad skills, yo'? I think I'm starting to understand some of your odd phrases, and why you say them."

"Alright. I asked for that." We both laughed as I started getting dressed in one of the pairs of street clothes left behind in the packs abandoned by the White Wardens. The shirt was too tight, and the pants were too short, but at least they were clean. "What do you think, leave now, and follow the river up to the city?"

"That's probably for the best. We can make camp when we reach the river, and travel north at sunrise." Cross looked back to where the others were working. "The roads are going to be watched, and showing up to the gates with a bunch of horses and gear that belong to a missing group of White Wardens is certainly going to bring the wrong kind of attention. If we can flag down a passing barge, there's less chance of them connecting our group with them after all this time." The corner of his mouth lifted for a moment, so fast I almost doubted that it happened. He was back to his regular stoic self in a flash. "Taking unnecessary risks is something we should avoid if possible."

I looked toward the man, curious about what had his attention. Cross hardly ever smiled, and I was curious about what could have cracked his hardened shell.

Murphy was double-checking all the tie-downs on the horses, hard at work as always. His hands moved with practiced efficiency, ensuring nothing would shift and rub our horses' backs on our march. Even a small pack could cause a serious sore or rubbing injury in a short time, and Murphy wasn't the type of man who wanted to see something like that happen to an innocent animal.

Leedy was doing some kind of weird kung-fu thing with a crossbow in one hand and his sword in the other, practicing against an invisible enemy twice his size. Somehow, it didn't look as dumb as it sounded, but that's not saying much. It was still pretty goofy, especially when he reloaded the crossbow with his ear. At least he was practicing, I guess, and there was no doubt his sword moved in a lethal blur around him.

Jess was helping Murphy, occasionally sneaking the horses some slices of an apple she was eating. They munched happily on the treats without complaint, long-since used to the dangerous smell of the shifter woman. She was no longer the serving girl worried about her place in the world, but was already a powerful earth mage still coming into her own strength. As long as she held onto the conviction in her heart, Jess would be a force for good on this planet, and I felt bad for anyone in the future that stood against her.

After looking at the three of them, I could see why Cross had the urge to smile. I thought about what we had gone through and what we still had to face, and went back to getting my gear ready to go.

"Oh, the guilds are going to figure out we're connected to the missing Wardens, there's no doubt about that." I shook my head, thinking about all the times I'd failed at political intrigue in the past. "Once we sell off all that gear and equipment, no matter how much we spread it out through the city, pawning pieces here and there, word is going to get around. People will start asking questions, and once they put two and two together…"

"The truth will come out." Cross frowned, rubbing his chin in thought. "What if we dump everything in the river? Wouldn't being anonymous be better than the extra gold?"

I snorted, unable to keep in my sense of amusement. "Spoken like a man who's never had to pay for the restructuring of a governmental system out of his own pocket before." I finished strapping on my punctured armor, having to use my pocket knife to scrape off a few splinters to keep it from stabbing me before cinching it on tight. "Overthrowing the guilds isn't going to be cheap. Besides, we wouldn't be hiding in the shadows for very long. They'd learn who we are soon enough, and then we'd be exposed *and* broke, instead of exposed and rich." I shrugged my pack into place, finally ready to go. "Trust me, if you have the option, always choose to be exposed and rich."

"Somehow, that does make sense." Cross shook his head as we walked toward the others. "If we can't get a barge to stop, we'll have to wait for dark, and try to sneak up to the land entrance near the docks. It's a narrow strip of ground, so it won't be easy."

"We'll figure it out, don't you worry." I motioned toward Jess, and lowered my voice. "Also, don't forget, when we enter Greendown, the Button Guild is most likely going to be hunting her and I as well. We're going to have to keep an eye out for any traps or engineered 'accidents' they might arrange."

Cross grimaced, clenching the fist of his non-blackened hand hard enough to crack his knuckles. He was clearly remembering it was his fault the secretive guild of assassins might even know about her in the first place. "I will *personally* search for their guild headquarters, and burn it to the ground if they don't agree to drop the contract on her head." He very carefully didn't look at me as his voice remained deadpan. "I might mention dropping your contract as well, but I don't know if I'd burn down their building for you. I might tip over a candle or two, if they're nearby, but that's about the best I could do. Not because I don't like you."

"Of course not. That's crazy talk." I agreed easily, thinking about my many qualities that made it downright impossible for anyone to dislike me.

Cross continued as though I'd never said a word. "It's just, with the Green Wardens in the city to reinforce the contract, I don't think they're going to stop coming after you for anything."

Back when Cross had been 'Captain Cross, Leader of the Greendown Hunter's Guild contingent of Blue Wardens', he had been sent to kill me, and anyone with me. He had managed to send a message back to the city that had named Jess, and gave a good enough description that she would be easily recognized by a group of accomplished assassins.

After cutting off his hand and showing him the error of his ways, Cross felt very bad about what he had done. Now, he had a new hand, and was a Judge in his own right. If I could get him trained up, and keep him from becoming corrupted before whatever the darkness the lich had infected him with could finish its job, all the better.

"How kind of you." I smiled, nudging his shoulder. "I'll leave that little bit of excitement to you, then." I cracked my own knuckles, feeling the new power of seventy points in my Strength stat pulse through my hands. "I'm sure there's going to be plenty of other things to deal with."

"Definitely. After we set up a base of operations, you'll have to deliver the letters to those guilds from the villagers, and try to speak with the Sailor's Guild, and then–" Cross was cut off by a faint rumble that shook the ground. He looked at me with a raised eyebrow.

"That wasn't me. Not this time, anyway." Another rumble shook the ground, causing us both to whip our heads to the west. In the far distance, treetops were swaying, like something big was moving in our direction. In my vision, a screen with bright red letters popped up.

****Warning!****

One of the Icons of Wrath sent by an angered god is approaching your location. Leaving the area immediately is strongly advised.

As the screen disappeared, I felt the exhaustion of the day wash away in a flood of adrenaline. I grabbed Cross and pulled him toward the line of horses, where the others waited.

"So, I know this is going to sound crazy, but a god wants to kill me, and we've got to run. Right now."

Oddly enough, they didn't argue. We took off without looking back, the rumbling steps from the Icon trailing far behind us.

CHAPTER 9

Our run through the dark started as a nightmare. Not because it was hard terrain necessarily, but because we just so happened to run into a section of forest that had become absolutely *infested* by some kind of bug that created webs. Are webs considered terrain? I set the question aside for a time when I wasn't actively being chased by the corporeal wrath of a deity.

Thankfully, it wasn't spiders. Unfortunately, my subconscious didn't care if it was a harmless silkworm, caterpillars, mites, or whatever else it might be. When a web touched me, I got the heebie-jeebies, and it was all I could do to not burn down the forest around me. That would be bad, because the Icon trying to track us down would see the beacon it would make from miles away.

While a throwdown with an Icon might be fun to test out my new stats on, we had already been fighting all day. It would be much better to get some rest and come at it fresh, hopefully after finding out what 'it' actually was in the first place. I had also noticed the plural use of the word 'icon,' meaning there was more than one of them running around out here. It would really suck to get rolled up by a whole group of god-enhanced monsters in the middle of the night.

A strand of thick webbing slapped me across the eyebrows, and I felt something squirming drop down my cheek. I slapped myself so hard it made my ears ring, and I wasn't even mad about it. Stupid bugs. Ugh. I felt like I was fighting invisible ninjas.

Our train of horses handled the night run through the forest without any problems. They were bred and trained for moments exactly like this, and even ignored the webs like the champions they were. Show offs.

Leedy was our point man, and after I had several fantasies of tossing him into an active volcano for leading us through the webbing zone, he brought us to a part of the forest that was more spread out and open.

It showed signs of having been logged in generations past, and the people had left the most impressive trees to continue to grow and dominate their little parcels of land. The dense canopy didn't allow as much sunlight to reach the ground, which kept the underbrush much thinner. Despite the darkness, we actually managed a quicker pace with the better footing.

After what felt like hours of moving as quickly as we could through the endless trees, we were forced to slow down and give the animals a rest. Not that the humans were doing any better. Everyone was tired, and the sounds of pursuit had trailed off enough for us to be able to afford the break. Which was good, because if we'd continued on at the same speed, we'd have been forced into a pause due to true exhaustion or a horse going lame at our frantic pace.

Leedy found us a place to stop where a creek small enough to easily step over traced the south edge of a small rise. The horses were able to get a drink while the five of us climbed the ridge to get a better idea of where we were, and possibly see if the Icon was still following us.

There was good news. The river leading to Greendown was within sight. We only had another thirty minutes of hard running before we made it to the ribbon of water that reflected the bright starlight that lit up the night sky.

Then there was the bad news. We could all see the Icon was most *definitely* still following us.

"What *is* that thing?" Murphy had both the fewest number of enchanted items and the least amount of magical knowledge in the group, meaning he was the only one unable to enhance his vision enough to get a good look at the creature as its head poked up between two shorter trees, giving us all a good look at what it was. "It kinda looked like a giant goose or something." He shuddered, obviously reliving some past trauma. "Please tell me we don't have to fight a giant goose."

"No, Murph." I gave him a pat on his shoulder, trying to ignore my own heart pounding in my chest. "Don't worry. It's not a huge goose, although maybe it's an ancestor of some kind." The others looked at me in confusion, clearly not read up on the whole 'evolution' thing. "If you ever want to hear about a guy named Darwin, I'll tell you all about him when we have some free time. They even have these awards they give out in his honor where I'm from and everything. Very prestigious." I held back a laugh, remembering some of the more ridiculous Darwin Awards I had heard about from my past. Taking a deep breath, I refocused. I might have been feeling a little light-headed after seeing what had revealed itself in the forest behind us. "Anyway, none of that's important. What *is* important, is that I'm pretty sure a freaking *tyrannosaurus rex* just stuck its head over those trees so it could get a better scent of our backtrail."

My only reply was the wind rustling through the trees. Murphy swallowed hard, his knuckles whitening on the shaft of his halberd. Curiously, knowing it wasn't a giant goose actually seemed to calm him down a little. Weird guy. Or, maybe there were giant geese running around that were more terrifying than the granddaddy of all dinosaurs.

"This doesn't change anything. We still need to reach the river, and use it to lead us into the city." Cross looked back to where the giant dinosaur was stalking through the trees, doing his best to gauge its speed. "Everybody knows a rex that size isn't very fast. It's not a burst predator, it's a long-distance stalker. All we have to do is outlast it. We're in for a long night, and an even longer day tomorrow, but we should be fine."

All of that was information I most definitely did *not* know until he said it. I looked down at the horses, some of which were already showing signs of exhaustion. There was no way all of them would make it through the night, and less than half would manage to keep going past noon.

"Sooo…" I said, overly casually. "Hypothetically speaking. Let's just say that you're right about the giant dinosaur being a long-distance hunter, and that our best bet would be to outlast the thing." Cross went from a confused face at me restating his information, into one of refined horror at my next words. "And, oh, I don't know.

For the sake of hashing out a totally hypothetical and nowhere near real possibility–let's say that said dinosaur had been blessed as an Icon by a nature god. Would you think it's possible for us to do it?"

"That… thing is an Icon?" Cross whispered.

I nodded.

"By the Trinity's six tits." Cross placed one entire palm over his face, rubbing at the very real stress he seemed to have found there.

I paused, my brain suffering a small short-circuit. I don't think I'd ever heard Cross curse like that before. Setting that thought aside with the many others, I nodded again, having expected the outcome.

"That's pretty much what I figured. We're either going to lose most of the horses, or we're going to have to fight the dinosaur. Considering the amount of wealth they're carrying, I *really* don't want to lose the horses." I saw Jess give a sharp nod of agreement. She didn't want to see them die for entirely different reasons, but I was happy for the support either way. "It would be a better idea if we could find a place to set up an ambush."

Cross shook his head as he pointed a blackened thumb toward the last place we had seen the tyrannosaurus. "You've never fought one of those things, have you? Otherwise, you'd know we'd need siege equipment to pierce its skin. They make those bone knight ghouls look like glass dolls in comparison." He looked back at the river, squinting in the distance. "The only way to save the horses is if we can get them on a barge that agrees to stop for us before that thing catches up. If not, we're going to have to start sacrificing the slowest ones as a distraction to buy us time."

I thought about it for a second, not liking any of those options. That was how life worked sometimes. You weren't always given good options, just bad and worse ones. Tying up a horse or two for the dinosaur to feed on here would certainly slow down the pursuit. The sacrifice of one to save the lives of many always felt dirty, no matter how many times it happened. Maybe. The thing was being divinely appointed after all, and there was no guarantee it would stop for a little snack, no matter how convenient I made the diversion.

A memory from my past bubbled to the surface, and I was forced to relive one of the worst days of my life on world four.

Blood-slicked cobblestones made our retreat even more dangerous, our shield line slipping with almost every step. The smell of death had long-since permeated the city, but now it was thick enough across the intersection to choke even the most stoic of the defenders. The mixture of howling attackers and screaming men made the full assault on my senses overwhelming, and I vomited off to the side. I wasn't the only one, just the first in my row to do it, earning shouts from the detachment sergeant and a glare from the knight standing beside me.

"Don't show weakness in the face of the enemy, James!" His gauntleted fist thumped my shoulder, almost causing me to drop my heavy tower shield. "We're the last line of defense between these heathens and the Nine Bishops. If they get through us, the clergy is as good as dead!"

The attempted breakout from behind the besieged castle walls had been doomed from the start, the heavy gilded carriages of the church were simply too much for the starving horses to pull at anything approaching a reasonable speed. Even now, the pride of the church leaders on this planet was too great to travel in anything less, and the people were so brainwashed after generations of belief that they even agreed with them. No matter what I did or said, there had been no way to change anything. I was too weak *to change anything.*

We had waited too long to try something like this anyway, even if they had listened to me. The food supplies had dwindled to the point where we were either going to have to eat the horses, or use them to try and escape the ring of 'barbarian heathens' surrounding us and their goblinoid slaves they used for fodder against our walls. The poor equines had been trapped and underfed in the stables for so long, it was a miracle the trio of carriages even made it over the drawbridge. We had barely made it a quarter of the way through the city before the horde had swarmed us, forcing us to abandon the attempted escape, and sticking us in this intersection where we were trying to turn around and go back to the castle.

"It's not weakness, Sir Riety, it's the smell. I'm not as used to it as you are." I stomped dead a rat that scurried in front of us, their numbers so prolific after weeks of fighting that even our melee in the middle of the streets did nothing to deter them. They were the only winners in this siege, the rats and carrion eaters that picked over the piles of dead heaped against the sides of every building. "I won't flinch against the enemy, don't you worry."

"Ha! We'll make a knight out of you yet!" Sir Riety gave me another bruising thump before falling out of line. "Help hold here, while I see what's taking so long. By the Saints, turning three carriages shouldn't take this long."

The boisterous knight left, checking on a problem I could have already told him the answer to. We were trying to hold in an intersection that would have barely been big enough for one of the clergy's oversized transports to turn around on a perfect day, with a team of eight well-fed horses to do the task.

Right now, there were only six horses per carriage, and three of them were crammed into the space, along with all of their escorts. There was no way they were going to get them to turn around before we were overwhelmed. The bishops were going to have to abandon their fancy wagons, stuffed to overflowing with gold and precious stones from the cathedral's hidden depths. It was our only chance for survival, and it was the one thing they wouldn't lower themselves to do. Despite the reality of their situation staring them in the face, they were too blind to see it.

"To our left! They're coming through the alley!" The archer who shouted the warning suddenly sprouted at least four enemy arrows from his body, spinning him in place before a lance of fire ripped him in half. Apparently, the barbarians had brought a spellcaster.

My detachment sergeant didn't hesitate, shouting for our squad to shift into position. We moved with practiced precision, slamming our tower shields into an impenetrable wall of steel that completely blocked the narrow entrance. We would be able to hold, but only as long as the magic in our tower shields held against the enemy spellcaster. There was no way to know how much time that would be, given the history of this world.

All of the weapons and armor used by the church had been created a long time ago, during a great war with a demonic race that invaded from another plane of existence. Their god had blessed every bit of metal, empowering their warriors and allowing their armies to wipe out the evil after a century of warfare. That was a long, long time ago.

The magic that was left in all the armor and weapons of this planet's church was fading, and had been for generations. They hadn't been used to fight against true evil, and whether that factored into the decline of the equipment, or it was simply the silence of their god, I couldn't be sure. Instead, the weapons and armor were tools for political expansion and power, spreading the church, its influence, and its wealth far beyond the role that any religious organization should ever hold. As their political power waxed, their true power waned, and now the current generation got to reap what the past generations had sown.

For some reason, the magic of their god remained the strongest in their shields, which was the only reason why we weren't melted into slag when another wave of fire washed over our line of troops. I could see a few men wince in pain as their shields grew hot to the touch, while others remained perfectly fine. The defenders holding the center were the first to fall, and there was nothing I could do to help them.

I had ended up being the right-most anchor when we had shifted, meaning I could lean against the wall of the building beside me for support. When the mass of goblins slammed into our line, it was all I could do to hold on, digging my heel into the ridge of the cornerstone beside me.

My only weapon was the single-edged short sword given to me by the church, and I used it to good effect, stabbing over the top of my shield into the exposed heads of the shorter humanoids trying to push their way through our line. I got lost in the rush for a moment, until another wash of flames served to clear out the goblins, while also causing two of our seven men to scream in pain as their shields turned red from the heat. Neither dropped their shields though, their training and toughness holding through, despite the sizzle of their flesh. If they were closer to me, I might have been able to heal them, but that would mean exposing my ability to do magic, and they would burn me at the stake as a heathen. They would just have to deal with the pain.

Our center started to bow as a second wave of goblins rushed forward, the fodder gleefully sacrificing themselves against our blades. Behind them, I knew the barbarians were waiting for their turn. Once we were softened up enough, they would come, and the real fight would start.

"Hold!" Sir Riety was there as if by magic, supporting the center of our line like he had never left. "Hold the line, men! For God and Glory!"

"For God and Glory!"

Our answering call was echoed by all the men around the intersection. There were far fewer voices than there should have been. I looked back, noticing for the first time that there were nine horses missing from their harnesses. From there, the mental math was rather simple. There had been nine bishops in the carriages.

I guess I had been wrong about them being too blind to see reason. Though, I gotta say, it was too bad they waited until I was stuck in the middle of an enemy horde for them to actually see the light.

Everywhere I looked, it was only a single line of soldiers holding back the enemy, with a lone knight provided for support. The rest of the protection detail had left with the bishops, running back the way we had come. The bishops had left us behind to die, so they could live.

They had left us as a sacrifice.

"Why is a god trying to kill you?" Murphy's voice snapped me out of my flashback, popping the old memory like a soap bubble.

"We never got a chance to hear the details about how you knew a god was angry with you, and why they wanted to kill you in the first place."

I gave my head a shake, trying to clear it of the past. World four had been a long time ago, and I was not the same man that I'd been then. After taking a deep breath and letting it out slowly, I made eye contact with Murphy, trying to express to him how serious I was being. "I can't tell you *how* I knew there was a god sending something after me, but the *reason* is because I kept tearing up the forest. I'm pretty sure it's some kind of nature or forest god, and they want to punish me for destroying so much of this pristine land."

"Oh." Murphy gave me a thumbs up, relaxing his grip on his halberd with his other hand. "That makes sense. You really have messed up a bunch of trees. If I was a forest god, I'd be mad at you too."

"Thanks, Murph. I appreciate your honesty." I checked our backtrail one last time, trying to get another glimpse of the dinosaur following us. "We should hurry this along. The river isn't far, and we can take another break when we get there."

As the others started back down the rise, Jess stopped and grabbed my arm. "What about the plan to leave some of the horses behind? Are you going to do it?"

I could tell the plan bothered her, at least more than it did me. Cold practicality had begun to prioritize the lives of sentient, thinking people over those of animals long ago. I wasn't heartless, or unnecessarily cruel, either. "No. Not unless we have to. We'll think of something else. I don't want to sacrifice anyone, even if it is just a horse." My memories had only driven home how awful such a practice was. "It's one thing if someone *chooses* to sacrifice themselves for a cause, or for someone they care about. That's something noble, and worthy of praise. It's completely different if they are forced to do it. The horses can't make that choice, so I really don't want to force it on them if I don't have to."

She gave me a sharp nod of agreement, relief clear on her face. "Thank you. It's probably dumb, but I like all of them."

"That isn't dumb. It just means you have a heart." I patted my own chest as we started walking down the small hill to join the others. "Don't ever lose that. It's your guide, to help tell you the difference between what's right and wrong. The stronger you become, the more important that guide will be. Make sure to listen to it."

Jess thought quietly for a few heartbeats before looking over where Murphy was already getting the horses back in line. "I'll do my best."

"For the sake of this world, I sure hope so. You're going to be a strong and influential leader one of these days, and you can't forget that compassion is the one thing that makes you worthy of that power." I pointed at Murphy before leaning in and lowering my voice to a whisper. "Look, I'm not saying depending on others to be your conscience is a bad thing, but you still have to depend on yourself as well. With the way you feel about the–"

A trumpeting roar from far in the distance echoed through the forest, causing everything around us to go still. The tyrannosaurus rex had found our scent again, and was back on the hunt.

It was time to find a barge.

CHAPTER 10

Standing in open daylight made Gleason's skin tingle. It wasn't painful. He was beyond that now, but it was certainly another reminder that he wasn't the same man that he used to be. As he watched the pair of green-cloaked figures enter the Hunter's Guild, the throbbing black veins that pulsed across his clenched fists were an even better one. Gleason would not be cowed by his past. He was not the same scared little boy who had stood by while his father got massacred by a trio of Green Wardens. They would pay for who they were, what they represented, and he would be the one holding the collection plate.

"Anything else for you, sir?"

Gleason's attention was forced back to the street vendor selling the skewers of spiced vegetables. "No. Keep the change." Always magnanimous, he flicked the man a full bronze piece, and walked away, picking at the food to better blend in with the crowd. He needed to wait a few minutes until the Wardens made it to his uncle's office, the Commandant, before he cast his spell to eavesdrop on what they were up to, and eating food was one of the best ways to make it look like you belonged. Considering how crowded the streets were with the influx from the surrounding farms and smaller hamlets, it wasn't too hard to blend in as long as he didn't stare at any one place for too long.

The city wasn't fully under siege yet, but it was already starting to feel the pinch from reduced trade as the supplies from outlying villages were slowly being cut off. Normally, there would be meat included with the skewers, but the vendor had supplemented it with hearty chunks of mushrooms. Rooftop gardens and the city greenhouses would have to start picking up the slack, until they would fail to produce enough as well. Street vendors would keep going for as long as they could, using whatever they could find, adding new spices to keep customers buying what they offered. The one he bit into had a thick crust of seasonings that was meant to make the mushrooms taste more like venison.

All of it tasted like ash to his tongue.

Ever since the arrival of the Green Wardens in the city three days ago, his complete attention had been absorbed by their presence. His existing plans had still moved forward, of course, and the new arms and armor he had wanted were well on their way to completion. The only things he needed now were the few missing ingredients and components to some minor items and he would be all but unstoppable when the time came to cleanse the city of its filth and sin.

Capitalizing on any new opportunities had been impossible for Gleason, however, and he knew he was close to failing his mission given to him by the Trinity. The gods had blessed him, given too much, for Gleason to fail them now. He had to focus on what was important, and find a way to ignore the distraction the Green Wardens represented.

Most of their time was spent outside the city anyway, fighting against the encroaching army that even now closed its grip on the city. Once Greendown was encircled, Gleason's opportunity to strike would be on a countdown. Eventually, either the defenders would be overrun, causing him to lose his chance to enact the will of the Trinity, or the siege would fail, and those trapped in the city would scatter like the rats they were. He couldn't allow either of those outcomes before his ultimate scheme came to fruition.

He might even be able to time things so he could destroy both the sinners inside the city and the undead corruption outside its walls, if the gods willed it. Fire and devastation would rain down on them all, and he would be the architect that brought forth the storm. Vivid images of what was possible flashed through his mind, as if cast there by another. Screams filled his ears, and the smell of smoke and cooked flesh was so vivid it was almost real. This wasn't the first time he had received visions, but these were certainly the most tangible.

It had to be a message sent from the Trinity, telling Gleason they still had faith in him. His skewers of food dropped from nerveless fingers. The thought of so much pain and destruction was nearly orgasmic, and he had to stop and lean against a parked wagon to let the visions pass and allow his mind to settle. The black veins under the skin of his knuckles writhed in counter-beat to his pounding heart as he hunched over and clutched at the hem of his dirty robes, trying to bring himself back under control. The dark veins were black river eels, excited by the scent of blood in the water. Somehow, that thought didn't seem to bother him.

"Hey! Get away from there!" A pair of barrel-chested men wearing the rough brown woolen clothes of the Porter's Guild came stomping up the street, pushing through the crowd of people that became onlookers to the sudden entertainment. One of the men with a jagged scar running down his cheek pointed a finger at Gleason, and shouted at him again. "We don't need any bums getting sick on our cargo!"

For a brief moment, Gleason looked for the street drunk the man was yelling at. Once he noticed the load of crates in the back of the wagon, he realized the porter was talking to him. A flash of rage provided the clarity he needed to clear his head.

Gleason stood up straight and faced the two men, his eyes sparking an eldritch green as the black veins in his pale face squirmed to the surface, causing the porters to pause. Both heavily-muscled workers were smart enough to understand the man in front of them was a different kind of threat, and far beyond a simple drunk.

Instead of reacting in anger like his more basic urges demanded, Gleason looked down at himself. He was used to looking like a White Warden, in spotless robes and shining armor. Right now, his appearance was that of a mercenary that had fallen on hard times, like many others in the city. Battered and mismatched armor, dirty clothes covered with questionable stains, and exuding the faint odor of the sewers, certainly no one from his past life would ever recognize him. Even *Gleason* didn't recognize who he was becoming.

Gleason waved a hand in apology. "Sorry. My mistake." As he walked toward them, they backed away, neither wanting to pick a fight with the suddenly imposing man.

Remembering their faces, he quickly walked away from the immediate area. It was too open, and in broad daylight. A confrontation this close to the Hunter's Guild and Warden's Headquarters was asking for trouble he didn't need at the moment.

Now that he knew their faces, he could visit the men in the dark of night at his leisure, and take his time showing them how upset they had made him. Perhaps he could add them and their families to his growing collection of useful individuals under the city. A few porters might make moving the heavier items around a bit easier on his Blood Wardens.

For now, anyway. Once the alchemist finished finding a way to concentrate the formula into either an elixir or a pill, his men wouldn't be found lacking in strength ever again. The thought of what he would be able to do with them under his command made his anger evaporate.

Even the mistakes the alchemist made would be useful as well, especially once they were combined together and added to the water supply. No control, but sometimes chaos was a certain kind of control all on its own. It would be glorious to see the results.

"Focus on the now." Gleason admonished himself out loud, causing a few bystanders to stare at him oddly as he passed by. "The fun will start soon enough."

The incident with the porters made his last location a poor choice for his eavesdropping spell, so Gleason had to change where he would cast from. It was a simple spell of his own creation that used almost no mana, meaning even someone as powerful as his uncle–or even a Green Warden–would find it nearly impossible to detect. The only limitations were its range, and the need to be in the same line of sight of whatever the spell was aiming toward.

After finding an alley that had a view of the Hunter's Guild where Gleason could hide behind a pile of forgotten crates, he cast his spell, aiming at where he knew his uncle's office window was. Once the tiny flow of mana snapped into place, he could hear the voices of the Green Wardens and the Commandant as if he was standing in the room with them. They were already deep in a debate about the city's disposition.

"I understand your position, Chief Warden Tew, but the life of one man doesn't hold a candle to the importance of the safety of this city." Gleason's uncle, the Commandant, sounded tired. He could imagine the dark circles under the older man's eyes, and the threat of the siege causing his wide shoulders to droop. "Your presence on the battlefield has already extended our timeline to bring in more supplies, and we both know how many lives that extra food is going to save before this is over."

"Hmm." The deep grunt, most certainly from the larger of the two Green Wardens Gleason had seen, didn't sound happy despite the positive news his uncle delivered. "The *Oracle* doesn't give orders lightly, and to have so many come so quickly about the same person is almost unheard of. The threat that must represent is greater than our understanding. All I'm saying is, it would be foolish to ignore something so important."

"No one is saying–"

"Why don't we do both?" A third voice, this time one much younger, and feminine, interrupted the two older men. "I am more than capable enough to handle the fighting outside the city. Chief Warden Tew can focus on hunting down the target inside the city."

The young woman's idea was met with silence at first, and then the two older men started grumbling to themselves as they thought it over. Gleason had to physically restrain himself from jumping with excitement. If they voluntarily split themselves apart, it would make several of his possible aspirations much more likely to come to fruition.

"Oriana, are you sure about this?" Tew's concern seemed genuine, and Gleason could hear him shifting in the leather chair inside the Commandant's office. "There's an entire army of undead out there, on top of all those witches. Even a more experienced Green Warden would pause against such a threat."

"Give me most of our guard contingent, if you are that worried." Oriana sounded eager to Gleason's ears, which only made him happier. He knew young, eager, and inexperienced was an excellent combination for him to exploit. "You won't need that many against one man. Besides, we both know those witches don't have their heart in this battle. Otherwise, we'd have triple the number of orcs and goblins out there. Plus, they haven't cast a single great working against the city. If they were truly trying, we should have seen several by now. Like I've been telling you, something is off. With *all* of this." She paused, as if gathering her thoughts. "It's like they're being forced to attack, and all of it's a show for someone else's benefit. We're only seeing a part of what's going on, and I think there might be a third party behind all of it."

"Until you have more proof of your conspiracy theories, trainee, keep them to yourself. The Commandant has enough on his plate without you adding to it." Tew's voice softened a bit, losing most of its sternness. "However, as for the rest of your plan, I think if the Commandant is willing to add a squad of archers to your guard detail, I'd be willing to agree with it."

Gleason could well imagine the sense of relief his uncle felt when he realized he was getting to keep a Green Warden on the front lines, as well as another running around the city in search of some other target. It was no surprise when the Commandant agreed. "I'll assign a mixed squad of bowmen and crossbowmen as scouts and close escorts to be mixed in with your existing team. As for your search of the city, I wish you luck, Chief Tew."

"I make my own luck, Commandant." The sounds of the chairs scooting about signaled the meeting was coming to an end, and the visiting Green Wardens were getting ready to leave. Tew's confident voice got harder to hear as it moved away from Gleason's spell, but he could still make out what he said. "If he's anywhere in the city, I'll have James Holden captured and executed in no time. Then we can get back to fixing your undead problem in full force."

"That sounds excellent. I'll look forward to it." The Commandant let out a deep sigh, and the sound of his bottom drawer squeaking open was plain to Gleason's ear. It was where the old man kept his bottle of rotgut whiskey, the kind he drank when he meant to get truly drunk. "I've lost enough to that foolish mission already."

Gleason cut the spell, his mind whirling with what he had just heard. If the older Green Warden really was here for James Holden, then maybe he should wait before he killed them. But, if he waited, he would lose his chance to face the Greens while they were separated. He could also follow Tew until he found the man who had broken his arms and legs, and then swoop in to kill both of his most hated enemies after they had weakened each other. Knowing which option to choose was nearly impossible at the moment, especially since he didn't have any of his completed equipment. He wasn't prepared to handle someone with the kind of power that James Holden had at his disposal, nor he suspected, the Green Warden Tew. Not yet.

"One thing at a time. I'll just have to properly *motivate* the crafters to finish their jobs. Then, I'll be ready." Deciding that his best course of action was to return to his base to think things over, Gleason didn't notice the green sparks that fell to the ground from his fingertips, lit by his excitement.

He also didn't see the shadow that followed him along the edge of the rooftop, their careful footsteps making no sound.

CHAPTER 11

We made it to the river the first night without any further problems. The Icon following our trail didn't gain any ground, but we all knew it would keep following us without fail. None of my past experience told me how to best fight a giant dinosaur, so I fought down the urge to double back and take it on by myself.

Whatever else Alexander Cross was, he was a capable man, and when he started talking about siege equipment being needed to take down such an enemy, I'll admit that I was hesitant to ask whether he meant a normal t-rex or if he was taking into account it being empowered by a god. I wasn't sure that I really wanted to know the answer, and so I decided to keep my dumb decisions to a minimum. Really switch things up for a change. Variety is the spice of life, after all. Instead, we made a cold camp on the riverbank and got what rest we could.

Since it was my first time seeing the Mighty Reka, it was quite a surprise to witness how big it was up close. Huge is a good description, but it didn't do it justice.

It was easily comparable to any of the great rivers from my home world, like the Nile, Amazon, or Mississippi. The banks were far enough apart that the other side was hard to make out with any detail, beyond it also being heavily forested, and maybe having a little bigger trees.

The current moved at a deceivingly fast clip, and it made me wonder how a barge could travel upstream against the flow toward Greendown. There was no way a team of rowers could manage it, and there wasn't enough wind for a sail to make any discernible difference. It was the first thing I asked about when we packed up our few items and started out for the day as the sun crested the horizon.

"Oh, the barges use several ways. Most use poles they stick in the ground to walk up the river, and they work in teams." Leedy used his hands to pantomime straining against an invisible pole. "There's several teams on every barge that trade off as they go. It's hard work, but they're paid well for it. Others use riding contraptions that are man-powered as well, but I don't know as much about those."

"I'll have to see it in action. I'm having a hard time picturing how it would work." I thought about how effective a steam-powered paddle boat would be on such a wide river, and shook my head at the waste. "Too bad you guys don't have steam engines yet."

"What?" Leedy rubbed at his ears, as if trying to clean them. "I have no idea what you're talking about."

"Don't worry, I don't know either." I shrugged. It wasn't like I knew how to build a steam engine. And even if I did, I was only on each world for a year. That definitely wasn't enough time to instigate an industrial revolution, so I had never bothered to try. I suppose I could get across the basic principles involved and let someone else figure out the rest. I'd have to think about it. Failures on past worlds made me hesitant to even waste my time. "Let's get moving. We don't want that t-rex sneaking up on us."

As we made our way upriver, I managed to bring down a deer. I thought spreading around the blood and carcass to throw the Icon off our trail might buy us some time. At the very least, the dinosaur wouldn't be as hungry if he caught up. The deer was unlikely to work for long, but needed to be done simply due to the possibility that even the smallest distraction could make the difference between us making it into the city and becoming dino chow.

The entire time we traveled the first day, there wasn't a single barge, ship, or boat to be seen. According to Cross, that wasn't normal, but with the increase in undead activity through the region, it wasn't that big of a surprise. No crew wanted to risk their lives and livelihood if they didn't need to, and there weren't many risks bigger than a bunch of undead.

Somehow, our entire group–including the horses–managed to keep going the entire day despite a pace that pushed at the edge of our collective endurance with almost no breaks. It was as if the beasts of burden understood that to fall behind was to die.

Each of us took turns rotating to the rear, trying to get some idea of how close the giant dinosaur was to catching up with us. Even after climbing the tallest trees we could find, there was no sign of the Icon following our trail. Despite that, no one doubted it was out there, still hunting us.

As the daylight was starting to fade, Cross dropped back from his place in the front to talk with me. “We should find a place to camp. There’s an area not far from here I know about, where river traffic stops sometimes to forage and get fresh water. Now that we’re closer to the city, it isn’t safe to drink from the river anymore. It’s as good a spot as any to hope for a ride. As much as I hate to say it, we need to light a fire.” He pointed a thumb at the river, once again making me realize how empty it was. “If we don’t, a barge might see us and think we’re trying to hide. They’ll never stop and talk to us if that happens.”

“Fine.” I looked at the forest behind us, still not seeing any signs of the tyrannosaurus rex. “We’ll be a beacon to the Icon, but if we keep the fire small it might not notice us. I’m still holding out hope that the deer I killed distracted it long enough that we managed to get away.”

“Not likely, but you never know. I’ll get us heading to the right place.” Cross shrugged, before jogging off to the front of our group.

I couldn’t help but notice the thick black veins that were running up his arm as he left, longer now than they had been a week ago. Whatever the lich had infected him with was speeding up, growing more each day. Figuring out how to get rid of it was going to be one of the first things I did as soon as we had a few spare moments in Greendown. My skills in alchemy were extensive, especially since it was the second profession I’d earned. If I could get some time to study both Cross and the various unique ingredients of this planet, I was confident something would come to me.

Once we got to the area Cross mentioned, it was obvious that the location saw a lot of activity. It wasn’t as built-up as a waypoint in the woods like the ones the guilds set up and maintained, but it wasn’t far from it, either. It also made sense. Any large barges or ships should, by definition, carry enough supplies to outfit themselves for any trip, including sleeping space, and should just need whatever odds and ends they'd gone short of on their trips. Which meant that many of the facilities catered to the needs of smaller vessels and groups and therefore needed a smaller infrastructure to handle it.

Unless you were a merchant caravan, roadside waystations catered to the needs of nearly everyone on a given road and needed more manpower to protect and police. Waterways weren't known for their large, leafy obstructions, for example–which meant most, if not all interactions on the river were done in plain sight of anyone with eyes. The literal visibility meant that crimes of opportunity on the riverway were probably minimal and normally only required a token presence from the guilds to police. Things would absolutely be different if it weren't for the truly massive scale of the river. Bandits simply couldn't ambush vessels from the tree-enshrouded shoreline. The distances were just too large to make such an effort make any sense.

A series of logs used as benches were placed around stone circles along the river, worn smooth over time from both weather and people. There were several posts hammered into the ground where we could tie up the horses, and a rock-lined well in the center supplied clean water, with empty wooden troughs ready to water draft animals. It only took us a short time to get the animals secured, and Jess and Murphy started rotating them through to get a drink.

My Mind stat had increased with the rest of my stats, which greatly modified my perception of the environment. I'd often gotten headaches, despite the Mind stat also increasing my capability to process the expanded senses, it still took weeks to attune myself to my growing sensory grasp on the world around me. The recent boost had once again elevated those capabilities and meant that I could smell the evidence of a very recently dampened fire in the rest area we'd chosen. Combined with the lack of any other evidence of a group quickly packing their things away and escaping ahead of our arrival meant that the group was small and lacking equipment. Refugees, most likely.

After determining that the threat level of this group was minimal, if not non-existent, I pushed them to the back of my mind.

While the others were dealing with the animals and getting supplies unpacked for a meal, I did a quick walk around the perimeter to check for signs of any undead passing through the area recently. There were plenty of tracks of all kinds, but none that were fresh. Though, I did confirm the existence of a small group that validated my suspicions about the refugees that had been here before. The constant mud from the daily rains made it hard to tell what was a few days old, and what was brand new, but I was confident there was nothing around that would constitute a hazard for us.

"James, could you come here please?" Murphy's voice sounded more polite than normal, which put me on edge. Something was wrong. Great. Let's see what you got, Murph. "We need some help over here."

"Sure, Murph. On my way." I curled in my index finger while spreading my other digits wide, and swung my arm as I cast a spell that was barely more than a cantrip. I whispered the activation word, and kept the mana I pushed into the spellform low enough that no one watching should be able to see it. "*Spark Shield*."

Each time I swung my arm, it created a long thin line that settled onto the ground, and the makeshift tripwire would activate the spell as soon as something crossed it. The minor jolt wouldn't do much harm, but the shooting sparks would create light which would draw attention and allow us to see even an invisible or camouflaged enemy sneaking into our camp.

"What's the problem?" As I knelt down next to Murphy, keeping my voice low, all he had to do was shift a pile of ashes next to the fire he already had going. I raised my eyebrows, feigning surprise. "Damn. That's fresh."

"It's not just fresh, the coals are still hot. Someone else is here, most likely watching us." Murphy surreptitiously looked to the trees in the direction of Greendown. "Not many, since the fire was small. I imagine only a few. Probably hiding somewhere over in that mess of brush." I gave him a tiny nod of agreement, not seeing anywhere else they could have run to when we came walking up. "What do you want to do?"

"I'm not sure," I hedged. "What do you think?"

"Considering the lack of gear they left behind, and the fact we didn't smell any food cooking when we got here, I bet they're refugees from the city. Probably starving, and hoping for a ride on a boat out of here." Murphy said, carefully not looking around.

It was a good assessment. Similar to my own. I tried to extend my senses to feel if there was anyone strong enough to sense, but I still wasn't picking up on anything. "I think you're right," I said, encouragingly. "What would you do in this situation?"

"Let's wait and see what their reaction is to us. There's no reason to attack someone if all they are doing is hiding because they're afraid. I'll start cooking something nice, make sure that it smells really good to see if we can't draw them out on their own. It would be nice to talk to someone from the city to find out what the situation is like inside the walls. We could also warn them about the dinosaur roaming the area, so they know not to make themselves an easy target."

"You got it." I agreed easily. I was glad to hear Murphy's reasoning behind his decisions. They were right on target with what I was hoping to instill in the man and the group as a whole. I gave him a mental thumbs up and made sure to move about casually to not ruin the man's plan.

Murphy immediately got to work, banging pots and pans around and generally putting on a show for anyone who might be watching.

I explained the plan to the others, and they quickly agreed. Jess helped with the cooking, while both Cross and Leedy split up to climb nearby trees, loudly stating they were going on lookout duty. Their job was to keep an eye out for any vessels coming up the river, and make sure the Icon didn't somehow manage to surprise us.

While everyone else was occupied, I took a turn looking over the horses. My internal mana generator had finally settled down after absorbing the bone fragments, and my energy levels were feeling higher than ever. It would be a good chance to heal any problems the animals might have, before they could become a bigger issue if we had to go on a long march tomorrow.

That was when I figured out how we had managed to keep all of the horses up to this point. Someone–it had to be Jess–had been magically boosting them. All the animals had faint traces of earth, water, and nature mana running through their bodies, which provided extra stamina, flexibility, and healing over time.

It was an extreme waste of personal mana, and she must have almost bottomed out her reserves several times a day to pull this off. Tactically, and as a leader, it was about the most stupid move Jess could have made. Personally, I was proud of her. It would be hard for a person who did something like this to turn into a power-hungry monster, and it alleviated a lot of the underlying concerns I'd been having about what she would become after I left this world.

When I looked over at Jess, I noticed how dark the circles under her cat-like eyes were, and how lethargic she was acting. She was too tired and drained to be of much use for anything other than moral support at the moment. There was a lesson here, and I hoped she learned it without someone losing their life first. Prioritizing the animals over the safety of not just herself, but the group as well, could lead to a deadly outcome.

If her actions were because she realized on her own that our lives were tied directly to those of our horses, given the nature of the thing chasing us, and that their condition would rapidly and dangerously affect the group if too many were to go lame, and then determined that the best use of her time and energy would be used in keeping the horses healthy… Well, in that case, she was growing as a strategic leader.

Soon enough, the smells coming out of our cookpot were enough to make any sane person's mouth water. Murphy had outdone himself.

As I finished up with the horses and made my way back to our small fire, I heard hushed whispers from farther back in the brush. I enhanced my hearing, allowing me to fully hear what was being said. The voices sounded much younger than I expected.

"But they could kill us!"

"It don't matter if we starve to death, does it?"

"What about Pa?"

"He ain't moved in a long time, Davey. A long time."

"Well, I ain't gonna leave him."

"I ain't said we was gonna leave him, did I? We'll just look for some food, and come right back here."

"Stealin's wrong, but–"

"No more buts. We ain't had real food in forever. If we don't eat soon, I don't think we're gonna make it. Besides, we ain't gotta steal nothin'. Maybe we can take whatever they don't finish for their supper."

"Okay, Pete. But if they kill us dead, I get to say I told you so."

The voices were clearly from two young boys. Even though I hadn't met them in person, they reminded me of my own brother and I at that age, which made the sharp pain of homesickness that stabbed me surprisingly deep and jagged. Pushing my feelings aside, I sat down next to Murphy and Jess, but kept my voice low enough that the approaching kids wouldn't hear me. "Expect two kids–little–from their voices I'd say one might be ten, the other a year or two younger. They're going to be hungry. A third person, their father, is either unconscious or dead." I locked eyes with Murphy. "What do you think we should do?"

He looked surprised. "Why are you asking me? What do *you* think we should do? You're pretty much the boss here and everyone knows it."

"I know what *I'd* do." I smiled. "I want to know what you'd do. You found the fire and planned out the meal to draw them out. What do we do next?"

"Well," Murphy scratched the back of his neck, his face breaking out into a blush under our attention, though I was sure that I had little to do with Murph's current state. "You said one was injured or dead, and if they got this far with the man, I bet they're going to be pretty hesitant all around. It'll probably be tough enough to convince them to come eat a meal, much less convince them to let us take a look at their injured father if that's who's back there. Let's try and talk to them and if we can't convince them to let you take a look at the man with them, why don't you sneak back around and check on him while we feed the kids and keep them distracted."

I nodded. It was a good plan. "That's what we'll do, then."

Murphy immediately started loading up heaping plates of food for them, while Jess went to tell Cross and Leedy what was going on. She gave Murphy a pat of approval on his shoulder as she walked by, obviously pleased that we were helping a family in need.

We would do whatever we could for them. As long as the Icon didn't show up while we were feeding them, there was no reason not to help. I mean, come on. Hungry kids.

As they got closer to the camp, I got ready to do a little bit of acting. The two kids moved surprisingly quietly through the forest, which explained how they were still alive. Making it all the way down here, at least two days' hard hike from the city through undead-infested forest, was quite a feat for most people, least of all kids. Despite their skills, they had no way of sensing my tripwires.

Since I didn't want to scare the bejeezus out of them–only a minor jump scare–I pulled the mana from all the spells but one, and adjusted the remaining one to shoot colored balls of light. As soon as they set it off, the red and blue flares that shot up caused the boys to freeze in place, and I jumped over to where they could see me with both hands raised in what I hoped was an unthreatening manner. They were poised to sprint back into the brush, but I spoke calmly before they could disappear.

"Hold up there, kids. We aren't going to hurt you." I looked both of them over, noting each only had sharpened sticks for weapons thrust through their belts in a crude imitation of daggers. They looked more than half-starved, and their clothes were well past the point of salvaging. It was clear they had been through a rough ordeal. "You look like you have a tale to share." I took on a stern expression. It was obvious that whatever these kids had been through had worn out their trust for other people, otherwise they would never have felt more safe outside of the city than in it. They were more likely to trust a man with a clear and understandable agenda than a suspicious level of kindness from a stranger. "Now, I'm not one to give handouts out of the kindness of my heart, understand? My granddad taught me to always give and take something in return, you get me?" The kids nodded, their posture less wary but still waiting to hear what terms I'd have. "Why don't you come and tell us about the dangers you might have seen, and for payment we'll share our meal? Food for information, the more you tell us, the more you get. How does that sound?"

At first, it looked like I was going to lose them, but as soon as I mentioned a way for them to *earn* some food, I could tell I had them. Both boys gave each other a subtle nod before the older of the two–Pete, if I remembered correctly–stepped forward with his hand on the rough hilt of his makeshift wooden dagger.

"We get *three* meals. Big ones, no matter what." He scuffed a ragged boot missing its laces through the dried mud of the campsite. "And nobody touches us."

Behind him, his little brother gave a sharp upward tilt of his chin in challenge, silently backing up everything his older brother had said. Their brown eyes and dark hair made them almost mirror images of one another, the only noticeable difference between the two was a few inches in height. Even their mannerisms were basically the same, the two of them against the world. There was no way anyone could doubt they were related.

"We *start* with two meals, and I'll throw in the third if your information is good and there's enough of it. Take it or leave it." There was no way I wasn't giving these kids that third meal, but this was the language they understood. It was the sort of response they could accept and understand. 'Nothing came free in this world', seemed to be a lesson beaten into their bones. I would know. I'd majored in that same lesson and had it hammered into the very fabric of my existence. Perhaps that was the thing that struck me with such force about these boys.

In their eyes, I saw myself.

The boys locked gazes with each other and whole conversations were had at that moment. They turned back to me and nodded as one.

I swept my arm toward the campfire, where Murphy sat waiting with their already prepared meals. "Please, sit."

Somehow, they managed to clean their plates before I even managed to get settled down by the fire and ask my first question. "Wow. You might want to slow down some. I'd hate for you to choke on your food."

"Do ya have any milk?" The younger of the two, Davey, looked over at Murphy with a hopeful face.

Murphy tossed over a wineskin with a shrug. "Sorry. Best I can do is some watered wine. It's basically grape juice."

They grabbed it and started passing it back and forth, happy to have something besides plain water.

"So, now that you've eaten something, how about you tell us how you got here?" Jess took their plates from them and refilled them while she talked, playing her part perfectly. "Are you refugees from one of the farms around here?"

Both of them looked at one another, obviously silently debating on how much they should reveal. Pete took another sip from the wineskin before he answered.

"We're from the city. Ya prob'ly ain't going to believe us none, but we was kidnapped by Wardens. *Bad* Wardens." Pete grimaced, staring down at his ragged boots. He was decidedly *not* looking at Murphy's Warden gear. "Our Pa, he makes boats. Not even good boats, but not because Pa's bad with wood. He's the best, e'rry one says so. Well, not long ago, the bad men came. They took us to make him do things. They'd hurt us when he din't listen to them good as they'd want."

"Bad Wardens?" Murphy was on the edge of his seat, practically vibrating in anger. Both of the boys backed up in fear, almost dropping the second round of food Jess had handed them. "Sorry, I'm not mad at either of you. I'm mad at the thought of a Warden doing something bad to children. Can you tell us what they looked like? Which branch of the Wardens they belonged to, or maybe their names?"

Davey nodded, happy to not be in trouble. "They wore the white robes, but all dirty. And the one they was all scared to talk to was Gleasy. He had them black veins runnin' through his body, an' when he'd yell at folks the black would grow bigger. Like when grandmama use ta get mad at grandad fer drinkin' too much, an' the veins in her fo'head would pop out real big."

"More like *Greasy*," Pete muttered with a scowl, his mouth more than half-full of food.

Now, it was my turn to be on the edge of my seat. I had a pretty good idea I knew *exactly* who the boy was talking about. "Do you mean Gleason?" The sound of both Cross and Leedy quietly making their way closer reached my ears. They must have been listening in from their places in the trees, and had started making their way down as soon as they heard there were Wardens involved with what had happened to the children. When I said the name Gleason, both of them froze on the edge of the firelight. "It's very important that you get this right. Was his name Gleasy, or Gleason?"

The last time I had seen Gleason, the leader of the White Wardens, we had fought a very one-sided battle. I had shattered all of his limbs right before he had been yanked into a dark hole by an undead tentacle horror. The prevailing theory had understandably been that he had died a horrible death, one that the little psycho had earned fair and square. Instead, it sounded like the cockroach was somehow still alive. Worse, it sounded like he'd been infected by the lich in a similar way that Cross was, but throughout his whole body. Both Cross and I made eye contact while he hid just out of the boys' sight, and he raised an eyebrow in an obvious question. I gave him a slight shake of my head, silently telling him to wait.

Davey shrugged his boney shoulders, oblivious to the two newcomers to our fire. "It could'a been Gleason. I don' know." He speared a chunk of bright yellow root vegetable with his fork before stuffing it into his mouth. The little boy hemmed and hawed while he thought, acting out his thought process as only a kid his age could manage to do. "They was keepin' us in the sewers cause he was in trouble, and all these black veins runnin' through his body was scary. There was other Wardens who din't seem to mind and was followin' his every word. It's how we knew for sure they was bad Wardens for real, and not pretendin' or somethin' else. We ran 'cause we din't think anyone would believe us."

"Well, if you couldn't tell, we've met Gleason before, and we *do* believe you." My eyes flickered over to where Cross was tensely waiting in the shadows. "The last time we saw him, there were no black veins like you talked about. Can you tell us anything more about them?"

"Our Pa might know, but he won't wake up." Davey went to stand, but his brother pulled him back down. He pushed back at Pete in frustration, tears welling up in his eyes. "Maybe they could help him!"

Pete opened his mouth to argue, an instant fight about to erupt between the two. Fear and frustration on the older boy's face was plain to see, and it pulled at my heartstrings. The pressure to hold it together for his younger brother must have been immense, and the strain was starting to show.

"Instead of fighting, you could give us a chance. From the way it sounds, I don't think I could do any worse by taking a look." I made a flicking motion with my wrist, and a green wave of healing energy washed over the boys, visibly helping their exposed scrapes and bruises. "There's a chance I could help your dad, if you'll let me."

"The Healer's Guild?" Davey jumped to his feet, and he would have dumped his remaining food on the ground if his brother hadn't managed to snatch it off his lap at the last second. "You've gotta come! He's this way!"

Pete only had a brief moment of hope I could see in his young face before it was buried in skepticism. He grabbed a large hunk of orange-looking meat from his plate and pointed it at me like it was a weapon.

"Don't go gettin' his hopes up for no reason. I seen what happened to our Ma when the Healer's Guild came to fix her." Pete's eyes misted at the memory, and I was once again reminded of my own brother and I at that age. "Pa is worse than Ma ever was, so I don't expect you can do much."

The doctors on my world hadn't done my mother much good either. It's why my first profession had been healer, after seeing the few options given to me by the system when I was selected–*some* people might uncharitably say kidnapped–to be a world-hopping judge.

It's me. I'm some people.

"I'm not promising anything. I'm no miracle worker." I offered my hand to the boy, hauling him to his feet. "But I can *definitely* say you've never met a healer like me, kid. You could say, we're worlds apart from one another."

The system had never given me a pun title of some kind, which I felt was unfair. That one was solid, as far as word-play goes. Oh well, it wasn't as though I was ever going to stop trying for that one in any case, whether it actually existed or not. I took a deep breath, letting it out slowly.

It was time to try and save a life.

CHAPTER 12

The man was so starved and dehydrated, I would have bet all the gold in my pouch he was deader than a doornail. He smelled faintly of old sewer and rot, with a heavy dose of death. Add the obvious signs of torture with the infection from being blinded by a dirty blade, and the only thing that told me the boys' father was still alive was the rattling breath he took as I knelt to look him over.

I had seen mummies with more life in them. No, really. Specifically, on world two, where demons had a bad habit of possessing the dead. It was a great planet to earn my Warrior Class, but the mummies were always dusty when they were busted apart, making it a nasty experience all the way around. It was like sand getting in all the bad places you don't want it, but instead of sand, it was the ashes of possessed dead people instead. Super gross.

Both of the boys watched me closely as I laid a hand on their father's chest. At first, I went slow, taking it easy and sending out a light probe of healing energy to see if he was as bad as he looked. It almost finished him off.

Normally, a healing spell used the body's own energy stores to help provide the regenerated tissues brought on by injury or illness. There wasn't any spare fat or energy for the man to give up, and the spell stole what it needed from his muscles and organs.

His heart stopped, and I cursed under my breath as I forced a burst of power into his body to get it beating again. As his heart shuddered back to life, the feedback from the spell told me he was as bad of a case as I had ever seen.

I could see the infection where his eyes used to be, but he'd also had his tongue cut out. The dehydration and starvation had allowed the sickness to spread throughout most of his body, and a fever was cooking his brain. Only the sheer will to live had kept this man from death's final grasp.

"This is going to take a minute." I glanced back at Murphy, who was the closest to the camp. "Bring me as much broth as you can.

And he's going to need some clean clothes, food, and water once I'm done."

If I'd had more time and resources, I knew that I could make an intravenous quality saline solution using my Alchemy skills. It would quickly alleviate the dehydration and make the healing process much smoother. Creating it required distillation and a very specific zero-point-nine percent solution of purified salt to match the body's natural ph ranges. Honestly, I'd never had anyone complain about just rounding up to one percent, but I hadn't exactly had the opportunity to consult many doctors or nurses about my back-of-the-napkin math, either.

As Murphy hurried away, I planned out what I was going to have to do. Delving too deeply into another person's body could cause me to harm myself, and the risk was great enough that I normally wouldn't risk healing someone this far gone. Especially since I would be the one providing all of the energy to heal him. However, the newly regenerated and robust mana generator inside me might make enough of a difference that I wouldn't be risking my own life. I hoped. Add to that, the bump across the board to my stats and I was actually looking forward to challenging my new capabilities, to say nothing of the fact that the two brothers struck a deep chord inside of me. The two kids deserved to have a father, and I'd be damned if I let Gleason take him away from them.

When Murphy got back with the cookpot and a ladle, I started feeding the boy's father some broth, and he managed a few swallows without choking, which I took to be a good sign. It meant his brain wasn't completely fried by the high fever.

"Okay. This is going to take a while, and I'm going to need someone to keep giving him broth and water as I work." I handed the ladle off to Murphy, who positioned himself across from me. He gave me a thumbs up, while Jess had an arm wrapped around each of the boys a few paces away. "Here goes."

I put a cupped hand on my patient's forehead, and a flat palm on his chest above his heart. The first thing I needed to attack was the infection, and the fever it was causing. With it spread all throughout his body, it meant I couldn't brute-force a healing spell. A surge of energy directly into his body would strengthen him, however, because of how widespread it was and the fact that sepsis fed off of the energy of the host they were attacking, it might do the same for the bacteria causing the infection. Some extra finesse and control would be necessary, so one hand would gently push in the energy while the other pulled it out, creating a loop that connected the two of us and reducing the amount of lost energy. I had never tried this before on someone so sick, and I hoped it would work to give me the time necessary to heal him.

A trickle of energy went directly into his head, soothing the swollen brain tissue. I was careful not to dive into his actual brain functions, and kept my focus on the bigger picture. As his swelling went down, I guided the energy over his eyes, tongue, and optic nerves, where the infection had started. The smell that hit me as the damaged tissue was stirred up was a physical force that nearly pushed me away, but I exhaled sharply and re-doubled my concentration.

Tears of blood and far worse substances oozed from his ruined sockets and leaked from his mouth. Murphy mercifully rinsed them away with the occasional dribble of water and a piece of cloth while I worked without me having to tell him, keeping the worst of the smell down and helping cleanse the area.

Some unknown amount of time passed, and I kept the measured flow of the energy pushing into the infected area steady and smooth. New, clean flesh started to grow, and Murphy concentrated on keeping any debris out of the affected area. As the diseased flesh and pus was pushed out of his face, it caused a secondary spike of fever, and his heart fluttered in his chest against my splayed palm.

"Damn it. This is taking too long." I needed reinforcements. Even I couldn't win this particular war alone. I cut off the bit of power that was going toward regrowing his eyes and tongue, and sent it questing deeper into the man's body. Stimulating his kidneys, liver, and spleen helped keep his blood clean, and boosting his blood marrow increased red and white cell production. Allowing his body to fight for itself would make sure anything I missed was handled without my help. It also meant I was finally able to make the full connection, and start looping energy through both of us.

Once the connection was formed, it didn't work like I had planned. Instead of the draw on my body lessening, it grew worse. Much worse. Somehow, the connection meant our two systems tried to find a balance, and given his condition, the imbalance in strength skewed enormously in his favor, and against mine. Like a chamber holding two different levels of water, the door that separated us suddenly opening meant the sloshing waves of power were an uncontrollable mess that I had no chance to seal. The flood of power hit the man like a tidal wave.

The mana generator in my body went into overdrive, with electrical sparks shooting out of it as if an angry elemental decided to throw a temper tantrum. The storm contained inside the purple crystal walls swirled into a tornado, and I did my best to ride out the unexpected violence.

A series of rattling coughs shook my patient, and he groaned in pain when I kept him from rolling onto his side. Just as I feared, the uncontrolled wave of power certainly strengthened him, but it made the infection stronger as well. The only thing that probably saved his life was that I had cleansed the majority of the invasive taint from his head and nearby gray matter, which meant I could keep his brain from getting eaten as everything from the neck down was suddenly riddled with a virulent super-bacteria.

It was something I hadn't been prepared for back in the beginning of my profession as a Healer, though perhaps I should have expected it. In a magical world, *everything* was affected and enhanced in some way by that same magic, even microbes. In fact, there were a host of diseases that could never exist on my home planet because they got every ounce of their energy from magical means. Flooding the man with power not only provided him strength, which the infection could draw on in a way more familiar to modern medicinal expectations, but more worryingly, it empowered the microbes directly. It was a delicate and difficult balance to strike, and one that had become familiar to me over the years.

The second the waves of power between us settled, I started identifying things that didn't belong inside his body and helped his immune system target them. The truth was, I actually did surprisingly little in terms of conscious effort. The body was more of an expert at identifying foreign invaders than I'd ever be, and could even be *too* good at that sort of thing. One of the major difficulties involved with organ transplants was keeping the body from attacking the new replacement that was helping to keep the body alive. I mostly provided energy and an adjustment in priorities since the body's immune system tended to be more genocidal than an ogre with a toothache. Both basically held the idea of 'smash bad thing' as their central driving motivation, and were similarly focused on whatever was right in front of them at the time. The fever tried spiking again, but our connection was strong enough now that it was little more than a thought for me to keep it under control.

While that was great for his healing, it was bad for me. We were getting too closely linked. My only options were to back off, cut the connection, and let him die, or speed up and try to finish before I started losing the connection with my own body. Images of Pete and Davey blended with those of my own brother and I in my memories, and the thought of allowing them to grow up as orphans physically nauseated me.

I chose to speed up.

Since the extra rattle in his lungs was the opposite of a good thing, I focused there next. I allowed the fever that wanted to rage through his body to take hold in his chest, and the phlegm and gunk loosened with the sudden heat. The increased localized fever was simply an indication of an adjustment in priority for his immune system. Through a more focused effort, the microbes in his lungs were suddenly flanked and ambushed mercilessly. If anything, the presence of phlegm and mucus had increased a lot in the aftermath of the small war that had taken place there. Removing it from his body after that was trivial, and he coughed it out in one long fit.

After clearing his airway, his color improved immediately, and his body stopped drawing on mine by a marked difference.

That was the turning point. The infection ravaging him was clearly on the back foot after he could draw a full, complete breath, and I gave more energy to his lymphatic system to help boost it over the top. His muscles started cramping from his dehydration, and I could feel them as if they were my own. I was too connected, and it was time to back off, no matter how badly I wanted to heal him.

"Give him more water." My own voice sounded raspy to my ears, and as I pulled away from the boys' father, a wave of exhaustion hit me like a ton of bricks.

Despite the obvious impact the healing had on me, I could tell that my increased stats had allowed me to go further, endure more, and as tired as I was–kept me on my feet.

I was right in assuming that the higher my stats increased, the more each gain represented. The gains seemed to be cumulative, as though the improvements grew from the baseline of previous capabilities. Meaning that going from a sixty-five to a seventy was an order of magnitude different from when I'd gone from a fifteen to a twenty in a given stat. A strength of fifteen, for example, was only moderately higher than an average person, while a strength stat of sixty-five was simply incomparable. I was happy with the changes, having seen its impact on a process that I was very familiar with as a benchmark test.

Still, healing was one of the most exhausting things a person could do and I was glad to set the burden down. The echoes of our connection remained like trailers of fog in my vision, and I could sense his will to live was even stronger than it was before. It had been a powerful ember even in his weakened state. Now, it was a blazing inferno that I could feel even without being connected to the man.

I exhaled heavily. "I did what I could. The rest is up to him."

"So, you didn't save him?" Pete stood next to Jess, his eyes wet from unshed tears. Davey was asleep in her lap, and the deep darkness of the night told me I'd been at it for several hours. Pete had stayed awake the whole time, despite his exhaustion and the heavy bags under his eyes. "I shoulda known."

"No, kid. I was never trying to 'save' your father. That's just not how it works. Your dad is strong. He's saving himself. I just gave him a little nudge in the right direction." Pete wasn't sure how to answer me, so he stomped back toward the fire, where Leedy was now tending it. "Come on, let's get settled and try to get what sleep we can. We're going to have to have someone feed him at every shift change. He's going to need all the energy he can get."

I helped Murphy shift the man closer to our camp, and cleaned him up as best as I could with what we had on hand. Then I made my way down to the river and took a bath, getting the stink of sickness off of me. It brought back more memories than I wanted to remember, and from more than one point in my life.

"You're awfully brave, risking a bath in the river like this. There's no telling what's out there." Cross appearing out of the darkness nearly made me launch a lightning bolt in reflex, which was both annoying and surprising. First of all, when had Cross gotten as sneaky as Jess? And second, since when was lightning my go-to reflex spell? I was literally standing in one of the most conductive mediums on the planet. He didn't seem to notice how close he came to getting blasted, and crouched by my pack at the edge of the water.

Instead of letting the man realize that he'd gotten one over on me, I yawned dramatically. I wasn't sure if he was talking about the fact that we were downstream of a large city and that human waste contained human pathogens, or if he was simply referring to any oogie-boogies that might lurk beneath the waters. My answer was the same for both. I cocked a thumb at myself casually. "Healer, remember?"

Cross nodded just as casually. "Hard to forget, after what you just did." There was a small silence at Cross' acknowledgement of my accomplishment. I accepted it for the praise that it was as Cross continued. "What are we going to do with them?"

"We take them with us. Making a litter better than the ones the kids had for the dad won't be hard, and the boys are light enough the horses won't even notice them." I scrubbed at myself one last time before getting out of the water, and started digging through my pack for a fresh set of clothing. "Leaving them isn't an option."

"Are you sure taking them with us is the safer option?" Cross motioned back into the trees, where shadows made it impossible to see what might be hiding in the woods. "There's a giant dinosaur coming after us, and once we get to Greendown, they aren't going to be any safer. If Gleason spots them, who knows what might happen."

"I know all of that, Cross. It doesn't change anything. We have to get them someplace safe, and despite everything, that means Greendown." I motioned back down the river, where I knew other cities hugged the banks several weeks' worth of travel downstream. "If we can catch a ride on a barge or boat, maybe they'll be willing to take them somewhere safer. Otherwise, it's up to us."

Cross grunted as he stood, and brushed off the seat of his pants. "About that. I came here to let you know I think I saw a light farther downstream, but I couldn't be sure. It was too far away, and I couldn't climb any higher in the trees." He grunted as he picked up my rucksack for me, and I hurriedly finished getting dressed. "If it was a boat, it would make it here in another hour or so. If it's a barge, I wouldn't expect it until first light. Either way, Leedy and I volunteered to keep watch while the rest of you got some sleep."

"Are you sure? I can stand the first watch." While I was exhausted from a long day and the extensive healing, the mana generator inside my body was still churning away, refilling itself as it steadily pulled in the ambient energy around us. It felt similar to missing out on a full night of sleep, and keeping yourself awake by chugging coffee and energy drinks. Unpleasant, but manageable. Ah, the joys of night shift. Almost like being back home. "Everyone needs to get at least *some* sleep."

"You should see yourself right now. It's obvious you need it more than the rest of us, even Jess, and she almost fell asleep in her bowl of stew." Cross tried to give me a stern look, but gave up when he realized I wasn't paying attention. "Seriously, you don't need to sacrifice your sleep right now. We can handle it."

"Fine. I'm not going to argue. I know when I'm beat." I mindlessly worked the straps and cinches of my gear. Sleeping in armor sucked, but it was better than waking up in an emergency and having nothing on but your birthday suit. Fighting naked wasn't as fun as it sounded, and that was coming from someone who'd done it enough times to be somewhat of an expert on the matter.

Seeing that I wasn't going to argue, Cross took his leave. "I'll get back in the trees, and wake everyone if it's necessary."

"Thanks Cross, I appreciate it." As we parted ways, I was once again surprised at how easily he disappeared into the shadows. That wasn't something he could do before the lich had cursed him, and it was more concerning than I wanted to admit. Later. I'd have to worry about it later, after all the other pressing emergencies were done trying to kill us all.

It felt like I'd barely laid my head down and fallen asleep next to the fire when I was woken up by the sound of distant screams. "One time. I can't have one time where I wake up like a normal person."

The screams were far enough away that no one else could probably hear them yet, but that would change. The brightening skies told me dawn wasn't far off, and by the sound of it, this promised to be a bloody one. Not a new experience for me, but one I never enjoyed.

Something I liked even less was the screen that popped into my vision as I sat up and saw I was the first person awake. To say I was in a bad mood would be the understatement of the year. Worst mood of the year for this planet, anyway.

****Warning!****

One of the Icons of Wrath sent by an angered god is approaching your location. Leaving the area immediately is strongly advised.

Of course. Stupid dinosaurs and their stupid faces. I guess it was time for our showdown.

CHAPTER 13

"Everyone, get up! The barge is under attack!" Leedy came tearing through our campsite, dirt flying under his heels as he ran for the river. "It's a monster!"

I grabbed my mace and sword before giving orders to the others. "Murphy, protect the kids and their dad. Jess, you're with the rest of us." The boys' father was still breathing, but there was no time to check on him. Jess and Murphy were still untangling themselves from their bedrolls, so I started running for the sounds of battle without them. "Catch up as soon as you can!"

Blowing past Leedy was easy, since he wasn't using any of the physical boosts from his armor. He shouted something at me, but I didn't understand a word he said over the pounding of my own heart in my ears. The mana generator inside me was reacting as well, shooting sparks of energy through my body that made me feel jittery and overstimulated. That was something I would need to get under control, because I didn't need to go into battle with the shakes like I was some kind of rookie. I had twenty years of experience. It was a lot of fighting, to say the least. Not twenty years of fighting freaking dinosaurs, but close enough.

As I neared the riverbank, it was obvious I wasn't dealing with the dinosaur I thought I would be fighting. Looking over the update from the system again, it didn't specify *which* Icon of Wrath had found me, and this one wasn't a t-rex. It was the biggest damn crocodile I'd ever seen.

"*Kill it*! Kill it with *fire*!" As a general principle, I agreed wholeheartedly with the high-pitched screams that were coming from the frail-looking man teetering on top of the stacked crates of the barge, which looked to have been run aground by the massive beast terrorizing the men and women scrambling for cover. In my experience, if you wanted something dead, killing it with fire was usually an ideal way to get the job done.

Neither the cover nor the fire appeared to be doing them much good, considering the furiously splashing beast was pushing thirty feet long, and probably closer to three tons than two. Which is a whole lot of angry crocodile, not to mention that the Reka itself was as impressive in its own way. It was a whole lot of water, which tended to put a bit of a damper on any attempts to 'kill it with fire', as the thin man had so eloquently put it.

Leedy's shout from behind me put voice to the same thought I was having. "What in all the Holy Trinity's three heavens and six hells is a crocodile doing here? This is *fresh*water, not *salt*water!" As he finally caught up to me, Leedy looked at his rather diminutive-looking sword and compared it to the giant reptile. "I don't think I'm going to be much good in this fight."

"Sure you can." I pushed him toward the one-sided battle, causing him to stumble a bit. "See if you can help get those people to safety while I distract it. Where's Cross? This seems like a good excuse for him to use some magic. I don't think this is a situation where we're going to be able to hold back. We'll worry about his curse later."

"He was the one who flagged down the barge. I don't know why he isn't here." Leedy pointed with his sword at the edge of the river, where the bank had been badly torn up and frayed. There were a few splashes of blood with a few scorch marks among the reeds. It looked suspiciously as if there'd been a battle between a single warrior and a humongous crocodile. I was sure it was all a coincidence, though. Probably just some other cursed Warden and school bus sized croc that had a minor disagreement here. "Last I saw, he was standing there. When the crocodile came out of the river and attacked the barge, Cross started using the spear you gave him to shoot fire darts at it. When I jumped down from the tree I was in, I lost sight of him."

While I didn't want to count Cross out, it definitely didn't look good. If he had hurt the croc badly enough to draw its attention down on him, a one-on-one fight with something that massive would be hard for anyone to stand against. Yep. Only a real idiot who was a glutton for punishment, pain, and suffering would go down in those waters and against *that* thing. I mean, I'm talking about the sort of dumb on the level of poking a wasp nest with a stick while naked levels of stupid here.

Naturally, I made my way down toward the besieged boat.

The shoe fit, after all. I am not always a smart man.

Another visceral scream echoed through the trees as the crocodile knocked over another stack of crates, upending the thin man that had been perched at their peak. The barge rocked precariously from side to side as the heavy creature tried to throw itself higher onto the deck, where the noisy snack it wanted was trying to get out from under the pile of debris. Somehow, the scrawny guy didn't understand he was making himself a target by creating so much noise.

"We'll figure out where Cross is later. Right now, we need to get those people to safety. And if we can, I'd like to keep the barge in one piece." I concentrated on drawing the power flowing through my body into my blessed starmetal mace. As it started to glow a faint blue, sparks jumped between the blades, and the jitters that had been plaguing me leveled out. "Once I draw it away, you get the barge secure, and the crew far enough away that the croc won't come after them."

"Are you sure about this? Going by yourself, I mean. I can go with you." Leedy's knuckles were white as they gripped his sword. He was afraid, and I didn't blame him. I was a little scared too. "I could use my armor to boost my body, and fight with you."

"No. That boost doesn't last forever. Besides, no matter how badass a few–" I looked over at the massive croc again, adjusting my words, "hundred new pairs of crocodile skin boots might be, the people and the barge are the priority." I flexed my knees, getting ready to sprint into the fight. "Now, let's go."

The ground under my foot cratered a few inches as I shoved off. There was no holding back any of my strength this time, not against something like this. Streamers of light blurred from my mace as I raised it over my head, telegraphing my attack. I flipped my ninjatō around into a reverse grip, ready to stab downward into the crocodile.

By the time I closed the distance, the Icon was more than three-quarters up onto the deck, and the whole thing was tilted a few feet out of the shallow water on the far side. A loud crack came from the barge, and the large vessel groaned as it settled deeper into the thick mud of the riverbed.

"Hey, handbag! Yeah, I'm talking to you! Stop breaking my ride!" I kicked off a fallen log, leaping into the air. Below me, the croc had almost nosed its way to the screaming man, but my shout caused it to tilt its head to the side, probably to see what new snack was coming to present itself for breakfast. Instead of an easy meal, the crocodile got a bit more than it was expecting.

I hit the oversized reptile like a freaking meteor strike.

My momentum, combined with the downward snapping swing of my mace, created a thunderous explosion of kinetic energy that blasted against the side of the monster's head. The sound of cracking bone accompanied the shuddering jolt of electrical discharge that had built up in the mace. I tried aiming my sword for its eye, but the massive eyebrow ridge was too thick to pierce and it deflected off with only a minor scratch in the heavy scales.

Without my planned handhold from my ninjatō, the only thing holding me on the croc was my balance on its freshly damaged snout. Unfortunately, none of my past worlds gave me experience as a rodeo clown. Meaning, I was unprepared for how *twisty* things got.

I was able to handle the first turn, but then the crocodile started to *roll.* It knocked me into the air in an awkward spin, stopping me from being able to dodge as it somehow batted me away with the thrashing of its gigantic tail. After I took a few hard bounces off the ground, both the crocodile and I were covered by a thick wave of muddy water as the barge bobbed free of the Icon's prodigious weight. The Icon let loose a hissing roar as it writhed in surprised agony from my attack, while I concentrated on trying to fill my lungs with air.

"Probably… should… have planned… that better." I grimaced in pain as I sat up. There was something wrong with my chest, and taking a full breath was physically impossible. Since I hadn't felt any bones break, I'd probably dislocated some ribs. Not as bad as a break, but still nasty. Being a ridiculously high level didn't seem to mean much when you had to fight things that outweighed you by a factor of twelve.

The good news was, the croc was in an even worse condition. The Icon's jaw was misshapen badly enough it couldn't close its mouth anymore, and it looked like the front left leg wasn't working correctly as it flopped around. It snarled and rolled twice before settling back onto its belly, angled toward me with its wounded side tilted away.

Despite the damage I had done, the sheer size of the crocodile meant it was still in decent fighting shape. It just had too much mass for me to damage before it would start to have a serious effect.

Between the two of us, in terms of pure physical fighting capability, I'd have to say I had actually come away the loser in our brief exchange, even though I was the ambusher. What should have been a killing blow had only wounded the Icon, and now it wasn't playfully poking around. It was angry *before* I joined the battle.

Now it was fucking pissed.

This was the exact reason why I hadn't wanted to fight the tyrannosaurus rex, either. No matter how great a machine gun was, it would always lose to a tank. I didn't like not being the tank.

A quick pulse of unfocused healing energy through my body drained my reserves by nearly a quarter, but it was necessary if I wanted to have a chance at leading the croc away from the barge. It was definitely ready to chase me, so I needed to be able to breathe. The tight feeling in my chest started to relax, and I drew in a deep breath through my nose with another wince of pain. Good enough.

"Alright, scaly. Papa needs a new pair of boots." Since my ninjatō wasn't working, I sheathed it with a flourish, and then pointed my tri-barreled gauntlet at the croc. "Come on, time to chase me."

I fired the center barrel, aiming for the eyeball. We were too far apart for the heavy round to be accurate enough to hit the basketball-sized target at that distance, but it still carried enough power that it plowed a long bloody furrow right at the corner of its mouth. The Icon let loose another hissing roar, and I took off at a dead sprint along the riverbank, leading it farther upstream.

For once, my inflated stats counted for something. While the croc was certainly fast, it didn't have the kind of speed and acceleration I had. After it was almost out of sight, I slowed to a stop to allow it to catch up to me.

At first, I was afraid I had run too far away, and the beast would give up and go back to the easy meal waiting on the barge. I shouldn't have doubted my ability to piss off something to the point of unreasonable rage. Maybe the whole mandate from a nature god played into things to some extent, but I was putting my money on it mainly being a result of my special gift for egregious annoyance.

The crocodile charged down the muddy riverbank, sending up a plume of mud in its wake. Its injured limb didn't seem to slow it down much, and its whipping tail left a trail of destruction as it slammed craters into the ground on either side of its body. It would reach me in less than a minute.

"Not enough time to make a pit trap, and it would just jump in the river if I used fire." Lightning was an option, of course, but I was *also* standing in the muddy water and I didn't think that we were quite at the level of relying on mutually assured destruction quite yet. Though, the day was still young. In the distance, I watched as the heavy monster destroyed the riverbank as it grew closer and closer. "The only way through that thick skin was to use its own weight against it. But how?" Thinking furiously of a plan, I clipped my mace to my belt and held out both hands. Sometimes, doing *something* is better than just standing around doing nothing, so I went with my instincts.

To my left, just under the surface of the water, I started forming two rows of the densest stone my spike spell could conjure. The thick mud and layers of river rock combined into eight short, thick spikes of a magically reinforced brown quartz, which barely poked out from the top of the water.

With my other hand, I cupped my palm and curled in both my index finger and held my thumb over the second knuckle, and concentrated on a fist-sized lump of driftwood that was sitting in the path of the crocodile. Most of the time, I didn't need to cast an actual spell to force energy into anything and I rarely ever tried in any case, since my starmetal mace was the only material I had found that didn't blow up when holding mana for any length of time–unless it was enchanted with runes, of course, but even that required special materials. Just because I didn't use the spell very often, didn't mean I had forgotten what Lizbeth had taught me on world seven. The White Witch had been an excellent instructor, in some ways more knowledgeable even than the elves on world eight. "*Imbue Lightning*."

The amount of energy I was shoving out of my body from both hands made my arms vibrate and ache with the strain. There wasn't enough time to take a more measured approach, so I had to dump as much energy into the spells as fast as I could. I would be too drained to move for a few moments once they completed, so timing this right was incredibly important. I'd told myself that I wasn't at the point of needing to sacrifice myself for victory, and that hadn't changed. I wasn't electrifying the water specifically, so it wouldn't be a big deal. There was definitely no problem with what I was about to do. I was plenty far away. Almost *too* far, in fact. Everything was fine.

I kept repeating that to myself in a way that was suspiciously similar to a prayer.

I knew the wood was a terrible option for holding all that lightning energy. That's exactly why I picked it. As the monstrous beast came rumbling closer, the chunk of wood started to shake against the ground. I gave the spell one last push as the Icon caught up to me, opening its mouth in a snarl of rotting meat and fresh blood. The spells were a heartbeat from finishing, and there was no way I would be able to dodge. Everything boiled down to twenty years of instincts and timing.

Also, the structural integrity of a chunk of driftwood.

Until very recently, lightning had been one of the elements I was weakest in, and I tended to avoid it. Now, it flowed easier than any of the others, almost to the level that it was hard to get it to stop. I intellectually understood that lightning was negatively charged free electrons traveling along the path of least resistance to a positively charged area, but *magic lightning* didn't give two shits about any of that. It still followed the same rules of grounding and conduction and all that, but so many little things were different. Maybe the cognitive dissonance is why I had so many problems with it in the past, and my increased power pushed it beyond my mental hangups. Or, maybe I didn't understand lightning like I thought I did.

Either way, when the giant crocodile's misaligned jaws were about to clamp down on me, the empowered wood gave out and the explosion of lightning energy blew both of us high into the air.

Everything was going according to plan.

CHAPTER 14

Nothing went according to plan.

I hadn't accounted for one *small* variable.

I must have blacked out for a second, because the impact with the freezing cold river was the next thing I remembered. Hitting water at high speeds feels a whole lot like landing on concrete, with the added bonus of drowning. I came to the surface spluttering and confused, until I saw the words floating in my vision.

Title Upgraded: Send Them into Orbit III
-Your ingenuity and willingness to blow yourself up alongside your enemies deserves special acknowledgement. The ability to cause more destruction! Keep up the chaos, and soon enough you'll find all new paths to glory!
Skill Imparted: Primary explosions are 55% → 60% more powerful. Secondary explosions now carry a 10% chance to also carry the same bonus as the primary explosion. This chance applies to each secondary explosion individually, not cumulatively. Can now be used at any time, up to four times in any thirty-day period. Explosions are still dangerous to both friends and enemies.

The stupid explosion skill. I had forgotten all about it during all of the excitement. It explained why I had come ashore far downriver, covered in blood, mud, and scorch marks, instead of being knocked back a few feet when the spell overloaded the piece of wood. There were more than a few injuries to go with the damage to my clothes and already mangled armor. My right arm didn't want to bend properly at the elbow, and my back and pelvis were more sore and tender than the *night that shall not be named* back on world three. I've never looked at brothels quite the same.

Since my energy reserves were nearly empty, I would have to recover using my natural regeneration for the moment. What was far more important was figuring out what happened to the crocodile. I was on the wrong side of the barge now, unless the crocodile had been washed farther downriver than I had been. It could get to the vessel–or our campsite–before I had a chance to get there. Despite my injuries and lack of mana, I started running.

The barge was eerily quiet when I finally got to it, with no signs of life nearby. Hoping that just maybe my last-minute hairbrained plan had actually worked, I ran even harder toward the site of the explosion.

When I got there, the crater was still smoking. It was surprisingly shallow considering how large the overloaded explosion had been, but since it was a surface explosion, I guess the force went mostly up and out. As the croc and I had found out through personal experience.

All of the spikes that I had made were designed to not be crushed by the weight of the Icon, with the hope that its massive weight would provide the necessary surface tension to puncture through its tough skin, and kill it. As it turned out, I was a little off on a number of factors.

I had been blown far out into the river, given my smaller size and weight. The three-ton crocodile was merely flipped onto its back, landing neatly onto the spikes, where it still thrashed as it was held out of the water with the pointed ends barely poking into its thick hide. Like a human laying on a bed of nails, the number of spikes allowed the weight to be distributed evenly enough that it didn't puncture all the way through. I was lucky enough that no matter how it tossed and turned, there was no way it was going to free itself without getting impaled on the other portion of spikes it was leveraging its weight against. One way or another, the Icon was doomed.

Not only had the exploding driftwood knocked the croc onto its back, but it had burned and scorched its underside heavily. Blood leaked through cracked scales, and it seemed to be in immense pain from all of its accumulated injuries.

All of this was caused by more stupid gods meddling in things they should leave well enough alone. My whole life story was basically a bunch of gods acting like big-headed assholes and regular people dealing with the fallout. Bunch of jerks.

Since I'm not the kind of person that likes to see an animal suffer–even if that animal is a man-eating creature sent by an angry god to kill me–I knelt down and placed a palm on the ground, connecting to the stone spikes I had formed. Carefully and without risking it escaping, I slowly pulled down every other spike, allowing those remaining to finally pierce the Icon and put it out of its misery.

****Warning****

Killing an Icon of Wrath has changed your status from 'angered' to 'enraged' for one of the gods of this world! They have dispatched additional Icons of Wrath for your immediate execution. Leaving their area of influence as soon as possible is strongly advised.

Yeah, thanks a ton. I was going to keep this place at the top of my vacation go-to list, right next to haunted graveyards and active volcanoes, but I guess I'm not welcome here anymore.

"James! Thank the Trinity you're alive!" Jess came tearing out of the woods, with mana swirling around both of her fists. "We were helping Leedy with all these people when there was this loud boom, and then we couldn't find Cross, and we were afraid–"

"Cross. Damn. I almost forgot about him going missing." I got back to my feet with a groan of pain, my back and hips still hurting from the impact with the water. "We need to figure out what happened to him quickly, before more giant monsters show up."

"More? What do you mean?" Jess went from one kind of worried to another, her cat-slitted eyes widening in alarm. "Is the dinosaur going to catch us?"

"Well, there's a good chance it heard that explosion as well, so I imagine it's not far away." Not to mention that the thing had found its way exactly to where I had first received the notification that a god was sending minions after me, and now I had a second such message. Chances were that this place had just become a beacon to any and all Icons of this particular god. I started walking back to the last place Leedy saw Cross. "Let's just say there might be even more big and nasties nearby, and getting to Greendown sooner rather than later would be a really good idea."

"Okay…" Jess looked around with her mana flowing even more urgently, checking our surroundings for threats with all of her senses, even the arcane. "While you look for Cross, I'll go back and warn the others, and let them know the creature is dead. I'm sure the barge master will be happy to give the people who saved his life a ride. There should be enough room for all of us, plus the horses, if we help them rearrange the crates and items that were knocked around during the attack."

"Were any of them injured?" I finally had enough of the lightning-enshrouded mist built up in my mana generator to set it spinning again, and it started pulling in the ambient energy around me more insistently. It wouldn't be long before it held enough to heal my own injuries, and then I could help anyone else that might be hurt. "I can heal them after everyone eats a small meal, if it's necessary."

"Only some bumps and bruises." Jess waved a hand, brushing away the thought. "There isn't anything that needs a healing spell." She turned to leave, before spinning back to me. "Oh! I almost forgot to tell you. In all the excitement, the boys' father woke up. He seems confused, but the kids are happy."

"That's good to hear." I would have to check him over later, and see how much he remembered about his time with our wayward White Warden. "Now hurry up. I might need help finding Cross, and with your shifter senses, you have a better chance to see something I could miss."

She was gone in the blink of an eye, disappearing back into the forest like a shadow. It was a quiet reminder of her ability to be exceedingly sneaky when she wanted.

I was just happy she hadn't been creeping up and scaring the crap out of me recently. That little trick had worn on my nerves. The last thing I needed to do was to reflexively blast half of our campsite with lightning, and while I had been suffering from soul strain Jess had thankfully been treating me with kid gloves. I guess now that I was healed, I might have to start worrying about her again.

The location where Cross had fought with the giant crocodile was a mess. Now that I was taking a closer look at the area, it definitely looked like he had used some kind of fire magic to attack the monster before it devolved into a physical altercation. Considering the lack of burns that I had seen on the Icon, none of his spells had worked, beyond drawing its attention.

"Hmm…" I pushed aside some taller reeds on the riverbank, seeing a single boot print with the toe pointed toward the river, and the heel barely filled with blood-tinted water. "Injured, jumped into the water at a sprint. The croc didn't follow because the guy on the barge was probably screaming at the top of his lungs, which was far more interesting at the time." I stood up and moved to the edge of the bank, looking downriver. "He's either drowned, got washed farther downstream than I was, or…" I looked across the incredibly wide river at the far bank, where the distance was so great it was almost impossible to make out any details. "The only thing that would keep him from coming back right away would be somehow getting stuck on the far side."

I definitely didn't want to make that swim myself, so Cross would have to wait for us to load up the barge and make our way down. To make sure my guess was correct, I took a long walk farther downstream while I healed all my injuries. There were no signs of anyone coming ashore, beyond the lone pair of tracks from when I woke up in the shallows.

That meant Cross either abandoned us, or got turned around and swam to the wrong riverbank. I was going to give him the benefit of the doubt and go with the latter assumption until I heard otherwise. He was a Judge now, and had turned over a new leaf. Abandoning people to be eaten by monsters wasn't something he would do on purpose.

Unless he did, and then I would have to pass judgment on a Judge.

CHAPTER 15

"Sir, it's ready for testing."

Gleason sat up, rubbing at his face. He had fallen asleep at his desk again. It was a recent habit and Gleason knew deep down it wasn't good for him, but he wouldn't give up the extra time staying up late gave him to plan. Wiping away the puddle of drool from the warped wood of his desk, he looked up at his Blood Warden who had interrupted his sleep. Something the Warden saw in his eyes made the man wince, and he started blabbering before Gleason could ask what he wanted.

"Two test subjects are already prepared, and we have several materials laid out for–"

Gleason interrupted him with a simple raised hand, along with a slight push of air pressure from his palm. Nonsense. The man had interrupted him with useless nonsense. Gleason realized then that he was going to have to do some retraining on top of all the other issues he was faced with. There was a brief distraction as he calmly considered the magic bleeding off of himself. He had noticed that power was unintentionally leaking from him more often, but it was a minor concern compared to his current problems. Especially since the Green Wardens had proven to be so ineffective against the hordes of encroaching undead combined with the witches' orcs, and goblins.

The two Wardens had proven to be little more than a distraction, the older unwilling to abandon his search for James Holden most days, while the younger could only be at one place at a time. The witches' leadership skills were far more advanced than anyone anticipated, and they adapted to the new dynamic quickly and efficiently, moving their important troops out of the line of fire while sacrificing goblin fodder to the powerful warriors.

By the next sunset, all those dead goblins were more undead for the horde the defenders would have to face. Their failure to have any true effect on the oncoming siege had forced the timeline of his plans forward drastically, and no matter how hard he pushed his captives, he just wasn't ready.

Gleason sighed, and shook his head to clear his thoughts. The quiet whispers that filled his mind when he was alone had warned him that time was running out, but the messages from the gods had yet to provide any tangible assistance beyond their insistence that he hurry. "Did the undead finally encircle the city? Has the siege started?"

"Not yet, sir. The Green Wardens managed to shatter the large troop concentrations built up along the riverbanks last night, allowing fresh supplies to come in from that ship that was anchored in the middle of the Reka." Gleason's Blood Warden quickly scurried over to the ancient and outdated map moldering on the wall of the old sewer office, where he pointed at the faded blue line that disappeared to the south of the city. "Word on the street is, there are at least two more barges supposed to be coming in the next few days, so that's been their mission. They've got the rest of the city surrounded, though." The Blood Warden pointed out the major intersections around the city, and their corresponding gates. Everything that had been built up outside Greendown's walls over the past hundred years had already burned to ash, so the old map was surprisingly accurate, barring a few new roads and checkpoints. "It's only a matter of time before the witches come in person, and the Green Wardens won't be able to leave the city without risking it falling. Everybody knows that hill witches can weaken city walls in a blink, with their dark magic and entropy spells. Only the Green Wardens have a chance of stopping them, so they'll have to stay inside and watch the docks burn."

"Fool. Greendown's walls are warded by *old* magic. Only the gates could suffer such an instant collapse." Gleason scratched at the stubble on his jaw. "I suppose that doesn't change the end results, though. The old man and his snot-nosed apprentice will be stuck protecting the gates, while the jaws snap closed on the city. Then, in a fortnight, when starvation begins to weaken their resolve, along with their arms, we *strike*. That's when they'll learn. They'll all be taught how wrong they've been, all this time ignoring the edicts of the gods..."

"That's why I'm here, sir." The Blood Warden shifted his stance so he wouldn't have to meet the suddenly feverish gaze of his leader. He cleared his throat, and indicated the open doorway. "As I was saying, the weapon, shield, and armor are finally ready for you to test."

Gleason closed his eyes and took a slow, deep breath before jumping quickly to his feet. "The Trinity truly do stand behind me. If these are of masterwork quality, nothing can stand in our way."

The two men quickly marched down the dank and dark tunnels, toward the sounds of clanging metal and smells of stinking chemicals. They were led only by the burning ball of darkened fire that Gleason barely remembered flicking into existence, any vermin long since having learned to avoid the area his group had claimed. The prisoners had proven to be better than barnyard cats in keeping the vermin down. None of them appeared to want to miss the opportunity for an extra meal, after all.

Little workings of magic that would drain a normal wizard or mage had long been easy for him, but recently they had become trivial. If he didn't know better, it was almost as if he had the power of a warlock, or even a sorcerer, but Gleason knew he hadn't made a deal with a dark god, demon, or daemon. The gods he served stood firmly in the light.

Black smoke from his ball of flames made the Blood Warden cough and drop back as they got closer to the door, forcing him to stand in darkness while only Gleason stood in the light. The fitting symbolism made Gleason smile, and he could feel his mood improving even more as they got closer to their destination. Occasional screams from those still resisting his orders echoed out from other hallways they passed, telling him that the rest of the Blood Wardens were hard at work, as they should be.

Before Gleason pushed open the heavy rust and iron door that led to the testing chamber, he stopped and looked back at the man following him. "What of the other tasks? Has the alchemist learned to focus, and put his full effort into our cause?"

"He seems to be giving it his all, sir. We hope to have the final results soon. We'll update you as soon as there is news." The Blood Warden tried to step closer, but something about the dark red light and grasping fingers of black smoke hugging the ground made him hold back. "Everything should be ready for you inside, Commander. I–I'll go check on the progress of the others."

"Yes, you do that." Gleason turned, already forgetting the man's face. All of his Blood Wardens were the same to him now. They were little more than useless, barely able to accomplish the most basic of tasks he set before them. Soon, with the help of the alchemist, that would all change…

Any thoughts of the future flew out of his mind the moment he saw what was laid out on the table near the entrance of the testing chamber. It was everything he had asked for, and more.

The deadly armor of darkened plate alloy was twice as thick as his ancestral armor. Memories of James Holden somehow shattering his father's enchanted shining steel plate flashed through his thoughts, but he banished them to the hole where he put all the other injustices that motivated him during the silent moments when doubt tried to sneak in.

A white fist on a blue background enameled onto the oversized round shield placed carefully next to the spiked armor was the only concession to his history as a White Warden, and even that was surrounded by the embossed edge of dark alloy that was itself a weapon of sharpened spikes long enough to punch through hardened leather.

It was paired with an enchanted, plain-looking heavy baton of bone, wood, and steel that would shatter both blades and limbs with little effort. Gleason could already envision himself tearing through a platoon of Blue Wardens without breaking a sweat. The weapon was designed similarly to the metal rod he had recently been favoring, so his fighting style wouldn't need much additional training to adjust.

Last, but not least, was the final piece Gleason needed to stand against the witches, his uncle, the Green Wardens, the corrupt guilds, and possibly James Holden, if the man ever showed himself.

In the place of prominence, laid out on top of the glorious, blackened platemail, was a piece of braided steel and leather that was so encrusted with runes and enchantments that it sparked where it rested against the plain wood of the table. A masterwork whip unlike anything Gleason had ever seen before, and it called to him.

As he picked it up, Gleason felt a corner of his mind clear, and the mumbling voices he hadn't even noticed speaking to him fell silent. This was *right*. This was *proper*. This was everything he had been *missing*, without even knowing he needed something *more*.

Feeling more whole than he had in a long time, Gleason turned to face the rest of the room. "Ah, what a treat. Do you remember me?"

The two men who had been gagged and shackled to the wall could only shake their heads in fear as he approached. Both were in good shape, and lacked the signs of starvation that the rest of Gleason's captives shared. A distinctive jagged scar running down the cheek of the man to the right made the former White Warden focus on him.

"You don't recall our last meeting? It's no matter. You probably forgot speaking to me the moment I left your sight." Gleason cracked the whip to either side three times, fascinated by the way it seemed to move without any effort beyond the barest flicker of his wrist. It had unspooled so fast that the explosive triple cracking sound seemed to be only one long assault to the senses. "But just because you forgot *me*, doesn't mean *I* forgot *you*."

The next few whip cracks weren't aimed to the side, and Gleason quickly learned how lethal his newest weapon truly was. He didn't even have time to properly show the porters that had spoken to him so disrespectfully why it had been such a mistake. He shouted for an attendant to come, and while he waited, Gleason carefully observed the dismembered corpses in front of him. The whip would take some practice if he didn't want to cut straight through unprotected flesh and bone.

"You called, Commander?" The man who opened the door carefully avoided looking at what was behind Gleason, while also making sure not to make eye contact with him. It was a careful dance that many of the men had quickly learned to master.

"The man who came to my quarters earlier, he was the one to find these two test subjects?" Gleason was mostly certain the Blood Warden in front of him wasn't the same man as before, but he wasn't completely sure. Not that it mattered. The Warden nodded quickly, seeming to assume that Gleason had found some fault with the two men, and was quick to pass the blame off on another. "Find him, and tell him that I would like the families of these two men brought to me. All of them."

"*All* of them, sir?" Forgetting himself, the Blood Warden made eye contact with Gleason before flinching away. He paled in fear, knowing the mistake would only bring pain.

"Unless you would rather take their place?" Gleason cracked his whip, tearing a furrow out of the stone wall beside him.

"N-no, Commander. I'll personally make sure you have them here as soon as possible." The Blood Warden visibly shuddered, unable to keep himself from glancing at the pile of limbs and gore that had once been two men in their prime.

"Good. See that you do." Gleason looked at the targets lining the far wall, where a series of materials from cloth to enchanted steel were ready for him to test. "I'll be busy with this for the next hour or so, learning how to master my control. After that, I hope for your sake I don't have to go looking for new things to test my skills on."

The Blood Warden disappeared, already running for help from his brethren. Soon, Gleason would have live subjects again, and the fine control he'd require could be polished and perfected. First, he would need to put on the armor to test it for a proper fit and mark any adjustments.

As he set the whip down, Gleason barely noticed the return of the whispers to his mind, as the spell connecting him to a far-away location snapped back into place.

While Gleason was busy putting on the armor, the shadow watching him stretched out to try and grasp the heavily enchanted weapon, but it was forced back by the condensed power in the masterwork. Instead, it reached for the shield, and managed to grasp it to leave a mark of its kind before disappearing out of sight once more.

Gleason noticed none of it, absorbed in his thoughts of the future chaos that was to come.

CHAPTER 16

Cross was waiting for us when we finally managed to make it over to the other side. It took us a lot longer to reach it than anyone expected, but the damage done by the giant crocodile had to be fixed before the barge was able to float.

In a true case of serendipity, the boys' father–a carpenter named Zach–had been healed enough to help guide the necessary repairs. He was entirely too weak to do any of the physical labor, but he was a master shipwright, and seemed to instinctively know exactly what to do to fix the broken barge.

On the downside, Zach had completely forgotten any and all details that might help us figure out what Gleason might be up to, and where he was hiding in the city. The only thing the fever hadn't cooked out of his head was that the demented Warden was a sadist of the highest order, and we already knew that by looking at what was done to Zach when we found him.

The memories were still buried somewhere in his subconscious, because when Zach realized we were going back to Greendown, he had a full-blown panic attack and Leedy had to sedate him. If you want to call bonking him on the head with an oar before he could jump overboard with a screaming kid under each arm being 'sedated'. As a Healer, which made me the best thing to a medical professional on the planet, I could–in good conscience, state that Nurse Leedy's application of tenderly induced anesthesia was both necessary and highly effective.

Shortly after I healed his head injury, we saw Cross waving at us from the riverbank. The crew of the barge had quickly adapted to having several horses on board, and despite the crowding, had managed to steer the unwieldy beasts to the opposite side in short order.

By that point, I had almost regained my full strength, and jumped over to where Cross stood. He was lucky we were able to see him in the first place, as his entire body was covered from head to toe in mud. Wondering if the lich's curse had finally pulled him into a full blown madness, I slowly walked up to what looked like something that came from a cheesy horror film, instead of my apprentice Judge.

"Why are you covered in mud?" I did a quick scan of our immediate area, and only noticed some bug swarms hovering deeper into the forest.

Cross looked at me with bloodshot eyes, one arm hanging limply while the other grasped the spear I had lent him tightly. "You just wait. When those bloodsuckers come for you, I bet you'll end up looking exactly like I do."

I glanced back at the insect swarms I had seen a moment ago, and paid closer attention this time. They were similar to mosquitoes from my home world, but their size was at least triple what I was used to seeing, and the poky bit was far more robust. Plus, they had stingers, like a freaking wasp. What kind of planet has super mosquitoes with wasp stingers? A terrible one, that's what.

"Okay, I think I see your point. So, do you want to tell me what happened?" I held back from pulling on the mantle of a Judge, deciding that hearing him out first was the better option. "How did you even get over here?"

Cross cleared his throat, and cracked his neck before looking me in the eye. "So, what had happened was…" As he trailed off, Cross dropped his gaze to his mud-covered feet, and hunched his shoulders in shame. "I lost control of my magic."

"You *what*?" I looked at the arm that was hanging limply at his side, and finally realized it was the one that was blackened by the curse of the lich. The mud covering him had hidden it from me, and I had no way of knowing how far the dark veins had crawled up his limb. "How bad is it?"

"Not as bad as you'd think." Cross shrugged, causing the arm to flop bonelessly against his side. "I saw the monster coming for the barge, and rushed down to the river to stop it. There was no time to get help from anyone else. At first, I was winning the fight against the monster with no problem, but then my magic suddenly stopped listening to me. The spells kept getting bigger and bigger without me telling them to, and I couldn't stop casting. So, to avoid blowing myself up along with the barge and its crew, I jumped in the river. That only traded one problem for another, though. The spells kept on blasting me over the water like someone skipping a stone. Before I knew it, I was already across the entire river. I think I got smashed into one of the trees and lost consciousness. I woke up swarmed by those damned devil-bugs." He gestured at himself. "The mud keeps them away though."

"Well, your powers of attraction might not work on the ladies, but you've found something out there attracted to you." Yep. Still got it. I had begun to worry that everyone was becoming immune to my jokes and pop culture references. I reached out a hand to grab him, but he pulled away. "Let me see if I can heal you, Cross. This isn't the time for pride to step in and hold you back."

"Just *listen.* Please." Cross planted his spear in the mud before rubbing at his shoulder, then finally looked me in the eyes. What I saw there was fear, mixed with a healthy dose of determination. "I heard a voice whispering to me, telling me to do things. It sounded like the lich, but…" As he trailed off, his eyes glazed over, seeing something that wasn't physically here with us.

"But what, Cross?" My palms itched to grab my sword and cut off his arm–or maybe even his head–before the echoes of a dead lich could take over his mind. I only held back because I knew for certain the lich *couldn't* come back. I had destroyed its phylactery myself, and there was no coming back from that for a creature that abused its soul in such a manner. Cross was cursed, sure, but possession was all but impossible. At least, not from the lich. "What is it?"

Cross shook his head clear and focused on me once again, grabbing his spear and pulling it free of the riverbank. "I don't think it was actually the lich speaking. It was something else, some*body* else, using the curse the lich left behind as a doorway to get to me." He frowned in thought, this time not losing himself. "The thing is, I don't think I'm the actual target. I'm only getting the echoes of whatever is going on. Nothing it said makes sense. I couldn't understand everything, but what I did hear was nonsense. 'Time grows short. Prepare for the cleansing of the sinners,' and 'Punish them for what they've done.' Then my magic went wild. None of that feels directed toward me."

"Huh. So, what you're saying is that you think that your brain is a magical antenna picking up the *eeeviiilll* radio waves." I drew out the word evil as I nudged him with my elbow, trying to make him feel better. "That is a whole bucket of crazy you're talking about, Cross." I held out my hand, preparing a healing spell. "Still, now that I know to look for a connection to something, how about you let me check for it?"

"You promise not to take my arm again?" Cross held himself back, the drying mud on his face flaking off as he dramatically raised an eyebrow.

"Hey!" I retorted, offended. "Who gave you that thing in the first place? I'm not promising anything, but I won't do anything drastic without talking to you about it first." I definitely didn't cross my fingers when I said it. I might have crossed some toes. There's no way to be sure since I was wearing boots.

"Fine." Cross finally relented and stepped closer, allowing me to grab ahold of his mud-covered arm. He winced at the contact, and tried to pull away, but I had already started pushing my mana into the cursed flesh of his injured limb. "That stings."

"Hold still, you big baby." I did a quick pulse on the surface to scan his whole body, and noticed a good-sized knot on his head that I healed absently. Minor concussion, no long-term damage, some tinnitus that I fixed with another small burst of crackling energy. I guess he really did hit his head. Some blisters on his feet he was ignoring that were becoming infected, so I took care of those too. Soldiers should always take care of their feet, and Cross knew better. He must have been very distracted with everything else going on. "Okay, that should've helped with the basic healing. Get ready for the not-so-fun stuff."

I didn't wait for an answer, and dove straight into his arm. My mana generator reacted violently to the blackened veins of flesh that

I ran into, its spinning storm shooting lightning that arced down my arm and into Cross before I could stop it.

This was the first time I had inspected him since I had cured my soul strain, and upgraded the crystal walls of my mana generator. It apparently didn't appreciate the dark feelers pushing into clean, unblemished tissue, and acted on its own to try and curtail its advance. While I didn't appreciate something inside me acting without my consent once again, it certainly acted with my intent, which I suppose was still a win.

Since the last time I had checked, the curse had wormed its way much farther than before, with small capillary-like strands reaching all the way into his shoulder joint. With the unexpected jolt of electric shock, the curse curled back onto itself, drawing back to protect its frail appendages from being destroyed.

Not willing to give up such an unexpected advantage, I used my healing energy to chase the seemingly sentient curse farther down his arm. It kept retreating, curling back on itself and leaving empty channels that my healing spell quickly replaced with healthy tissue. The backward withdrawal started to slow partway down his humerus, and the two energies finally crashed against one another at his elbow.

Cross grunted in pain as I leaned against him for support. Without realizing it, I had almost completely emptied my energy reserves once again. I had done it so many times in such a short period of time, without giving myself enough time to recover, that I could feel a familiar ache reminiscent of soul strain. Instinctively, I knew I was close to causing myself another injury that would take a long time to heal.

"Are you okay?" Cross held me up, using the arm that had been useless only minutes before. "You look really pale, James."

"I'm fine." I mentally grabbed the few wisps of fog in my mana generator and set them spinning, forcing them to pull in the ambient power around us. It hurt to do so, but the ache of leaving it stagnant was worse. While I was focused inward, I still noticed the heavy drone of insect wings seemed louder than before, so I pulled on

Cross to drag him toward where the barge was waiting. “It should be me asking you that, not the other way around, but neither of us is going to care if those mosquito-wasp-mutant-abomination-things decide they want a snack. Let’s go.”

We made it back on board, where Cross was quickly assaulted by Leedy and Murphy. The three of them had a complicated relationship, and I didn’t bother to try and understand their dynamic. Instead, I went to check on Jess, who had nominally been put in charge of wrangling the barge captain to do our bidding. It was a job I definitely didn’t envy, especially considering how fervently the man had tried to keep us from bringing the horses along. To say that he and Jess didn’t get along would be an understatement. It was nothing that a stern glare and an admonishment couldn’t fix. We had not only saved the captain's life, his crew, and his goods, but provided the expertise needed to repair his ship afterward. I’d set the man straight that I was neither a pushover, nor a storybook hero and informed him under no uncertain terms that he owed us, and that I was there to collect.

“Everything okay, Jess?” I grabbed a bowl of crocodile stew from the cook’s station set up near the rear of the barge on my way to talk to her, where the captain’s quarters used to be. They had been mostly destroyed during the fight, and then cannibalized for parts to repair damages elsewhere. That might have been part of the reason why the captain didn’t like our group so much. It’s hard to put a finger on these kinds of things, though. “You look stressed.”

“Me? You’re the one bleeding.” Jess grabbed a handkerchief from somewhere and wiped at my nose, showing me the bloody cloth. “Did you get punched in the face?”

“Um, sure.” I hurriedly checked myself over again, making sure I hadn’t done any permanent damage. There were definite signs of strain, but nothing was beyond the point of no return. “I’m fine though, seriously. How are things with the barge captain? Will he get us to Greendown anytime soon, or do I need to have another little chat with him?”

"Oh, he's going to do us one better." Jess smiled, brandishing a ribbon that I was probably supposed to recognize. "The captain is so ready to get rid of us that he's willing to use a *very* expensive and rare water travel scroll to boost our speed throughout the night. By the time we wake up, Greendown should be in sight."

"That's great! What made him decide to use his fancy scroll?" I took a bite of crocodile stew, and immediately regretted it. Murphy definitely didn't cook this. If rubber had a baby with cardboard-flavored fish, I just found out what it would taste like. "Nevermind. Mystery solved. I bet there's a great burger place in the city he wants to get to in a hurry. Can't fault the man's priorities."

Jess laughed before tucking the ribbon away. "No, the captain agreed to a deadline for some of his cargo–considering how nervous he is, I'm pretty sure it's contraband of some sort–and the delays have put him too far behind to make up the time without the help of magical assistance." She stood, swaying with the motion of the barge. "I'll go get Cross to supervise the activation. I'm sure he's got some kind of experience with similar items. You should try and get some rest. It looks like you need it."

I waved her off, instead concentrating on the personal challenge of finishing the bowl of rubber pretending to be food. The enemy had returned, it seemed, and stronger than before. I hadn't let the crocodile beat me in combat, and I wouldn't let it beat me now.

After choking down the concoction masquerading as food, I found a few bales of fabric to lay out on to try and rest. I knew once we made it to the city, things were only going to get crazier. Humans tended to make things harder than they needed to be in my experience.

While I was being rocked to sleep by the motion of the river, I looked inward once again at the condition of the storm inside my mana generator. The rapid emptying and filling had stressed the hollow crystal, and it seemed to have thickened as a result. I checked my stats sheet to see if there had been any changes to represent the growth.

Name: James Holden (Earth v7.2)
Title: Chief Justice/Arbiter/Justicar/Executioner/etc…
Level: 100/MAX
Rank: 2.1/10
Age: 27 (Physical) 47 (Actual)
Class: Warrior/Soldier/Knight/Paladin/Mage (5/5)
Profession: Healer/Alchemist/Blacksmith/Runesmith/Judge (5/5)

Status:
Strength- 71
Flexibility- 70
Vigor- 71
Mind- 72

Mission:
Mythical Quest: Deliver Justice - World Count 20/???
Legendary Quest: Return Home - Requirements not met
Epic Quest: Find out why - Requirements not met
Rare Quest: Track down Silver Star - Ongoing
Unique Upgrade Quest: Find ten places of power - 2/10

The few extra stat points in strength, vigor, and mind were a welcome sight. So was the slight increase in my rank, even if it was only by point one. The uneven change was probably brought on because the increase didn't involve a place of power like my previous upgrades, or was the result of something major like healing a damaged soul. Either way, improvement was improvement, and it made me happy to see.

I wasn't sure when I finally fell asleep, but I was jerked awake by the sudden sound of screams and smell of smoke. The horses were stomping and pulling at their bits and traces, and generally making a racket that made it impossible for me to figure out what was going on.

Opening my eyes to the stinging cinders in the air, I realized quickly that it was well past midnight. I jumped to the highest stack of crates I could see, blinking away the tears that blurred my vision with my mace in one hand and a spell ready to manipulate the water around us in the other. If the barge was on fire, it would need to be put out quickly.

As my vision cleared, I realized it wasn't the barge that was on fire. We had finally made it to Greendown.

And the city was burning.

CHAPTER 17

"We need to turn around!" The scrawny, loud man who was somehow the captain of the barge was running up and down the middle of the vessel in a panic, waving his arms around like his hair was on fire. "Hurry! Turn us around, before we all die!"

If there weren't so many flammable objects around, I might have set a spark on the top of his head just so he had a reason to act like the raging lunatic he was portraying. Speaking of flammable objects, I grabbed a small cask a little larger than my fist from a pile covered in warning labels and tucked it into my belt pouch. It barely fit, but after rearranging some things I managed. The rest of it I would have to come back for later. I considered it payment for saving the barge and its crew, even though they hadn't offered us any.

"Somebody catch that idiot, before he trips over something and breaks his fool neck." Cross immediately jumped into the pit where the steering functions were located and pointed us straight for Greendown. "I'll get us around the docks. I think the ones farther upstream aren't burning yet."

While I approved of the initiative, I wasn't sure about getting us so close to the burning docks that stuck far out into the river like the fingers of an angry god. Then a gust of wind swirled the smoke clear for a second, and I saw what was waiting on the riverbanks. He was definitely making the right call.

"I've got him!" Jess darted after the suddenly nimble captain, who apparently didn't want to get caught. They ran around the deck of the barge while everyone else either tried to keep the horses calm, or ensure the barge was moving in the right direction.

The magic from the spell scroll must have already worn off while I was sleeping, because we were barely moving forward at a slow crawl. While I hadn't closely inspected the means of propulsion they used earlier, it seemed to be some kind of stationary bike-like system hooked up to either a propeller or paddle wheel that churned the water to the rear. Three of the barge crewmembers were seated at stations near the front–I guessed they were placed there so it was easier for the crew to see and steer during less stressful times–pedaling for all they were worth. As close as we were to the city and its docks, the fast rushing water had stilled as we neared the shore. It seemed that the contraptions being pedaled were used to adjust the large boat's position and for fine adjustments while docking–and apparently, for picking up speed in an emergency. Every other free hand had one of the long poles used to steadily work their way upriver against the current and were now using them to push the barge as quickly as possible toward the closest available and unburned dock.

It wasn't going to be enough.

Now that I had a better idea of what was going on, I realized that it wasn't all of Greendown that was burning. Several outbuildings, warehouses, and the docks farthest from the city's walls were all an inferno. It was impossible to see in the dark, but there had to be defenders keeping the flames from getting too close to the looming gatehouse that overlooked the river.

What I *could* see clearly, however, were the invaders who had set the fires. Bunched together all along the riverbank were groups of undead, along with a few more organized clusters of what I assumed were this world's version of goblins and orcs. The goblins were smaller and more wiry than I was used to seeing, while the few orcs I spotted through the flickering firelight were larger and more robust. All of them were gleefully causing destruction, their hoots and howls echoing eerily over the water.

It was strange to me how some traits seemed to be universal, no matter the world, while others could be drastically different. On world fifteen, orcs had an advanced society that rivaled humans in its complexity, and their culture was more civilized than anything I had seen on world eleven. Despite their civilized society, some things were still the same. They still howled when excited, and tended to burn things when they got riled up.

Their coalition with humans to fight against goblins and monster kind was so strong and deep-rooted, I had only gained two levels on world fifteen–since everyone else was doing all the fighting–along with failing my assigned mission to reduce the scale of the conflict that raged across every city and kingdom. The urge to fight was simply too strong for the orcs, and generations of battle had made human culture no different.

It still remained the least successful I'd been of all the worlds I had visited when purely considering the mission that had been given to me, even though the planet itself wasn't all that bad to begin with. Certainly nothing as bad as world eleven, or even as rough as world one turned out to be in the end–as long as you didn't mind being a fighter, of course.

The issue had been that the culture and bureaucracy of war was so deeply ingrained into every sentient creature on the planet that nothing I had tried or done had managed to move the needle even slightly toward the direction of peace. It was one of those things that required education, effort, and time. Things which were difficult to establish in a society that only seemed to respect and admire the physically strong. While intellectuals were certainly repressed and devalued in their society, on the bright side it kept the lawyers in check.

I had been forced to spend the majority of my time, as ironically as it sounded, creating a rebellious underground faction whose 'extremist' views were centered around the value of education and free thinking. That's right. The 'nerds' had become the fringe activists trying to change the world with their fanatic ideology. It hadn't left me with much time to gain levels and I'd had to leave long before I could see any of my efforts see success in the orcish society where the revolution had begun.

These orcs, though, seemed to have absolutely nothing in common with their more sophisticated cousins I had seen before, and appeared to be little more than rabid beasts in comparison.

"Gotcha!" My thoughts were interrupted as Jess performed an impressive flying tackle that brought down the barge's captain, and his incessant hollering finally stopped. He put up a token struggle as they rolled around between the crates of goods, but was no match for the former barmaid. She had him restrained and muffled in less than a minute, and plopped him down next to Pete and Davey amidst the horses in the center of the barge.

"Nice job." I hopped down from my perch, landing beside her just as a flight of crude arrows passed over where I had been standing. The goblins must have spotted us. I had no idea how accurate they normally were, but odds were it wouldn't be long until they found their range and started dropping volleys on our heads. "Now, I think it's up to the two of us to provide a little help to get us around the docks."

I didn't wait for an answer, instead juking around crates and bundles to get to the rear. Both Leedy and Murphy were already strapping our equipment and spoils on the horses, keeping them calm while also preparing them for a fast exit once we managed to reach a safe dock. Jess stopped to say something to Murphy, but I didn't stay and listen. I let the young couple have their quiet moment in the chaos.

"Mighty wizard! Are you here to save us? Are we about to die? Do you think we'll be turned into the undead, like those poor buggers over there?" One of the barge crew was hiding near the back edge of the barge, where the water was being churned furiously by the underwater propulsion. I was pretty sure he was hard at work having a mental breakdown. He looked like a shorter, younger, and rounder version of the captain, which made me think it was either a cousin or brother.

"First, I'm a mage, not a wizard." Seriously, I hated when people messed that up. "Second, who are you, and what's your job on the crew?" I asked him simple questions to try and get him to calm down.

While he swallowed air and tried to process the answers, I started prying up a section of decking roughly the size of two people. The pegs holding the boards in place were half-rotted and covered with a thin veneer of varnish, so popping them loose only took a little effort.

"I–I'm Warrinton, the cook. My family runs this barge for the Sailor's Guild." He dropped to the deck as another flight of arrows buzzed overhead like a swarm of angry bees. Or, I guess on this planet, it could be a swarm of mutant wasp-squitos. A few of the crudely made arrows thunked into the deck at the farthest edge, barely managing to hit with plunging arcs of fire. Their aim was getting closer. Warrinton looked at the hunk of wood in my hands and pointed a shaking finger at the hole in the deck. "Why are you tearing up the ship?"

"The cook, huh?" After tasting his food earlier, I had no doubt his family was very important to the Sailor's guild. Nepotism was the *only* way he was able to keep his job. "I'm tearing up the ship because I want you to hold this chunk of wood up and provide cover while we try and get this thing moving a bit faster. Sound like a plan?"

"Me?" Warrinton tried scooting back, but there was nowhere for him to go. Unless he fancied a swim, of course. "I could certainly find someone more capab–"

"Why would you need to get anyone else? After all, you'd be safely behind cover, all while standing next to two of the most powerful magic users in a dozen miles." I held out the wood planks, waiting for my words to settle in his brain.

When the revelation that being brave was actually the safest option to him hit, it was visible to any observer–like me–because his eyes widened and he sat up from his crouch. If a lightbulb had been floating over his head, it would have flickered on with an audible dinging sound.

"I'll do it!" Warrinton practically ripped the makeshift tower shield out of my hands as he hurried to the corner of the barge, knocking a few bales of straw off the back as he went. "Not one arrow will make it past me, Master Druid! You'll see!"

"Mage, not druid, dickcheese." I mumbled it to myself this time, giving up on correcting the man. My experience with a certain nature god on this planet had made me particularly sensitive to any association with *those* types. Ultimately, I decided that he wasn't worth the frustration. He also wasn't quite bad enough of a cook to warrant judgment, either, but it was a near thing. One more meal of the quality I'd experienced from the man and I was prepared to stake my reputation on accusing him of inhumane acts against another sentient being.

Another loud buzzing filled the air as a cloud of goblin arrows fell out of the night sky. They had the range dialed in this time, but they fell to our rear. A few strays thunked into the wood Warrinton was holding, and he yelped in surprise as he nearly dropped it into the river. I wanted to save the charge on my shield bracelet for when we made the landing, which is why I was using this idiot as a replacement.

"Don't lose your shield. It would be a shame if you had to become the thing that blocks the arrows." My deadpan tone of voice accurately conveyed the moral crisis I was experiencing at the thought of him versus the plank of wood taking the full brunt of the barrage. Jess arrived at the perfect time, and I could tell by the upturned corner of her mouth that she perfectly understood the situation the moment she arrived.

"Glad you could make it." I waved her toward the open section of decking a few feet away from me. "I was about to get started without you."

Jess dropped to a knee and grabbed a section of splintered railing to steady herself before lifting her right hand, palm pointed at an angle perpendicular with the surface of the water. "Shall we?"

"You provide the force, I'll try to steer us." It was a good thing she had shown up. The rest I had gotten certainly helped, but based on the ache surrounding the area where my mana generator rested, I was a long way from being back to normal. As much as I had joked about doing it without her, I legitimately didn't know if I could have held on to a spell powerful enough to push the barge long enough to make a noticeable difference without hurting myself. Small bursts to help direct it, though? That I could certainly do. "Whatever you do, make sure you cut off your spell when we pass by the last burning set of docks. We don't want to slam into the pier going too fast, or this tub will shatter under our feet."

"Got it." Jess swallowed hard at the thought. The river wasn't moving incredibly swiftly, but it looked especially deep all around the wharf. "That would be bad."

"Very bad. Now, let's get to it. Remember to anchor yourself with the spell into the frame of the ship, not just your own body, or you'll go flying, trust me–it is just as embarrassing and dangerous as it sounds. And, for the most acceleration, try to keep your element ratio to about one third fire, two-thirds wind magic." I gave her a reassuring smile, and Jess gave me a quick nod before she closed her eyes to help her concentrate. We had practiced a lot of things over the past few weeks, and I had no doubt she could handle something like this, even though she was strongest in earth magic.

As the power in her spellform started to build, I stood up to look toward where Cross was still steering, and used a bit of mana to boost my voice. "Heads up! You might want to hold on to something!"

That was all the warning I could give, because we were out of time. Arrows fell out of the sky like angry rain, and I heard the screams of both humans and horses. There wasn't anything I could do for the injured at the moment that would be more productive than getting us out of the kill zone, so I followed my own advice and dropped back to one knee and got ready for the explosion of power I could feel building inside of Jess.

It only took a few more seconds for the energy to reach its peak. It erupted from her outstretched hand in a cone of yellow and orange fire that turned night into day, and even though I was ready for it, I was still almost knocked onto my stomach. The shove against the rear of the barge tilted its nose to the sky, and it caused more screams of surprise and pain from the passengers and crew onboard.

Surprisingly, the cook managed to hold on, and even kept the makeshift shield in position. Which was a good thing, because our sudden movement put the next volley of goblin arrows right on top of where the three of us were crouched at the rear. If we hadn't moved, it would have hit the barge perfectly amidships, devastating the already injured and wounded laid out on the deck.

Once the buzzing rain of arrows stopped falling, I peeked over our cover to see how we were progressing. The barge was on track to clip the edge of the dock sticking out the farthest into the river, so I wound up a spellform of my own to move us out of harm's way.

Two small bursts of wind power–unintentionally laced with traces of lightning–allowed us to barely clear the edge of the burning jetty. I felt the strain of the spells, but it wasn't as bad as I was expecting. Even the small amount of rest I'd taken had been enough to allow me to recover more than I ever had in the past, meaning the boost in rank was already proving its worth.

Now that we were past the worst of the danger, I realized it was time to start slowing down. The intact docks were closing quickly. "Okay Jess, cut it!" When the mana powering the spellform didn't cut off, I looked over to see her eyes open to the sky, tears streaming down her face as her magic ran rampant.

Yeah, I mentally said to myself while nodding calmly. *This feels about right.* She'd lost control, and now we were blasting toward a stone dock at ludicrous speeds.

I looked up to the sky, opening my arms up into a 'why me' gesture.

"This is fun for you? This is how you get your kicks? Why can't you just have a normal hobby, like knitting or detonating supernovae in distant regions of space? Why does it always have to involve tormenting *me*?"

Which was exactly when I took an arrow to the knee. *Yep*, I thought. *That's about what I expected. There goes my adventuring career. Town guard, here I come.*

Sometimes, it's just better when you don't even bother to get out of bed.

CHAPTER 18

One thing about goblins you can always count on is their penchant for using poisoned arrows. These seemed to be no exception, considering the gnarled stick with an obsidian-pointed tip jutting from my joint, and the stinging pain that was already working its way through my bloodstream. *How* they poison them is something I'd rather not think about.

Poop. It was poop.

Goblins were some genuinely nasty creatures. Unfortunately, the arrow wasn't my highest priority.

I knew I had been pushing Jess to advance quickly, but I hadn't realized how close to the edge she was riding. For her to lose control of a spell that used so much of her mana meant I couldn't just knock her out to stop it. The backlash might actually kill her, or at the very least burn out her ability to cast magic.

Right now, the safest option for Jess was to let her run out of mana and allow the spell to die off naturally. She would have a monster headache from mana deprivation afterwards, and probably wouldn't be able to cast any big spells for a few days, but that was a minor concern compared to the impending collision with the stone dock.

Most people, when asked, tend to hold to the utilitarian viewpoint that the lives of the many outweigh the lives of the few. If I was a more drastic type of person, I would knock her out, slow the barge, allow us to dock safely, and keep everyone safe and sound. That's not what I decided to do at all.

Instead, I cast two spells of my own in rapid succession. One created a major burst of force to redirect us so we would pass by the dock entirely, and the second to lift a screen of river water as close to Jess as possible. She continued to channel the spell which was a mixture of wind and fire mana that now impacted the wall of water, robbing it of both heat and kinetic energy. The resulting eruption of steam created a fog that obscured everything in the immediate area, as well as raising the temperature to sweltering levels instantly.

My weak water spell wasn't enough to cancel out the force of the spell being powered by Jess, but it was enough to lower our speed to the point that Cross could once again take effective control at the barge's rudder. All he needed to do was ensure we didn't hit anything until we lost our forward momentum, and we could use the current and the strange, bicycle contraptions to bring us back to the docks in no time.

With the sudden fog providing concealment, the goblins couldn't effectively target us, and the rain of buzzing poisoned arrows finally stopped. Jess started wobbling as I limped over to her, and she collapsed into my outstretched arms when her mana levels hit bottom.

I flopped onto the deck, making sure she didn't hit her head in the process. Catching my breath felt like the most important thing in the world at the moment, and it was a struggle to do against the pain. The glass-like obsidian arrowhead had shattered inside my knee joint, and I could feel it tearing apart my internal tissues as if dozens of miniature scalpels had been set loose by a mad surgeon on my leg. Coupled with the poison burning through me, on top of my natural vigor stat trying to heal everything in a very inefficient manner, and I was feeling downright shitty at the moment. Pun intended.

"What happened? Is Jess okay?" Leedy's head poking over a nearby crate shook me out of my stupor. He looked a lot like how I felt, with a thick gash on his forehead painting most of his face red as fresh blood leaked freely, tracing trails all the way under his breastplate. "Do you need anything?"

"Let Cross know he should be fine to guide us into the docks, if he can see them. Jess will be fine after some rest. The spell got away from her, and she needs some time to recover." I grabbed the shaft of the arrow and yanked it free, which isn't exactly what you're supposed to do, but I didn't give a damn. "Look in my pack for one of those stoneskin and healing potions. If you pour some in any open wounds, it should help close them, and hopefully push out any debris at the same time. The arrows were all poisoned, so everyone is going to either need a few drops of potion, or I'm going to have to heal them. After I get my own knee fixed."

I looked at the fletchings of the one that had hit me for any distinctive markings. There were only two feathers, and both were solid black, probably from either a crow or raven. Some odd hollow burrs in the wood stuck out along the shaft, which is where the buzzing sound most likely came from. Nothing else stood out to me, so I tossed it into the river.

"Got it." Leedy disappeared, already on it. The man certainly handled himself well in an emergency, and I appreciated him for it. It was too bad he wasn't a natural mage. Both him and Murphy would have been excellent additions to the Judge profession, if only they could hold the mantle.

Since there wasn't anything I could do for Jess at the moment, I focused on healing my knee. Pushing out the shards of obsidian was the opposite of fun, so I did it as quickly as possible to try and minimize the agony. It was always crazy to me how joint injuries hurt so much worse than a wound only a few inches lower or higher on the same limb. Next time, I wouldn't trust a bad cook to cover me, and I'd use my shield bracelet. It's why I had the stupid thing in the first place, and trying to save up the charge for the landing would do me no good if I was too injured to get into the city.

After the volcanic glass was removed, I could take care of the goblin poison. The revulsion of knowing exactly what was infecting my body nearly made me gag, but this wasn't my first time dealing with poop making me sick. Third world sanitation led to a whole lot of situations where a person had to deal with contamination from feces, and a lack of plumbing had been a nearly universal issue on all twenty worlds I had been forced to visit.

My mana flushed through my body and crushed the poison in short order, leaving me feeling shaky and drained. I needed food, and more importantly, I needed rest. It seemed like ever since I had arrived on this planet, I was in a constant state of exhaustion.

Considering the city was in flames, and we were already starting to drift back toward it, I didn't see much of a rest coming anytime soon.

Without looking, I yelled over at the cook. "Get that shield back up, Warrinton. We're going to be in range again soon." The sound of wood scraping told me I had guessed correctly. He'd taken a break, thinking we were in the clear.

I grabbed Jess and pulled her between some crates to provide better protection, even placing a few bales of hay across them to give her a modicum of overhead cover. The steam that had hidden us from the goblin archers was thinning out enough now that vague shapes were visible through the mist. A few shouts from Cross set the water churning under the barge as the men up front got to work on their stationary bikes, slowing our approach towards the wharf.

As we got closer, I provided a few more bursts of wind power to ensure we didn't come in too fast. The extra effort had me sweating from the strain, but the mana generator in the center of my body was already working double-time to pull in all the extra energy that filled the atmosphere around us. All of our earlier spellcasting had seemed to supercharge the river with mana, stirring up what was already there on top of adding more, and the density was far higher than normal. It had a certain 'flavor' that was different from the forest, but my body didn't have any problems absorbing it.

"Master Warlock?" I opened my mouth to give the cook a piece of my mind when I caught sight of the fact that Warrinton was pointing at a distinctly feminine figure near the front of the goblin ranks holding a staff, with the tip putting out a silvery light that gave the area around her a washed-out look. "What's that?" His voice quavered. The warehouse district behind her burned, outlining the outstretched hand that seemed to wave at us as we came closer. "Do you think she needs help?"

"Call me a warlock again, Warrinton, and I'll kick you in the nuts so hard your scrotum will only be useful as a dust flap for your asshole." 'Warlock' was an unflattering term for a spellcaster, to say the least. Calling me a sociopath who sacrifices people to perform magic was far worse than calling me a ritual-focused wizard or tree-hugging druid.

While I let him digest that comment–or threat, I suppose–I focused on the woman. My earlier bursts of power to slow the barge had set the remnants of steam swirling, and the smoke from all the burning buildings didn't improve visibility much either, making it impossible to make out any specific details. Still, with her holding such a bright source of light, I could plainly see she wasn't fighting the goblins. She was commanding them. "That's not a damsel in distress, Warrinton. That's one of the enemy commanders."

"You think it's one of the witches?" Warrinton gulped heavily, pulling out a necklace of the Holy Trinity with his free hand and kissing it before quickly tucking it away again. "We're doomed, then. Their coven will take over our minds, and have us all drown ourselves in the river before we can get off the barge!"

"Mind control? Not likely. Witches aren't mind flayers, and unless you drink one of their potions you should be fine." I tried sensing what the woman was doing so I could prepare a response, but it was like running my hands over a pane of frosted glass. Smooth, lifeless, and cold, with no flexibility. It didn't feel like any witch's magic I had dealt with before. It was another step of confirmation toward a sense that'd been building inside of me that there might be more layers to this onion than we knew about. Whatever she was up to over there, it didn't feel pleasant. On the upside, I didn't feel any other spellcasters in the enemy ranks at the moment. "I'm not sure what she's doing, but she's definitely alone. There isn't a whole coven waiting for us to land."

"It looks like we're going to be fine either way. The Trinity protects! Look, that's a Green Warden!" Warrinton was hopping up and down in excitement, his weight causing the barge to rock slightly as we grew ever closer to docking. His shield leaned against the railing, forgotten once again in the excitement as one of the heroes of the realm came charging out of the city's gate, leading a force of at least two hundred heavily armed and armored warriors. It probably represented the majority of Greendown's elite fighting force, if not all of them. "In all my days, I'd never thought to see one in person."

"You better get that shield back up, or you won't live to meet them." As Warrinton scrambled to get back in position, I felt the focus of the woman's spellcasting change from us to the new threat. I let out a genuine sigh of relief. We did not need the added problem of being targeted by whatever spell the stranger had been preparing. I could tell by the size of the person in the green cloak that it had to be Tew leading the charge, meaning Oriana was probably still in the city. If I were them, I would have the rookie wait just inside the gate to stop anything powerful from getting through the opening in the defenses. "Good luck Tew, I think you're going to need it."

A single flight of arrows hit the barge again before we managed to dock–and by dock, I mean slam into the stone pier–but this time it was much less concentrated. The majority of the goblin archers were focused on the city defenders rushing their quickly forming lines. Obsidian arrowheads shattered like glass against upraised shields and steel armor, doing nothing to the charging forces of Greendown.

Undead shambled into rough lines in front of the woman spellcaster, herded by a smattering of bone knights and swift-moving vampires that acted like shepherds over their flock of stinking mobile corpses. The raging fires funneled the undead toward the banks of the river, closer to the wharf where we were tying off, and kept them from flanking the humans as they positioned themselves to provide a corridor to Greendown.

The battlefield was a mixture of burning buildings, rubble-filled streets, and empty warehouses waiting for their turn to add to the conflagration. Ash fell from the smoke-filled sky like snow, while the moans of zombies and grunting howls of hunting orcs fought to be heard over the crackle of the flames and shouts of officers and sergeants as they ordered their warriors into position.

Once the warriors of Greendown got into place, both sides paused. The main street that led from the docks to the gate of the city was twice as wide as the others I had seen, and it served as the proverbial line in the sand, the demarcation zone between the living and the dead. One side burned, already falling to ash and rubble, while the other still stood, although small groups of raiders could be heard smashing windows and setting fires in the distance. It was also the most direct path we needed to take to get into the city.

In front of the humans stood Tew, casually meeting the eyes of the woman who led the undead, his magical dagger with its mighty green gemstone glittering brightly as it steadily gathered power. The woman, who I now could see had silver hair and wore a form-fitting black dress, stood behind a veritable horde of zombies and greenskins. Her staff had been gathering mana for far longer than Tew's dagger, and her forces outnumbered his own several times over.

The lull in the battle didn't last long.

A flash of green light from the gem in Tew's dagger staggered their front ranks, and the two sides collided with a crash of flesh and steel. The Green Warden tried cutting his way to the silver-haired woman initially, but was quickly met by a bone knight that was strong enough to hold him in check with the help of countless zombies constantly getting in his way.

As the Warden single-handedly locked down the leading elites, Greendown's forces cut through the enemy with abandon, shattering skeletal undead into pieces and cutting down the fresher corpses as if they were little more than training dummies. Beyond the single ghoul fighting Tew, the smattering of greater undead stayed clear, content to let the unthinking fodder wear down their human enemies as they ordered more freshly turned corpses into the grinder.

The distracted humans were also unable to watch for goblin arrows, and were steadily peppered with the poisoned shafts as they fought. While they might not have been instantly fatal, the long-term damage it would cause the city's defenders would be extensive. They might still hold the line, but there would be a time limit as the infection took hold, or as the healers exhausted themselves combatting the added complication of sepsis along with the rest of their duties.

It was plain to see that while Greendown's warriors were certainly winning for the moment, the sheer number of enemy forces would eventually wear them down, making them easy targets for the more deadly and powerful combatants hiding in the rear. On top of that, every fallen ally was now a potential source of reinforcements for the enemy.

"Now's our chance! They're holding the line so we can get to the gate. Grab what you can, and get inside the city!" Cross was shouting at the onlookers to get them moving, and had everyone on their way the moment we were secure. A second group of people with wheelbarrows and hand carts were already on their way from the gate to help strip the barge of anything useful, their lightly-armored escorts holding up shields to defend them as they ran. "Hurry, before their archers realize we're in the open!"

That thought sent everyone sprinting. Murphy and Leedy had already loaded our horses down with as much as they could carry, and despite a few being wounded, the well-trained warhorses followed the pair across the wharf in a steady line. Murphy had grabbed Jess at some point, and had her slung across his shoulders as he led the way, with Leedy bringing up the rear alongside the boys and their father. The barge crew was more of a gaggle, moving as an overloaded cluster of humanity in their own group to the side of our horses. None of them had stuck around to help the city folk load the cargo, especially the captain and cook. At least Warrinton had remembered to grab some items before running for the gates. The captain didn't have anything with him but the clothes on his back. I'm sure the Sailor's Guild wasn't going to be happy with him about that.

Cross stepped onto the dock next to me, handing me my things. I noticed he had gloves on to hide that one of his hands wasn't normal, which was probably a good idea. Advertising you were different was usually a bad idea in every pre-industrial society. Post-industrial society too, really. I guess human nature applies to all societies.

As I shouldered my ruck, I finished what I had been concentrating on doing while all the other excitement had been going on. He looked at what I held in my hands and raised an eyebrow in surprise. "Are you sure about this? I thought you wanted to keep a low profile until we were more established inside the city."

"I'm sure. Besides, I have a feeling that Green Warden is going to need some help soon, and while I know they're hunting me, the city needs them if it's going to stand." I hefted the small cask I had taken earlier and looked it over, inspecting the enhancing runes I had carved into the wood. "Did you happen to grab any more of these from their stockpile?"

"There's two in your pack, and two in mine. The rest are divided evenly among the horses. After seeing how useful fire powder can be, Leedy and I thought it best to procure as much of it as we could for our own needs once we stumbled upon it. After all, their captain didn't offer to pay us for saving them. And, helping out the war effort is important to the captain, I'm sure."

I made one final scratch with my pocket knife, cleaning up the fire rune on top of the cask so it was as pristine as possible. The way his thought process matched mine about procurement of goods for repayment made it hard not to smile. "Good. Smart thinking. While you call it fire powder, Cross, I call it something else. Gunpowder. And it's about to make those goblins and undead have a very bad night."

CHAPTER 19

I used *Inspect* on the cask I was holding, hoping it would give me some idea of the blast radius it would produce. With my new title upgrade to explosions, that kind of information could mean the difference between showing up as the city's newest hero, or the killer of a Green Warden.

Item: Enhanced Gunpowder Concussive Cask Grenade
Type: Runed Wood with Black Powder
Grade: 2/3
Description: A rune-covered keg of gunpowder that explodes shortly after ignition with a shock wave designed to cause serious damage to soft tissue. Rune quality is at significantly high values given the materials, boosting the intensity of the initial blast. Secondary effects include disorientation, loss of hearing, loss of vision, memory loss, and extreme nausea. Effects are intensified in enclosed environments. Inorganic enemies receive drastically reduced damage. Area of effect is twenty paces. Recommend being far away when detonation occurs.

Well, that's definitely exciting. Twenty paces was something like fifty feet, and my title made explosions sixty percent more effective. That put the blast area of the little keg I was holding at somewhere around eighty feet, maybe more. I'd also had quite a lot of experience with prompts at this point and understood that this one wasn't actually giving all of the relevant information. The 'area of effect' description of an explosion referred to damage exceeding a threshold that the system considered generally fatal. Meaning most things would, unsurprisingly, not survive within the immediate blast radius.

However, there were secondary effects outside of that range that I'd argue deserved their own consolation mention prompts about explosions, given those effects still had the capacity to greatly injure, even permanently. The most obvious of which would be the hearing of anyone within a quarter mile, though I'll admit that I was working off of an educated guess with that estimate. Given the amount of things I'd made go 'boom' over the years, though, I'd say my guess would be a pretty good one. I would have to put some serious effort into my throw to make sure I wasn't blowing myself up with it. Not just that, if I were to wrap some nails and ball bearings around the outside, the concussion would quickly change to shrapnel damage, but there wasn't time to work on it more.

Our people were already shuffling inside the gate, and the runners sent from inside the city were almost done loading up their handcarts. They had done an efficient job stripping what was available, prioritizing food over everything else. The only thing that was going to be left on the barge were building materials and a few random crates without labels. I hoped for the captain's sake his smuggled goods weren't left behind, because the orcs and goblins would certainly take anything still here as spoils.

"Shall we?" Cross was still eyeballing the cask in my hands, making sure to keep some distance between the two of us. "I can help get everyone safely back inside the city while you do... whatever it is you're going to do."

Before I could answer, we both felt a sudden flare of energy from the escalating battle going on a few hundred yards away from us. The woman was finally releasing her spell.

Cross and I sprinted for the center of the human line, when a thin column of glittering green energy shot out from where Tew fought the largest cluster of undead to intercept the cone of cold silver trying to wash over the line of humans. I activated my shield bracelet at full power and pulled Cross behind me, afraid that I was too late. Night turned to day as the two energies met, and the ground shuddered under our feet. As I blinked my vision clear, I expected to see that Tew was dead, along with the majority of the humans. Thankfully, I was wrong.

Somehow, despite the difference in power levels, Tew had managed to disrupt the silver spell before it could reach the humans. It also made me happy I hadn't fought the old man in the forest. I guess all that experience as a Green Warden had to count for something.

Where it *had* touched was a field of destruction, with needle-thin clusters of shining crystals coating the ground and the undead ranks waiting to attack. Everything they were embedded in smoked from the immense cold they emitted, making even the air around them seem brittle as the frozen effect spread.

"What in all the hells was *that*?" Cross shook himself free of my grip as we stood, looking around in amazement at the devastation in front of us. "I've never seen *anything* like that before."

I shook my head, feeling a grim oppression from the after-effects of the woman's spell. The sharp crystals were sinking into whatever surface they rested on, cracking and shattering stone as easily as they did flesh. Instead of dissipating like shards of ice, the incredibly cold needles seemed like indestructible diamonds that appeared permanent, not conjured. That was definitely something new for me. All conjured constructs such as ice, fire, or lightning survived in this world on the mana provided by the caster of the spell. When that mana was used up the construct would dissolve and any remnants of magical power would diffuse into the ambient mana of the area the spell had been cast in. Magical constructs simply didn't *stay*. "Neither have I, Cross. We don't want to stick around for her to try again, either."

Tew had fallen back after stopping the spell, allowing the men around him to capitalize on the suddenly frozen and brittle undead while he took a breather. Their weapons shattered the zombies like glass, and even the bone knight was quickly killed by the disciplined troops. The biting cold of the woman's spell was also affecting the humans, but only those who pushed too deep into the frozen ranks risked their lives.

As the two of us ran up to him, I saw how bad off Tew truly was. He was breathing raggedly, his complexion was gray from mana deprivation, and wounds covered his arms and chest. More than one of them already showed signs of poison, and even the mighty Green Warden looked like he was about to pass out.

Evidence of his prowess during the fight was spread out around him, proving he had put in some work before blowing apart the mega-spell. I had only seen him fighting the one bone knight, but there were four dead ones nearby–and two vampires–meaning Tew had been chewing through several, not just one. For an old guy, he could throw down.

"Paladin? I'm surprised to see you." Tew tried to stand, but collapsed back onto the pile of rubble that was holding him up.

Even though the Warden was my enemy on paper, our goals were actually not all that dissimilar. While I didn't care for the various indications of corruption among the Wardens, I did admit that the root of the problem appeared to be this so-called 'Oracle', and not specifically with each and every Warden. Like Cross, Leedy, and Murphy–I'd decided to deal with each of them on a case by case basis instead of painting the whole organization with the same brush. I may have to fight against Wardens in the future, but for me at least, it wouldn't be personal. Matters with the Oracle on the other hand, would get *very* personal.

"Perhaps you haven't heard, Warden Tew," I said with a casual smile, choosing the same words he had spoken to me before. "But a Paladin is meant to fight against the undead."

The Warden nodded with a strained chuckle. "I actually did hear something along those lines, in truth. I'm glad that it is not empty sentiment. Looking around, it seems that now is as good a time as any for you to make your grand appearance." We all felt it as the ambient power started to once again begin to be pulled toward the back line of the enemy. The woman was preparing to cast her spell for a second time. "Might I recommend you get behind the wards of the city walls. I don't think I have it in me to stop another one of those castings."

As much as I didn't want to do it, I held up a hand and cast one of the spells that I hated. Being in character really sucked sometimes. "*Blessing*." The pure white light that erupted from my palm washed over him, as well as a few dozen of the city's warriors beyond him. All of them perked up immediately, redoubling their efforts and pushing the enemy back hard. Tew still looked rough, but his color was already improving. Unlike other spells or abilities, the strain on my own body was minimal, since it came from one of my classes. Instead, I paid the price by way of my own discomfort. The disconnected feeling that settled on me wasn't welcome, but I pushed it aside. "Now's not the time to lie down on the job. The city still needs you."

I held out my hand, and he took it. Cross gave me a questioning look as I pulled the Green Warden to his feet, but a quick shake of my head had him focused back on our surroundings.

"While I appreciate the assistance, Paladin, my advice still stands. You should get to the city walls before it's too late." Tew took a deep breath, and pulled free his dagger. Seriously, I *really* wanted to steal that thing. Being a Judge sucked sometimes. If he tried to kill me though, that thing was free game. "I'll make a run for their leader. If I can end such a strong spellcaster now, it might save many lives in the future. Tell Oriana to finish our mission, and immediately return to our headquarters to report what has happened here. They need to know."

I grabbed his shoulder as he turned to leave. Despite his weakened state, I was surprised at how much strength it took to stop him. Tew turned to look at me, equally surprised I was able to keep him from his suicide mission. "Or…" I held up the rune-covered cask and gave it a spin. "We could blow them up, and all live to see the sunrise."

Tew obviously hadn't dealt with explosives very often, and it took a few minutes to explain things to him. Once Cross corroborated the effects it could cause, he grudgingly agreed to the plan. I half suspected Tew only agreed to it because he wasn't sure he could actually kill the woman in his weakened state before he went out in a blaze of glory.

"By ranks of two, fall back!" Tew's orders went up and down the line as soon as the last of the recovery crews were back inside the city. The walking wounded were dragging litters filled with warriors unable to retreat on their own, while those most rested and the few touched by my blessing spell fell to the rear and took the brunt of the attack as they executed a fighting retreat.

Cross jumped in with those holding back the horde, his spear darting in and out of the gaps in the line with practiced ease. I stayed out of the way, especially since I didn't have any practice with their unique style of fighting. Every unit has specific quirks that make it dangerous for an outsider to jump in a line, especially if they're trained in a different set of tactics. I didn't want to cause a problem by making the wrong move at the worst time, and end up getting someone killed unnecessarily.

Once the undead and greenskins were finally out from the cover of the buildings and onto the road, I got ready to throw. Most of our people were inside the gates now, and were just waiting for a chance to break contact. If the enemy would just group up a bit more…

"Paladin, the woman!" Tew was beside me, pulling me behind him with his dagger sputtering green light as he raised it in front of him. "She's casting early!"

At the rear of their forces, I saw the tip of a glowing staff raised high. I mentally kicked myself for not expecting her to do something like this. Just because she used a full-powered spell last time didn't mean it was *necessary* for the spell to be cast.

I took a step back and slammed the enhancement runes along the length of the cask with mana until they glowed with azure light, overloading them with power. As the silver lightning in my mana crackled along the channels that connected them to the ignition runes, I cocked back my arm and threw it as hard as the wooden container could handle.

"Everybody, get *down*!" I pulled Tew to the ground, and this time he didn't fight me. I activated my shield bracelet, trying to cover as many people around me as I could.

I saw Cross pull back the front rank of warriors and throw up an earthen shield to hold back the enemy troops for the barest of heartbeats.

The silver cone of frozen destruction broke free from the end of the upraised staff, sweeping away everything in front of it.

Until the arcing grenade I had thrown finally detonated.

When I carved the enhancement runes into the wooden cask, I used a rotating pattern focused on increasing the size of whatever effect was in their range, a rune that boosted the temperature of fire, and a rune that magnified force. The combination of the three runes were a tried-and-true set I had used several times before. However, I had never used them with my newly upgraded *title* before.

The explosion outright *evaporated* everything directly beneath it.

As the shockwave moved outward in a dome, it shoved aside the silver cone of crystal needles and shattered the spellform like a piece of spun sugar, causing a nasty backlash that the enemy spellcaster would be regretting for a long time, if she managed to survive.

Undead flesh was stripped from bone, and goblin brains were liquified inside their overly thick skulls. Rubble-strewn alleys were blown clear of debris, and teetering buildings were blasted free from their foundations, collapsing to the ground in storms of dust. Nearby fires were blown out, and those worn down to embers were reignited as burning cinders were thrown far and wide. Guards atop the city walls were knocked off their feet, and the warriors still outside the gates had their eardrums blown out.

As I got to my feet, I looked around, surveying the destruction.

Yep, definitely making more of those.

"What in the name of the Trinity *was* that," whispered the hoarse voice of Tew, shocked and staring at the destruction while still on the ground.

"That," I said proudly, "was my *Holy Hand Grenade*."

CHAPTER 20

"The latest rumors from the battle last night near the riverside regions of the city are each as unbelievable as the next, Commander." The Blood Warden standing in front of Gleason's desk was scratching at his neck, where a boil was forming at the edge of his collar. "No official reports have been filed yet, so we haven't been able to tell the truth from fiction. With the siege finally in place, there probably won't be one anytime soon."

"Mmhmm."

"We *can* confirm through our own visual inspections that there were some minor damages to the gatehouse and walls, and a large number of supplies were brought in from the final barge. Not enough to make a lasting difference, but it probably added at least another week of food to the city's surplus." The man pulled out a ledger and placed it on Gleason's desk, where a stack of similar reports already sat. "Our own supplies are still at acceptable levels, and we will be able to survive on siege rations for far longer than the rest of the city."

"Mmhmm."

"The number of refugees sneaking into the sewer system continues to grow, and the city watch has done nothing to curtail crime among those living on the streets. Their focus, and the focus of the Wardens and Hunter's Guild, is to hold the city walls and gates. Other guild forces have attempted to fill in this gap, but they aren't adequate for the sheer number of people crowding the streets."

Gleason was barely listening to the man speak, instead drumming his fingernails along the edge of his desk and thinking over the next steps of his plan. His latest round of experiments with the alchemical solutions mixed into the food and drink of his men had gone completely unnoticed, and the only side effect had been the occasional boil or pustule like the man before him was suffering from. If the captive alchemist was to be trusted, all Gleason needed to do now was get his men to ingest the final ingredient in three days' time. Then, he would be able to move forward with the first phase of his operation, and it would be too late for anyone to stop him.

"So, what's your decision, Commander?"

"What?" Gleason snapped out of his daydream, finally focusing on the man debriefing him. "My decision on what, Exsanguinator?" The new name he had decided on for the rank of his two lieutenants still gave him a thrill when he said it. Soon enough, the word would mean more than just a title.

"Sir, on what we should do about the refugees making incursions into the sewers to find shelter. The overcrowding in the city is so bad now that the gates are permanently closed, even the sewers are more appealing to some than sleeping on the streets." The Blood Warden scratched once again at the angry boil on his neck before continuing. "They're nearly guaranteed to get a knife in the ribs if they rest in a dark alley. At least in the sewers, it's only a possibility."

"It sounds to me like you have two options, Exsanguinator." Gleason stood from his desk and walked over to the hand-drawn map of the sewer system his men had recently pinned in place. It was crude, but far more current than the version left by the people that last used the abandoned facilities. "You could start patrolling the surface, and make it safe enough that the rabble above us don't feel the need to seek shelter in our tunnels."

"But Commander, there aren't nearly enough of us to–"

"Or, you could make it obvious that sewers are *far* more dangerous than anything lurking in the dark alleys of Greendown." Gleason's grim smile was all the Exsanguinator needed to see to know which option the man preferred. "In fact, by taking those unfortunate enough to enter our domain, it would provide far more test subjects for the alchemists'… more *unique* concoctions, don't you think?"

The Blood Warden shuddered, happy that he wasn't one of the prisoners forced to drink the foul brews Gleason had demanded the captive alchemist to make. It never crossed the man's mind that there might be tasteless and odorless versions available, since all he had seen were the stinking and bubbling vials that killed more often than not.

"I'll let you figure out how to best go about your task. As long as you don't allow anyone to accidentally get into here, here, or here." Gleason pointed out specific locations on the map, ensuring the Blood Warden understood his mission. "Now go, and be sure to send me any new information you might learn about what happened at the riverside gate the moment you verify it's more than rumor."

"As you say, Commander." The Exsanguinator gave Gleason a sharp salute before marching out of his office.

While their uniforms weren't as pristine as they once were, discipline had taken a sharp turn for the better after Gleason had made another example. Sloppy salutes and escaped prisoners were a thing of the past, and soon, he wouldn't even need to give them orders. They would enact his will simply by existing.

Time draws near
Great enemies surround
Corruption must be cleansed
Do not fail

"Shut *up*!" Gleason grabbed his head, the voices sending a stabbing pain through his temples. The whispers had gotten louder, and now they shouted at him when he least expected it. "I know all of that. You don't have to keep repeating it."

Time draws near
Great enemies surr–

"I said *shut up*! If you're going to talk to me, at least say something useful!" Gleason didn't expect anything different to happen. The voices had been saying the same thing to him for ages, urging him to hurry, watch for enemies, cleanse the city, and warning him not to fail. He even heard the voices in his dreams, repeating the same thing, over and over again.

Talking to it had changed nothing. That didn't mean he stopped trying, though. It felt unnatural not to speak to the voices inside his own head. Sometimes it sounded like his long-dead father, sometimes many voices at once, but most often it sounded like his uncle, the Commandant, chastising him for not doing enough. When the voices stayed quiet, he relaxed, hoping they had quieted for a time. "And you don't have to be so loud. I can hear you."

Gleason sat back down at his desk, pulling out a sheaf of papers. They outlined the second phase of his plans, along with diagrams of the city water supply and grain storage facilities. His stockpile of alchemical solutions wasn't nearly enough to permanently affect the whole city, but he could focus on one district and it would cause lasting changes. Or, he could temporarily affect all of Greendown, causing short-lived side-effects at the opportune moment. Choosing which option would best serve his needs was the hard part.

Once he knew which course to take, phase three would start. The army surrounding Greendown would have to play their part, but as long as they took the bait he dangled in front of them, their unclean stain would–

You are hunted

Gleason's thoughts came to a crashing halt. The voices had said something different. He jumped to his feet, sending his chair crashing to the floor. "Who is hunting me? Where are they? What do they know?"

You are hunted

Do not fail

"I'm not going to fail, damn it!" Gleason stomped over to his armor stand and started strapping on pieces, doing his best to ignore the throbbing pain in his head. The black veins running under his skin flushed to the surface as power flooded his body and adrenaline made his heart pound in his chest. "The city gates are closed, and no one can leave. They think I'm trapped, but instead they're the ones who've been cornered."

His other plans couldn't be ignored, but he had some time before the next dose could be used. Scouring the streets for this new threat would be a good excuse to get some fresh air. Gleason's first stop would be to see who his uncle was talking to, and then check on the Green Wardens and their activities. If someone was hunting him, perhaps that old bastard of an uncle could prove useful for once in his pathetic life and give Gleason a hint about their identity.

Whoever they were, he would find them, and he would kill them first.

CHAPTER 21

Greendown was a nightmare. The city streets were overflowing with refugees, and everyone looked lean and hungry. Disease was only one bad cough away from tearing through this place like a wildfire. With the almost daily rains keeping everything damp, it was a matter of 'when,' not 'if.'

"This place is a tinderbox if I've ever seen one." I had meant to keep the thought to myself, but Tew gave me a sharp look as he walked beside me. "Tell me I'm wrong, then, if you disagree."

After a long introspective look around us, the thickly-built Green Warden shook his head with a sigh of defeat. "No, it's not that you're wrong. It's only that I don't enjoy hearing the hard truth of it." The warriors in front of us–the highest ranking members of the Hunter's Guild who still remained in Greendown, I had learned–cleared our path as we marched for the city center. "Once you meet with the Commandant, you'll see how hard we've all been working to keep things as good as they are. I shudder to think how bad it would be without such a capable man leading the defense."

"I'm sure you've all been doing as much as you can." I tried to give Tew a convincing smile, but it was made even more difficult by the washed-out feeling my earlier Paladin spell was causing me. "Hopefully my group and I can find a way to help."

Tew's tired face sagged for a heartbeat before the mask of a strong, indomitable hero fell back into place. "If a Paladin and his people can't provide aid, I don't think anyone would be able to help." He looked behind us, back to where we had left Cross, Jess, Leedy, and Murphy to wrangle our horses. "Are you sure it's okay to leave the rest of your party? Greendown isn't as safe as it should be at the moment."

"Oh, don't worry about them. I tend to surround myself with capable allies." I waved away his concerns, slapped the man on the back as if to include him in the complement, and shifted the heavy pack that was cutting into my shoulders. "They've got plenty of tasks to keep them busy and out of trouble."

While that was true, it was also vitally important that Cross and the Commandant didn't see each other face-to-face. He would be immediately recognized, and then all kinds of unwanted questions would surface.

Shortly after we had collected everyone and closed the city gates, representatives from the Healer's Guild had shown up and tried fixing everyone. They were absolutely useless when it came to repairing damaged eardrums, so I had to do it by myself, and left them to the more mundane injuries. The Healer's Guild wasn't happy about a Paladin that could heal, but the two of us had a date with destiny soon anyway. A date they wouldn't enjoy, if things went my way.

Thankfully, they *did* have a magical form of treatment for the goblin poison, as long as it wasn't too far advanced, so most warriors were back in fighting shape after several hours of waiting.

I shuddered as I considered how often the Healer's must have dealt with poo-inflicted injuries to have a treatment on hand, but was grateful that I didn't have to deal with *that* particular trauma–which included both the injured and my own psyche.

The lull provided by the Healers had given our group enough time to recover, and more importantly, start to plan, especially since we hadn't prepared for this kind of arrival. We hadn't been completely caught by surprise, however. There were rough contingencies in place, even for something as unlikely as making it into the city under the protection of the Green Wardens. While Jess and Murphy sold off as much merchandise and extra equipment as possible, Cross and Leedy would secure a base of operations for the foreseeable future, and hopefully get the boys and their father someplace safe. At least, as safe as you can be in a city about to be overrun by the undead.

Replacing our tattered and broken gear–like my poor armor–would be a task for later. Most likely tomorrow, at the rate things were going. All I needed to do was ensure we weren't made an integral part of Greendown's siege defenses. Or, at the very least, an *active* part.

"Once you meet with the Commandant, you should visit Oriana and I in our quarters. There's something else I'd like to discuss with you." Tew leaned in close, looking around at the people huddled against the rain that had started to fall. "Something dark stalks the streets, taking people with impunity. A Paladin might be uniquely suited to stopping it, before it gets worse."

"I make no promises, but I'll certainly stop by to talk." Considering the odds were high I already knew what the problem was, it would be good to get whatever intel they had on hand. "We have enough going on outside the walls. Worrying about a monster within them does us no favors, so I'll hunt it down immediately."

"Exactly my thoughts on the matter." Tew thumped me on the shoulder, almost causing me to stagger. The man was certainly no weakling. "After what you did to that group outside the gate, I almost feel bad for whatever gets in your way."

"Yeah, you bet." I gave him another half-hearted smile and we fell into a companionable silence as we made our way through the city, the crowds only getting thicker the deeper we went.

It was quickly apparent why so many people were huddled deeper into the city. The old town had a working sewer system, which included fountains that provided fresh water, and a higher level of cleanliness. It was also where the next set of my major enemies were located. The damned guild houses.

Most of the guild houses were closed off to anyone seeking shelter, but many did offer food from the entrances to their compounds to those less fortunate. Only if they still had a few coppers left to pay for the thin soup or gruel, of course, but something was far better than nothing. From what I had seen, just the religious institutions were handing out food for free, and it looked like broth so thin it was practically discolored hot water. The only well-fed people in the city seemed to be the ones hiding inside each of the compounds that housed the guilds, and they weren't sharing. Somehow, I wasn't surprised. It was one more indicator of why I needed to either crush the guilds, or fix them.

Once we made it to the Hunter's Guild, it was plain that the place was controlled chaos. Men and women were running all over the place, most loaded down with equipment or supplies, and a few younger warriors–barely more than teens–carried messenger bags to and from the door that was labeled as the headquarters. That was the entrance Tew took me toward, and everyone moved out of his way like he was a force of nature. In a way, he kind of was.

"Is he in?" Tew had us stop and wait to the side of a busy waiting room that reminded me of a doctor's office. Everyone had a nervous kind of energy, where they knew they *needed* to be there, but they didn't necessarily *want* to be there.

The secretary guarding the door was a badly scarred man in the uniform of a Black Warden–this world's version of a firefighter and safety inspector–who had been burned sometime in the distant past. Despite his disfigurement, the man carried himself with a quiet sense of pride that I appreciated. I thought about offering to do my best to heal him, but I didn't get a chance.

"Is that Warden Tew? Send him in!" The strong voice of the Commandant was the kind that brooked no argument. He was clearly a man used to giving orders, and having them followed.

Both the Green Warden and I were hurried into the room by the secretary, and the door was shut behind us with a quiet but firm click. If I had been a lesser man, it would have been hard not to make a nervous swallow at the sudden onset of nerves that tried to rush over me. It was like being escorted to the principal's office for setting off fireworks on the playground in elementary school all over again, except this time the explosion I had set off had been a lot more than a couple of cherry bombs.

"Well, Tew. I've read the reports, and talked to your apprentice, but we both know that's no substitute for speaking to the men who were on the front lines. Why don't you tell me your side of things?" The Commandant was an older man, probably a good ten or fifteen years older than my actual age. To my eyes, he wore his years well, and kept himself in good shape. "And introduce me to your friend, while you're at it."

"Sir, it all started when the guards on watch reported seeing a barge approaching while enemy forces were burning the outer river districts. We knew how vital the supplies they carried would be for the city, so a plan was quickly formed and executed to safely provide them escort into the city." Tew pulled out a list of hastily scrawled names and passed it over. "Surprisingly, only a few died in the engagement, but several were wounded severely enough that they will require a longer recovery time than the city is likely to last."

Tew's retelling went more in depth, so I stopped paying attention and started looking around the office. What it showed me was a city on the brink. A well-worn cot poking out from behind a temporary screen in a corner proved that the Commandant was sleeping here more often than not, and a stack of discarded maps of the surrounding area with markings that showed skirmishes from before the city was encircled still sat on top of a table alongside a neat stack of dirty dishes. Lists of supplies covered in an ominous shade of red ink were tacked in place next to the map of the city hung on the wall, and the Commandant himself hadn't shaved in a day or two. I had seen signs like this before. It all added up to a leader barely holding his forces together.

"And then, the Paladin threw the Holy Hand Grenade, and smote the undead and their caster with the most powerful explosion I've ever witnessed!" Tew's voice rose in excitement, and I started paying attention to what they were saying again. "The permanent death of so many enemies was glorious to behold." He took a short breath to calm down, and laid a heavy hand on my shoulder. "I believe you can trust this man. He is not only a Paladin, but a warrior of the highest level. We should include him in our plans, especially those involving our 'mystery' problem."

Of course, I gave myself a pat on the back for getting the stoic Green Warden to say 'Holy Hand Grenade' while managing to keep a straight face. It didn't matter that I was the only person on the whole planet who got the joke, I had to take the little wins where I could find them.

"Sir Paladin, it sounds like I owe you my thanks for saving so many of the Hunter's Guild, and for bringing much-needed supplies to the city." The Commandant held out a well-calloused hand for me to shake. "You can call me Beck. I'm glad you happened to be on that barge. I would hate to think what could have happened otherwise."

"The barge wasn't my doing, Commandant Beck, just a happy chance encounter. Saving your men was only the right thing to do, considering they were risking their lives to save my own people." I nodded my head toward the map on the wall, trying to steer the conversation in the direction I wanted. "Are things truly that bad already, or does it only look that way on the surface?"

Beck grimaced, accentuating the wrinkles on his face. "You noticed that, did you? I wouldn't say we're at risk of the city falling to an outside force anytime soon, but…" As he trailed off, his eyes drifted to the stack of dirty dishes on his side table. "Food is going to become a problem soon. There are too many mouths to feed, and this attack came at the worst possible time. We weren't able to bring in all the harvests, and what we did bring in went first into the guild warehouses, and only the mandatory fifth went to the city."

"So, if the guilds have a bunch of food stored, why don't they help take care of the people? Aren't most of the refugees citizens of the guilds?" I stepped over to better inspect the pages outlining the situation. I knew a few nature spells that could help speed plant growth at the cost of soil depletion, but with the guilds holding on to a ready food supply I would hold the idea as a last resort. Especially since it would most likely be Jess, Cross, and me doing all the heavy lifting for the spellwork to make it happen. This would be a good way to bend the guilds to my way of thinking anyway. "I would think they would want to take care of their own."

"It's more than that." Beck sighed as he joined me, shuffling his feet. "Even with the undead trying to knock down our gates, some of the more foolish guilds can't help but play at politics. They want concessions, incentives, and bonuses that will ruin this city as sure as the horde outside. None of the less ambitious guilds will weaken themselves in the others' eyes by shifting position while there are holdouts, and Greendown's civil leadership is more useless than a short sword when hunting kraken. Anyone considered 'royal' enough to settle things abandoned the city weeks ago, taking their men and supplies with them. On top of that, I've got people from every station, from the highest of the high to the lowest of the low, going missing at all hours of the day and night, and not a single clue to figure out what's happening to them. Now, there's rumors spreading about monsters in the sewers, which means the undead may have already found a way into the city we don't know about! I'm stuck between a boar hog swarm and a wendigo, with nothing but a belt knife and my knickers!"

Beck had gotten more and more animated as he went on, and by the end of his rant he was nearly shouting. He took a deep breath to calm himself down and then shrugged in defeat.

Tew walked over and gave the old man a solid pat on the back. "Cheer up, Commandant. You're handling things far better than anyone in your position could have ever expected. Now that we have a Paladin here to help, perhaps there's something that can be taken off your shoulders." Tew turned to the map and pointed at a cluster of yellow dots marked a little to the southwest of the city center. "While Oriana stays on the walls and I search the slums one last time for James Holden, I thought the Paladin could check the densest knot of those reported missing and–"

"Sir, is everything all right in here? I could hear someone yelling." The secretary opened the door to the office, and a burly man that I hadn't seen waiting when we were outside tried poking his head in to see what the commotion was about. The secretary turned back in annoyance to glare at the man before looking back at the Commandant. "Also, that mayor from one of the outlying villages you wanted to speak to is here to see you."

"Everything's fine, thank you. Tell the mayor I'll see him in a moment." Beck turned back to the map. "Now, you were mentioning–"

"It's *you*! I'd know that smell anywhere!" The man from outside shoved aside the secretary and came barging into the office. He was pointing a finger right at me. "Everything that happened is your fault!"

"What? What's my fault? I didn't do anything." I had no idea what the man was talking about, until he let out a roar of equal parts pain and rage as he shifted into a giant bear. Ah, crap. The werebear mayor I had a disagreement with over a month ago. I looked around frantically for something to defend myself with. Preferably an industrial-sized newspaper that I could roll up. Unfortunately, there was nothing useful nearby. "Now, hold on just a second. You don't want to–"

His flying tackle took both of us out of the office window.

CHAPTER 22

I barely had time to activate my shield bracelet before we hit the ground. Since the bubble of energy only had a moment to form, it wasn't ready to take the hit when I landed on my back. It *certainly* wasn't ready for the extremely angry grizzly bear that pancaked me right afterward, either.

Having a Vigor stat over seventy did come with some benefits though, including being tougher than an old leather boot. Instead of broken bones and a shattered rib cage, all I got was the wind knocked out of me.

The werebear on top of me got up with a groan, and shook his head to clear it. He looked down, probably expecting to see me as nothing more than a red smear on the cobblestone courtyard. What he got instead was a knuckle sandwich.

"Hello to you too, *Mister* Mayor." My punch had knocked him off of me, and he fell to the side with an earth-shaking thud. "I've got to admit, it's a *surprise* to see you." I gave him a solid kick to the ribs, sending him sliding across the ground. I had to take a few moments to unbuckle one of the clasps on my breastplate. When he had squished me, it had bent into a position that didn't allow me to take a full breath. I seriously needed new armor.

"Are you okay?" Tew was poking his head out of the bear-sized hole in the wall where a window used to be. "Do you need any help?"

"I'm good, Warden. This lycan just needs to be taught a lesson on manners before–" I was slammed from behind, causing me to bite my tongue as I smacked into the edge of the building and tumbled into a decorative bush trimmed in the shape of a giant pigeon. I sat up and spat out a mouthful of blood, casting a quick and dirty healing spell to take care of all the bumps and bruises along with the damage to my mouth. "Man, who knew a charging bear could be so quiet?"

The werebear didn't feel like answering. Instead, the angry lycan made another jumping leap for me, trying to pin me back into the pigeon bush. His claws tore through my loose breastplate like paper as I dodged to the side, ripping it off in one swipe.

I thought about pulling a weapon, but I held back. A subtle warning flared from my Judge Mantle and told me it would be wrong. I punched him in the ribs before he could right himself, causing the werebear to fall into the bush. "Stay down, bear-man. Don't get out of the giant pigeon, or I'll have to hurt you." Which, honestly, might have been one of the weirdest things I'd ever said out loud.

Of course, he didn't listen and came charging at me once again, destroying the topiary in the process. I jumped out of his way, pulling our fight off to the side of the building. He pulled a parkour move on me that I wasn't expecting and catapulted himself off the corner of the guild hall, tearing through stone with his claws. The lycan showed no signs of being slowed from my earlier hits, his advanced healing keeping him in top form.

I managed to catch him by his jaws with my hands as he slammed into me, his teeth digging into my fingers. His weight was enough to bend me backward, and I had to brace myself against the curb behind me to keep from sliding. Stone crunched under my heels as the werebear pushed his weight down on me. Blood dripped down my arms from my torn fingers while he did his best to crush my head with his muzzle. Since my hands weren't free, I had to activate my shield bracelet once more and mentally shape it to focus on my torso before he could shred me with his claws. He quickly gave up his attempts to disembowel me and placed both of his arms on my shoulders, pushing down on me even harder as I tried to shove him off of me.

"I don't know why you're so mad at me, but I'm over this. Last chance before I stop holding back." The urge to shoot a stone spike from the ground right in between his legs was nearly overwhelming. I mean, it was a *wide open* free shot.

His only reply was another growl, and he redoubled his efforts to bite my face off.

"Fine, have it your way, fur ball." I couldn't actually cast the stone spike spell because my hands were preoccupied, but one quick and easy cantrip was always available. "*Spark.*"

The barrel of my wrist gun closest to my index finger was pointed straight along the side of his head. The other two were aimed at more vital locations, like his eye socket and up his nose, but my Judge Mantle still wouldn't let me outright kill him. And since the bullets in my wrist gun were silver, it *would* kill him.

So, I blew off his ear.

He roared in pain as he tumbled off of me. I raised a hand and curled in both my pinky and index finger as I forced out a heavy burst of mana and made a backhand slapping motion. "*Push.*"

A dense fist of wind magic punched the bear man away from me, knocking him even further away from the guild house. I followed that up with another healing spell to seal up my torn hands and wrenched back muscles, then started charging up a lightning bolt spell to zap the ever-loving bejeezus out of this guy.

The werebear tried getting to his feet, but suddenly losing an ear had thrown off his balance. Inner ear trauma played merry hell with a person's equilibrium. He stumbled around a bit before falling onto his side, swiping at his wound.

"Ready to talk instead of fight?" I held back from actually casting the charged lightning spell, but I didn't let the spellform go. "I'm willing to calm down if you are."

Instead of an intelligent answer, he roared and made another swipe at me. His heavy paws tore loose a cobblestone that smacked me in the shin, breaking one of my last pieces of armor and bruising my leg.

"Alright, I'm about done playing. Remember, you asked for it". I released the lightning spell at his chest, which sent him flying.

He hit the ground and rolled to a stop in a heaping pile of smoking hair and scorched limbs. As his regeneration started to kick in, he slowly shifted from a bear back into a man.

I walked up to him, once again casting a healing spell to fix my leg. The strain on my mana channels was much lighter after the past few days, meaning I had probably leveled up a small amount once again. I didn't bother checking my stats at the moment, considering I had a bleeding naked man who still looked like he wanted to fight me that I needed to deal with first.

"You! Everything went wrong after you showed up." The mayor was holding his hand against the side of his head, which didn't do much to slow the bleeding. "What did you do to me? I'm not getting better."

"Silver bullet, genius." I waggled my wrist gun as I started reloading it from one of the pouches on my belt. "I could have killed you at any time, but I seriously have no idea why you're so mad at me. The last time we saw each other you gave me a cold farewell from your little village and passed off some letters to my friends to deliver. Is that why you're so mad? Because we haven't delivered the letters yet? If that's the case, you should know we had to kill a lich, and it put us *teensy* bit behind schedule, otherwise we would have handed them off a long time ago. Being a mailman has been far down my list of priorities, I'm afraid."

"It's not about stupid letters!" The mayor swayed a bit before sitting down on a patch of grass. "I-I'm not feeling well."

"You're losing a lot of blood, but I can help. Promise not to bite me?" I held a hand out, and the mayor gritted his teeth as he nodded his head. "This is probably going to feel weird."

The healing spell took a little longer to take hold, most likely because of his reluctance to have me touch him causing a weak connection, but it did its job and he had a fully regrown ear in less than a minute. He touched his ear in wonder, jumping to his feet in a hurry.

"Healing like this changes *everything*. You have to come with me." He turned, and his blood-smeared face was no longer angry, but pure desperation. "*Please*. I was wrong before. My temper got the best of me. Now that I don't have the mayor's medallion to help me control it, that happens a lot. That's not what's important right now. Things happened after you left. Bad things. You might not understand yet, but you will."

"Fine. I'll go with you, but you might want to do something about being so… naked." I motioned at his lack of clothing, and he looked around at the crowd that had gathered to watch us fight. "I should also let the Commandant and Green Warden know what happened before I run off without saying anything. You *did* throw me through a window, after all."

He shook his head while looking around the street we were on. "No, there isn't time. You'll see why soon." A dirty blanket next to a trash heap was quickly transformed into the world's nastiest toga. "Come, before somebody important tries to stop us."

If he was willing to put on that blanket for whatever kind of emergency he was talking about, I wasn't going to turn him down. Tew would certainly be able to find me again if he truly needed me, and I had already seen the location where most of the people had gone missing, so I felt okay about leaving with him.

We ran through a warren of twisting streets and narrow alleys, most of which were packed with refugees on the edge of starvation. Neither of us said anything to one another, mostly because there wasn't much of a chance to speak in the loud and cramped spaces everywhere you looked. In a rapidly short amount of time, we were on the opposite side of the city from where I had made my dramatic entrance through the river gate.

This side of Greendown faced the forest, farms, and mountains, which was where the majority of the enemy forces were located. The smell of undead faintly drifted over the city when the wind blew just right, and no one could doubt there was an army fresh from the grave waiting to expand their ranks on the other side of the wall.

"In here." The mayor pulled back the curtain on a shack that probably once held gardening equipment, but now served as a house for a family of three. "Now you can see why I was so upset. This is what happened to my family after you left. Men came–calling themselves White Wardens–and they were looking for you. When we couldn't give them answers, they did this."

Two people looked out from the dim interior, covering their eyes from the sudden light. Inside, I saw exactly why the werebear had been so angry. The mayor's wife and daughter were inside the shack, and both were heavily scarred. While his wife was striped across her face and arms by an obvious whipping, the daughter was much worse. It looked like she had been whipped, and then burned, and then whipped again, creating layers of scars that must have made even the simplest of tasks extremely painful for the poor girl.

I was reminded of a title upgrade that I had received while hunting for the lich about unintended consequences, and I had to be looking at them. By simply walking into their village, that one act had led these people to untold amounts of pain. The urge to rip Gleason's throat out and violently shove it up his pee hole caused sparks to jump off of the knuckles of my clenched fists.

"Give me a little bit, and I should be able to fix this. I can heal damage this bad, but it takes time." I knelt next to the mother first, and she tried to push me away.

Her fingernails shifted into claws, digging into my arm. She shook her head, adamantly pointing at her daughter and grunting, her eyes imploring me to heal her daughter first.

"He…" The Mayor whispered. "The White Warden's men cut out her tongue and… they forced each of us to rely on our natural regeneration, but that can only do so much."

I nodded grimly and gently plucked the woman's nails free, doing my best to ensure they didn't cut me. Both of them looked equal parts frightened and hopeful, and I didn't hold the fresh wounds against her. "I agree, she's in much worse shape, which means that she is going to take significantly more time and energy and will need someone to care for her. I don't know bear shifter bodies very well, so I'd rather make any mistakes on you. Wouldn't you agree?"

She thought for a moment before giving a short nod of agreement, still sending fearful glances toward the younger woman.

I could tell that she was conflicted about allowing me to heal her first. "Don't worry." I consoled the woman. "I'll have plenty of energy to take care of her too."

She finally seemed to relax as small tears welled up at the corners of her eyes.

"I'll pay whatever price, as long as you heal them." The Mayor croaked, his throat seeming to have gone dry with emotion. "Even our family connections haven't been able to help, and we've all but given up hope."

"I'm a Judge. I only charge for healing when the guilty require it." Grabbing her arm, I started the healing spell immediately by pushing it into her bone and deep muscle tissue and began mapping her anatomy with my magic. Shifter bodies were weird compared to a normal human's. They felt like they were made of layers, and each layer required a separate form of healing.

Connecting to the damaged skin and deeper scar tissue was relatively easy once I cleared up the minor problems she was dealing with, like a sore back and a minor infection in her gums. Getting her tongue to go back to normal wasn't as easy. It had been scar tissue for long enough that her body had started to see it as the 'correct' form it should take, so coaxing it into regular healthy tissue required a deeper connection than I wanted to make.

Diving deeper into the woman, my mana began to stretch throughout her body. Power resonated like a plucked string, vibrating her bones. I made mistakes and corrected them as I went, learning the ins and outs of the werebear's biology.

Stepping back from the mom once it was done, I sat down hard on one of the sleeping mats. I was drained and my mana generator was throbbing once again as it strained to refill itself, but my body wasn't hurting nearly as bad as before. Definitely had another level up recently.

"By the grace of the Trinity!" The mom was holding out her arms, looking at the lack of scars. Her hands suddenly jumped to her mouth and restored tongue as the words spilled out with her tears. "I can't believe it. You're a *real* healer, not one of those pretenders."

"Like I said, I'm just a Judge, but I may know a few things here and there." I gave her a tired smile before backing away to let her husband and daughter look her over. I looked inward, and saw my body was working better than it ever had before. My mana generator was already spinning furiously on its own, so I would be ready to try to heal the daughter after a short break, and there were no signs of soul damage. The fight outside the gates had been good for my development.

"Thank you." The mayor plopped down heavily next to me when I opened my eyes. "No one would know she was even hurt by that bastard and his men."

"Can you tell me what happened now?" I had a pretty good idea, but I wanted to make sure I wasn't jumping to conclusions.

"Not much to tell, really. As I said, a group of those White Wardens came looking for you, and they used my family and I as an example. They handed off the mayor title to that troublemaker you had a fight with before they left, and the members of the village with more than half a brain in their skull came to Greendown with my family and me to seek justice from the Guild." He waved around at the dirty shacks and tents surrounding his own. "Not that it's done us much good. With the enemy on the doorstep, we haven't been a priority."

"What about your village? Any word on what happened to it after you left?" I knew that roving packs of undead had been seen pushing through every part of the forest, but I didn't know if they had made it as far as his old village.

"As far as I know, it still stands." He shrugged before standing back up. "Not that it concerns me much anymore. The people there made their choice, and it wasn't a good one. I'll not be returning, even after this all blows over."

"That's fair, I suppose." I stood as well, and motioned for the daughter to move into the fading daylight. "Come on, let's get you healed up. Once you're good to go, I've got a mystery to solve, and some guilds to knock around."

After seeing the daughter's scars in the light, as well as her destroyed eye, I was really looking forward to finding Gleason. He got away from me last time, but I wasn't going to make that mistake this time around.

CHAPTER 23

The lights in this part of the city seemed dim compared to everywhere else I had been over the past few hours. A heavy drizzle had turned into a steady rain, making the few oil-wick street lamps that hadn't been stolen even less effective at fighting back the night.

Healing the mayor's daughter had taken even less time than I expected, especially after having the experience of fixing her mother. The transformation that the poor girl had undergone was dramatic–from a scarred half-blind and horrible existence into a young and beautiful girl–and only reinforced the need to find Gleason and put his sadistic urges into an early grave. My Judge mantle was practically screaming for it.

Shortly afterward, the very thankful mayor had helped by taking me to the armorer's district. I had seen Cross and the others selling off our stockpile while I was there, but I stayed away from them for now. We each had tasks to focus on, and I didn't want to distract them. Not only that, but the Button Guild–a group of assassins that made killings look like an accident–might have already realized that Jess was in the city, and I wanted to remain a wildcard to mess up any plans they might have for her. If I wasn't seen with her, maybe they wouldn't realize I would come to her aid.

With a siege going on, most of the armor that was available was either more decorative than useful, or the dregs left behind after everyone had already taken the best choices. I'd been lucky enough to find a set of equipment that the former owner didn't need anymore. Their blood had still stained parts of the leg armor until I cleaned it off with a mixture of heat and water spells, and the gear smelled like an old boot, but it was far better than my last set, the Woodsman Scouting Uniform, had been.

Item: Orc Hunter's Armor (Leather and Steel with Copper reinforcement)
Type: Medium Armor
Grade: 8/10
Description: Full medium armor that covers the chest, back, shoulders, forearms, thighs, and shins. Meant to withstand heavy blows from strong opponents without sacrificing range of movement. No bonuses to camouflage. No additional protection to mana-based attacks. Does not restrict spell formations or casting from the wearer.

Adding runes to boost the mana protection and spellcasting would be necessary, but there wasn't time for that at the moment. Hunting the assholes that were making people disappear was far more important.

That was why I was currently doing my best caped crusader impression, hiding on a rooftop in the darkest part of the city. Rain was soaking the filth-strewn alley ways. It had to be close to three in the morning, and I was one of the only things still awake. A few roving street gangs had moved through earlier without causing any problems, so I let them go by unmolested. It felt more like a poorly formed neighborhood watch than anything nefarious. It still made me happy to see the people doing something to try and protect their own, even if they didn't know exactly what they were doing.

Just as I was about to give up for the night and return to speak with Tew and Beck, I heard a scuffle a few alleys over. I leapt over rooftops to see what was going on, only to see the sewer grate next to an empty building drop into place with a heavy thud. To have an empty building of any kind in a city filled to the brim with refugees was already suspicious. It meant the people in the area knew to avoid the place, either through instinct or experience.

I briefly thought about going to get more men in the city watch, but that would risk losing the trail of whoever had just been taken.

That wasn't something I was okay with accepting. Instead, I dropped down and looked through the grate, hoping to see some kind of clue.

The rain was actively washing away everything that could have possibly given me any idea of what I was dealing with, be it Gleason, a group, or some kind of monster. I wrenched the grate free and dropped down below with my mace already in hand, its blue glow casting enough light to see by in the dark tunnel.

Dirty water rushed by at knee height, nearly knocking me over with the slick rocks under the swift-moving stream that made it impossible for my boots to get a good grip. I did some impressive breakdance moves as I slipped and slid to get over to the edge where there was a narrow walkway. It was nearly as slimy as the rocks under the water, but I wasn't getting shoved around while trying to walk.

Now that I was in the sewers, I could easily see a trail on the wall where someone had scraped the layers of slime and moss off at shoulder height as they had walked by. That meant someone in armor, and not a monster. From the varied levels of scrapings, there were at least four. Probably more, considering it was likely they were of similar heights or not all of them had pointy shoulder armor pieces.

Either Gleason wasn't working alone, or this wasn't him at all. I knew he had to be down here somewhere though, especially after I had talked to the boys and their dad. Odds were, I had found his trail. The glow from the power I was leaking into my mace intensified as I let my anger get the best of me for a moment. I couldn't wait to crush his stupid face in.

I didn't know which direction to take, so I picked the one that headed toward the more central part of Greendown and started jogging. If the kidnappers weren't expecting to be followed, I might be able to catch up to them before they got back to their base and question them.

The sewer tunnels were surprisingly well-built, and I didn't have any problems beyond the precarious footing. It wasn't long before I heard the sounds of people talking, and the flickering of torchlight coming from farther up the tunnel.

I cut the flow of mana to my mace and did my best to sneak up on the group. It wasn't difficult. They weren't looking behind them at all. They had been snatching people with impunity for so long, they'd become complacent in their arrogance. While they were still out of sight around a sharp bend, I finally caught their conversation as they stopped to take a break at a juncture of six tunnels.

"How many more test subjects do you think he needs?" The first voice was higher-pitched, and sounded young to my ears.

"I don't know, I just don't want to be one of them. Did you see the last batch? I'd rather be torn apart by the horde than end up like that. They looked… melted, from the inside." This one sounded more raspy, and a quick look around the corner revealed him to be a tall, scrawny man in bloodstained robes and armor.

"Shut up, you two. You never know when he might show up. If he hears you, we'll all get the lash. Is that what you want?" The last speaker was the only one who looked somewhat healthy, despite a smattering of boils around his neck and ears. He was clearly the leader of the trio. "This should be the final one. After this, it's on to the last stage of his plan."

"We're supposed to be Blood Wardens, not whipping boys. When is this going to end?" The youngest looked jaundiced, with yellowed skin that hadn't seen enough sun.

"The city is going to fall in another week or two. After that, I say we get our cut of what's left of the city and guild coffers, and go our separate ways. We never have to see him again once this business is done and over." Scrawny guy was scratching at his nether regions, which definitely couldn't be a good sign.

"Where are you fellas off to?" The youngest's armor was the only one not covered in dents and rust, but the amount of bloodstains covering his formerly white robes made up for it.

"My sister has a place down south, near the border with the desert kingdoms. I figure nobody will have heard of Greendown that far away. I'll disappear, maybe start over as a guard or something." The leader had a nervous habit of rubbing at his boils when he talked, which was even more disgusting than it sounded.

"You want some company? I've got no better sounding plans than that one." The young one sounded like a lost puppy, and I *almost* felt bad for him.

"Same. My brother is a Black Warden to the east, and he wouldn't welcome me any." The scrawny one stopped scratching at himself to sniff at his fingers and winced, which was saying something considering we were standing in a sewer system.

"We'll see what kind of riches we can dig up in the aftermath first, boys. You might have enough that you don't want to go that far south with lil' old me. Now, enough jawing, let's get this one up and get 'em back to the holding cells. The first dose will be wearing off soon." The leader motioned at the man on a litter, who hadn't moved the entire time they were talking. It looked like they had grabbed a heavily muscled laborer, dressed in the rough clothing of a refugee down on his luck. Someone that wouldn't be missed.

"Yes, Exsanguinator. We'll get him there beforehand. We don't want him raging out on us and getting loose in the tunnels like the last one." The scrawny man bent and picked up his end of the litter, and I chose that moment to strike.

As I took a step out from around the corner, a shadow across from me detached itself from the wall and dove at my face. Even with my enhanced speed and reflexes, I barely had enough time to get my mace up in time to block the attack.

Both my shadow attacker and I went tumbling into the rushing water, and my back slammed into the slick rock as I was washed away from my intended targets. The darkness was absolute, and I lost all sense of direction as slimy tendrils wrapped around my neck and started to squeeze.

Despite the situation, my main focus in that moment was on not opening my mouth and letting in the sewer water. I pushed a flood of power into my mace, lighting it up with a burst of blue sparks that flared underwater bright enough I could see them through my closed eyelids.

A surprised screech from my attacker at the sudden light lessened their grip on my throat, and I punched downward at the ground hard enough to pop myself back out of the water. I finally got a look at my attacker, and I was disgusted to see it was a vampire that had been turned when they were a child.

It was hard to tell given the slower growth rates of people in worlds like this one, but they were probably somewhere between the ages of twelve and fifteen. An adult in the eyes of some on this world, depending on the region, but still a child to me. Given our size disparity, now that the element of surprise was gone I was easily able to pry it off of me and snatch the little bloodsucker by the back of its neck and hold it up like an angry kitten.

An evil, bloodsucking, murdering kitten with the strength of two grown men and claws and fangs as strong as steel. I might have slammed it in the face with my mace a time or two to get it to stop struggling so much, but we quickly reached an understanding.

"So, the Destitute is helping Gleason, is he? How many of you bloodsuckers does he have helping him?" I didn't get an answer, so I held a pointy part of my mace to his face and let it glow extra bright. "Answer me, or you won't like the alternative."

"*Nooonnee…*" The creepy little leech hissed like a snake, so I bounced his face off the wall.

"Knock off the act. You aren't fooling anyone with that crap. I feel for you getting turned so young, but I'll still turn you to ash in a heartbeat if you aren't useful to me." Another flare from my mace served to accentuate my point.

"Fine, fine. No need to get nasty." The kid crossed his arms and pouted at me. "I'm not working with that crazy fella. I'm only watchin' him for the Lady. She's got plans, an she wants to know what he's up to."

"This isn't the first time I've heard about this 'Lady' from the mouth of an undead." I flared the light around my mace once more and growled. "Spill. Who is she, and what are her plans?" I pulled my mace back, giving him some space to answer.

"I can't say nothin' about her without me head blowin' up. It's a curse, and a compellin' she laid on me. As for plans, that, I got no idea. I'm only a watcher. Me an' one other in the city that I know of. With them Greens runnin' about, the Lady can't risk more." The little vampire shrugged, wincing with the motion. "I ha' ta stop ya from keepin' them from gettin' that fella back to their base. Ya don't want him runnin' loose in the city. They do somethin' to their blood, make it smell rotten, an' then they go looney. The sheep'd be all kinds a' scared if they seen that, an we don't need 'em more afraid right now, goin' into a panic."

"Sheep? You mean regular *people*?" The little vampire gave me a quick nod, realizing he might have said the wrong thing. "Well, what are you going to tell your 'Lady' if I let you go?"

"Nothin' that I seen so far she needs to know, ya? You was just pokin' about in the sewers like a bunch before ya been doin' since things got bad." He grinned at me, showing off stunted fangs.

My first instinct was to simply kill the kid and be done with it. That would mean the 'Lady' would know her spy was caught, and she might act out because of it, or try and send in a bunch more to replace him. Right now, I had a known quantity with this vamp, and since no vampire victims had popped up he was probably surviving off of small animals, or only snacking, not killing. His replacement might not be so kind to the populace.

"Fine. I can agree to that. But I need to get a closer look at this operation, and find out for sure if a man named Gleason is running it. If he is, I need to kill him, and shut it down now, before it gets any further out of hand." I set the vampire kid down, ready to smash his skull in if he acted up. He surprised me when he didn't misbehave at all.

"Ya ain't gonna like this, big fella. Gleason's the man yer lookin' for, sure nuff, but he ain't here." The vamp raised his hand and slowly pulled out a sopping wet stack of papers from an inner vest pocket. "He run off to the surface, an ain't been back. That there was the last grab. They're gonna get up to their evil soon enough, but that Gleason is doin' other bad."

He handed me the papers, and I took them carefully. Sometimes, I seriously missed hand sanitizer. "Okay. So, you're saying I need to hunt down Gleason–wherever he's disappeared to–and *then* come back and finish these assholes off before they can get up to no good."

"If'n I was in boots that were a lot like the ones on ya feet, then yes." The vampire kid gave me another fang-filled grin and a little salute. "Luck to ya, big fella. If ya can break my bond, I'd be mighty happy." He disappeared down the tunnel, off to do whatever bidding his evil overlord wanted him to do.

Oddly enough, my Judge Mantle had been silent during my entire interaction with the little vampire. I don't think it knew what to think of the little leech either. I was pretty sure the vampire saw me as a way to get out from under the thumb of the person controlling it, especially after we had fought. I saw it as a way to find and kill Gleason and his men, and eventually I would have to put the little vampire down.

For now, my hunt was back on the surface.

After I had a bath.

CHAPTER 24

Reviewing the random scribbles on the papers the vampire kid had given me was a lesson in frustration. The ink had run, and it wasn't like I could read the written word of this planet in the first place. A few diagrams that pictured various reactions to medicinal and alchemical combinations were more than a little alarming, but beyond Gleason building himself a bunch of mindless shock troops I didn't see how it mattered.

I felt some conviction about going back down into the sewers and tearing apart the little hideout Gleason's 'Blood Wardens' had set up, but taking off the head of the snake had to be the priority. The risk of him escaping to recreate his twisted plans was too high. I had seen Gleason's type before. Fanatical. Their instability always escalated and the horrors they would inflict would grow until it consumed the entire world. No. I needed to stop him right here, right now. I knew there had to be some way to get him to show his face, and I figured putting myself on display was the best way to do it. If word got back to him, he'd come to me.

"Anything else for you, sir?" The old woman who I had woken up by banging on the door of the bathhouse before the sun had even come up wasn't exactly happy about the early hour, and even less so about the state of my current hygiene, but the flash of a gold coin had cooled any hot feelings. It unfortunately hadn't warmed up the water in her bathhouse much. Still, a bath was a heaven-sent miracle when you smelled like a sewer, and cleaning my clothes and armor was included with the price. Besides, I had my own magic to heat up the water when she wasn't looking.

"I'm good, thank you." I got out of the bath and started putting on the still-damp clothing. It was raining hard outside, so I was going to be wet soon anyway. That didn't make putting the sodden clothes on any more comfortable, and I was quickly discovering the chafing issues the heavier armor was causing me in a few places. A memory hit me from my time on world four, where I had gained my Knight Class.

"This armor chafes me in all the wrong places, Sir Riety. I don't think I'm cut out to be a knight. I'm just a simple soldier, not some fancy guy like the rest of you." I rubbed at my shoulder, where the edge of my breastplate was digging into me. "My only accomplishment was making it out of that mess alive."

"No, my young friend, you did far more than that." Sir Riety gave me a hand, adjusting the straps on my new armor. "That battle was one of the worst I've ever seen, and once the bishops left for the castle, even I thought we weren't long for this world. If you hadn't managed to get our men to the rooftops, no one would have survived. Knighthood is the smallest reward you have earned."

"I'm sure the common people seeing the reward for returning a bunch of blessed armor and shields to the clergy being so high has nothing to do with it?" I tried really hard to keep the sarcasm out of my voice. I truly did, considering how devout Sir Riety was to his church and its leaders. Even after they had abandoned him to die, he still saw them as the end-all, be-all of his universe. Generations of brainwashing and programming don't get reversed overnight. "And everyone else getting commendations isn't buying their silence so they won't speak of the cowardice of the clergy in the face of the enemy, right?"

"Of course that's part of the reason you are getting rewarded, Sir James. Why wouldn't it be? You didn't have to bring back all of those heavy shields, but you did, and without orders. They are going to save many lives." Sir Riety finished tightening up my straps before moving to fix up his own armor and equipment for the award ceremony. "If others follow your example in the future, who knows how many people the Church can save with the blessed metal from God. As for buying the silence of the devout? That's just nonsense. The Nine Bishops have only to command, and we will willingly lay down our lives. It is our duty and obligation to protect them. I

considered that duty fulfilled when they were able to escape while we bought them the time to do so."

I gave up trying to explain what I meant, and decided to focus on helping Sir Riety instead. He just didn't see it. While I was being officially knighted, Sir Riety was getting some type of commendation medal alongside the rest of the survivors of the debacle left behind by the bishops. All three of them.

Not that I needed to be officially knighted by the clergy. My system had given me the class as soon as I had returned to the castle, and the four new skills it imparted would be a huge help in the coming weeks and months of the barbarian siege. Defend, Shield Bash, Chivalrous Might, and Taunt were all powerful tools that I couldn't wait to try in a real fight. The new stat points helped too, especially the increase in strength if I was going to be walking around in heavy plate armor all the time.

"Any word from the messenger eagles?" I rubbed a polishing cloth across the ridge of my visor. There was a scratch from an enemy blade that would need to be buffed out later, but it would have to do for now. "Reinforcements and resupply would be very welcome."

"The bishops haven't said much since they returned from our failed mission, Sir James. If an eagle made it through the gauntlet of the enemy spellcasters and archers, they haven't told the rank and file." Sir Riety belted on his sword and picked up his shield, and motioned for me to do the same. "Now, why don't you finish up here so we can go to the courtyard and get our just rewards?"

"You go on ahead. I'll catch up in a minute. I just want to polish my shield one last time." I didn't know if anyone had caught on yet, but I was the only person that had both a shield and blade that still held a full blessing from their god. So many had died that it was easy to pick up the best ones off the ground and claim them as my own. They worked best when they were polished til they practically glowed, so I made sure they were spotless before hurrying down to the inner courtyard.

When I got there, I was surprised to see that the stage they had set up for the award ceremony didn't look like a regular stage. I couldn't put my finger on it, but it didn't look right. Instead of walking out there, I stopped at the arched doorway, hiding in the shadow of the gilded door. Stupid excessive church. Who in their right mind puts gilding on a plain door to an inner courtyard? The excessively rotund bishop that needed help getting up on the stage for his speech. That's who.

"Good people, we have gathered here today to see the execution of those responsible for the great loss of life we suffered a few weeks ago." The bishop's pointy hat was red with gold trim, except for a few places where grease stains had darkened the material. He probably put it on and took it off while eating, and his ridiculous hat suffered the consequences. "We have received word that a contingent of the Cardinal's Cavalry is on their way to put down the barbarians and their goblin allies, and it would be far more merciful for the guilty parties to die by our hand than by those of the Cardinal. They might not be as understanding, or as swift in carrying out justice."

Several hooded men marched out behind the fat bishop carrying out wooden beams and ropes, and in only a few minutes five sets of vertical crosses with a single arm were set up and ready with crude nooses tied in place. I hadn't been looking at a stage. I had been looking at a gallows.

The people gathered in the courtyard had slowly gotten more and more agitated as time went on. At first, I thought they were going to revolt against the bishop. I was an idiot.

"As a trial was already held in private, there is no need to review the facts. Bring out the guilty!" The bishop's yell was like flipping a light switch. People went from quiet, holy, reverent observers, to bloodthirsty monsters screaming for the death of others.

"Kill them!"

"It's all their fault!"

"Make them pay!"

"They took our jobs!"

"Send them to the pit!"

Food, rocks, manure, and whatever wasn't nailed down was thrown at the four bravest men I knew on this cursed world. Their hands were tied behind their backs, and they were roughly shoved up on stage by hooded men in the same uniform the lower clergy liked to wear.

Literal priests were sending innocent men to their deaths, because the bishops didn't want the truth of the bloodiest day of the siege to get out when the Cardinal's men arrived. Their cowardice knew no bounds. I had joked about it, but I never believed they'd actually do it.

The hoods were ripped off the four men, and they blinked at the sudden brightness. None of them were young, as only the truly tough and experienced veterans had managed to fight free of the barbarians when the bishops left us to die. True to form, none of them bothered begging for their lives, and they all stood stoically as the rough hemp ropes were fitted around their necks.

Four men in full armor–exactly like I was wearing–came up on stage to whisper in the ear of the bishop. His face turned almost as red as his hat, and he grabbed one of them by his tabard and pulled him down to his eye level. "I don't want excuses, find him*! He's got to be somewhere inside the castle. Once you find him, don't bother bringing him to me. Kill him, and dump his body over the wall into the moat. The nightcrabs need to eat as well."*

The armored men ran off, obviously searching for me. Sir Riety noticed the interaction and searched the crowd of people throwing things at him, and I stepped out of the shadows just far enough to allow the sun to glint off my gauntlet and aim it into his eyes. He probably could only see a darkened doorway, but he knew I was there. Even from the distance we were apart from one another, I could see him mouth the four words to me we had said to one another on the battlefield. 'For God and Glory.'

"As they are guilty of cowardice, they do not get the grace of speaking last words. May God grant their souls mercy." The bishop

yanked a wooden pole on the stage and all four men dropped out of sight.

That bishop didn't know it yet, but he hadn't just killed the four bravest men in this castle. He'd killed himself and every member of his clergy I could find before the Cardinal got here. We did agree on one thing, him and I.

There damn sure wouldn't be any fucking mercy.

World four had seriously sucked goat balls. At least I had gotten a ton of practice using my Knight skills after that. I splashed some water on my face to help clear away the old memories, besides the few ideas that popped up from being in a siege again.

There were definitely some lessons learned that I could apply to my current situation. Chief among them being to never allow those in power to have *ultimate* power, and to strip the guilds of as much control as possible.

After refocusing on the now, I made a quick plan. The most densely populated part of the city was the area around the guilds, so that's where I decided to go. If Gleason had spies out, they were bound to see me eventually. I also had a bunch of letters to deliver from the village the mayor had been in charge of, even if they were a little late. It gave me an excuse to walk around the area, and I still wanted a face-to-face meeting with the Sailor's Guild leadership.

One of the letters I had was a message for the Vice-Admiral, and while I couldn't read it myself, it was supposed to mention that I was a good candidate for a clandestine group they had which focused on reducing the power of the guilds over the common people. That was *definitely* something I was interested in talking to them about.

Dropping off the various letters to most of the guilds went quickly, especially since I wasn't even allowed to take a step through their front gates. The guards out front took the sealed envelopes and scrolls without even checking who the senders were, or asking my name. I didn't hold out great hope that the people in charge would see the messages anytime soon. Or at all.

Since I wasn't offering a bribe, none of them took me seriously. It was more nails for the coffin of the guild system of government. Their inflated sense of self-importance made me sick to my stomach. It needed to go, and the sooner, the better.

When I approached the Sailor's Guild, I took a different approach. It was the last letter I had to deliver, so I decided to make a nuisance of myself. Being seen was a major part of the reason why I was in the area anyway, so it served both purposes nicely.

"I need to deliver this to your Vice-Admiral." I held up the letter in front of the quartet of gate guards, who all seemed equally annoyed that I was speaking to them. "Now would be good, please."

"Hand it over, and we'll pass it on as soon as the guild leadership becomes available." The only guard in armor stuck his arm through the wrought-iron fence to take the letter. "I'm sure they'll get right to it, whoever you are."

"You didn't hear me. I said I need to give this to the Vice-Admiral myself. Go get him, and I'll be on my way." I crossed my arms, and kept the letter out of reach. "Trust me, he's going to want to see this, and speak with me after he reads it."

"Sure he will. The second most powerful man in the second most powerful guild wants to talk to some random guy off the street he's never seen before." The guard turned to the other guards and pointed a thumb at me. "You guys hearing this?"

They laughed. I laughed. A few passersby laughed.

Then I grabbed the bars of the gate and ripped it off.

They all stopped laughing.

I didn't.

"What in the Trinity are you doing?!" The armored guard tripped over his own feet as he fell backward, dropping the cudgel he was trying to pull free from his belt in the process. "That, that's…"

"A great reason to get the Vice-Admiral? I agree." I tossed the gate to the side with a clatter of torn metal and broken cobblestone. Hiding the wince from the torn back muscles I had caused myself when I twisted to toss it to the side made things less funny, so I stopped smiling. "Hurry up, I don't have all day."

They scurried off, leaving me alone at the front entrance. I didn't think the people in charge would be happy about all of them abandoning their post, but that was their problem, not mine. Maybe they'd decide to be better guards while they were installing a new gate.

After a very short wait, a not-so-surprisingly large contingent of guards wearing guild colors came out, all with weapons in hand. They were led by a man wearing a peaked hat with an impressive feather poking out the top. He was smaller than I expected one of the most influential men in the city to be, but he carried himself well.

The Vice-Admiral looked at the bent and warped gate before sizing me up, and boldly walked up to me while motioning for his men to stay back. "I heard you wanted to see me?"

"You heard correctly. It was tough at first getting your guards to take me seriously, but I think we found a way to communicate effectively in the end."

He glanced back at the torn gate. "So I see."

I gave him a grin and held out the letter. "Why don't we go inside and talk about some things? I promise to play nice, as long as you do the same."

"Fine." He snatched the letter from my hand and turned back to his headquarters.

Quick hands. If he knew how to use a dagger, this man would be deadly up close.

He might have been showing off a bit. "Come on, then. I'll have some tea prepared for you while I read this, then we can talk about… things."

I followed him into the guild hall, where even more guards were waiting inside. It was as opulent as you would expect the economic powerhouse of a major city to be, with enough gaudy gold and polished marble to give an interior decorator an aneurism. There were a few hidden alcoves with crossbowmen on the upper story, and combined with the extra guards, I was feeling a little outnumbered. My shield bracelet was ready in case they wanted to start something, but a servant came and led me to a library before anything could get spicy. I guess they didn't want me wrecking their nice place.

The servant led me into a library that was impressive for a world that didn't have a printing press. Three full floor-to-ceiling bookshelves were loaded down with books, leatherbound ship's logs, charts, and scrolls. A few padded chairs surrounded a cluster of small tables intricately carved with polished bone and mother of pearl inlay. It was definitely fancy. "The Vice Admiral will see you shortly, sir. Until then, please make yourself comfortable." The servant filled a few cups of tea before leaving, shutting the door behind him.

I didn't sit down immediately, instead taking the chance to look over what a stocked library might look like. While I couldn't read the spines, context clues let me know that most of the subject matter covered ships, sailing, and water-based monsters. As I finished looking at the final bookshelf, I moved a scroll to find a dust-covered book that looked old. Really old.

The cover was made from some kind of rough material that felt like sharkskin. As I picked it up, I felt the slight indentations of runes embossed on the edges. It was a repeating pattern that was meant to preserve the book–which, now that I had a closer look, I was pretty sure was a journal–as well as a way to seal it from anyone not allowed to read it.

"What are you doing?"

I looked up to see the Vice-Admiral had finally decided to grace me with his presence. The tea had gone cold a long time ago, and a lesser man might think he was trying to show dominance by making them wait. Lucky for me I wasn't a lesser man, and I figured he just had to go to the bathroom or something.

"How old is this book?" Instead of answering his question, I held up the silvery-gray journal and popped the rune that allowed it to open. "It feels ancient, but I could be wrong."

"Wha–" The Vice-Admiral stepped forward, holding up his hand. "How did you–?" He took a moment to collect himself, and took off his hat to toss it on the nearest table. "A sorcerer. Well, this isn't going to go anything like I planned, is it? You walk in here and rip our front gate off like it's nothing. Then, you open one of the sealed journals from the first Guild Leader that no one has been able to access in living memory."

"Mage, not a sorcerer. Big difference. Especially in how we make an entrance." Seriously, is it that hard to get it right? "Anyway, what were you planning?" I took a seat across from him and idly flipped through the journal. "I take it you read the letter from your family members, and it recommended me for some kind of underground organization that you wanted to feel me out for yourself?"

"So you read it? I should have guessed." He sat down as well, and took a sip of the tea before making a face and putting it roughly back on the table. "I hate it when they use the cheap stuff." He got up and pulled a rope next to the door that must have let someone know to bring more refreshments. "Yes, I wanted to get some sense of you before I risk my reputation, my position, and very possibly my life."

"That's entirely fair, Admiral. How about we lay all our cards on the table, and then–" I paused as I saw a drawing inside the book that caught my eye. For a second, I thought I was seeing things, because there was no way this 'plumbing-is-a-miracle' backwater of a planet would have something like this, but there was no mistake. It was an airship. A straight-up, steampunk-style blend of zeppelin and pirate galleon kind of airship. "And then, you're going to read this journal to me, out loud, from cover to cover."

"What? Why would I do that? Just read it yourself." The Vice-Admiral seemed genuinely confused, which was the only reason why I hadn't left with the book already to find Jess or one of the others and had them read it to me instead.

I took another deep breath to calm myself down. "Because I can't read or write your language. I'm from *very* far away, and I'm using an advanced form of magic to even be able to speak with you. Like I said, full disclosure time." At least, as full disclosure as I could get without blowing his mind. "The reason I'm here is because I have two quests. One is to bring justice to the people. That's because I'm a Judge, and it's pretty much my job to tear down corrupt institutions like your guild. Which, in case you hadn't put it together, sounds a whole lot like what your secret club of misfits is trying to do."

He gave me a slight nod to show he was following me. He probably didn't trust me yet, but I certainly had him interested.

"My other quest is to find something called the 'Silver Star,' which I only recently found out is a lost airship." I laid out the journal on the table and pointed to the drawing. "And I don't know about you, but that looks a whole lot like an airship."

"By the Trinity!" The Vice-Admiral bent over the book and pointed at a line of text under the drawing. "This *is* the Silver Star! Do you understand what this is? What this means?"

I tried to answer, but he was entirely too excited to give me a chance to talk.

"This isn't the journal of the first Guild Leader. It's the journal of the engineer that built the Silver Star! We might be able to make our *own* airships!"

My system made a dinging sound, and a screen flashed across my vision.

Quest Update!

Rare Quest: Track down Silver Star - Ongoing

-You have discovered a clue to the location of the lost airship. Continue to gather information and items that will help you solve the mystery behind what caused this world's greatest invention–and future ruler–to disappear.

Rare Quest: Track down Silver Star – Ongoing

Sub-quests:

-Find the Key to the Silver Star

-Find the Enhancing Gem

-Close the Demon Gate

He tried to snatch the journal from me while I was distracted, but I was ready for his quick hands this time. I pulled it out of reach and his happy attitude went angry almost as fast as his hands were. "That's not your property. Just because you opened it, doesn't mean you get to keep it."

"I don't want to keep it. I want you to read it to me, out loud. Every. Last. Word."

The Vice-Admiral paused for a long moment, as if considering. He pinched the top of his nose between finger and thumb as though trying to relieve a headache. His long, drawn-out sigh was of a man conceding.

"We're going to need more tea."

CHAPTER 25

The giant hole in the wall of the Hunter's Guild was perplexing Gleason. There hadn't been any of those undead bone knights or a band of orcs that made it inside the city, so how it got there was a mystery he didn't unravel.

"Would you like a shoe shine, sir?"

A street kid wearing a hooded robe tried touching his boot, so Gleason kicked him away. "Get close to me again, rat, and I'll skin you alive right after I've killed your whole family. Filth like you should know where it belongs." The boy jerked back like he had touched a hot stove, but only where the weak sunlight coming through the spotty clouds had touched him as his robe shifted when he was kicked. "Learn your place, or suffer the consequences."

Forgetting the interaction almost immediately, Gleason continued down the street to get a better look at the Hunter's Guild, completely missing the fanged smile of the boy who watched him walk away.

The reason for Gleason's distraction was the extreme amount of damage in the city's center. There were several places where infighting had taken place due to so many people getting crammed into such a comparatively small location, but the whole area had certainly been roughed up worse than anywhere else inside the walls of Greendown, especially along the wing of the building that belonged to the Wardens. A missing window, the grounds and street torn up, and even a destroyed bush. There had definitely been a serious fight.

Finding another place where it was possible to cast his listening spell was far easier this time around, since the recent violence had encouraged most people to leave the area. Gleason quickly found an empty food vendor's shop to hide in that had a window overlooking the side of the building where the new hole was located. Once he was safely hidden, Gleason settled in place before he cast his spell and patiently waited for something important to happen. He didn't have to wait long.

A faint knock on his uncle's door sounded before the voice of his secretary announced Lieutenant Lucente had arrived for the daily debriefing.

It made Gleason sick to hear the only member of the Wardens present in such an important task was a member of the Blue. No White Wardens, Green Wardens, and not even a member of the hapless Black Wardens were present. Only the Blue, and a woman at that! His uncle was a traitor to his blood that allowed politics and position to override the importance of family–which is why his father was dead–but now he was allowing the fabric of the Wardens to unravel at its most basic levels. Soon, they would be no different than the rabble that made up the rest of the Hunter's Guild.

"Ah, Lieutenant. Glad you could make it. Have there been any changes I should know about?" Commandant Beck's voice sounded like he was tired and worn down. It made Gleason happy to hear that the old man's age was finally catching up to him.

"Nothing beyond a few probing attacks, sir. We're still seeing more of those wardstone pillars being erected around the city, so I'd imagine the witches will be doing some great spell working to bring down our protections soon enough." To Gleason's ears, the Lieutenant sounded even more weary than his uncle. Defending a city was too much for her, and the fact his uncle couldn't see it was more proof for Gleason that he was in the right.

"Well, we knew it was only a matter of time. They're keeping these wardstones out of range of our siege weapons and the few spellcasters we have?" The sound of tea being poured from a pot was all Gleason needed to know that his uncle had been up all night. He only drank tea when he was overly-exhausted.

"Yes sir, but they will have to bring them closer to the river side. Unless they plan on dropping them into the Reka." Lucente must have taken a cup for herself, since Gleason could hear her pause to take a sip. "We won't be able to hold the walls if they do."

"I've talked to the Green Wardens about that, and they assure me they won't be able to do something so simple. The flow of the river would disrupt their magic, and it would keep them from forming the spell structure. They would have to set up a stationary barge on the river itself, or go to the opposite bank." Gleason scoffed at his uncle's statement. Any leader worth his salt should have known something so basic. "That's not an option for them either, because it would make the wardstone circle so large, they could never power it." More teacup on saucer sounds made Gleason wince as his spell made them sound louder than need be in his ears.

"So, the real battle will be to keep them from erecting the wardstones along the wharf. If we can prevent them from encircling the city, the ritual magic those heathens are trying to put together will fail. Their forces will be in range of our warriors on the walls, and we can reap them like wheat." Now Gleason had the true information he wanted. The Lieutenant might be useless, but she did have it right that the final battle would be fought at the river gate.

Somehow, he felt it was poetic, as the river gate saw the lifeblood of Greendown–its trade–flow through it for generations, and now it would see Greendown's final generation shed its lifeblood to defend it.

"Call it an old man's intuition, but I'm afraid it won't be that easy, Lucente. Despite that, prepare the Wardens you have remaining. They'll make their move soon. I can feel it in my bones. The end is coming quickly, one way or another." Gleason smiled at his uncle's words. He had no idea how right he was.

Just as the listening spell was about to end, Gleason heard his uncle say something that quickly caught his attention. His heart hammered in his chest as Beck's words brought everything into a beautiful tableau. The Gods were truly with him. Everything was falling right into place.

"Oh, I nearly forgot. Inform your men there is a Paladin in the city. He left my office rather… abruptly, but I'm sure he's already carrying out the mission we discussed. The man is hunting down whatever is taking our citizens, and should have it captured or killed soon. He seemed very capable, from the little time we had together. If you see him yourself, have him–"

The spell connection snapped as Gleason's rage exploded, and he jumped to his feet. "A *what*? Some holy warrior thinks they can stand against *me*? I was the one *chosen* by the Trinity!" Blackened veins came to the surface as they throbbed at his temples, and oily smoke dripped from his clenched fists as sparks dribbled to the ground.

Knowing he was losing control, Gleason took long, deep breaths to calm himself. It would be fine. He could handle this. Some holy warrior with a few spells couldn't–

You are hunted

Do not fail

"*Shut up*!" Gleason punched the wall next to him, sending flaming bits of wood and debris everywhere. "I'm *not* going to fail!"

"It looks to me like you might."

With a flare of dark fire, the robe covering Gleason's new armor disintegrated into ash. His whip lashed out at where the voice had spoken, and another section of wall was destroyed.

"Temper, temper." The voice cooed, undeterred by his actions. "Lashing out like that at strangers might get you in trouble, you know."

Gleason spun around again, looking for the person hiding in the building with him. It was only a simple vendor's station, with two rooms and a display area, so there weren't many places for them to hide. He slid his shield off his back and onto his arm, and snapped his whip at the center of the room with a threatening crack. "Whoever you are, I welcome the chance to show you why sneaking up on me was a poor decision."

"I've been following you for weeks, Bloodletter. That's your new title, no? Your Exsanguinators should have named you such, if you haven't named yourself this. Know this, former Warden. If I wished you ill, I would have reported your activities to the Wardens when you were hiding in the sewers." A shadow dropped from the ceiling, and pulled back the hood on their cloak, revealing the pale skin and fangs of a vampire. "But, I do not wish you harm. In fact, now that you already know of the Paladin, I came here to warn of the witches."

"A greater undead? Why should I listen to you?" Gleason lowered his shield arm, but didn't release the grip on his whip. "You serve the forces outside the wall."

"We are not enemies, Bloodletter. You and I have no need to work at cross purposes." The vampire pulled his hood back up and stepped more fully into the light. "The witches are working faster than Beck expects. I have learned enough of *your* plans to understand they need several days to work. If you want them to complete it in time to matter, start now. Today. Otherwise, you will fail, and your work will bear no fruit."

"Let's say I believe you. I did hear Beck making plans to stop the witches. How do you know he won't succeed? If I move too early, there's no going back." Gleason finally stowed his whip, wrapping it in a loop before securing it on his belt. "Now that there is a Paladin hunting me, I have to be even more careful."

"Beck is a fool, and only sees what the Lady wants him to see." The vampire pointed a gloved hand at the Hunter's Guild, and Gleason looked outside to see Beck leaving with an entourage of Wardens surrounding him. "He will be one of the last to die, along with the Paladin, so they can see everything they worked for, fall. Once the wards fail, neither will be able to hide for long."

"Fine. I'll move forward with my plans, but then, I want to speak with this 'lady' you mentioned." Gleason turned to look back at the vampire, only to discover it was gone. "Sneaky one, are you? We'll just have to see about that."

Giving up on finding his stalker, Gleason made his way to the northern section of the city. Normally, the guard presence around city infrastructure was well-regulated and tightly monitored, but with the undead army surrounding Greendown those standards had dropped. It was far too easy for Gleason to pull several barrels from a nearby storage shed over to the city's water supply, and tip the viscous substances within over the stone lip of the cisterns.

The cisterns were filled by the river, which was fed by the snow capped mountains barely visible in the distance. Wards carved into the sides of the walls ensured the water was safe to drink, and kept disease from spreading through the population.

Finding a way to affect the water supply without the wards destroying what was added to the cisterns had been the most difficult part of the task Gleason had given the alchemist he'd taken. Threatening the man's family had been enough motivation for him to find a way.

It required three doses of a special concoction given in a specific order. Given the risks, and the warning of time growing short, Gleason dumped the first two doses into the city's water supply at the same time. There might be some adverse reactions for a few people instead of it staying completely hidden, but the average citizen wouldn't notice anything at all.

After dumping several barrels into each cistern, Gleason returned the empty barrels to their storage shed. There was one final barrel for each cistern, so he laid them out near the entrance for easy retrieval once the time came. It would take at least three days for the first two doses to settle, and then he could add the last set of ingredients. Once people even *touched* the water, the city would be cleansed, and Gleason's task would be complete.

"Now, to make the leaders of my future uprising." Smiling to himself, Gleason found the nearest entrance to the sewers. His Exsanguinators making the change early would give them time to get used to their new existence, and make taking charge even easier.

As soon as Gleason swept into his headquarters, he started shouting orders for his men to meet him in the central chamber, and to bring goblets and wine. It was located next to where the prisoners were kept, and while he didn't want to miss giving his men their final dose, he couldn't afford for the prisoners to be unguarded.

Preparing the mixture was easy. He followed the instructions the alchemist had given him, dropping in a pinch of powder along with a single drop of his own blood to ensure he would be able to control them when the change was done. All that was left was to have them drink it.

"You called for us, sir?" One of his Exsanguinators approached Gleason after all of them were gathered in the central area. "Is something wrong?"

"Nothing is wrong, my Blood Wardens. Everyone come and take a glass of wine. It's time to celebrate. Time grows short, and all we have worked toward comes to an end." Gleason thought for a second, and made a decision about his own title. "Call me Bloodletter, instead of Commander. We are the newest and most powerful order of the Wardens, and should all have proper titles to show the difference. Soon, all shall know of our power!"

His men all gave thoughtful nods, with a few in the back rows seeming disinterested. He brushed off their lacking enthusiasm with grace. It wouldn't matter how much they cared once they drank the wine he had prepared.

"A toast, to the Bloodletter!" His most senior Exsanguinator did his work for him, and all the men raised their glasses and drank deeply.

Gleason smiled as a few of them started coughing, and one of his men even fell to his knees. "Stay calm. You will soon feel some changes, but don't be alarmed. They are natural. Once the transformation is complete, you will be ready to lead my cleansing wave over this city, and–"

Anything else Gleason wanted to say was interrupted when the screaming started. Men clawed at their own faces as their bodies spasmed, and muscles bulged under their clothing and armor as the concoction did its work. Boils burst as skin became too tight to contain the new dense muscle tissue, and hair fell out in clumps as they writhed in pain on the dirty stone floor. Some even tried smashing their own heads in, but the new strengthened bones his concoction gave them made it impossible.

As the first of his newly formed Blood Wardens got to their feet, Gleason was happy to see they had grown at least a foot in height, and double that in width. Scraps of armor fell away, leaving them completely naked. Their new size would require different clothing and armor, but he had prepared for it. Sections of skin had torn open, weeping blood and clear fluids while revealing the new, compact muscle underneath. The wounds were already closing, leaving shining strips of scar tissue up and down their bodies.

Yellowed eyes met his own, and the madness he saw there made Gleason pause. He had added a drop of his blood to each goblet. Had it not been enough? Had the alchemist lied to him? As more and more of the changed men stood, Gleason stepped forward to give them their orders.

"On your feet, Blood Wardens. Go into the first storage room and put on fresh clothing. Then, you will all file through the armory to get new armor and weapons. Once that's complete, we'll–" Gleason was once again unable to finish his sentence, as the door behind him creaked open. It was the one holding all the prisoners, and one of them must have wanted to peek outside to see what all the screaming was about.

All of his Blood Wardens saw the frightened face of the prisoner dart back behind the door, and they acted as one, charging the retreating individual like they were prey. Nothing Gleason said or did could stop them.

Within minutes, there were no more prisoners remaining underground. His new creations were little more than mindless predators, and seeing something run from them had activated instincts that wouldn't be denied. Gleason couldn't even question the alchemist about what had gone wrong, because he too was torn limb from limb like the rest of the prisoners.

Once their grisly work was done, the Blood Wardens had disappeared, scattering into the tunnels to avoid Gleason's anger, his whip, and above all–his commands. The only thing his blood seemed to have done was make it impossible for them to attack him.

Alone in his headquarters, Gleason shrugged to himself. "I guess the chaos they will bring to the city is almost as good. Yes, this is an acceptable alternative. I'll just have to adjust my plans accordingly."

"What will you do now?" The shadowy watcher seemed to materialize out of the shadows above Gleason, clinging to the ceiling like a spider. It dropped to the ground when Gleason didn't react with violence, and drew closer to him, lowering its hood to reveal its fanged smile. "Your plans never accounted for something like this, Bloodletter."

"I'll think of something." Gleason tapped at his chin, deep in thought. "The incubation period is long enough that I might be able to find the Paladin. I think hunting the hunter would be a good way to spend the time waiting."

"Oh, the last report has him in the guild quarter. Another watcher is–"

Gleason's hand snapped out, grabbing the vampire by the throat. Dark flames erupted from his palm, tearing through the surprised undead before it had a chance to protest. Its ashes fell in a clump at Gleason's feet, and he turned to leave the sewers.

"Filthy thing. Foolish to think I would let it live."

CHAPTER 26

The journal had been enlightening, to say the least. Both the Vice-Admiral and I were surprised to find out the Silver Star had been on a mission to close a tear in their world they called a Demon Gate. Reading between the lines, it was obvious they had failed in their mission, leaving me to pick up the pieces.

According to the Vice-Admiral, the legends that still survive today about the Silver Star were mainly focused on the beauty of the lost princess, and the sadness of the kingdom when she never returned. The journal revealed she was only included on the mission because she was a spoiled brat who thought it would be a pleasure cruise, and officially because she had the magical ability to use the enhancing gem that powered the ship.

One line in the book told me exactly how the mission had failed, though. When the Vice-Admiral had read it out loud, even he was upset at the discovery.

"*The First Mate has been acting strange ever since attending the commencement party with Duchess Frost and her new consort. He only comes out to inspect the final preparations during the night shift, and finds excuses to avoid any daytime exercises. The Captain is displeased with him, and believes the man to be heavily in his cups. As his father is the Earl of South Harbor, there's no way to replace him so close to departure. At least the night shift will have a capable man at the helm, if his current schedule continues when they leave tomorrow. There is nothing to fear concerning the state of the ship or navigation, even by a drunkard. The Silver Star is a wonder that practically flies itself. It would take a great cataclysm to bring down a ship this powerful, and even a First Mate in his cups won't do too much damage to the Star.*"

"Vampire." We both said it at almost the same time. The first mate had been corrupted, and brought the ship down from within. How they managed to miss something so obvious all those years ago was a mystery I'd never know the answers to, but they had paid the ultimate price for the mistake.

With my new quest updates, I had a better idea of what direction to go once the siege was over. Since that wasn't anything I could deal with right away, I had doubled down on making plans with the Sailor's Guild.

As one of the four major guilds–the Sailor's, Healer's, Farmer's, and Hunter's Guilds controlled the trade, health, food, and security–getting a promise from them to support any proposed changes in the way things functioned was vitally important. Thankfully, the Vice-Admiral was all for it, and agreed to endorse anything that wasn't too crazy. All I had to do was convince the other three major players, and the rest would fall into line.

The fact it would only apply to Greendown didn't bother me. Once proof of concept was a success, word would spread, and citizens would demand change on their own. It wouldn't happen overnight, but the change would become inevitable. Other cities trying to suppress the new ideas would only make them spread faster, and the downfall of the guilds was a given. With a few more Judges to help the process along, this world should be a better place for everyone within a generation.

Hence, why I was currently standing in front of the Healer's Guild, waiting once again to be seen by somebody important. Word had spread about me ripping the gate off of the Sailor's Guild entrance, so I wasn't given the same runaround by the guards this time. They had sent word to someone important, and asked politely for me to wait outside. I spent a little time eavesdropping on them, and got some insight on what to expect when I got inside.

"I can't believe the stones on this guy. Walking right up to the front gate of the guild after healing people inside the city without permission? That's a kind of crazy I've never even heard of."

"He probably thinks he's safe because he's friends with the Wardens. I bet the elders show him how little that matters. They don't even care about the attacks on the walls getting worse."

The sounds of fighting from the walls and warning bells tolled throughout the city, but no one in the guild district seemed to care. Attacks seemed to be picking up both in frequency and scale, and a sense of urgency made finishing this task even more important. I was keeping myself busy by carving some runes into the inner copper layer of my bracers when someone finally came to grab me.

"They're ready for you, sir Paladin."

I looked up from a ring of carvings that would boost mana flow to see a woman that could have graced the cover of any fashion magazine back on my world. Black hair, brown eyes, perfect teeth–which was certainly done by magic–and a tight red dress that looked like it made it impossible for her to take a deep breath. She gave me a smile that said she knew exactly how good she looked, and it was hard not to roll my eyes. Just because I looked like I was in my twenties, didn't mean I was ruled by my hormones. Those mistakes had already been made a long time ago. That didn't mean I wouldn't put on an act for them, though.

"Well, we don't want to keep anyone important waiting, do we?" I gave her a smile of my own, and put a bit of smolder into it. I knew the game, and I could play it too. "Tell me, who will I be meeting with?"

The woman's smile faltered a bit before coming back even stronger. "Since you didn't specify exactly what subject you wished to speak about, the full conclave of those present within the guild are waiting to see you." She waved a hand forward as if presenting the best thing since sliced bread. "I'm sure you'll be able to solve whatever problems you might have with so many great minds in one place."

"Oh, of that I have no doubt." My thoughts on how this was going to go were more than a little jaded given what I had seen and heard about the Healer's Guild so far. There was a reason I was approaching them second, after all. The Sailor's Guild meeting was the carrot. I had a feeling the Healer's Guild meeting would be the stick. It would give the other two big guilds plenty to think about before I came by to see them.

If I had thought the Sailor's Guild was opulent, the Healer's Guild reset the gauge. Gold, gems, ivory, statues, paintings, fine china, you name it, and they had it on display. An enterprising thief could retire from the spoils of a single room. And yet, this guild still chose to charge people for food and healing during a siege. It was enough to make me want to burn it all down on principle alone.

My guide led me up thickly carpeted stairs to a set of golden doors–yes, pure gold doors, complete with golden hinges–before turning around with another perfectly white-toothed smile. "Here we are. Be sure to stop by and ask for me if you need anything at all." The woman slipped a card in my pouch before flouncing away back down the stairs.

I attempted to exchange a quick glance with the two guards standing on either side of the door, and based on where their eyes were now glued, they felt exactly the way I did. 'Flouncing' was definitely the right word.

They opened the heavy doors just far enough for me to enter the room, and slammed them closed in what was probably supposed to be an ominous boom the moment I entered. The fact the guards stayed outside, and only the elders waited for me on the inside, was surprising. They must have a lot of confidence in their own abilities. Theatrics aside, the room they had chosen for our meeting was impressive.

The nine elderly men arrayed before me were seated in a single row behind a table made from a single piece of dark wood that was so heavy it must have taken magic to move. Their chairs were carved pieces of the same wood, with gold inlay to match the doors. Thick silk cushions done in the same red that seemed to be a favorite color for the Healer's Guild were placed in all the chairs at varying levels to give them all the appearance of being exactly the same height. In front of them were crystal decanters of water that glowed with runes meant to chill the liquid inside. On the walls, tapestries displayed knights, queens, and kings bowing to healers with haloed hands as they benevolently cured the injured and ill.

Overall, it was incredibly impressive. If you had never seen a skyscraper. Or a toilet that could flush.

We looked at each other in silence for nearly a full minute before one of the guild elders finally broke the stalemate.

"So, the *Paladin* who can *heal* decides to grace us with his *mighty* presence. What is it you want to speak with us about? Asking forgiveness for healing without purchasing a permit, perhaps?" The elder who spoke was seated in the center, and had more white hair than the rest of them. He also was the only person in the room who I could sense was powerful enough to even come close to being a threat. His sarcasm set the tone for how this was going to go, so I rolled my shoulders to loosen them up a bit.

The others were a hodgepodge of magical strength that was hard to gauge. My guess was, they were a mix of mages and wizards, meaning their abilities would be all over the place. If all of them combined to attack, it would most likely be the equivalent of fighting the two Green Wardens. Not enough to make me worry for my life, but enough to stress my abilities and risk damage to my soul. Running counter to every role-playing game ever made, the fact that they were healers actually made them more dangerous than the average caster, considering they knew so much about the human body. I was the poster child for scary healers, after all. Of course, the threat they posed was all assuming that I played the same game they were playing.

Sweat on the brows of several of those seated at the table told me they had planned for this to go one way, and one way only. The men on the ends were trying to hide that they were holding wands in their laps, but the slight resonance of the enchanted tools couldn't be hidden by the presence of the pitchers that made water cold. A few other hidden enchanted objects were secreted about the room, but the wands were the most powerful. When the ambush started, I figured it would come from them.

"First off, I need to clarify something. I'm not *just* a Paladin, or a healer. I'm a Judge. I came here to see if the rumors were true about the Healer's Guild being run by a gang of reprobates who spend their time guzzling gallons of fermented bull semen. After seeing you disgusting heaps of human excrement in person, I can confirm that you do, in fact, guzzle bull semen, instead of helping the people that provide all the wealth you are happy to absorb like the leeches you are." As my Judge Mantle settled into place, I cast my verdict. "Second, and more importantly, I pronounce you *guilty*. Guilty of taking advantage of those you should be protecting. *Guilty* of risking the lives of innocents. And the most damning of all, you are all *guilty* of *cowardice* in the face of the undead, the natural enemy of *all* healers. For these sins, I sentence you to–"

The rod that contained the holding spell was hidden in the sleeve of the man to the right of the leader. It was probably intended to keep patients still when operating or performing delicate surgery, but it did a great job of freezing someone in place for an attack. Honestly, it was a very well-executed ambush that I didn't see coming.

Too bad for these assholes I shrugged off their weak-ass spell faster than you can say 'Blood Drain.' I know that specifically because one of the wands cast a spell called 'Blood Drain,' but I was already moving by the time the elder on the end had a chance to finish speaking the activation words.

My mace crushed his skull in a spray of pulped bone and gray matter that coated the two men to his right in gore. The shock of the suddenness and brutality of the attack froze them for a heartbeat, so I cut both their throats in one sweeping cut with my ninjatō as I slid across the table.

A twirl of my blade flung their blood into the faces of the remaining six elders, and I activated my shield bracelet in a dramatic flurry of sparks meant to cause them to flinch back in fear and surprise. "Death. I sentence you to death, you limp-dicked cockholsters."

"Kill him, you idiots!" The strongest elder tried casting some type of rot spell that would have been nasty to heal, but it rolled off my shield like water, ruining the nice table I was standing on. He tried to run for the tapestry hanging on the back wall. I didn't know what was there that was so important to the man, whether it might be a source of reinforcements or escape, but I didn't really care. He'd never make it. I threw my mace in a heavy overhand toss that crunched into his lower back and sent him to the floor in a heap.

The remaining five elders didn't even break my shield. One by one, I hacked off their hands, followed by their heads. There wasn't time to play politics with these idiots, and they had placed pride and wealth above the lives of the people. The battle was almost anticlimactic after hearing how tough these guys were. If I had stuck with a purely magical attack, maybe they'd have put up more of a fight, but they weren't prepared to go physical.

When I approached the strongest elder, I was surprised to find he was still alive. I turned him over as I ripped free my mace, and held my sword above his neck. "I have to know, why wouldn't you just do the right thing and help people? Don't you understand that all of you would die if the undead breach the walls?"

"Never… understand… how… the real… world… works…" He gasped in pain, trying to cast a healing spell on himself.

"Pathetic. The real world? You've been stuck in your ivory tower too long. You can't even heal yourself while in a little pain. Don't speak to me of the 'real' world. Your power games and politics are the world of fantasy and realm of little men who *wish* they were something more than puppets. Never doing, or creating. Just playing pretend in this house of gold built on the backs of real people who did real things that mattered. Die knowing you were as useless as you always knew deep down you truly were." My sword pierced his neck, severing his spine. I worked it back and forth to ensure he was good and dead before pulling it free and wiping it clean on his robes. "Judge. And *Executioner*."

The golden doors slammed open, and a flood of uniformed guards rushed in. They froze, staring in shock at what they found. I sheathed my sword and clipped my mace to my belt before turning and facing the man with the best armor.

"Your elders tried to ambush me. I defended myself. You might want to inform the next person in the chain of command that they got a promotion." I started pushing my way out of the room, none of them willing to stop me. They were smart enough to understand if I could do this to their elders, they wouldn't stand a chance. "Once the power struggles in the guild are settled, I'll be back to speak to whoever's in charge. I expect a more… friendly… reception next time. I also expect to see healers on the walls, helping in the defense of the city within the hour. Otherwise, there won't be a Healer's Guild anymore. Any questions?"

Nobody said anything, and I left the opulent meeting room unmolested. As I made my way down the stairs to the main entry hall, I heard a lot of raised voices and shouts, along with the unmistakable moans of sick people.

At first, I thought perhaps word of the elders getting wiped out had already spread. When I rounded the corner, I knew how wrong I was.

The entire entrance was overflowing with people trying to push their way inside, and the courtyard beyond was flooded with even more of the sick. The gates had been shoved aside by the mass of humanity, and all the guards could do was try and steer the masses in appropriate directions.

From what I could tell, most people seemed to be suffering from some kind of stomach flu, consisting of vomiting and severe nausea. There were enough with advanced symptoms that I already knew exactly what the problem was, though. Boils around the neck and ears that people scratched at incessantly.

I *might* have made a mistake.

CHAPTER 27

The decision to stay and heal people or try and stop the source of the problem was an easy one to make. If I didn't stop where the illness was coming from, the flood would never end. At least I knew exactly where to look. Even if it did mean getting all smelly again.

Going back down into the sewers was definitely going to suck, but this time I wasn't going to go by myself. I managed to find a small side gate to avoid the crush at the front, and went searching for Cross and the others. They should have finished selling off the excess gear and loot we didn't need, and hopefully were deep into completing the steps we had lined out before entering the city.

One of the first things on the to-do list was to get us our own headquarters set up. Initially, the plan was to try and buy a warehouse or empty shop near the wall somewhere to the northwest, closest to where the mountains were. We planned it that way because initially we thought that's where the enemy army would be assaulting from the most. Since the attacks from the undead and goblins had ramped up on the opposite side of the city, where the river was, I was hoping my team had adjusted without my input and found us a place near the southeast.

As I searched for my people, I started seeing signs that the illness was spreading. For some people, it seemed to manifest as a mild case of the flu. The worst cases had giant boils, weeping sores, and bleeding gums. I did stop to heal a young child that didn't look like they were going to make it without help. With my magic I found out that it wasn't an airborne disease. There were no unnatural substances involved, beyond their own immune system going crazy. Given the notes I had from the vampire kid, my best guess had this as some kind of alchemical reaction, but nothing hinted at a mundane or alchemical cure, or how to cut it off.

Wandering a crowded city all day while more and more people got sick was a dumb idea, so I started climbing on rooftops and doing something I knew would draw a lot of attention. Magic was frowned upon in cities, especially by the superstitious that thought it was all witchcraft or sorcery. That didn't stop me from shooting colorful bursts of wind and fire magic sporadically as I ran around. Eventually, either Cross or Jess would feel me casting, or Leedy or Murphy would see it. Except, after several hours, there was nothing.

After giving up searching the southeast section of the city, I started to swing straight south. If I had to make a full circuit of the city, I would cover the areas that were closest to the river first. Of course, just as I was thinking about stopping for an early supper, a pebble smacked me on the backplate.

"What are you doing? Trying to put on a show for the whole city?" Cross pulled himself up over the lip of the roof I was standing on. The building smelled like it used to be a brewery, but the hops and barley probably went to feed livestock weeks ago. Now, it smelled like fermentation and stale booze. Reminded me of a frat house I used to crash at when I visited some friends. "Hey, are you okay? You look like your mind wandered a bit there. What's going on?"

I thought about it for a second, replaying the events of the past few days, and suddenly everything clicked. "I think I might have made a mistake. A big one." I rubbed at my temples, casting every healing spell I knew to try and fix what had to be going on with me. Losing focus. Being obsessed with the minutiae of my surroundings. Letting the vampire kid go. Killing the healers instead of forcing them to work with me. And, the biggest mistake of all. Leaving the sewers before the job was done. "Where is everyone else? I'm going to need their help to undo my fuckups. At least, the ones that can still be fixed."

"Leedy is finishing up the list of everything we're supposed to be doing–except now he's moving the surprise to the river gate, since we're smart enough to switch from the other planned gates on our own–while Jess and Murphy are setting up our little headquarters and keeping out of sight." Cross pointed to a pile of rubble barely visible a few blocks over. "Remember the Button Guild, and how we know they're going to be after Jess? None of us can be sure it was them, but a building we were looking at collapsed while we were inside. Ever since then, we've been extra careful. Now, are you going to explain what your big mistake was?"

"Good call about Jess. Until we can find out more on the Button Guild, she needs to lay low." I let out a sigh, trying to frame how to explain the colossal series of screw ups I'd just made. "You know how I can cast Paladin spells?" Cross nodded, so I moved on. "Well, a normal Paladin uses their god, or faith, or giant invisible spaghetti monster, or whatever they have going on with a higher power, to provide the energy for their abilities."

It said something about Cross as a person that he didn't even react when I mentioned the giant invisible spaghetti monster. Was I… a bad influence? I rolled the thought around for a moment before emphatically denying it.

"Of course. That's what makes a Paladin special." Cross motioned to me. "Don't you do the same?"

"No. I have my Judge Mantle, which you obviously know about, and that pulls from a more… foundational power of the universe. My Paladin spells have to come from *me*. That means when I use them, I get… disconnected." I thought about how I had just killed eight of the strongest healers in the city instead of subduing them. During a *siege*. My mantle would have been okay with either decision, but I had chosen the lethal option. I was not here to be the Executioner unless it was necessary. It was an Authority given to me, to be used when appropriate. But justice was more to me than simply death. It was easier, and more cathartic, but it certainly didn't serve the greater good of the city. Absolutely stupid.

"And when you feel disconnected, it diminishes your decision-making process?" Cross leaned against the lip of the roof, resting his chin on his hand. "How bad is it?"

"I've never noticed it being this bad before. I've also never been recently recovered from soul strain, either." I pulled out the notes the vampire kid had given me and handed them over to him. "Case in point. I was given these by a vampire. In the sewers. Several hours ago. I didn't have them read to me, I didn't inspect the underground base where *Gleason* probably was, and I even let the vampire kid walk away. I don't even really know if it's a kid. Since it's a vampire, the blood-sucker could be hundreds of years old. It just *looks* like a kid, and I let it affect my judgment. I'm telling you Cross, I'm all over the place."

"What do you want to do about it? Do you need to go somewhere?" Cross flexed his pitch-black hand, possibly subconsciously, probably not. "Should I try and fix you with a spell?"

"Now that I'm aware of the problem, it should be fine. I think so, anyway." I tapped the papers in his hands. "What do these say?"

"It's hard to tell. Some of these are really waterlogged, and the ink has smeared." Cross held them closer to his face, trying to get a better look at one of the diagrams. "Ugh! Why do they smell so bad?"

"What, you thought the sewers would smell like a garden of roses? Stop complaining and read." I kept watch while he laid out the folded papers. The sounds of bells tolling around the city calling for more reinforcements for the walls told the tale of more attacks, but the most frequent ones were definitely from the southeast, where the river gate was located.

I thought back to when we entered the city, and when I cast my Paladin spells. From the moment I walked into Greendown, I'd been making risky choices. Splitting up the party? Going off with the Green Warden to meet the freaking Commandant? Even for me, that was ballsy. They still didn't know my name. All they did was call me 'Paladin' and called it good. Once that stopped working, there would be hell to pay.

"Okay, I've got something." Cross pulled me over and pointed out several rough sketches that were barely more than indentations on the pages. "See this? I think Gleason was taking people to enact some master plan to bring down the city from within. At first, everyone he grabbed was important. The *most* important was an alchemist. There are three lists of ingredients they stole after taking him, which either means three different potions, or one big potion with three stages."

"It could also be one potion and another that's two stages." I pointed to what I recognized as this world's version of a question mark. "Just saying."

"That's true." Cross nodded in agreement before tapping at another list. "But look here. Three identical loads of a very special kind of wood were taken. The kind necessary to hold alchemical ingredients without them degrading. But, you wouldn't know that unless you were in the military and served time in the quartermaster–something nobody in the White Wardens does–or a master carpenter. You remember how Pete and Davey's dad was a master shipwright? I'm just guessing on the dates here, but right after he would have escaped, they didn't kidnap another *carpenter*. They took a *cooper*."

"Cooper. They make barrels, right?" I thought about everything for a bit. "So, you're saying they needed the carpenter to tell them the type of wood to use, and when he escaped, instead of grabbing another big name from the Sailor's Guild, they just grabbed the best barrel maker they could find."

"Because all three of the alchemist's concoctions need to go into barrels. And if the amount of wood they took is any indication, it's a *lot* of barrels."

"Damn." I mentally kicked myself again. "I need to get underground. Now."

Cross grabbed me before I could jump over the side of the roof. "That's not everything. Do you see this?" He pointed to a few diagrams that outlined what looked like armor and weapons. "Gleason has some new upgrades. Be sure to watch out if you see him down there."

"Me? You aren't coming with me?" I shook my sword in its scabbard to make sure it would draw cleanly. "Gleason is supposed to be your nemesis, not mine, remember?"

"As much as I would love to go crawling around in the sewers with you, I'm actually helping in another way." Cross pulled the spear I had loaned him off his back and gave it a little spin. "Remember that Green Warden, Tew? He came looking for you, and wanted your help hunting down some guy named James Holden. Claimed it was the last chance to get the greatest threat the world has ever seen before it's too late. I told him I hadn't seen you, but I was willing to help. I thought it would be a great opportunity to steer him toward Gleason if we see him running around anywhere."

"Fine. That's actually a good way to spend your time." I thought for a second about all the things I still had to do, and all the mistakes I'd made. "Before you go, I've got something else to put on your plate."

"Keeping a Green Warden busy, hunting a madman, and looking out for hidden assassins isn't enough for you to give me?" Cross smiled, shaking out his numb hand. "Sounds about right."

"You and the others know the laws and customs of this world better than I do. I've already got the Sailor's Guild on our side, and scared the Healer's Guild into submission. What I need now is something to show the Farmer's Guild and Hunter's Guild so I can start the conversation about ratifying the change this city needs in the way its government works." I tapped my forehead before pointing at him. "You're smart, and a Judge. Listen to what your Mantle tells you is right and wrong. Talk things over with the others. Each rule change you think about can stand or fall based upon the combination of all of you. Like a decision by a Jury. Just don't mess it up. It's probably only the future of the people on your whole planet on the line."

"Of course. No pressure." Cross gave me an unreadable look as I crossed the rooftop, looking for a sewer entrance. "Are you sure you trust me with something this big?"

"Right now, it's sink or swim time. Do or die. All or nothing. Make or break. Everything or nothing. Be all that you can be. You are what you eat. I'm going to stop talking now." I gave him a thumbs up and jumped off the roof. I'm pretty sure he got the point.

While he had his tasks, I had mine.

It was time to go back underground.

Alone.

CHAPTER 28

Finding the underground headquarters took longer than it should have. Not because it was well-hidden, but because I had no idea Greendown had two sewer systems. The more central part of the city, where I needed to be, wasn't connected to the part I'd jumped into like an idiot.

Once I finally figured out my mistake, it had gone full dark outside, and the attacks on the gates were in full swing. I *almost* went and joined in the city's defense, but one look down any street at all the refugees showing symptoms of the disease told me I had to stick to my priorities.

The only positive thing about smelling like the sewers is that getting through crowded city streets and alleys was incredibly easy. People automatically get out of your way, without you even having to try. It made getting to the proper sewer grate very easy, and I was back underground, this time with several sets of torches.

While I would normally be concerned with setting off methane gas, the number of people down here before me with torches made it a non-issue. I was also pretty sure the wards that protected the city also circulated the air down here to some extent, otherwise there certainly would have been an explosion at some point in the long history of the city.

Using torches allowed me to keep my magical senses focused outward without any interference from powering my own mace for a source of light. Following the scrapes on the walls left behind by the Blood Wardens was my best clue to find the headquarters, but I was hoping they would have some kind of magic going that would allow me to find them without having to search every single tunnel someone else had scratched up in the last few weeks.

As I reached the major junction where I had last seen the Blood Wardens–and met the vampire kid–I started feeling a tingling from tunnels that angled deeper underground. They looked even older than the other tunnels, with more cracks in the stone roof and thicker layers of sludge running over the slick bottom. It certainly piqued my interest, but now wasn't the time for exploring.

I focused on the tunnel that had seen the most traffic, and carefully crept my way into the dark. There should have been some kind of light for me to run into at some point if the tunnels and chambers were occupied, which was what I kept looking for.

Unfortunately, it wasn't another light source that told me I'd found the headquarters. It was the magical residue. And the blood. So, so much blood.

The space they had used looked like it had once been its own miniature underground village, complete with a smithy, the expected alchemist station, workshops, offices, and a cafeteria– which is super gross, because we were in a freaking sewer.

It had been repurposed into a war camp, complete with storage for dry goods, spare armor, weapons, and since Gleason was involved, a few torture chambers. It was all abandoned, as if everyone had just decided to step outside for lunch and never come back. Except for their prison area.

I quickly found the place where they had kept the prisoners. It was like someone had sent an entire butcher's shop through a buzz saw. A whole bunch of buzz saws. I didn't bother spending the time to check, but there'd been at least twenty people in there. Probably more.

Guilt hit me like a freight train. If I had come down here instead of running around trying to find Gleason without any plan whatsoever, these people would still be alive. Intellectually, I understood that I wasn't the one who kidnapped and killed these people. I owed them nothing, and saving them wasn't my responsibility. That didn't change how I felt.

Very quickly that guilt switched to anger, and then rage. It was plain to see these people had been killed by some kind of beast, or monster. Some of the remains had been gnawed on, but too much was left for it to be a natural predator. They wouldn't leave so much meat behind.

Gleason and his Blood Wardens had taken these people, and then when they were done with them, they let some beast inside to rip them apart. I was going to return the favor, with gratuitous amounts of pain and violence.

After locking the makeshift tomb, I went to inspect the alchemist station to look for any clues. There were a few scraps of paper with scribbled notes that I couldn't read, so I grabbed them and stuffed them in my pouch.

My next step was to check out the room that looked like an office. It was another dead-end. Someone had taken the time to clean up, and all that remained was a pile of oily ash in the far corner of the room.

Frustrated, angry, and about to give up, I slammed open the door of the office. Instead of hitting the stone wall with a resounding boom, it rebounded off of the distinct sound of flesh and breaking bone.

Whatever I hit was instantly pissed, and it let out an inhuman roar as it tackled me through the doorway. My torch went flying, sending shadows dancing before it went out entirely, plunging the room into absolute darkness.

Heavy claws scraped across my breastplate before getting caught in a groove along my side, and it used the grip to throw me, sending my pack one direction and me another. I was flung into a wall hard enough to see stars, but instinct and years of fighting had taken over.

At some point, I had pulled my sword and stuck it all the way to the hilt into my attacker. Belatedly, I activated my shield bracelet, and the dim sparks it shot off provided a kaleidoscope of colors I could barely see by. A heavy fist pounded into my face out of the darkness, but my shield took it instead of my nose.

The hit was strong enough to cause it to flicker after only the first punch, which made this a very dangerous enemy. I managed to unclip my mace and I dumped enough mana into it to cause the glow effect to flare brightly.

My attacker wasn't expecting the visual assault, and reared back in surprise. It finally gave me a look at what I was fighting, and it wasn't the kind of monster I expected.

This thing looked like the Incredible Hulk, if the Hulk wasn't green, had torn skin that didn't fit the bulging muscles that tried to rip free from its overstressed bones, nails thick enough to be claws, and covered in clumps of thick hair like a diseased werewolf with a bad case of the mange. It also had the twisted features of a man driven insane by pain. Features that reminded me a whole lot of one of the Blood Wardens I had seen carrying the drugged man through the sewers. The one that had the boils on his neck.

I now knew what happened when the sick people got the final dose of Gleason's concoction.

"Oh, you poor bastard." I flicked my wrist, casting a quick lightning bolt meant to stun the raging human. The magic-eating sword buried in its ribs drew in the magic, focusing the spell and burning a hole through its side.

The rager didn't like that very much, and tried swinging a haymaker of a punch at me. I swung my mace to meet his fist, and the shockwave shattered my shield like glass. The mutated Blood Warden didn't even react to its ruined fist, and stomp-kicked me in the chest before I could react, bouncing me off the stone wall again. He managed to backhand me on the rebound, and I slammed against a bunch of stone shelves, turning them into gravel as my left arm bent the wrong direction with a sickening crack of shattered bone.

Getting smacked around by giant mutants wasn't my idea of a good time. The small office space favored the brawling style of the rager, and I needed to get into a more open space before I got turned into mincemeat. The only reason I was still conscious was because my armor and shield bracelet had soaked up a bunch of damage.

I rolled behind a desk as a massive foot blistered by my face. Damn, these things were ridiculously fast. Its stat points had to be at least five or ten points higher than mine, which was insane. The rager had to be tearing itself apart on the inside to be moving and hitting like this, but it just didn't care. I had seen the insanity in its eyes, and all semblance of humanity was completely gone.

As it slipped in the gravel, I managed to dive out of the open doorway as the desk behind me was crushed by another sweeping kick. Now that I was in the open, I had a chance to change things around.

Snapping my arm back into place made me see spots and hear white noise for a heartbeat, but I started dumping mana into a healing spell to try and get it at least a little functional. If I could get the arm working, I could aim with my wrist gun.

At some point I had gotten to my feet, and the glow from my mace was wobbling erratically. I steadied the flow of power going to it, and for the first time in a *very* long time, I used one of my four Knight Class abilities. "*Chivalrous Might*."

My stats would now be boosted by a quarter across the board for five minutes. The downside was after it wore off, I would be weakened by half for five hours. Right now, that seemed like a fair tradeoff.

The rager made a diving leap for me out of the door, and this time I was ready for him. Since my left arm still was made of bone shards and agony, I could only swing my mace one-handed. I swung that thing like the bases were loaded and it was the bottom of the ninth inning. It connected with a hollow-sounding knock, and my mace was ripped out of my hands as a heavy outstretched arm knocked me off my feet.

Once again, the light was cut off, but I banished the shadows with a snap of my fingers. Three orbs of bright yellow light spread out from my upraised hand, revealing the nearly decapitated mutant splayed out on the ground beside me.

My temporarily increased stats had allowed me to swing hard and fast enough to finish the fight in one hit, and the boost to my Vigor stat meant I was feeling better and better as my natural healing kicked in. It still didn't feel good when I tried using my left arm, so I rolled the body over using a little flick of earth magic instead.

"You deserved to die, but I don't think anyone deserves to die like this." I was talking to a corpse, so maybe I'd gotten a concussion. That didn't make it any less true. Retrieving both of my weapons and my pack only took a short time, but I was already on the clock. Once my five minutes were up, I would feel weak and sapped of strength for a long time. Unfortunately, there wasn't time to rest, even if I was operating at half my regular abilities.

Inspecting the body of the rager up close didn't reveal anything I didn't already know. It was incredibly strong, fast, and tough. The skeleton and skin hadn't upgraded as much as the muscles had, which was the only thing keeping this monstrosity from being a perfect killer. That, and the madness, of course. It'd still managed to hunt me down in pure darkness, meaning it had advanced senses, along with predator instincts. If the whole city turned into these things, nothing would be left standing.

I had to stop it, before the city was wiped out.

CHAPTER 29

Heading back to the surface took a bit longer than I wanted. A big part of that was because the hit to my stats when my Knight ability wore off. I had to stumble around a little bit while I got used to the changes, and even then it felt unnatural. It was why, like Paladin, I seldom used my class abilities unless it was an emergency.

Knight, like Paladin, only had four, and *Shield Bash* was basically useless for me since I didn't normally carry one. That left *Chivalrous Might*, *Defend*, and *Taunt*.

Defend worked without a shield, but it definitely wasn't great, considering it planted my feet in the ground and made me immobile for a few seconds, no matter what hit me. I preferred to dodge attacks from giants, not meet them head on. If I could combine it with *Shield Bash*–which could knock away an enemy ten times my size with no effort–it would be a great combination attack, but shields were heavy and cumbersome to carry around all the time, and like I said, I preferred to dodge attacks if at all possible.

Taunt only worked on weak-willed enemies, meaning goblins and lesser undead were perfect for it. The problem was, since I normally ended up being the biggest, flashiest threat anyway, I really hadn't needed to use it since gaining Mage, which was way back on world nine.

While *Chivalrous Might* had the nastiest cooldown, the others had them as well. Even though they lasted for minutes instead of hours, that's still a lifetime on the battlefield. Only *Shield Bash* had a somewhat reasonable thirty-second cooldown, but since I hardly ever carried one, I didn't really get to try it out.

Maybe I should try getting a ring with a miniature shield on it? If the ability would still count the tiny shield, I would have a super punch. Definitely visiting a jewelry shop when I got back to the surface. That's an experiment I should have tried out ages ago, but I hadn't ever thought about using my older abilities in new ways like that. I would have to rethink all my other skills at some point to see if there was anything else I could try to exploit.

Distracting myself from the discomfort of walking around with stats in the mid-thirties was going well, until I passed by the section of sewer tunnels where I had gotten the tingling feeling. Despite my lowered perception, the feeling was even more intense. I poked my head into the tunnel where the feeling was strongest, and got a quest update.

Quest Update!

Place of Power Detected

Unique Upgrade Quest: Find ten places of power - 2/10

-Absorb the power built up at the location to increase your level.

***Note - This place of power is being utilized in a ritual, causing it to be strongly aspected. Disturbing it may lead to unexpected consequences. Proceed with caution.**

Damn. Considering the last two times I had dealt with a place of power I had been knocked for a loop, right now didn't feel like the right time to poke the bear. It wasn't going anywhere though, and now I knew where it was. I also had a good inkling that I'd just discovered what was powering the wards that protected the city as well, especially since there hadn't been anyone on the walls doing it the entire time I'd been in Greendown.

Ignoring the place of power for now, I finally made my way back to the surface. Where, of course, it was a total shitshow.

Smoke choked the air and people were screaming as fire filled the sky. I started running for the nearest gate, dodging people running from the areas closest to the walls.

At first, I thought the city had fallen, and the enemy had breached the defenses. Then, as I got closer, I realized things weren't as bad as I thought. The smoke was from the other side of the walls, and the fire was from spells being cast by Oriana.

She was giving it to the bad guys hard. I hadn't seen her since I had made it inside the city, and I had never seen her throw down. There was a reason she was a Green Warden, and it wasn't because she looked good in the uniform.

Her control of the flame lances she fired from the top of a tower was beyond impressive. Even from all the way down on the ground, I recognized the mastery over both wind and fire magic. She was creating tubes of spinning air, and launching relatively small fireballs down them at the undead forces on the other side of the wall. The flames were enhanced by the wind spells, and by the time the lances of flame arced over the wall, the intensity was magnified to ridiculous levels. The beauty of using two small spells to create one massive attack wasn't lost on me, and I appreciated the art of what she was doing. It wasn't anything extraordinary to combine fire and air, but her execution was flawless. If there were other combinations like this she had up her sleeves, I was very happy I hadn't picked a fight with her.

"Hey, Paladin! Up here!"

I looked around and I was surprised to see both Tew and Cross on the wall above me. They pointed to the side where a makeshift rope ladder had been staked down, probably so guards didn't have to use the gatehouses for shift changes. I waved to show I understood, and started climbing my way up to meet them.

"Oh, by the dozen hells, Paladin. You smell like an outhouse!" Tew backed away from me, and both him and Cross quickly swapped positions with me once I got to my feet. "No offense, but you should stay downwind."

"None taken." I sniffed myself, not noticing anything. Definitely noseblind. "I'm surprised to see you both up here. I thought you were hunting someone, like I've been?"

"We were, until this started." Tew pointed at a cluster of orcs in heavy armor struggling to move some kind of marble obelisk. They were surrounded by hundreds of goblins and undead, and protected by a bubble of energy centered around a palanquin carried by another group of orcs. "The witches are making their move. That's a wardstone, and once it's in place, they'll have the spell circle formed to begin the ritual to drain the city's protections."

"Well, shitfuck." I knew exactly how nasty ritual magic could be. World-warping, mind-melting, civilization-destroying levels of nasty. I'd seen it happen on world seven, and it was all kinds of bad. Also, if I was right about the city's wards being connected to the place of power, it would be impossible for me to drain it for myself and gain more stats.

I needed to stop this assault, break their ritual before it could begin, drain the place of power–but leave just enough to keep the wards from failing–and then make sure the city was protected long enough for the place of power to recharge. Or, maybe a better plan would be to absorb the power, and then give it right back. I only needed it long enough to expand and grow my body and mana generator. Keeping it wasn't necessary.

"How did things go for you?" Cross broke me out of my train of thought, and when our eyes met, I could tell he wanted to get away from Tew to hear all the details I could give him. "Were you successful in your hunt?"

"Yes and no. These were all I could find where the alchemist station was located." I pulled out the scraps of paper I had found and passed them over so he could read them for me. "I found a full underground hideout, along with a very nasty mutant that almost killed me. It had already killed everyone else. I'm still recovering from the fight."

"But you killed it? So that means the kidnappings will stop?" Tew went to clap me on the shoulder, but stopped when he smelled me again. "I knew you could do it!"

Shaking my head, I thought about how many Blood Wardens there were supposed to be according to what Pete and Davey had told us. "I don't know if there was more than one of those mutant monsters or not. I'm also sure the sickness in the city is being caused by this group."

"It's definitely not over." Cross held out a slip of paper for Tew to read. He didn't bother trying to hand it to me, and just told me what it said. “It says, ‘make enough for entire city supply.’ I don’t know about you, but that sounds bad.”

“Nothing about what city supply they were targeting? It could be food, water, the granaries, literally anything.” I thought about all the sick people that were affected. “My money’s on the water. With everyone getting sick, it’s the only explanation for the speed of the spread.”

“That’s impossible.” Tew scuffed a boot across a palm-sized carving near the base of the crenelations on the wall. “See these engravings? These are the wards that protect the city. The cisterns have *hundreds* of them carved into their walls and pipes, for this exact reason. You can’t poison the city water supply.”

“What about the fountains individually? Are each of them warded the same? Or, even worse, what if they broke it up into stages? Each individual ingredient isn’t poison, but when they combine, the end result is terrible. That’s possible, right?” Cross was still flipping through the scraps of paper, so he didn’t see Tew’s face slowly grow more and more pale as he asked his questions.

“You need to go to Beck and warn him. Now, before it’s too late.” I set my pack down on the wall and started stretching. “There needs to be a wall of guards around Greendown’s water supply. Probably the food and grain as well. I’ll see what I can do about the witches.”

“Are you sure you can handle this by yourself?” Tew looked doubtful, and eyed my dented and scuffed armor. “You already said you were still recovering from fighting below the city.”

“I’m not anywhere near where my strength is normally, but it’s going to have to be enough.” I pointed at Oriana, who had just renewed her spells for what had to be the tenth time since I had come up on the wall. “Plus, I’ve got help.”

Cross dug in his pack for a moment before handing me another of the small powder kegs. “Here. I know it won’t take you long to carve this, so you can have an easy way to destroy their big rock.”

“Thanks.” I took his keg, and swapped it out for the last keg I had in my pack. One that already had the necessary carvings on it. “I’ll hold onto that one for later. Right now, we don’t have the time for me to sit around whittling. It looks like the orcs are about to start setting up the wardstone."

"You sure you don't need us?" Cross cocked an eyebrow before subtly tapping his temple. "You're thinking clearly and everything?"

"Get out of here already." I went to grab them, but both backed away from my smelly reach. "Each task is equally important. Enemies from both inside and out are about to destroy Greendown. We need to keep that from happening. Don't be afraid to grab the others if you need to. This threat needs everyone to stop it."

"Jess, Leedy, and Murphy are already on the wall. They're helping to hold the mountain gate." Cross pointed to the north, where the occasional flash of light indicated the wards stopping a spell from breaching the walls. "The other spellcaster, with the nasty staff that freezes people, is pushing the gate with their bone knights."

"Damn. Okay then." We were spread thin, and I felt weaker than a kitten. Subjectively, of course. I was still about on par with a single Green Warden at the moment, which meant I wasn't a pushover, but it would be at least three more hours until I was back to full strength, and I hadn't slept or eaten in a very long time. It didn't matter. Now was the time when you pushed through. Besides, if it was easy, everybody would be doing it. "It's up to us, then. Good luck, you two. I'll see you soon."

"I'll let Oriana and the men at the gatehouse know you're out there before we see the Commandant. They'll keep an eye out for you, but don't expect a rescue mission if something goes wrong." Tew held out his hand and we clasped wrists in a warrior's handshake, despite how bad I smelled.

He wasn't all bad, for a Green Warden. I still wanted his dagger, though.

They took off, and I waited for the next wave of fire from Oriana to clear me some space to jump down from the wall. There weren't as many enemy troops on the ground as there were when the barge landed, but the ones that were here consisted of a higher quality than what we faced last time. This would have to be fast, otherwise I would get bogged down and eventually torn to shreds. Once she blasted a lane for me, I took off at a dead sprint, using a burst of wind to help speed me along.

I hit the ground running–literally–and aimed right for the ring of orcs trying to lift the obelisk into place. They were under the bubble shield being maintained by the witches, but right at the edge of it. One of the orcs noticed me, and turned to face me head on with a giant club in hand. I leapt at the last moment, aiming a flying kick for its face. And then broke my foot on the shield.

"Mother-son-of-a-stupid–" Flopping onto the ground, I rapid-cast two healing spells to try and fix my foot. Apparently, the shield could tell the difference between greenskin and human. Fine. I can work around that.

The orc was laughing its stupid face off at me, doubled over and slapping its knee as snot dribbled out of its nose.

"We'll see who gets the last laugh, chuckles." I tried my magic-eating sword against the bubble, but all it did was create a small puncture around the blade itself that was closed the moment I pulled it free. The shield would be drained eventually, except I didn't have all night. Already, I had been noticed, and small groups were being sent in my direction. I limped over to the nearest body, which was a goblin that had been burned all over the back half of its body. Died running, and died tired. Like most goblins.

It would work for my purposes.

My sword cut through the abdomen with one smooth stroke, and I stuffed the enchanted keg of gunpowder inside, leaving the end with the ignition rune barely visible. It was disgusting, but it should do the trick.

The laughing orc had seen what I had done, and was now mildly concerned about my actions. It shouted something, and nudged the two orcs to either side of it that were busy situating the obelisk. When they saw me, they turned back to their business, ignoring their partner. They were almost done, and wanted to finish.

I limped up to the shield and started swinging the dead body in a circular motion, like it was a shot put. Once I had enough momentum built up, I cast the spark spell on the ignition rune and let the dead goblin go.

As it soared through the air, I had a brief moment of worry that it wouldn't go through the shield. When it passed through like nothing was there it was my turn to give the orc a smile. My aim was a little off. Instead of the body landing at the base of the obelisk, it landed just to the side. Close enough. The orc yelled something, but I didn't see the rest of what happened because I used an earth spell to erect a thick wall between me and where I had thrown the body.

When the bomb went off, it tipped the obelisk over. I didn't know that the witches had already empowered it–empowered it with enough juice to bring down city walls–so when the rock tower snapped, the excessive amount of stored magical energy also exploded. This counted as a secondary explosion, and my explosions enhancement title had a ten percent chance of increasing the size of it by sixty percent as well.

Of course, it did.

My earthen wall wasn't nearly big enough.

CHAPTER 30

Gleason was very possibly the most miserable he could ever remember being. He was cold, tired, dirty, and hungry, like some commoner living on the street. It was disgusting.

Ever since leaving the sewers, he'd felt eyes on his back. No matter what he did, or where he went, someone was watching him, and it made his skin crawl. When he tried stopping to rest, there were always people there, waiting, staring, ready for the moment he let down his guard. Their eyes followed him everywhere, searching for a weak spot so they could pounce.

If there was one thing Gleason would prove to everyone, it was that he wasn't prey. No, he was the hunter, and the hunter wasn't afraid to act, no matter the time and place.

The sun was just starting to show over the horizon, marking it as the second day since he'd dropped his first dose in the city water supply. Dark clouds on the horizon were already strangling the morning light, but it was still another day gone. Another day closer to his goal.

Last night a great explosion had rocked the city, causing both sides to pause in their attacks while they tried to figure out what'd happened. It gave the defenders a much-needed rest, which only meant Gleason had an even harder day in front of him. Those hunting him probably had a chance to rest, while he was forced to wander the cursed city of Greendown to avoid the eyes that followed him.

Rain started falling in heavy sheets shortly after Gleason finally felt like he'd lost his tail, forcing the beggars and riff-raff to find cover. The heavy cloud cover made it feel as if the night would never end. Perhaps that was how the world would end. One long night that never stopped, filled with nightmares and the dead that haunted the living.

Now that Gleason didn't sense the gaze following him anymore, he took a short break to lean against a covered doorway. Only a quick breather, so he could think through his next steps.

Finding the Paladin had been all but impossible for him. It was like the man wasn't even inside the walls of Greendown. To make matters worse, his connections to gather information in the city were gone. He'd never actually handled any of the espionage aspects of his mission himself, choosing to delegate that task to a few Exsanguinators he trusted more than the others. Now that they were all… changed, he had no way to reach their contacts.

As Gleason was about to leave his little doorway, a pair of Black Wardens walked by, wearing full plate armor instead of their normal light leathers. The two were deep in conversation, and didn't notice the man slumped in a shadowed doorway.

"This is crazy, right? We both know there's no way somebody would poison the water. Even if they wanted, they *can't* with all the old magic protectin' the city."

"Not them fountains. That's why we've gotta guard 'em. If a bad fellas got a bunch o' luck, and they're mean enough, they could poison a whole bunch o' fountains and get the job done. That's why all the Black Wardens got yanked from fire duty to be put on water watch."

"Kinda ironic, ain't it? Goin' from watchin' for fires ta watchin' water?"

"Maybe. I jus' want this shift over fast. I got these boils formin' on the back o' me neck I want the healers gettin' a look at. They itch like a sailor's nethers after a visit to the Tainted Rose."

"Hey! Them girls ain't all bad."

"If you're sayin' that, you need to see the healers too. We might be lucky an' sneak in to see 'em durin' lunch. Jus' be glad you ain't on the search crews with the regular Hunters. They don' even get a lunch. Now come on, our guard spot's right up here."

Gleason missed the rest of their conversation, because he was too busy having a minor panic attack. They knew. Not everything, but enough that they might stop the most important part of his plan. It was too late to try a different way to give the concoction to the people, but too early to give them the last dose.

Silently cursing to himself, Gleason started working his way through the back alleys and empty streets to the shack where the barrels of his mixture were held. He needed to move them to a more secure location, away from anything important. They were too close to the cisterns to not get caught in the search the two idiots had been talking about. First, he would need a covered wagon to hide the barrels in, and then he could–

You are hunted

Do not fail

"I know!" Gleason rubbed at his temples, the voices making his already stressed mind throb in pain. "You don't have to tell me."

You are hunted

Do not fail

The intensity of the voices was even higher, causing Gleason to drop to one knee in pain. "Stop, please. You're too loud."

You are hunted

Do not fail

"Stop!" Gleason screamed as the voice of his father thundered in his head. Blood shot out of his nose and ears, while red streaks leaked from the corners of his eyes as he unconsciously cried blood that tinted his vision red. He didn't remember falling on his face, but as he stood up, he had to use the alley wall to support him. "I'm not going to fail. You don't have to keep reminding me to–"

You. Are. Hunted.

Your. Enemies. Draw. Near.

Do. Not. Fail. Us.

Gleason woke up on his back with a splitting headache. He couldn't have been out for more than a few minutes, because the blood covering his front hadn't dried enough to become tacky. As he went to rub his face, he realized he was holding his whip. The enchanted weapon that severed the connection with the voices in his head. He unconsciously shivered at the thought of what could have happened if he hadn't grabbed it.

"To the hundred hells of damnation with this!" Gleason placed the whip around his neck like a piece of jewelry so it would stay in contact with his skin. The voices had never done anything like that before. If Gleason was being honest with himself, he might realize that fear was driving his decisions. Instead, he tried to pretend it was anger that made his choice. "Fine. I'm done planning. The last barrels can go in *now*."

Patrols of Hunters and Black Wardens were everywhere, and Gleason's paranoia made getting to his secret shed even more difficult. Reaching the shack where the barrels were stored became much easier when he moved to the city rooftops. Not many of the patrols bothered to look up, and he finally got to the shed around the time the guards were rotating through lunch.

Loading the barrels into a cart was much easier this time, especially since he only needed one barrel per cistern. They were also smaller than the others, as the final dose of his alchemical solution was far more concentrated than the other two had been.

The mix was almost sludge-like, and Gleason decided he would simply knock the lids off and toss the casks in. He didn't want to stand around waiting for it to take forever as it slowly poured into the water. The barrels would sink to the bottom and seep into the city's water over the next several hours, allowing him to move on with the next phase of his plan.

Even though he was doing this before the incubation period of his first two concoctions were over, Gleason knew there would still be strong changes to the people of Greendown. Sinners would still be punished. Their rotten insides would be exposed on the outside. It just wouldn't be as powerful, or permanent. The chaos it created should still be enough for the army outside the gates to cleanse the city for him, especially if he could complete his second plan.

Killing the Green Wardens.

Surprisingly, there were only a few Black Wardens guarding the actual cisterns, and it was easy for Gleason to sneak past them by causing a small fire one street over. The simple men couldn't resist the chance to do their normal jobs, abandoning their posts as they rushed to put it out.

As he dropped the final barrel over the side of the last cistern with a splash, Gleason pulled a knife free to slice his palm. The final ingredient was his blood. After the fiasco with his Blood Wardens, he knew it wouldn't allow him to control anyone, but like his Blood Wardens, it should keep the changed riff-raff from attacking him as he moved throughout the city.

Before he could make the slice, he heard the scuffling of a boot behind him and he spun around just in time to draw his baton and knock aside a spear thrust that would have taken him in the neck.

"I *knew* you would be here."

Gleason jumped back and managed to get his helmet in place before the spear-wielder could make another thrust at his unprotected face. The rest of him was already covered by his armor, and he ripped away the bulky robes that hid them from casual observers.

"What have you done, Gleason? What did you put in the water?"

Laughing, Gleason finally recognized the man he was facing. "Cross? *The* Captain Cross, finest Blue Warden the city of Greendown has ever known. I'm surprised to see you here, and out of uniform. Tell me, was it hard returning to my uncle in disgrace?" Gleason laughed as Cross shifted uncomfortably at his words. "Oh, I see. He doesn't even know you've returned. You've been hiding who you are. Is it because you don't want them to know you disobeyed the *Oracle*, and instead joined forces with the man you were sent to kill?"

"The orders were wrong, Gleason." Cross drifted to the side, obviously looking for a weak spot in Gleason's new armor. It was thick, and covered in spikes, making it a weapon by itself. "He's only a threat to the power of the guilds, not to the people, or the Trinity. If anything, *you* are the one who needs to be put down. You've always been a rabid dog, but now you decided to bite the hand that feeds you."

"A *rabid dog*?! I've been *chosen*! You wouldn't understand what I've been through!" Gleason pulled his whip free, while keeping his sword in his off hand. "I'm going to crush you, flay your skin from your bones, and laugh as you beg for death!"

"See? That's exactly what I'm talking about, Gleason. You're a madman, but not so mad that you don't understand what you're doing." Cross seemed to change, and the faint outline of a familiar dark cloak appeared around him, causing Gleason to take a step back in fear. "You have been Judged guilty once for your crimes, and I Judge you doubly so again. Your sentence is death, to be carried out immediately."

"T-that's the same thing Holden does. Are you like him? An *abomination*?" Gleason spit at Cross, snapping his whip so suddenly that it trailed smoky flames. "Only the *gods* can judge me, not some mortal."

"You live among people, and can certainly be judged by them, Gleason. Now, before you die, will you at least tell me the cure to what you've done to everyone?"

"Cure?" Gleason's laugh was that of a man completely unhinged. "There is no cure. I made sure there couldn't *be* a cure. Greendown is filled with sinners, and now it will be cleansed of their filth."

"*Bastard*." Cross thrust his spear for Gleason's eyes, but was forced back by the cracking whip that nearly took off his nose. "All those women and children, the elderly, they're defenseless!"

"Wait until you see what they can do *now*." Gleason did a quick shuffle-step to the side, forcing Cross to put his back against the lip of the cistern. "You'll join their ranks as well, don't worry. Or you would have, if I'd allow you to live."

His baton blurred forward in a trio of slashes, and three waves of red fire flashed from its edge toward Cross.

Unwilling to be pushed into the poisoned water, Cross held up his blackened hand and a spike of ice shot forth into the smoky flames.

The collision of the two elements created a burst of ashy steam that blocked the vision of both combatants. Cross tried rushing into the burning cloud, his spear tip leading, only to find that Gleason had already backed away into the narrow entrance that led to the cistern access area.

Another exchange of spells created a second steam cloud, making visibility almost impossible. Gleason knew it favored him greatly, since his armor was much better than the kind Cross was wearing. Now that he had the advantage, Gleason waded in for the real fight.

Cross had earned his rank in the Wardens, and knew how to fight. In a proper duel, Cross might even be Gleason's superior due to his speed. He'd gotten even better during his time with James Holden, and his magic was much stronger than Gleason remembered it ever being. That didn't mean they were equals, and this *certainly* wasn't a duel.

Gleason used his whip to control the narrow entranceway, and punished Cross with it anytime he tried to get too close. His baton was more than enough to keep the darting spear from finding the few weak points in his armor, and all Gleason had to do was wait for Cross to wear himself out. He was content to let it go on until there was an opening that allowed him to throw the former Blue Warden into the cistern, but that was all ruined when they were interrupted.

"Surrender yourself now, and I will do my best to see that you avoid the noose. Men, surround him."

"Tew, no! Get those men out of here! Don't give him a chance to toss–"

Gleason didn't hesitate, cracking his whip through the steam and wrapping its burning length tightly around the Green Warden's neck. "The Trinity have truly smiled on me this day. My old nemesis, and one of my father's killers, all at the same time? I couldn't have asked for more."

Tew tried grabbing his dagger to cut himself free while casting a spell to knock Gleason away from him, but the burning whip was cutting off his airway and the flow of blood to his brain, making his hands dumb and his magic failed. No one had warned him of the danger this man posed, and as a result he wasn't prepared. He had drastically underestimated his opponent, expecting only a simple bandit or disgruntled citizen, and now he was paying the price. Tew fell to his knees, trying to squeeze his fingers between the fiery whip and his throat.

Cross tried renewing his assault now that Gleason couldn't use his whip, but the men Tew brought with him got in the way. They tried to save the Green Warden, and instead were launched one at a time into the poisoned water of the cistern.

"Now, it's just the three of us. Before we go any further, I would *very* much like to know where James Holden is, Captain Cross of the Blue Wardens." Gleason laughed as Tew's bulging eyes flickered to Cross, giving away his surprise. "Oh, he doesn't know the truth about you either? I didn't think so. That makes this so much sweeter." When Cross didn't answer, Gleason yanked on the whip, causing Tew to gag. "Come now, Cross. Now isn't the time to give me the silent treatment. Tell me where Holden is, and I promise all I'll do is throw you in the cistern and walk away. Everything that happens afterward is up to the gods. You might even survive the process." The screams coming from the men he had thrown in earlier were still going on, and it sounded every bit as awful as it had down in the sewers with the Blood Wardens. "Living with yourself after what you do when you've changed, however… that's up to you."

Instead of answering, Cross took a diving leap at the whip choking Tew, trying to cut the man free. Gleason ripped the weapon out of his reach, tearing apart the Green Warden's throat in the process. Cross was forced to drop his spear and clamp his hands on Tew's throat to slow the bleeding and start using the strongest healing spell he knew, otherwise the man would be dead in seconds.

Gleason walked over and picked up the spear. Even though he was less than two feet away from him, Cross couldn't do anything, otherwise Tew would die. Gleason looked down at him and smiled. "This used to be his, didn't it?" He gave it a twist, and the paper-thin blade disappeared back into the handle with a quiet *snick*. "It certainly didn't come from anywhere around here. With this, I don't need you to tell me anything."

A series of low growls echoed from the cistern, and both Gleason and Cross looked over to see thick, hairy arms struggling to find purchase on the smooth stone lip that surrounded the water storage area. Soon another pair of arms popped over the edge, then another, and another.

"Oh, this is perfect." Gleason used his whip to expertly snatch a beautiful dagger from the belt of the Green Warden, leaving both men with only their miniscule boot knives. Cross wasn't anywhere close to being done healing Tew, and the changed men would be over the edge of the cistern in a matter of seconds. "I'll be leaving now, I think. You have fun with the sinners of Greendown, Cross. I'm sure we'll never see each other again, especially since the change leaves them very, *very* hungry."

Laughing, Gleason slammed closed the iron gate that led to the cisterns and bent the locking bar in place. Only one Green Warden was left in the city, and they were young and inexperienced. He would have fun hunting her down, right after he'd *talked* with his uncle.

First, there was something more important to do. With a few ingredients he could pick up in the city, Gleason could put together a quick tracking ritual.

Hefting the spear that belonged to James Holden, Gleason twisted it again, sending the blade shooting out of the tip.

Oh yes. Today was a very good day.

Today, James Holden would finally die.

CHAPTER 31

When I opened my eyes, I wished I was dead. Everything hurt, and the cold rain falling on my face only made it worse. The sun was just starting to come up, meaning I had been unconscious for several hours. Pushing aside the rubble covering me revealed I didn't have broken bones anymore, but I most definitely had a few before I had been knocked out in the explosion. Natural healing could be a lifesaver. Literally.

"By the moon, he lives! Danika, hurry, we need to make a circle before he can use another of those cursed objects that destroyed the pillar!"

I looked behind me to see a pair of old crones hunched over the remains of the obelisk I had destroyed. They were obviously afraid to see me, and were already pointing knobby wands in my general direction. Honestly, I couldn't blame them. That last explosion had been a doozy, even for me. I was a little shocked not to see another title upgrade when I woke up because of it. Probably needed a few more explosions to get to the next level.

"Witches. Of course it's the witches." I got to my feet gingerly, testing to see how much juice was in my shield bracelet at the same time. "Any chance you want to turn around and go home? Leave the city alone, and we can just forget this whole thing happened?"

"Huh?" The older-looking of the two witches lowered her wand a bit. I was a little surprised she could hold it steady in the first place. Both of them looked like they'd been run through the wringer sideways. The explosion had probably shattered their bubble shield, and they were suffering from the backlash. "Aren't you afraid of us, boy? We could turn you into a toad."

"No, you can't. Even a full coven doesn't have that kind of power, and even then, you'd need my consent, which you certainly don't have." I heard footsteps behind me, and saw a third witch picking her way through the rubble.

She was much younger than the other two, with long black hair instead of white, and spotless skin that was somehow still tanned, like she spent a lot of time out in the sun. I don't know how she managed that with all the rain around here, but it made her look exotic. And pretty. She was also obviously very tired.

"Danika! He knows we can't turn him into a toad." The old crone waved the younger witch back with her free hand. "I think he's dealt with witches before, so don't get too close."

"Is there just the three of you? Where's the one with the silver hair and the big staff?" My mana generator was finally waking up, and it was pulling in the energy around me as quickly as it could in preparation for a fight. It'd probably emptied itself trying to heal me while I was knocked out. "I know it takes at least four to make a coven, one for each cardinal direction."

Danika ignored the more senior witch and got several steps closer before she stopped, finding a nice lump of burnt stone to wearily take a seat. "She's not a witch, she's our jailor." The black-haired beauty squinted carefully at me, trying to gauge me with her eyes. "Did you mean what you said earlier? I could hear you, when you mentioned us leaving, and everything being forgotten."

"Your jailor? You're prisoners?" I was still a little out of it, but my mind was doing a decent job of putting things together on the fly. "You mean to tell me the *vampires* are running the show? Why don't you fight them? Even a coven short one member should be able to take down one vampire mage."

"We *did* have a full coven. It wasn't enough. The staff the Lady wields is like nothing I've ever seen." The old crone finally lowered her wand once she realized we weren't going to fight. "We think she wants to turn us all into vampires as well. Make us her thralls, to serve her in undeath."

"The Lady, huh? Was it her that killed your friend?" All three nodded. "Damn. I'm sorry." I looked around at the torn and shredded bodies of orcs and goblins around me. "So, I take it you don't *want* to attack Greendown, then?"

"Why would we want to wipe out a whole city?" Danika flopped her arms in an exasperated manner. "Other cities would band together and seek revenge. We would be dead within the year. Most importantly, they've done nothing to us, so we have no *reason* to attack."

"Okay, so run." I shrugged my shoulders, not seeing the problem. "Aren't you the people in charge of the greenskins? Have them attack the vampires during the day while you make a run for it."

"The Destitute would find us." The witch that hadn't spoken yet, finally decided to talk. She looked more like a friendly old grandma, which was probably why she dressed the most like a witch. She was wearing an actual pointed hat and everything. "He's far more powerful than anything you've ever imagined."

"I can imagine a lot, lady." Like mushroom clouds and nuclear bombs, baby. If I had a cell phone that worked, I would most definitely lie to the government of a certain freedom-loving superpower about there being vast oil reserves here, and they'd show this Destitute guy some real power.

Man, I really had hit my head.

I cast a quick healing spell to make sure I was okay and focused back on the witches.

"How about this? When the showdown between me and the 'Lady' happens, you pull your troops out and make a run for it. After I kill her, you can point me toward this guy, and I'll take care of him, too." I tapped my starmetal mace on my belt, causing it to ring lightly. "I have a history of showing people with stupid one-word names why they should leave people alone."

The three of them walked off together to discuss my proposal, and I took the opportunity to try and knock out some of the dents in my armor. It had gotten roughed up, but was thankfully still in one piece.

"We've made a decision." Danika walked back over by herself, leaving the older two to rest by the broken obelisk. "We won't promise anything, but if it looks like your side is winning, we will do as you suggested."

"So, you're saying you'll pick the winning side, and stick with them." I gave her a thumbs up. "Survivor. Can't fault you for that." I dropped my joking tone, and went completely serious. "I can tell you, if you go inside Greendown's walls, I'll kill you. There are no second chances." I relaxed, and dropped the steel from my voice. "Anything you can tell me about this 'Lady' vampire? Something I can use to take her down, maybe?"

"Understood, about Greendown." Danika took a hesitant step backward before stopping herself. "The Lady used to be someone important, a long time ago. It's why she knows such odd magic. The staff she carries is from the same time, and it makes her more powerful than she truly is. If you can take it from her, you will have a much easier time fighting her."

"Thanks." I stood up, brushing myself off. "Any way you guys can draw out this wardstone business? Give me a day or two before you try it again?" If they agreed, it would give me plenty of time to drain the place of power, and allow it to recover.

"Oh, that would happen no matter what. We're going to have to create a new one, and then power it. That will take at least three days." Danika smiled, and I definitely didn't check her out when she did. Why were witch girls always so hot? "Will that be enough time for you to do whatever it is you need?"

"Definitely." I held out a hand for her to shake, and she stared at it awkwardly. "Oookay then, that happened." I turned around to head back for the city, giving her a wave instead. "Hopefully I'll see you around, Danika."

"You too, odd man." She waved back before returning to the other two members of her coven.

The three of them immediately put their heads together and started whispering furiously, occasionally looking in my direction, but I couldn't hear anything despite my advanced senses. They must've put up some kind of barrier to block sound.

If there was any chance they went along with the plan, we could pull off a surprise win against the undead even if they got inside the city. If not, I wasn't sure Greendown could hold once a gate or wall went down. There just weren't enough defenders to secure a gap in the defenses in addition to continuing the general defense of the wall and gatehouses. We would have to hold, no matter what.

Getting back inside the city was easy. There were no attacks going on near the river gate, so I just walked up and knocked. They were surprised to see me, but quickly let me in. A sergeant asked me to wait for some lieutenant to come and talk to me, and I had to let him down gently by informing him I wasn't in the chain of command, and I was a very busy man.

No one tried to stop me as I left, and since it was close to lunch, I found a man selling meat pies next to the sewer entrance I knew I was about to have to go down again. There was no time like the present, after all, and I still smelled pretty bad. Might as well get it over with.

I did ask the mystery meat guy where a jewelry store was, and he pointed me to a place nearby that sold trinkets and cheap junk. I decided it was time to try out my idea for the *Shield Bash* ability, and needed something quick and easy to play with. The old guy running the place soldered a cheap piece of tin that vaguely looked like a shield to a strand of braided copper wire he sized for a ring, and I had my first super-punch experimental device to try out when I wasn't surrounded by a bunch of people. I asked him to make some nicer examples using silver–just in case it worked–and he told me to get stuffed.

Guess I'd make my own pieces later if it was a success.

My third trip down through the sewers made the first two seem much nicer. If any trip through a pre-industrial society's sewer system could be considered nice at all, anyway.

The rains on the surface had gotten much heavier, which made the tunnels underground much harder to navigate. Dirty water frequently tried to knock me down as it rushed over the edge of the channel, and the lack of handholds along with the increased slipperiness of the narrow walkway made the trip even more precarious.

I finally made it to the intersection that led to the ancient tunnel sections, and started shuffling my way down the sludge-covered shaft. The light my mace gave off seemed to get dimmer the deeper I got, as if the darkness had an oppressing aura built by untold centuries of being undisturbed. There were a few disturbed places in the muck where it looked like the Blood Wardens might have come this way, but they must have given up when they didn't find anything interesting. Either that, or the smell of centuries of congealed excrement was too much for them. I could understand why they felt that way.

The sewer channel eventually veered off underground, splitting into two different tunnels. I took the path that wasn't covered in poop, leaving me in a dry underground shaft that was reinforced with stone arches every twenty feet. It reminded me of an old mine, or some kind of forgotten catacombs under an ancient cathedral, forever waiting for the bodies meant to fill its empty halls.

Damn, my mind was drifting again. Stupid Paladin spells.

I could see faint rune markings on the keystones of each arch, but if there was any kind of power flowing through them, I couldn't feel it. The footprints I left in the dust on the ground were deep, and mine were the only set visible. It was practically like walking in snow, except I had to be very careful not to stir it up and choke myself while coughing on the ensuing dust cloud. No one had been down here in a *long* time.

While the shaft had a downward angle, it wasn't very steep. Instead, it corkscrewed around the city, probably so the runes on the arches could link everything above ground. By the time it came to an end, I had probably lapped the city four or five times.

There were a few traps placed here and there along the way. Thankfully, they were so old and dilapidated the trigger mechanisms had dry-rotted or rusted to the point of uselessness, otherwise it would have taken even longer. One pitfall trap had been activated by either age, failure, or the weight of the thick layer of dust a long time ago, forcing me to hug the wall and shuffle along the narrow strip of stone that still remained. My bulky rucksack had to be moved to my front for a bit, but I managed to make it across without falling onto the spikes below.

A rusted portcullis finally came into view around the time I figured I was under the Hunter's Guild, right in the center of Greendown. There were a series of gears and levers on either side, most likely designed as some kind of code to keep out people that didn't know the proper combination. Some not-so-subtle holes in the walls to either side meant someone getting it wrong would get shot full of poisoned fire arrows, sprayed with acid, or some other medieval form of terrible death.

That would have been a concern a few centuries ago. The rusted metal was weak enough I was able to knock out a few sections of metal with a couple of well-placed kicks. It was easy to squeeze through the gap and continue on my way.

After only a few dozen feet, the tunnel that never ends finally opened up into a chamber that was completely different from everything else I had seen since entering the sewers. Instead of ancient crumbling stone with barely visible runes, the underground hall looked like it could have finished construction yesterday.

The room was a dome carved out of the bedrock, and covered in shining black marble. It was large enough to serve as a banquet hall or meeting chamber, but not quite big enough for the grand dance halls or throne rooms I had seen in castles and palaces on other worlds.

Every wall was decorated with mosaics of multicolored crystals, each laid out in rune patterns that created repeating enchantments. Most of them I understood, if not by form, then by the energy they put off. Several were meant for protection, energy focusing, and mana channeling. The one that was repeated for the majority of the patterns was preservation, which explained why everything looked new.

All of those preservation enchantments were focused on the huge piece of jagged clear crystal quartz thrust out of the center of the room. It shot a beam of power out of its tip into a hole in the ceiling, a beam that was so bright, I couldn't look directly at it. As I got closer to the lump of crystal, I realized it was taller than me by a good two or three feet, and at least twice as wide as I was at the shoulders. It was a huge hunk of crystal.

The amount of mana pushing through it made my skin tingle, and the mana generator in my gut swirled at the density around me. It gave off a refreshing feeling, making any sense of tiredness and exhaustion wash away. In a lesser way, I also felt steadier, like I was more centered. Nothing like the last two places of power I had found, but that certainly wasn't a bad thing.

From the little experience I had gained, places of power were all similar in that they were locations where mana was much denser than anywhere else in the world. By absorbing them, I stretched the limits of both my body and mana generator, increasing my stats and abilities.

They did more than that, though. I was pretty sure the environment around each place of power affected the type of mana it contained and produced. That's why after I absorbed the first place of power–a forest location frequently lashed by storms–I suddenly had a much stronger affinity for lightning spells, and my earth magic came easier.

My second place of power had been taken over by a lich, and was also in a location frequently hit by storms. After thinking about it for a long time, I think my mana generator was able to process death mana, which was why I was able to use the bone knight armor to heal my soul damage. My lightning affinity had grown once again, which explained why one of my weakest abilities was now one of my strongest. When I had absorbed the shards of the bone knights, my lightning had even taken on a silver tone that probably carried the death aspect.

This place of power was located over a city filled with tens of thousands of people, and had been that way for centuries. It was also underground, and that had to affect the kind of mana it produced. That's why I was almost positive the mana aspects I could gain from this spot would be life and earth mana. I was mildly concerned there could be a negative interaction between the death aspect I had already absorbed and the life aspect I was about to take in, but fortune favors the *bold*, not the scared.

Once I got closer to the center of the room, I could see the hole in the ceiling was surrounded by smaller clusters of crystals that helped funnel the mana upward. They seemed to act like a series of magnifying lenses, focusing the beam higher to a point somewhere above that probably powered the wards around the city.

Based on where I thought the underground chamber was located, the central distribution juncture had to be somewhere in the basement of the Hunter's Guild. If they even knew it was there or not, or if it was in some kind of hidden room or sub-basement, I had no idea. Someone monitoring the distribution point would certainly raise the alarm as soon as I started draining the mana from the place of power, but from what I had seen from the layers of dust, I didn't think anyone up above knew where the energy actually came from.

Taking a deep breath, I reached out and placed both hands on the giant crystal. A familiar screen once again popped up in my vision.

Quest Update!

Unique Upgrade Quest: Find ten places of power - 2/10

-Absorb the power built up at the location to increase your level.

***Note - This place of power is being utilized in a ritual, causing it to be strongly aspected (Life Mana Aspect 75%/Earth Mana Aspect 10%/Darkness Mana Aspect 8%/Water Mana Aspect 5%/Light Mana Aspect 2%). Disturbing it may lead to unexpected consequences. Proceed with caution.**

It seemed that by figuring out that places of power carried aspects, I'd unlocked the information in my system updates. There was sensible logic behind each of the aspects, except for one. How it had two percent light aspect made no sense to me, but there weren't instruction manuals laying around anywhere to help out. Not that I could read them if there was one. There also weren't any warnings about the life aspect interfering with the death aspect I'd already gained, so I pushed my concerns aside and started pulling in the energy the crystal contained.

After doing this two times already, I thought it'd make the third experience much easier to manage. I should've known better, but sometimes–and I do mean *very* rarely–I'm kind of an idiot. Like, for example, completely underestimating what a mana *type* could do in large quantities.

I kept my draw slow and steady, without allowing any large power spikes to overwhelm me. The beam of energy shooting out of the top of the quartz formation diminished in brightness slightly, but it continued to feed the crystals in the ceiling at a steady rate. My body started feeling feverish, but I pushed past the sensation and tried to concentrate on keeping the tornado of mana spinning inside the hardened purple walls of my mana generator steady. It was a storm that thrashed against the walls trying to contain it, and the strain made me grit my teeth in pain as a new type of golden lightning invaded my body, thrumming in cadence with my heartbeat.

While there hadn't been a warning about the death and life aspects clashing, it was now obvious to me that there was a problem with how they interacted in my body. When my mana generator was reshaped by absorbing the bone knight armor, it had hardened and thickened its walls. Now that life aspected mana was being introduced in such large amounts, there was no flexibility for the more robust and tumultuous energy. My mana generator felt brittle against the onslaught of the new kind of power. The cold silver lightning of death and vibrant gold lightning of life fought for dominance, and my body was the battlefield.

The whirlpool of energy inside me quickly became a typhoon despite my controlled consumption, pushing out into the mana channels that ran throughout my body. My mana generator wasn't large enough to contain the amount of life this mana carried, and the intensity and concentration of *vitality* burst free.

As the crystalline walls inside me shattered, the white-hot agony dropped me to my knees. I was no stranger to pain, but this wasn't pain. This was death. The uncontained whirlpool ripped through my body, tearing apart my insides. I vomited blood onto the quartz in front of me, changing a part of the white light it emitted into a warning strobe of red.

This was it. I was going to die. Casting a healing spell was impossible. With the mana generator shattered, I couldn't control my own magic. I also lost control of the influx of power pushing through my palms, and the beam of energy cut off completely as it shunted into me at full blast.

I would have been blown across the underground chamber if it weren't for the power welding my hands to the quartz. The only thing I could do in the moment was focus on the shattered remains of my mana generator, which had been ground down by the storm inside me to little more than sand.

More mana pushed through my palms, as if lava was pouring into me. I vomited blood once more, and I had no idea how I was even still alive. It felt like hours passed, and still I knelt, light and life dumping into my body like I was a pool at the bottom of a waterfall of lava.

Somehow, the life mana wouldn't allow me to die. Its constant flow through my destroyed channels kept me from death's door, combining with my Vigor stat to rejuvenate me just enough to stay alive. I wasn't even blessed by the sweet relief of unconsciousness. The torture of being burned and torn apart from the inside made me wish death would come. All the years of endless battles. Pointless struggle. Lost friends. Suffering for worlds not even my own. I pleaded for it to end.

A chime sounded in my head, and a screen blinked across my vision before I blinked it away. Now wasn't the time.

Then, a second chime, and with this one came a modicum of clarity. I ignored the second screen, and instead used the brief moment of lucidity to once again focus on what was left of my mana generator.

All that remained were scraps of purple sand and dust thrown throughout the wrecked and twisted channels in my body. There was no way to rebuild what was lost.

What I did have, however, was a storm of silver and gold lightning fighting one another for control. I took command of the thrashing bolts of power, forcing them to fill in the gap where my mana generator once rested. The two kinds of lightning were polar opposites and didn't want to blend, but like a magnet, I managed to find a way to twist and snap their polarities together into a cage that was three times the size of my old mana generator.

Once the skeletal framework of lightning was in place, it was as if the raging mana inside me *wanted* to reforge a new mana generator. The eye of the typhoon centered on the cage, and started pulling in the loose power tearing me apart. Walls started reforming, this time in layered sections like a scaled dragon, creating something flexible, yet strong and sturdy. The multicolored hue of the scales that formed represented each of the major aspects of mana, with a few minor ones that I didn't recognize.

The shape it built wasn't an orb, but it wasn't the sharp-edged square cage I had made, either. Instead, it was like an actual organ, a new heart with mana scales that mimicked a dragon, beating inside me.

Once my mana generator was reformed, my mana channels started to heal. The life mana pouring into me helped speed the process, and the remains of my old mana generator strengthened the channels to a whole new level of resilience and fortitude.

The last thing to heal was my body, and it was done in moments. The place of power had been nearly completely drained, and I was so stuffed with its energy I was literally glowing in the dark. Breathing without pain felt unnatural for a moment, until I stood and stretched, testing to make sure all my limbs still worked properly.

A scuff of boot on stone from the tunnel caused me to turn quickly, and I almost fell on my face. There had definitely been a boost to my stats, and I would need to get used to it. I unclipped my mace from my belt and took a careful step toward the tunnel entrance.

From the shadows walked the young vampire that had given me information on Gleason. It gave me a fang-filled smile and tipped an imaginary cap in my direction. "I gotta thank you. Followin' you around, watchin' you fight, learnin' everythin' I can about you for the Lady, it was startin' to get borin'. But gettin' down here, turnin' off the power? There's no way I coulda done all that on my own."

"What are you doing here, vamp?" I took another step forward, readying my mace. The vampire kid wasn't acting like he did before. He was far too confident, and I definitely didn't like hearing it was telling my secrets to its 'Lady'. "I thought you were supposed to be keeping an eye on the Blood Wardens."

"Oh, I have been. What's left of 'em, anyway. I led some of 'em down here, so they'll be here in just a little bit." The vampire flicked his wrist, and behind me I heard the sound of shattering glass. "First, I had to break that. Now the Lady can come through the gates when she wants, an' this will all be over."

I rushed for the vampire, swinging my mace for his head. It obviously didn't expect me to be as fast as I was with my new speed, and I smashed the creature's skull flat. It was dead, punished for its treachery, but I was too late. I looked at the ceiling to see the beam of light was no longer properly going into the hole cut for it. The vampire had thrown a knife at the crystals used to aim the beam, and shattered the largest of them. The city's wards would quickly run out of power, and soon after it would be at the mercy of the undead horde.

Greendown would fall, and it was all my fault.

CHAPTER 32

There wasn't time for me to beat myself up for past mistakes I'd made. I should have killed the young-looking vampire the first time we'd met, but I didn't, and now the city's defenses were destroyed. I'd led the bloodsucker straight down here. Then, I'd even drained the place of power enough that something as simple as a throwing knife could shatter the targeting crystals.

A quick check revealed there was no way for me to fix the broken lens. The knife the vampire had used was more of a spike with a handle than a regular knife, and it was covered with an enchantment that made it impossible to move once it was stuck in place. If I had a few days to gather supplies, build a scaffold, and then climb up there and study the runes used, I could probably disable it without destroying the other lenses. That wasn't something I could do right now.

I checked the body of the vamp, looking for any clues that might help me. All I found was a small notebook with some rough sketches that could have been a map, but I couldn't read the labels to be sure. Its body was quickly decomposing, meaning it was definitely older than it looked. Not that it mattered much, but it did make me feel a little better.

Since I had a few moments, I checked the screens that had tried to pop up while I was being ripped apart from the inside by the unknowable forces of the universe.

New Title Earned: Mythical Survivalist
-Your ability to not die even when you really, *really* should is already legendary. Now it's reached mythic proportions! Seriously, how are you not dead yet?
Skill Imparted: You are 5% more durable in every way possible.
Natural healing has increased by 5%.
Death takes one step back when it approaches your presence.

Title Upgraded: No Pain, All Gain VII
-Your ability to handle pain is downright masochistic! You might need to talk to someone. I'm not joking. Are you okay?
Skill Imparted: Pain sensation is reduced by 35%. Reflexes are not negatively impacted by this effect.

The new title was nice to have. A boost to my healing on top of a durability increase was a huge help, especially since the durability applied to *everything*. My soul would now be five percent tougher than it was before, which was something I had no idea how to strengthen in the first place.

My pain title getting upgraded to level seven wasn't a surprise, considering how much the process of rebuilding my mana generator had hurt. Each increase had given me a five percent jump in pain reduction, which now added up to over a third of all pain felt being ignored.

The last thing I needed to do was check my stat sheet. Whatever increases I'd gained, I knew they were going to be far greater than the last two places of power had given me based on the sheer amount of mana I had been forced to absorb.

Name: James Holden (Earth v7.4)
Title: Chief Justice/Arbiter/Justicar/Executioner/etc…
Level: 100/MAX
Rank: 4.8/10
Age: 27 (Physical) 47 (Actual)
Class: Warrior/Soldier/Knight/Paladin/Mage (5/5)
Profession: Healer/Alchemist/Blacksmith/Runesmith/Judge (5/5)

Status:
Strength- 71→96
Flexibility- 70→95

Vigor- 71→101
Mind- 72→112

Mission:
Mythical Quest: Deliver Justice - World Count 20/???
Legendary Quest: Return Home - Requirements not met
Epic Quest: Find out why - Requirements not met
Rare Quest: Track down Silver Star - Ongoing
-Sub-quests:
-Find the Key to the Silver Star
-Find the Enhancing Gem
-Close the Demon Gate

Unique Upgrade Quest: Find ten places of power - 3/10

Those changes were… insane. I had *never* jumped that many points at once. To go from seventy-two all the way to one hundred and twelve in my Mind stat? There was no frame of reference for me to put it in perspective. This was from more than the place of power. My new title explained the extra increase for Vigor, but not Mind. Recreating my mana generator had to be the cause.

I knew one thing for sure. The 'Lady' was about to get her shit wrecked.

A grunt came from the tunnel, forcing me to stop examining my screens. The Blood Wardens the vampire had led down here must have finally made their way through the portcullis.

Since fighting them in a place where they could destroy more of the enchantments felt like a bad idea, I decided to bring the fight to them. Charging inside the tunnel with my mace held high, I readied a basic windblade spell in my free hand. There was no building time to power the spellform. I simply thought of it being there, and with a flash of mana it was ready at full strength. Oohhh, baby.

The light from my mace flared arctic blue as I caught sight of the first Blood Warden. It was even bigger and nastier than the last one I had fought, with bulging muscles that rippled under the tight skin of the hulking monstrosity. Its teeth had all cracked and snapped off into jagged shards, making its snarl a bloody mess of horror. Dust fell as its head scraped the ceiling, and it was wide enough that the one coming up behind it couldn't squeeze by. If the rest of them were this size, the first guy I fought was the runt of the litter. Despite its massive size, it wasn't slow. It twitched from side to side, bouncing off the walls fast enough that a normal person would only see a blur of movement.

I flicked my wrist forward like I was skipping a stone, only the windblade that spun at the mutant Blood Warden was no stone. My mana generator had been remade with a framework of lightning, and my spell moved like it was infused with the speed of a lightning strike.

The Blood Warden only had a chance to open its disgusting mouth in surprise when my spell took it across the throat. The windblade didn't have the power to take its head off, but it was pretty close. The mutant fell backward as black blood fountained from its torn neck, falling into the second Blood Warden crowding it from behind.

I leapt over the tangled pair and smashed in the back of the head of the mutant trying to hold up its partner. To be safe, I kept hitting both of them with my mace until neither of their heads were anything more than a mess of pulped bone and gray matter.

Last time a fight with one of the Blood Wardens nearly killed me, and forced me to use a knight ability that weakened me for hours. This time, I killed two of them without breaking a sweat. My new stats were no joke.

There were no more Blood Wardens in the tunnel as I raced back to the surface. I had no idea how much time had actually passed, since the process of reforming my mana generator could have taken an hour or a day and I wouldn't know the difference. If it was still the same day, the witches would still be trying to build the wardstone to bring down the city's protections, and the army of undead would be hiding in the forest. If it was any longer than that, it was possible the vampire magic user could have changed plans already, and the city's defenders would have no idea their magical protections were about to crumble without warning. I had to let the Commandant know what was going to happen before it was too late to prepare.

Running back up the tunnel was so much faster, for a moment I thought I had made a mistake. My new speed had increased enough that the trip that'd taken me hours of circling the city underground now took less than thirty minutes when I wasn't holding back. Once I started though, I couldn't stop. The cumulative dust cloud I stirred up behind me would have choked me to death. At least it died down once I hit the sewers, giving me a chance to catch my breath.

Bursting out of the sewers, I was immediately confronted by a city in chaos. Again. People were running through the streets in packs, some in fear, some in rage. In the distance, I heard the roar of a Blood Warden, and the answering clash of steel.

Right in front of my eyes, a woman picked up a man twice her size and threw him through a brick wall. Her muscles strained against her skin just like the monstrous Blood Wardens, but not enough to cause the ripping and tearing the giant mutants had suffered. A boy no older than twelve ran screaming down the middle of the road swinging a wagon axle like it was a broomstick at imaginary enemies. I saw an older man huddled in an alley talking to himself, trying to keep calm as he crushed the cobblestones at his feet with his bare hands. Hundreds of similar instances must have been happening everywhere across Greendown.

Like I said, it was a city in chaos.

Whatever was going on, it looked like Gleason was successful.

I grabbed a man running across the street who was chasing a woman that was still normal, and picked him up by his throat. A burst of healing magic formed a connection between the two of us, and I tried to undo what had been done to him. The problem I saw was the lack of an invasive disease.

My new stats helped me get a better idea of what I was looking at, compared to the last time I checked one of Gleason's victims. This was caused by an alchemical solution that boosted natural chemicals and endorphins in the body to levels that should be lethal under normal circumstances. Like magical versions of steroids, cocaine, and hallucinogens all in one. Flushing his system would take forever, and there was no way I could track down everyone and save them before they managed to kill themselves.

Luckily, that wasn't necessary. His body was already doing it for him. Unlike the Blood Wardens, this change didn't seem like it would last long. I guessed by morning, he would wake up with the worst hangover of his life–and be insanely hungry and dehydrated–but he would be alive. If everyone was like this, the majority of the citizens of Greendown would survive. As long as they weren't eaten by zombies, of course.

To get clear of the insanity, I jumped onto the tallest roof I could find. It was an inn that I had seen full to bursting only a day ago. Now, it looked abandoned, and the doors and windows had been ripped free. At least I was able to get a good view of Greendown. Even if that view didn't show me anything I wanted to see.

The walls were nearly empty of troops, and the two gates I could see from the roof only had a token force of Wardens. Whether it was because the defenders were also going insane, or they had been pulled from the walls to try and control the citizens, it ultimately didn't matter. There was no way the besiegers hadn't noticed the change, and their leader had shown herself to be smart enough to capitalize on an opportunity like this. It was nearly sunset, meaning the vampires would soon be able to lead their troops personally. And they were going to lead them right for our throats.

Finding Beck was my number one priority. If he could rally his men to the gates, we might have a chance to last the night. If not, Greendown wouldn't exist the next time the sun rose.

As I jumped from rooftop to rooftop, making my way toward the Hunter's Guild, I saw how bad the city was suffering. It would take a concerted effort from everyone who cared about the welfare of the citizens to put Greendown back together once this was over. The guilds were going to get wrecked if they didn't play ball. I'd see to it personally.

When I finally made it to the Hunter's Guild, I found it abandoned. It was almost fully dark outside, and apparently the Commandant had taken everyone–even those in the infirmary–to defend the walls. In his office there was a big red flag pinned to the map where the northern gate was located. In some places, they call that a 'clue'.

I started north, running across the courtyard. A man in a full suit of spiked plate armor stepped out from behind a cluster of trees as I got to the edge of the Hunter's Guild property line, and I accidentally clipped him with my shoulder, sending him flying back into the fence. I couldn't see his face because of his helmet–and it was getting dark–but from his body language I could tell he was going to attack me. I figured he was either angry I bumped him, or under the influence of the rager madness alchemical solution.

He snarled something unintelligible, but it was impossible to understand him with his faceplate down and the screaming of so many crazy people running around the city. I tried to move around him, but he grabbed for a weapon on his belt. It was a nasty-looking whip that reminded me of something Gleason would use, but this guy wasn't wearing a white uniform like that psycho would have on. He also seemed to be suffering from the rager madness, which Gleason certainly wouldn't do to himself.

Before he could free his weapon, I gave him a solid shin kick to the ribs to put him down without having to hurt the guy too badly. Unfortunately, I still didn't have a good gauge on my new strength yet.

Spiky armor guy was blasted through the wrought-iron fence, in and out of the wooden guard shack next to the walking gate of the guildhouse, and smashed head-first into a brick building that was used to store fertilizer to help keep the lawn around the guild green. The impact was so hard the building swayed precariously before it collapsed onto the man, dumping hundreds of pounds of bricks and half-used fertilizer bags onto the man.

The smell of moldy manure permeated the area, and I was about to go check on him until I heard a faint groan under the pile of poop. He must have had some good armor, because it could take a serious pounding. Since I could hear the man was still alive, I left him where he was. I didn't feel like digging through a pile of crap just to fight a crazy person who might or might not even need healing. Besides, with him being so close to the Hunter's Guild, someone would find him quickly in the morning.

As I was running out of the hole in the fence made by the man, I noticed two interesting items in the debris of the guard shack. A very familiar spear-staff, and a thick-bladed dagger I'd been wanting ever since I'd laid eyes on it. How they got there, I didn't know. Maybe Cross and Tew had to check their weapons at the guard shack, and forgot to grab them in the excitement of the chaos? Stranger things had happened, I supposed.

I grabbed them as I ran, tucking them both away. The rest of my trip through the city was relatively uneventful, besides killing a Blood Warden I spotted with a bolt of silver lightning that was so intense it blew the hulking mutant's legs off, and left spots in my eyes so bright I had to use a healing spell to fix them.

When I jumped from a two-story laundry to a four-story dress shop, the northern gatehouse finally came into view. Standing on top of the battlements was the distinctive figure of Commandant Beck, and next to him was his scarred assistant wearing the leather armor of a Black Warden. They were yelling at one another, gesturing wildly at something at their feet. I also noticed there wasn't anyone else in sight to help guard the *entire* northern section of the wall. Or the gate. It was about to be a *long* night if that's all the help I was going to get tonight to protect the city.

I tried shouting to get their attention, but I was drowned out by the sudden boom of something slamming against the wooden gate. The metal crossbar jumped in its braces as a second impact knocked the thick timbers inward, and even from a hundred yards away, I heard the sound of wood splintering. A third impact shattered a corner of the right-hand gate door, and a massive eyeball peeked through the gap.

Even though I was nowhere near the gatehouse, and there was still an iron portcullis to get through, the giant eye managed to somehow make eye contact with me. I had seen it before. It was the god-damned tyrannosaurus rex. A ding sounded in my ear, and a very late and extremely unhelpful window popped up in my vision.

****Warning!****

One of the Icons of Wrath sent by an angered god is approaching your location. Leaving the area immediately is strongly advised.

"Oh, you don't say?"

CHAPTER 33

Considering running away wasn't an option, I ignored the mockingly obnoxious screen and sprinted for all I was worth. I needed to get to the tower and stop the dinosaur from breaking down the gate, otherwise it would rip through the city like it was wet tissue paper.

Another rattling boom shook the entire wall, forcing Beck and his assistant–a man wearing the uniform of a Black Warden–to stumble. A head of blonde hair poked up from between them, and I realized they hadn't been gesturing to the dinosaur while they were arguing. They were motioning to Oriana.

I couldn't quite make the jump from the ground all the way to the top of the gatehouse, so I had to monkey my way up the portcullis a bit before leaping to the battlements. Once there, I realized Oriana wasn't kneeling between the two men for no reason. She was hunched over the prone forms of both Cross and Tew, trying to heal them both.

The two men were in rough shape. Tew looked incredibly pale, like he didn't have enough blood to fill a thimble, and Cross was beaten black and blue over most of his body, making him unrecognizable. That was probably a good thing, because this wasn't the way we wanted Beck finding out Cross was back in the city. Neither Tew nor Cross were conscious, and Oriana looked nearly frantic as she tried pushing a crude–but powerful–healing spell into each of the men.

"Paladin! Where have you been?" Beck stumbled as another boom shook the gatehouse, and he grabbed his secretary to steady himself. "It's been outright stark raving mad since you disappeared over the wall to stop those witches. Everyone's lost their minds, and now there's a damnable *tyrannosaurus rex* trying to tear down my gate!"

I looked over the wall. The woman in the black dress was riding the freaking dinosaur like it was a horse, directing it with her glowing staff to slam itself against the thick timbers of the gate. Behind her was an army of vampires, bone knights, and zombies waiting to rush into the city. There were a few groups of orcs and goblins farther back, but not nearly enough to account for all of their numbers. The rest were probably spread around at the other gates. We were dealing with the main assault. I was mildly happy not to see the witches with this group, but at the same time it worried me that they could be magically assaulting the city somewhere else.

The woman with silver hair directed the t-rex to slam itself against the gates again, and the city's wards flared as the gatehouse was rocked. The light they gave off was dimmer, and the agitation in the undead ranks told me they noticed it too. We didn't have much time left.

"Yeah, I see that. Definitely a big-ass dinosaur. I wonder how they were able to find one of those around here? Pretty crazy." I knelt next to Oriana and started healing Cross. He wasn't as bad off, but major internal bruising like that could cause a blood clot. I didn't need him having a stroke right now. I also wanted to make sure that his face wasn't fixed all the way, so Beck wouldn't recognize him. "What happened to these two?"

"We're not sure. Some Hunters found your man dragging Tew down the middle of the street, barely standing. He collapsed before we could question him." Beck had to brace himself as the t-rex slammed into the gate again. "Oriana has been trying to heal them ever since."

"Healing isn't my strong suit. It's a good thing you're here." Oriana slumped as she dropped back onto her backside. "I'm surprised to see you again, Paladin. I thought you died when that wardstone exploded."

"Just surprised? I was hoping you'd be happy to see me." I gave her a wink and a smile, and she blushed before looking away. Yep. Still got it. I shifted my healing spell over to Tew, and immediately began stimulating his bone marrow to begin increasing production of his blood cells. "That's not important right now. What is important is figuring out how we're going to mount any kind of defense with what we have here."

"Where are the rest of the people you came here with? They seemed very capable." Oriana got to her feet slowly, obviously feeling more than a little exhaustion. She peeked over the side of the battlements to see what we were dealing with, and went pale as the gate took another hit. "We could certainly use whatever help they could lend us."

"If things are still going as planned, one of them is on a… *special* mission. I don't know how that's going with the rager infection in the people, but if he's successful, it's a very important task. The other two should be watching the river gate. They set up some surprises in case the enemy gets inside the city." I finished healing Tew while I talked, making sure he was completely healed. He had suffered from a serious neck wound, and fixing the nerve damage was finicky work. Before I absorbed the latest place of power, it would have taken all of my concentration. Now, I could hold a conversation while still actively healing. "What about the rest of the Wardens?"

"The ones not affected by this 'rager infection', as you call it, are trying to save those not under its influence." Beck let out a defeated sigh, and looked out over Greendown. Fires dotted the city, burning unchecked, and sounds of fighting were coming from everywhere. "I don't see how we can make it through this. Even if we hold the gates, there won't be much left to protect come sunrise."

"So, you just want to open the gates and let them in?" I sent a final pulse of energy into both Cross and Tew, hopefully rejuvenating them enough to get them back in the fight. "I thought you were protecting the people, not a bunch of buildings?"

"He's right." Oriana clenched her fists, causing wisps of flame to drift off of her knuckles. "Buildings can be rebuilt, but lives can't be replaced. We can't let despair take over."

Oriana's attempts to uplift the group came to a halt when the two unconscious people woke up.

"*You.*" Tew's mana-accentuated rumbling voice was emphasized by another booming impact against the gate. "Are you James Holden, the man I've been searching for?" His fists started glowing as he lifted himself to his feet. "*The Oracle* has demanded your execution, for crimes against the gods, and the threat you pose for all of humanity."

Beck and the others gasped, retreating quickly to get out of Tew's way. Both the Commandant and Oriana looked back and forth between the two of us in confusion, obviously conflicted at the sudden revelation. I hadn't been some raving monster, after all. They were clearly wondering why I needed to die.

"Don't do this!" Cross jumped in front of him, holding his hands up to show they were empty. "It isn't what you think."

"Get out of my way." Tew tried to push him aside, but Cross refused to be moved. "You knew I was searching for him, but said nothing. Some might say I should kill you as well."

Beck tried stepping forward to tug Cross out of the way as well. "Come on, young man. I understand notions of loyalty, and why you would want to defend him, but this is beyond you."

"No, *you* don't understand, sir." Cross quickly healed the remaining few bruises I had left, and Beck let go of him in shock once he recognized his former Captain.

"Cross? Is that really you?" Beck looked between Cross and I. "I thought perhaps James Holden had killed you."

"No, he *saved* me, Commandant. In more ways than one." Cross looked back at Tew. "And I saved your life, Green Warden. You can listen to me for a few moments, instead of threatening to kill me." Tew flinched, and slightly lowered his glowing fists. Cross gave him a grateful nod before motioning back at me. "The *Oracle* is wrong. It's been compromised, either by dark forces, or by someone in the guilds. I was sent to kill this man, and it was wrong to do so. He's done nothing that would threaten the Trinity, only the power the guilds hold over the people, and fight against evil when he sees it. Evil like Gleason, the one responsible for attacking us, and what is happening in the city."

"No. Gleason?" Beck looked shaken and slightly unstable, so his secretary helped support him. "I knew he had problems, but for my nephew to do all of *this*?"

"That much is true." Tew motioned to the empty scabbard on his belt. "I greatly underestimated him, and he managed to take me by surprise. Both Cross and I saw him putting something into the water supply, and he stole our weapons before leaving us to be killed by his creations. If it weren't for Cross, I would have died."

"*Gleason* had your weapons?" I slowly pulled out Tew's dagger and the spear-staff Cross had been using. "By chance, was he wearing this stupid-looking spiky armor? Almost impossible to understand him with his helmet on because his faceplate covered his mouth?"

"You fought him, didn't you?" Cross took the spear from me and checked it over to make sure it functioned properly. "Did you kill him?"

"Son of a *twatwaffle*!" Sparks of lightning jumped from my fists as I raged at myself internally. Of *course* the guy with a whip was Gleason. I'd let the little shitstain get away *again*. "No, I didn't kill him. I didn't recognize him without his stupid white uniform on. He's underneath a collapsed fertilizer shed by the Hunter's Guild. There's about three or four hundred pounds of shit holding him in place, so maybe he'll still be there when this is all over with."

"What is a twatwaffle, and why did you call my sister one?" Beck was frowning at me with his hand on his sword hilt.

Another booming hit rocked the gatehouse, and this time there was a shattering sound and a bright flash of light as the city's wards finally broke. A cheer went up from those waiting to invade Greendown. At least, the ones with throats that still worked cheered. A lot of the zombies and skeletons just waved their arms around like they were happily advertising for a used car dealership.

"The definition of a twatwaffle isn't important right now. What is important is knowing if we're all on the same page or not, because there is a really big undead army about to come through that gate, and I'm going to fight them, with or without you." I reluctantly held the hilt of Tew's dagger out to him. "Are you fighting me, or them?"

"May the Trinity understand. I'll fight them." Tew snatched his dagger and sheathed it with a small sigh of relief. I didn't blame him. It was a *seriously* nice weapon. "Now that we're all on the same side again, how should we do this?"

Beck stepped forward and immediately started giving orders. "I think this plan gives us the best chance of survival. Oriana, you're with the two of us." He motioned toward himself and his secretary. "We'll knock that woman off the tyrannosaurus rex as soon as she gets through. Then, we can take her down. Tew, you and Cross will have to keep the dinosaur distracted and away from us. Holden, you…" Beck looked over the wall at the horde of undead waiting to rush the gate. "You try to keep the rest of them from getting inside. We'll join you as soon as we can."

I cleared my throat and raised my hand. "I can't help but notice the numbers are a little skewed here. I'm taking on an entire army, while you guys are dealing with much smaller numbers. Are you sure you aren't trying to complete the 'Oracle's' orders in a less direct way?"

The Commandant shrugged. "None of the enemies in the larger army is much of a threat compared to the woman and the dinosaur. I figured a man like you could hold them off long enough for us to back you up. Twatwaffle."

I couldn't help but laugh. "Fair enough. It's as good a plan as any. Just remember, don't be afraid to adjust and adapt as they react to us." I stole a quote from my home world that had always proven itself to be true. "No plan survives first contact with the enemy."

Everyone mumbled in agreement. All of them had seen enough to know it was as true a statement as any.

Off in the distance, a massive explosion lit up the night sky. We all looked toward the river gate to see a great fireball rising into the air, and for a brief moment even the army outside the walls fell silent. The whole city held its breath, and then erupted back into violence with a roar of outrage at the interruption.

"What in all the three heavens and six hells was *that*?" Beck tried standing on his toes to see better. "Was that the river gate?"

"It looks like the enemy is inside the city. Remember the surprise I had my people prepare? That was Corporal Leedy's trap for anything breaking through the river gate." I was able to see flashes of magic coming from on top of the gatehouse. Jess was putting in work, and Murphy was probably standing right next to her. Leedy had better be doing his thing elsewhere, or him and I would have words. "Right now, it looks like there's just two of my people trying to finish off whatever survived the explosion."

"Damn. It looks like your words proved true, I just never expected it to happen so quickly." Beck closed his eyes for a moment before making a decision. "Oriana, go. Provide whatever support you can for them, and try to hold that gate." She gave him a quick salute before she was gone, sprinting along the top of the wall. He locked gazes with me. "Without her magic to help us, there's no way my secretary and I are going to get that woman off the back of that dinosaur. You're going to have to take her on, and we'll do your job and hold back the horde for as long as possible." His secretary gave a firm nod of agreement.

We all knew it was a death sentence for the two of them. They would be swept away in moments, and only their dead bodies might serve as tripping hazards for the zombies as they rushed to kill everyone inside Greendown. Still, I respected their decision, and I wouldn't stand between a man and his choice to go down fighting.

"If that's the way you want it, then that's how we'll do it." I pulled free the last two remaining enchanted gunpowder casks I had in my ruck and gave one to each of them. It only took a moment to charge two shards of rock with the *Spark* spell and I handed those over as well. "Here. Once you tap these stones on the symbol carved on the top, you've got about three seconds before they go boom. I would recommend throwing them very far away, and running like hell."

"The 'Holy Hand Grenades' I've heard so much about." Beck took his with a smile. "Thank you. I'm sure they'll be useful."

His secretary only gave me a nod. The stoic Warden tucked it into his leather armor and tied it in place. He clearly had no plans of throwing it if he needed to use it. That was a hard, hard man.

Tew looked over the side, and motioned us back. "While we've been talking, she's been charging a spell with her staff. It looks like this is the big one. We should–"

All of us were knocked from our feet as the gatehouse was rocked by another impact. The sound of wood shattering and metal screaming filled the air, and we all scrambled to our feet to inspect the damage.

The gate was destroyed, and the portcullis was ripped from its foundations, twisted to the side like it was made of clay. It made a gap just wide enough that the dinosaur could possibly squeeze through. The fight was on.

Cross and Tew jumped down immediately to face the onrushing horde, while I grabbed Beck and his secretary before joining them. The five of us stood tall as the first ranks rushed through, allowing the t-rex and its rider time to squeeze through unchallenged.

We easily mowed down the fast but weak vampires that were too eager to wait for the rest of their army, which gave me a chance to try and stop the dinosaur before it got through the remains of the gate. I cast several stone spike spells for the t-rex to step on. It was no use. The dinosaur's hide was too tough, and it crushed the spikes like they were made of balsa wood. I tried raising another stone wall in front of and behind the dinosaur, but the woman riding it unraveled my spells with a wave of her staff. She had some serious skill as a caster, and her staff was good at focusing and enhancing her power.

If magic wasn't going to work, it was time to get physical.

As I sprinted for the woman, Tew and Cross were right behind me. I could feel Tew's dagger powering up behind me, and Cross was already shooting stone darts at the t-rex's legs. Not that they were doing anything, but maybe the dinosaur thought they tickled.

I leapt as high as I could just as the tyrannosaurus cleared the gap. It stood tall and let loose an ear-splitting roar, and instead of landing on its back, I bounced off its chest. Not the smoothest start to a fight, but I'd had worse.

Cross managed to shut the dinosaur up by hitting the roof of its mouth with one of the stone darts he was shooting, and it made a strangled yelping sound as it ducked its head back down to protect itself. The dumb beast shook its head from side to side in pain, forcing the woman on its back to forget about the spell she was preparing and making her hang on instead.

That gave Tew the time he needed to finish his spell, and he let loose a green wave of energy from his blade that smacked the dinosaur across the snout, scoring its scales and forcing it to flinch and stumble to the side, where it crushed a small building as it fell against it just off the road.

Unfortunately, the dinosaur moving from the entrance only cleared the way for the rest of the undead horde.

At some point Beck and his secretary had managed to come around the opposite side of the road and were waiting for the swarm of soulless soldiers. They rushed into the narrow gap and met the tide of undead monsters without fear. Beck was wearing plate armor that provided good protection, but his secretary was only wearing leathers. Both men were well past their prime, and even though it was clear they were still in good shape, they wouldn't hold for long.

I refused to let their sacrifice be meaningless.

This time, I took a running start and used an abandoned wagon near the gate as a jumping block before leaping for the back of the dinosaur, sword in one hand, mace in the other. The woman–who I could now see was *definitely* a vampire–saw me coming, and had a spell ready to blast me once I was in the air, making it almost impossible to dodge. Almost. She was *not* ready for my magic-eating ninjatō to devour her spell like a shark going after brightly-clothed surfers.

She did manage to deflect my mace with her staff–which kept me from smashing her face in–but couldn't stop me from spear-tackling her off of her mount. The two of us tumbled onto the ground, and I managed to activate my shield bracelet in time to soften my hit onto a pile of rubble. The vampire woman handled the fall a little more gracefully, and sprang to her feet before she hit the wall of an abandoned smithy.

"Ah, it's you. The interloper. We finally meet face-to-face." The vampire brushed back silver hair, revealing regal features that would have stolen the heart of any man. At least, before she was a bloodsucker. Now, she would just eat their hearts. Literally. "I've been looking forward to this for a long time. There's someone who wishes to speak with you."

The tyrannosaurus rex roared somewhere off in the distance, followed by the muted booms of detonating spells. We both gave each other a small shrug. Dinosaurs gonna dinosaur.

"Well, I don't think we'd have much to talk about, considering the habit you and your friends have for trying to wipe out entire cities of innocent people." I pushed some mana into my starmetal mace, causing it to glow an intense blue as gold and silver lightning danced along its blades. My sword was ready in my other hand, and I crossed my arms, ready to deal a double backhanded strike. I knelt, prepared to sprint at her. "I'd rather you tell me where I can find this person, so I can turn their insides into their outsides after I'm done killing you."

"Such a violent man." She held up her staff, causing the clear diamond at its tip to glow. "I'm supposed to bring you in, but it doesn't matter in what condition. Perhaps losing some limbs will teach you some manners."

As she was releasing a spell, an explosion went off beside us, knocking us both off our feet, sending the needles of cold she cast far over my head. A second, closer blast followed shortly thereafter, shattering windows, and blowing free roof shingles from nearby buildings. Beck and his secretary had used their grenades.

"What is *with* this city? Everything keeps blowing up all the time!" The vampire was slower to her feet this time, and I rushed to close the distance between us.

My sword knocked her staff out of alignment, shooting sparks as the elven-made metal slid along the blackened ancient wood. She brought up her arm to block my mace, and seemed shocked as it crushed the bones in her forearm. I went for a follow-up blow as I tried for an uppercut with my mace, but she managed to kick me in the chest and create some separation between the two of us.

She shook her broken arm as it rapidly healed before my eyes. That's annoying. Now I knew what my enemies felt when I did it to them. She took her staff in both hands and held it like she knew how to fight with it. "I must admit, the reports I received from my little followers didn't do you justice, interloper. Your power is far greater than I expected."

"I'm full of surprises, princess." I flicked several wind blades at her to keep her honest. She easily defeated all of them, but it was good to keep her on her toes. "It's one of the things the ladies love about me."

"How did you know I'm the Princess?" Her formerly lackadaisical attitude dropped, and she turned ugly. Fangs long enough to mark her as a very powerful elder vampire extended from her mouth, and the glow from her staff turned much colder. "Who told you this?"

"It's a figure of speech, lady. Calm down." I paused, thinking about everything I knew from the legends of the Silver Star, and the secret of how it was overrun by vampires. "Wait. Are you *the* Princess Starnight? The one from the lost airship?"

She snarled, and blasted me with her ice needle spell. There was no more taking me prisoner on the table, apparently.

"I *detest* that name. I hate anyone who *uses* that name!" She hit me with another spell, this time shattering my shield.

We were done talking, and the gloves had come off. She had been holding back. As an elder vampire, the Princess had far more strength and speed than a regular vamp could ever hope to touch, and the years of practice meant she knew how to put it to good use. Her staff was like a viper, spinning and striking out at any openings with the weight of a sledgehammer. If that sledgehammer could also impart a freezing effect that would kill a normal person that didn't have an insane amount of life aspected mana flowing through their body, keeping them alive.

I was still new to my boosted stats, and in a high-level fight like this one, even the tiniest of mistakes could lead to massive punishments. I kept misjudging my own speed, and would time a block wrong, allowing her to slam the tip of her staff into my ribs. The aching cold it imparted slowed me down just enough that I was thrown off all over again, allowing more hits to pile up.

That's not to say I didn't get my own hits in. The Princess was looking pretty ragged as I managed to slice and dice her up pretty good with a few surprise cuts. She was very careful not to let me hit her with my mace, but my sword managed to hurt her several times.

All I needed to do was time it right, and I planned on blowing her head off with my wrist gun. I'd let her have it with all three barrels at once, and even an elder vampire wouldn't be able to come back from that. As soon as she was distracted and couldn't dodge or shield herself, I'd finish this fight in one blow.

My moment came when a group of bone knights tried to interfere in our fight. The undead army had been streaming past us as we fought, but there wasn't anything I could do to stop it until the Princess was dead. The bone knights tried rushing over to grab me, and I did a shuffling step backward, placing the smallest one between the Princess and where I was about to dodge. As I moved out of the way of her staff thrusting for my face, I lifted a small wall of dirt behind the bone knight and smacked him in the face with my mace.

The Princess dissolved my spell almost immediately, but it was too late. The bone knight tripped over the crumbling wall, and fell into her outstretched staff, knocking it far off to the side. Her eyes went off of me for just a moment, and I raised my arm and fired.

Smoke blocked my vision for a heartbeat, but when it cleared, I was shocked to see the Princess with her head still attached. My three oversized bullets were floating an inch from her face, and as they dropped to the ground a large medallion she was wearing shattered and crumbled into dust.

"Finally!" With a wave of her staff, all of the air around me disappeared. I couldn't breathe. My feet were floating an inch off the ground, so I couldn't move out of the airless bubble. "I was waiting for you to use that trump spell my spies told me about. I wasn't sure how it worked, all I knew was that it was powerful. I'm pretty sure it's how you killed the lich. That you had *three* of them? I don't think anyone knew that." She made a tisking sound with her tongue. "Replacing my protection medallion is going to make the Destitute angry. He won't be able to talk to me until we walk all the way to the mountains, and I can't tell you how angry he's going to be with you about that. I wouldn't want to be you when we get there."

I kept trying to cast spells, but she unraveled my spellforms the moment they formed. My weapons were yanked away by invisible hands, and I started to feel light-headed as my hands and legs were bound together. I grabbed at my throat, unable to make a gasping noise. Cold started creeping over me as the Princess cast her cold magic over me, wave after wave pushing against the life mana inside me that tried to fight it.

While I might've had knowledge from my home world, twenty years of experience fighting, and a little over a decade of practice using magic, the Princess was *ancient*. I should've planned things better. Fighting her face-to-face in a duel was stupid. She was probably killing people in droves when most of the people on my world were still convinced the world was flat.

I'd gotten high on my own power, and the new stats had made me overestimate my abilities. Now, Greendown was going to pay the price for my arrogance.

And the Princess was happy to rub it in.

"Once the city is turned, we'll outfit my new army and start our march north. It will only take two weeks to reach the caves. Undead armies don't have to stop for rest, or food. They're far more efficient than a living army. Once we arrive, you'll understand why all of this is necessary." The Princess waved to her side, where the last of her undead troops were funneling into the city. "Don't you see, interloper? It was foolish to fight the inevitable. Every man, woman, and child in this city will go on to serve a greater purpose. Isn't that nice?"

Keeping my eyes open against the invasive cold was a struggle. I couldn't cast spells. My weapons were taken. Air was running out. Listening to this psycho made me want to rip out my own eardrums with a rusty fork. It was turning out to be a really rough day.

Suddenly, a vampire went running past us, sprinting out of the city. It had one of its arms ripped off, and it was clutching the torn limb with its free hand. The look of fear on its face was unmistakable.

Another vampire came limping out of an alleyway, covered in blood with huge gaping holes all over its body. Before it could make it to the road, something in the shadows grabbed it and yanked it back. Its keening wails were cut off with a wet-sounding squelch.

"What is going on?" The Princess moved out into the road, dragging me with her. In the distance, we could both see groups of her zombies being torn limb from limb.

Regular citizens weren't cowering in fear at the sight of a zombie, like they normally would. They weren't being easily overpowered by both the greater and lesser undead. No, right now, the majority of Greendown's citizens were under the effects of the rager infection. And they were straight-up *waxing* the invaders like it was their most favorite thing to do in the whole wide world.

"What is *happening*?!" The Princess turned to me, stomping her foot like she was an unruly child. "Did you do this? Tell me right now!"

I opened and closed my mouth like a fish out of water. I wasn't putting on an act, either. In a few seconds, I really would pass out.

"Oh, yes. You need air to speak." She waved her staff, and I dropped to the ground in a shivering heap. "Now, tell me. What is going on in this city? These people should be ripe for the taking. Instead, they're putting up a fight!"

"Shhh… shhh…" I was shivering from the cold of her magic, and barely able to draw in enough air to speak. I also needed her to get closer, because there was only one last chance for this to work.

"You're too quiet. Speak louder, interloper." She knelt over me, putting her ear closer to my face. Where my hands were still clutching my throat.

"I sssaid… Shhh… *Shield Bash*!"

I had no idea if it would work. There hadn't been an opportunity to test it, and such a dinky little shield ring on my finger probably wouldn't be enough to do much anyway. Except it did.

The Knight Class ability activated, and it hit like a truck.

A very angry truck.

I had no idea if it was because of my increased stats, or if there was a set amount of energy used in the skill that was spread across the exposed face of whatever shield I was using–meaning the fingernail-sized surface area of the ring shield super-concentrated the shock wave–but when it hit her in the side of the face, it ripped her jaw clean off her head.

My finger broke with the recoil, and I kinda slapped myself in the face, but I barely felt any of it. The Princess, on the other hand, *definitely* felt what happened to her.

She dropped her staff in shock, and grabbed her face as she tried to scream. It came out as more of a wailing gurgle, and she fell back, trying to get away from me. Her tongue flopped around like it had a mind of its own, smearing blood all over her face and neck as it drooped disgustingly down her neckline.

The moment she had dropped her staff the spells holding me in place disappeared. I was still dealing with the invasive and punishing cold her spells pushed into me, but my mana generator was pushing life mana to drive it away. It made it possible for me to get to my feet, and I picked up her staff, finding it surprisingly heavy.

"Hey, Princess. Normally I'd go on this rant about you being guilty and stuff, but I'm tired and hurting, and you're disgusting and evil. So just die." I cocked back her staff like it was a baseball bat and swung for the fences. Her staff broke on the third or fourth hit. She was dust and ash by the fifth hit.

I made sure to stand upwind as she blew away. It was hard as hell to get ancient dead people dust out of your clothes.

CHAPTER 34

By the time sunrise came along, Beck's words had proven to be prophetic. Not much of Greendown was still standing, but thankfully most of its people had survived. A large part of that was thanks to the actions of Jess, Murphy, and Oriana at the river gate. The explosion that'd gone off had convinced the witches to keep their forces back, and when I killed the Princess they left in full retreat.

The rager infection had started to wear off for most people sometime around midnight, and by morning everyone but the Blood Wardens were back to normal. The remaining Blood Wardens had ended up taking on the bone knights, and the two groups had torn each other apart. Only the vampires smart enough to hide managed to survive the onslaught of the citizens under the influence of the rager infection. No other undead made it out of the city–for lack of a better word–alive.

At some point, Cross and Tew managed to kill the t-rex using a bunch of axle grease from a warehouse they found, combined with a wagonload of fruits that reminded me of watermelons from my world. I hadn't gotten the full story, but I gave them the full congratulations they deserved for completing such a difficult task. However they accomplished it, I considered it a job well done.

Teams of Wardens under the direction of Lieutenant Lucente were currently scouring the sewers, looking for any leftover Blood Wardens, bone knights, vampires, or zombies that might still be hiding in the dark warren of tunnels below the city. It would take weeks to ensure they were all clear. I was just happy I didn't have to do it.

After killing the Princess, I had spent most of my time healing people from afar. The process was much easier with all of the life aspect mana running through my mana generator, and it kept the majority of the crazed citizens from killing themselves while they hunted down any undead that had been unlucky enough not to escape from me. I hadn't found Gleason, but I hoped he'd been killed in the insanity of the night fighting. I wasn't holding my breath, though.

One of the bright spots had been discovering Beck still alive at the bottom of a pile of rubble next to the gate. He had somehow clung to life long enough for me to find him, and I had healed him back to full strength. His secretary had not been as lucky.

The man had willingly laid down his life for the people of Greendown, and took out a lot of the enemy in the process. According to what Beck told me, it was the second time the man had proven himself to be the hero that he was. They were going to build a statue of him by the gate once it was rebuilt. I promised to speak at the memorial if I was still in the city.

At the moment, I was resting against what remained of a jeweler just down the road from the rubble of the northern gatehouse, trying to piece together a better version of my new shield ring. I looked up when I heard footsteps, and I was surprised to see Tew.

"I suppose we should talk." The graying Green Warden sat down next to me with a grunt, holding a mug of something alcoholic. "I've been doing a lot of talking, and a lot of thinking."

After he didn't say anything for a few minutes, I prompted him to continue. "Talking to who, and about what?"

"Your pet Wardens. All three of them. And that shifter girl, too. The one with enough magic to give Oriana a run for her job." Tew took a drink before offering me some. I waved it away before he continued. "As hard as it is for me to believe, I think you and Cross might be right. The *Oracle* might be compromised. There's no good reason for the book to want me to kill you, unless it was controlled by a guild or something corrupted that wanted you gone. I've been around you enough to know you're not evil. Nothing about you would make the Trinity send out a kill order."

"Strong magic and a good sense of character? Tew, how would you like a job as a Judge?" I offered him a hand to shake, but he laughed and pushed my hand away.

"I'm about to retire. I don't need a whole new career hanging over my head, thank you very much." Tew stood, stretching out his lower back. "Either way, you don't have to worry about me coming after you. In fact, I think my official report is going to say something about James Holden dying in the siege of Greendown. It might not hold them off forever, but it should buy you some time."

"That's mighty kind of you, Tew." I finished with the pair of rings I was working on and slipped them on my fingers. "I greatly appreciate that."

"Don't mention it." Tew drained his mug and tossed it into a trash heap beside us. "Uh-oh, don't look now, but I think you might have some trouble heading this way. It looks like all the important leaders of Greendown are on their way, and they don't look happy."

"It's okay, I was expecting them." I pointed at Leedy, who was herding them from the rear. "That's my guy in the back. He's bringing them to me at my request."

"Your funeral. I've got reports to write. Have fun with… whatever this is." Tew shrugged, and made a hasty retreat. Lucky guy.

The people Leedy was herding toward me were a motley group of various sizes and levels of displayed wealth. Their one universal constant was how they carried themselves. Like a bunch of pretentious douchebags. If their noses had been stuck any higher in the air, birds might start trying to make nests on them.

"Is this the man who begs for death?" The woman leading the group was wearing more lace than I thought was possible to even get on a dress, and it somehow only accentuated how old and wrinkled she was. "Do you realize who we are, young man? Kidnapping us out of our homes and guilds will only end one way for you."

"Oh, I know exactly who you are. A bunch of thieving criminals who deserve to be killed for allowing the destruction and murder of the city and citizens they're charged with protecting." I stood, drawing my sword in a slow and dramatic motion. "None of this would have happened if you'd done your jobs. Instead, you hindered the Wardens at every turn, held back assistance for the people, kept powerful fighters to yourselves, hoarded food and supplies, all while vying for prestige, power, and position. You're responsible for everything that's happened here, and I'm going to make sure it doesn't happen again, one way or another."

"W-wait!" The old woman held up her hands, trying to melt back into the crowd. "It wasn't like that!"

"It's *exactly* like that. I've reviewed the actions of all the men and women here, and each and every one of you failed in your duties. For your crimes, I see only one option." I took a menacing step forward, lifting my sword over my head as it swallowed the lightning that bled off my armor.

"Paladin, stay your arm! There could be a way to save these people's lives, if you're willing to hear me out." Commandant Beck came out from behind a half-burnt stable, dressed in his full suit of shining plate armor. It had taken a good bit of magic to get it looking nice again, but I thought it would be important for him to look the part. His terrible acting job made his voice sound staged as all hell, but these people didn't seem to notice. Scary lightning man had them distracted. "Assistant, bring me the documents!"

Jess came running across the road, holding several stacks of parchment. I could tell she was fighting to not crack a smile, thankfully discipline won out and she managed to hold it together.

Beck took the first stack off the top and held it up like a talisman for everyone to see. "I hold here, in my hand, a new guild charter!"

"Why in Trinity's six tits would we–" A gruff-looking man I thought might be in the Farmer's Guild changed what he was going to say when I took another menacing step forward. "Ahem, I mean, what does the charter say?"

"It outlines new rules, regulations, and rights for citizens, as well as outlining the responsibilities and authorities of the guilds." Beck motioned for Jess to start handing the documents out to the people in the group. "The bottom line is, people will be able to do whatever they like, regardless of what guild they belong to, and without having to pay for permission from the guilds."

A small outburst was quickly quieted when a crackling burst of lightning erupted from me.

"There are also punishments and fines for guilds that don't follow the new rules, and limits on what they can do to their members." Beck looked at me again. "If they agreed to sign this new charter, and ratified it as fully legal, would you be willing to spare their lives?"

I let the lightning play along my armor for a few heartbeats before letting it drop. "I'll agree to this, but only if it's done within the hour. If a single guild doesn't sign, they *all* die."

Turning around, I could see Murphy and Cross hiding just out of sight of the guild leaders. Both of them were cracking up at our little performance, silently falling over one another as they pantomimed the scared faces on the city's leadership.

Cross, Jess, Murphy, and Leedy had done a great job putting together a new set of laws to help bring about real change to this planet. I had read over the charter several times to make sure there weren't any major loopholes, and added a few pieces about taxes, free speech, and personal protection. There would be changes and revisions as time went on, but it was the start of the avalanche, and I felt good about it.

The guild leaders would certainly realize they'd been played once things calmed down. It would be too late to do anything about it, but I didn't envy Beck's position over the next few months. He'd figure it out, especially since I was going to enchant some tools and equipment for him before I left for the north. I had a meeting with this Destitute guy I didn't want to miss, and I still had the quest to find the Silver Star.

After I took a break, of course. It had been a rough few months.

While I was walking back toward the gatehouse to try and find Tew–since he was retiring soon, maybe he'd be willing to part ways with his dagger–I noticed the broken staff the Princess had been carrying. I'd tossed it aside after the fight, but now I thought maybe I could fix it and give it to Jess. She could use a nice staff.

As I picked it up off the ground, the heavy diamond tip fell out of its mounting bracket and rolled a few steps away. A sudden sense of foreboding came over me as I bent down to grab it, but I ignored the silly feeling. Why would a shiny rock be dangerous?

Quest Update!

Rare Quest: Track down Silver Star - Ongoing
-You have found the Enhancing Gem, an important part of the lost airship! Find the Key, and locate the Silver Star before time runs out. [Time remaining: 60 days]
Rare Quest: Track down Silver Star - Ongoing
Sub-quests:
-Find the Key to the Silver Star
-Close the Demon Gate [86,398 minutes remaining]

"Oh, you twatwaffle."

EPILOGUE 1

The whip cracked against the orc's back, sending it snarling into the dirt.

"Hurry up, you!" Gleason would have to administer another dose of his mixture again soon, based on the angry look the orc gave him as it brushed the dirt off its fur vest. "We have to make it to the next trapper's shack before nightfall. I refuse to sleep in the dirt again. I'm not some animal, like the rest of you."

Gleason had woken up under a pile of rotting fertilizer to find Greendown burning. He had several broken ribs, and no way of knowing what happened to that *sinner* James Holden. With his mission to cleanse the city working successfully, he decided that it was the proper time to leave while he still could, especially with the injuries he was suffering from.

The fight with Holden hadn't gone as planned, but Gleason already knew what he'd done wrong. When he'd finished the spell to find where Holden was located, it had revealed the man to be right next to him. Gleason hadn't bothered setting up the spell in a secure area, or placing detection and protection wards to warn him if an enemy was approaching. He'd set up his tracking spell in the nearest copse of trees without thinking that his rival would be waiting for him.

With Holden gaining the element of surprise, it was obvious Gleason wouldn't be able to win. Next time, *he* would be the one waiting in ambush, and the ending would be much different. How dare he be so arrogant as to believe that he could get one over on the Trinity's chosen.

"Come on, you louts. Flankers to the sides, and make sure one of you idiots erases our tracks. Do I have to explain everything?" Gleason let out a heavy sigh of frustration. His plans had called for him to leave the city with his Blood Wardens as escorts, but that hadn't been possible.

Instead, Gleason had been forced to sneak out of the practically undefended western gate like a common criminal. There had been a small force of orcs hiding in the forest near the exit, and it had been easy for him to poison them with his alchemical mixture by dropping some of the pill forms created by his alchemist into their soup pot. It hadn't worked on them the same way it did humans, but it was enough for him to take control of the small warband and bring them under his banner. Those that were resistant fell into ranks with the liberal use of his whip, and an occasional bit of magic.

"Where go, stinky-angry master-man?" The orc that served as his second spoke a bit of proper language, and often had to translate more complicated ideas to the rest of the war party. Ideas like walking at a pace faster than a snail could crawl. "No city this way. Only forest."

"Yes, I know that." Gleason rubbed his face, feeling the stubble on his unshaven jaw. He hadn't even been able to wash off the manure from the fertilizer shed. "We go north, to the mountains. There's something there I must do, and you will help me do it."

"Mountains cold, stinky-angry master-man. We need warm fur if go there." The orc shied back as Gleason turned a glare on him. While they hadn't been together long, the orcs were all learning quickly to avoid Gleason's temper.

"I know that, idiot. Now go away, and get these idiots moving!" Gleason cracked his whip again, sending those closest to him scurrying.

A cool breeze blew across his face, calming Gleason slightly. He hadn't heard the voices in a while, but he somehow still knew where he was supposed to go. He was being drawn to the mountains like iron filings to a lodestone, and fighting the sensation was pointless.

Whatever the reason, Gleason knew he was hand-picked by the Trinity, and his final test awaited him in the cold and unforgiving heights of the northern mountain peaks. He was their chosen, and he would *not* fail.

EPILOGUE 2

The blue flames dancing in the fireplace didn't push back the chill of the snowstorm that hammered in vain against the arched windows of the Destitute's chambers. The ancient elder vampire was looking at the small figurines arrayed on the table in front of him when the broad-shouldered gray dwarf stomped his way into the room.

"Milord, I've returned from the Duergar Council. They agreed to your terms, but…" The rugged features of the engineer twisted in anger before settling back to a more neutral tone. "They unanimously agreed that this will be the last time."

"So be it." The Destitute waved his companion over to the table. "In a few months, I gauge there won't be a need for their support, one way or another." The elder vampire pointed to the table, where clusters of red figurines far outnumbered the white flags and black stones meant to denote different types of units. "The dragon grows more sedentary each day, allowing more demons to escape by its lair. It's only a matter of time until the tide grows too great for anyone to stop."

"But, Milord, the airship is now finished! We can use it to–" The Duergar stopped when the elder vampire held out his hand. In it rested a cracked medallion that was paired to only one other.

"I lost contact with the Princess. It's possible she's lost, and with her the ability to fly the airship." The Destitute crushed the medallion in his grip before tossing it onto the table. "We can still save this world, but I might have to use more… unconventional methods to do it."

"What do you mean? Would you like me to try and get a device from–"

"No, none of that. Breaking the Accords would only escalate the situation. If I must, working with the interloper is always an option, if I can come to some sort of agreement with them." The Destitute pulled out a glass fist figurine from his pocket, one that looked exactly like the symbol used by the Wardens. He rubbed it between his thumb and forefingers, feeling the faint connections it touched. "And if that doesn't work, I might have another way to stop the demon threat."

"Whatever it takes, Milord, I'll stand by you."

"Yes. Whatever it takes. To save the world."

END OF BOOK TWO

AUTHOR'S NOTE

Fever dream book two is complete. I hope you liked it. Personally, I felt like I grew a lot as an author during this one, and I hope that translates to the page.

As always, there's some people I need to say thank you to. Patrons, I love you. You support me no matter what, and that makes you the bestest. To my editing team, I put you through your paces on this one. Thanks for the hard work you put in. Family and friends, as always, thanks for putting up with the late nights and crazy conversations about whatever problem my characters are giving me. None of them listen, and I swear it's not my fault.

Amanda, you rock, and I love you.

If you want to check out some of the cool merch I've got, go to my website. There's links and stuff. Who doesn't like merch? Twatwaffles, that's who.

Posting about how much you like my stuff on the Facebook groups, Reddit Pages, and other social media sites is a huge help. Also, leaving a review would be great. I'd appreciate it, and it helps me sell more books. Selling more books means I get to keep writing more books. Writing more books means you get to read more books. It's a fun cycle where we all win.

Finally, and most importantly, if you've made it this far, just know that I appreciate you from the bottom of my heart, dear reader. You allow me to live this crazy dream job, and without your support I might be digging in actual mines instead of the proverbial word mines.

So, thanks. Seriously.

Until next time,
Michael

Sign up for my monthly newsletter, with updates on my progress and any new releases:

https://sendfox.com/author-michael-head

www.michaelheadauthor.com

PATRONS AND PATREON

The people who support me directly every month deserve some extra credit, and a whole lot of extra love. Those who support at the higher tiers, get even more. Thank you all so much for helping me do what I do.

Jeff Williams
Cromegas Flare
Justin Novak

If you would like to join their ranks, or check out my exclusive content you can go to:

www.patreon.com/michael_head

Thanks again, you legendary champions!

FACEBOOK AND SOCIAL MEDIA

Want to see silly memes and occasionally relevant information about books and author stuff? Check out my Author page on Facebook!

http://www.facebook.com/author.michael.head

There's also the Legion Facebook group to check out. It's got a bunch of great people, and plenty of book recommendations to look into if you want to find your next great read.

Only rules for joining are to spread the word about great new books, and don't be an asshat. There are also plenty of author interviews, including a few featuring yours truly.

http://www.facebook.com/groups/litrpglegion

I'm on Discord, and I even have my own place. Fair warning, it's not the most active place, but maybe you can help change that! Here's the link:

https://discord.gg/QSQHmSsGsx

ARC AND BETA READERS

ARC and Beta Readers are an integral part of turning a rough draft into a finished book, and the ones I had on this project were fantastic. If you see them out and about in the online community, be sure to poke them and say hello.

To each of you, all I can say is you are amazing.

Brian Nordon
Shawn Weeks
Scott Reid
Ben Oliver
Richard Griffiths
Jay Beraz

See you soon for book three!

QUEST ACADEMY

By Brian J. Nordon

A world infested by demons. An Academy designed to train Heroes to save humanity from annihilation. A new student's power could make all the difference.

Humans have been pushed to the brink of extinction by an ever-evolving demonic threat. Portals are opening faster than ever, Towers bursting into the skies and Dungeons being mined below the last safe havens of society. The demons are winning.

Quest Academy stands defiantly against them, as a place to train the next generation of Heroes. The Guild Association is holding the line, but are in dire need of new blood and the powerful abilities they could bring to the battlefront. To be the saviors that humanity needs, they need to surpass the limits of those that came before them.

In a war with everything on the line, every power matters. With an adaptive enemy, comes the need for a constant shift in tactics. A new age of strategy is emerging, with even the unlikeliest of Heroes making an impact.

Salvatore Argento has never seen a demon. He has never aspired to become a Hero. Yet his power might be the one to tip the odds in humanity's favor.

ARISE ALPHA

By Jez Cajiao

When you steal a hundred grand from some very bad people, the best way to survive is to stay small and quiet...

Possibly its not to save a pair of drowning girls, not go 'viral' on social media and certainly not to let the local police take your passport, trapping you on a small 'party' island in the middle of the Mediterranean Sea.

But Steve isn't the average guy, he's ex-military, ex-enforcer and ex-human. He's a one man nanite fueled nightmare for those that cross the line, and he's decided that it's time to clean up his act. He's going to make up for the things he's done, and save 'the little guys'.

It's a nice fantasy, but even he has to admit, it's really just a justification, because he's a very bad man, with horrifying abilities, and he's only just learning what he's capable of. He needs a reason to not go to the dark, and if that's hunting down the creatures of the night and beating them to death with their own femurs? Well, he's just the man for the job.

Stolen money. Greek Islands. Werewolves and Enforcers... What could possibly go wrong?

KNIGHTS OF ETERNITY

By Rachel Ní Chuirc

When Zara awoke in chains she thought she'd gone mad.

She was Zara the Fury - mistress of flame and fear. Her name was whispered across the land, from ramshackle taverns to the royal court. Even the heroic Gilded Knights thought twice before crossing her path.

She was feared—*respected*

Now she was curled up on a dirt floor on her fiancé's orders. Valerius, leader of the Gilded, mocks her cries for help. And the kingdom is on the brink of war over the missing Lady Eternity…

But that wasn't why Zara thought she had gone mad.

The reason why is that the last thing she remembered was blood, an arcade screen, and the gun that changed everything.

But no chains can hold the Fury, and when she gets out?

The world is going to *burn.*

LITRPG!

To learn more about LitRPG, talk to other authors including myself, and to just have an awesome time, please join the LitRPG Group

www.facebook.com/groups/LitRPGGroup

FACEBOOK

There's also a few really active Facebook groups I'd recommend you join, as you'll get to hear about great new books, new releases and interact with all your (new) favorite authors! (I may also be there, skulking at the back and enjoying the memes…)

www.facebook.com/groups/LitRPGsociety/

www.facebook.com/groups/LitRPG.books/

www.facebook.com/groups/LitRPGforum/

www.facebook.com/groups/gamelitsociety/

www.facebook.com/groups/litrpglegion